THE Shoreless River

J C SNOW

CONTENTS

PROLOGUE

IN THE CAVERN, there was a person being cut, over and over. The person lay on a stone couch, and the blood that flowed was caught in small drains carved into the stone, and from there fell into an open bowl, a thin waterfall.

The person was a young boy, about seven years old, with bright red hair and pale skin. If he opened his eyes, they were a clear green color, but he had kept them closed for a long time.

A creature sat near the stone couch, carving into the boy with his sharp claws. The creature looked something like a lizard, something like a cat; his edges were blurry and undefined, as though he wasn't quite sure what he wanted to be. His scales were silvery, and his wings and mane were like smoke. On his head were several small horns, pointing every which way like a thicket of ice.

Larger beings had come, cut harder, cut more often. For a long time, every time he cut the boy's skin it would heal. Now the wounds stayed open, and this creature, which was about the size of a large rabbit, could keep working on his own. As long as the boy was cut continually, the wounds wouldn't heal, so the process needed to not cease, day after day.

This was the creature's job.

It was a boring job.

One day, the creature got distracted, because his job was so boring, and how much blood did they really need, anyway? He went over to another part of the cavern and instead used his claws to make a design on the wall. The design looked like symbols and letters, although no one but the creature could read them.

"What's that?"

The creature whipped his head around. The boy had opened his eyes. The creature was struck by them; they were shaped in a fascinating way. He quickly calculated the degree of the angle between the bed and wall and leapt over. The creature liked to do math very much.

"Your eyes are the color of grass," he said.

"This time they are," the boy said, and closed them again as though he were very tired. "What are you drawing on the wall?"

"It's a system I worked out myself," he said proudly. "I can use it to calculate things precisely, angles and such, and predict where things will be at certain speeds within a certain period of time."

"Why do you want to know that?" the boy asked.

"Why not?" The creature brought his head back on his long neck like a snake getting ready to strike. "If I look at the stars at night, I see they are moving, and I thought it would be nice to know where they are and where they've been."

"Can't you just look?"

"No." The creature's head drooped. "I have to do this now. Just keep cutting you."

The boy actually laughed and turned his head to look closely at him. "Well, it's much worse for me. I can't see the stars either and I'm also getting cut all the time."

The creature looked at him curiously. He was very close to the green eyes now. Cautiously, he stretched out his neck and touched the boy's nose with his snout. The boy jerked back a little bit, but not much; he was restrained with silvery shackles around his wrists, neck, and ankles.

"Does it hurt?" the creature asked.

"Of course it hurts, idiot," said the boy. "Every time, it hurts."

"Oh," said the creature. "I didn't know. You never move or anything."

The boy sighed. "Well, better get on with it."

The creature lifted a claw and gently dragged it along his skin, but didn't cut into him. "Did that hurt?"

"No?"

The creature pressed harder. This time the claw sliced inside and drew blood. The boy frowned.

"That time it hurt, didn't it?"

The boy nodded.

The creature thought for a while. "A conundrum," he said at last. "I can't think of any way to do this without hurting you, but I have to do it. If I don't make sure you keep bleeding, the larger ones will kill me."

The boy didn't say anything.

The creature did his job and sliced him all over, making him bleed, but he noticed how the boy kept frowning, every time his claws cut. When he was done for the day, he went and curled up in another part of the cavern, thinking. Then, he drew on the wall some more, considering, and left.

After a while, a second boy entered the cavern and said, "Hello!"

The first boy opened his eyes, shocked.

The new boy was unconcerned that there was a person his own age tied up and bleeding on the stone couch. He sat on the edge and excitedly said, "Guess what!"

The first boy narrowed his green eyes. The second boy had black hair and eyes, and pale skin. "You are…"

"Look, it's me!"

The boy on the couch struggled and tried and failed to sit up, apparently forgetting that he had silvery bonds on all his limbs. "Why did you do that?"

"I can't hold it very long. This is my first time trying a mortal body." The other boy put his face down close so they could look at each other's eyes. "Is it good?"

Against his will, he smiled. "Very good."

The other boy's shape fluttered and dissolved, resolving itself back into the lizard-cat creature. "That takes a lot of energy," the creature said. "I have a plan to experiment with. I'll find a way to do this without hurting you. That's what the body is for. I'll test with it."

The red-haired boy looked at him pityingly. "Good luck with that."

"What's your name?"

"I don't have one," the boy said, "and I wouldn't tell you it if I did."

"Oh," the creature said. "I don't either. I'm not ranked high enough to be called anything yet."

The red-haired boy smiled. "I'll just call you demon, then."

"Then I'll call you phoenix." The creature sounded pleased, and began cutting the boy again. As he did so he said, "I asked why we have to have your blood, and they said that phoenix blood is the most powerful substance, useful for lots of things, spells and wards, and for cultivating power, and we need to cultivate so we can survive, although surviving really means we have to kill each other, it's all very confusing. Then they told me not to ask questions anymore."

Slice, slice. The boy frowned each time.

Talking more quickly, the creature said, "I've been cut a lot myself. I don't feel it anymore. That's why I didn't know it hurt you. If you let the big ones see that it hurts, they say you're a weak one and you should be culled, which means killing you. That happened to my friend, I had a friend once. There was a competition and he lost, so he's dead now."

Slice, slice.

The creature was getting a little frantic; he wanted to get it done quickly, but that meant he was getting sloppy with his technique and the cuts were deeper. The boy made a noise, and the creature instantly stopped.

"Are you all right?" the creature asked eventually.

"Of course I'm not all right, don't ask stupid questions," the boy said.

The creature noticed that there was water on his face. He reached out with his snout and gently licked the water off. It tasted salty. "What is that? The water?"

"It's crying. Shut up," the boy said.

The creature didn't come back for quite a while, perhaps several days although there wasn't a way to tell time. The green-eyed boy's cuts healed themselves, leaving pink scars.

When the creature returned, he was in his mortal body. "I have a solution," he said shyly.

The boy looked at him silently. There were dark bruises under his green eyes. He didn't ask if the green-eyed boy was all right because that was a stupid question.

"Here," he said, offering a cup of dark liquid.

The boy looked at him. "Have you not noticed that I'm tied up and can't use my hands?"

"Oh, I'll help you then?"

"What is it?"

"I made it. I tested it on this body," he said. "Look!" He took out a knife and drew it across his own arm without wincing. A great deal of blood immediately poured out.

The boy yelled, "Stop that! What are you doing?!"

"Don't you see?" he asked, crestfallen. "When you drink it, you can be cut and it doesn't hurt. And it also makes you bleed more, so I won't have to cut you as much."

The boy on the stone couch looked at him silently.

"Are you crying again?"

"Shut up."

He put the cup on the side of the couch, then transformed back into his normal self. "Will you drink it?"

The boy said, "No."

The creature curled up next to him. "You're warm," he said after a while. "I like being close to you."

The green-eyed boy turned his face to look at him. "I can tell it's you, demon," he said. "No matter what your body looks like, I think. You have the same expression in your eyes no matter what shape they are."

The creature put his head on the boy's arm and turned it to one side so he could see the green eyes better, considering.

The boy asked, "Do you know why they are making you do this? A little baby demon who doesn't understand what he's doing?"

"No? Why? I thought it was my job. I'm being punished for spending too much time looking at stars and making calculations. That's what they said, I need to be responsible."

"That's not why," the boy said, gently. "It's because they see that you are clever and will grow up to be strong if you can cultivate the demonic path. You can help make your clan more powerful, and thus make them more powerful, but they need to make you cruel as well. Otherwise, you're no good to them."

The creature stared into his eyes. "Am I not cruel?" he asked. "I'm a demon. I know…I know what we do…"

"Do you know what you have to do in order to become a true demon? To cultivate into your most powerful form?" the boy asked, still gently.

The creature looked at the ground, twisting his claw into one of the bloody channels in the couch. "They told me, but I don't really understand it."

"You can't do it if you're not cruel. You can't do it," the boy said, "so they need to make you hurt me, and get used to hurting me, and stomp out all the kindness you have. Anything that might rise up in you and resist — anything in you that is sad that you are cutting me and hurting me, they need that to be destroyed in your heart."

"I don't have a heart," he said immediately. "They said I don't."

The boy laughed. The sound was full of genuine pleasure.

The creature looked at him, unable to stop looking and listening.

"Everything has a heart," the green-eyed boy said, smiling at him. "You have one too."

"They don't know that I learned how to undo the wards," the creature said suddenly. "I watched them carefully when they captured you. I only need to see something once to remember it. I did the calculations already. I know how it can be undone."

"You figured that out before you came?"

The creature said, "I thought you might not drink it, so I planned ahead." He took his mortal form again. "But I don't want you to go. I wish we could stay together."

"Would you like to come with me?"

"I can't," he said. "I can't survive away from the clan yet. I haven't cultivated enough. I'd just be meat for other demons."

"Will they punish you?"

"Of course," he said, indifferent. He slashed his arm again, and blood gushed out. The boy gathered a handful and walked around the stone couch, murmuring in the demonic language, sprinkling the blood and wiping it on the shackles. The green-eyed boy watched and listened carefully.

The silver shackles disappeared and the boy sat up, rubbing his wrists and ankles. "Thank you," he said. "Be safe. I'll remember you." With visible effort, he transformed into a very small, red bird, the size of a hummingbird, and flew out of the cavern.

The black-eyed boy transformed back into his true body and went over to the cavern wall to continue his calculations.

CHAPTER 1
ZAI'AN

IN THE DEEP night of a quiet street, three people suddenly appeared from a blue-black slash in the air. They were a strange group: a young Daxian woman with gaping holes in the back of her shirt, a one-handed Daxian man dressed in travel-stained silk robes, his wide sleeves fluttering and long hair tangled, and a tall, dark-skinned man with a graceful bearing, dressed in an unremarkable shirt and pants that could have come from anywhere in any world.

Zhu Guiren looked around with distaste. "What a mess. This place reeks of resentment. And have they never rebuilt it?"

"It's called Zai'an now," said Liu Chenguang, putting her hair back behind her ears. Her voice sounded a little stuffy. "And yes, they've rebuilt it various times, but never again as it was under the Feng. Good job there."

"Enough," said Tainu in a calm, quiet voice. "Demon, can you find the array?"

Zhu Guiren closed his eyes and turned in a circle. "This place is…covered with arrays," he said. "Array on array…Some are very old. Those are the ones most likely to be associated with Hong Deming, but there are a lot. Any big, violent events here? What happened recently? There are some very strong new ones…"

"How recently?" asked Liu Chenguang.

He shrugged. "Past half-century or so?"

"Thousands of people in the Mitang quarter were killed here during the overthrow of the last dynasty," she said.

"That would do it. Hmmm…"

After a few moments of waiting, Tainu asked, "Hmmm what? What's happening? Can you find the array or not?"

"No," he said eventually. "Not…right now. Can we…sleep on it?" He looked a little abashed from what could be seen of his face in the moonlight. "I may need to do some reconnoitering. Talk to some people. The newer arrays have incorporated pieces of the ancient ones."

"By 'talk to people', do you mean talk to demons?" Tainu asked.

"Correct," he said. "For that, I need sleep first. In a bed. Do you realize that I haven't slept in a bed since…"

"Since last night?" Tainu asked dryly.

"That doesn't count. That was just a nap in Aili's uncomfortable abandoned house."

Liu Chenguang turned around and walked away down the darkened street.

"Wasn't she the one who decided to come and leave Aili?" Zhu Guiren asked.

"You are so…" Tainu shook his head. "Never mind. Come on, we'll find a place to sleep."

Quietly, Liu Chenguang called, "We should also get some decent clothes tomorrow. Especially him."

"Why?" Zhu Guiren looked down at himself. "What's wrong with this?"

"I think I'll just let you wander the streets like that tomorrow so you can find out." Liu Chenguang came back toward them. "I haven't been here since I left this area to look for Aili," she said in a steady voice. "About seven years ago now. The town has been through a lot, but it seems as though it's still Daxian territory–"

Zhu Guiren looked at her. "Of course it's Daxian territory."

"There's a war," she said. "Remember? A very complicated and protracted war with at least three sides, and the ordinary people are caught in the middle of it. There's been some kind of war or disaster constantly for the past hundred years, although not all of it affected Zai'an directly. Don't you read newspapers?"

"I've been in the Common Federation for centuries," he protested. "The newspapers don't have a lot about the Daxian Republic. Also, I've been doing other things. Also, since when do you know anything about politics? What did you do with Liu Chenguang?"

Tainu said, "Liu Chenguang, just take us to a place where we can sleep. Do you have money?"

"Not here. I don't even know what currency they're using now."

"Fine," Tainu replied. "Well, I agree with the demon. I'm tired. He and I can fly off and rest in a tree somewhere, but–"

"No," said Zhu Guiren. "No, I cannot. I want a bed and a bath."

"My goodness, people." Even in the dark, Tainu's eye roll was visible. "Demon, do you have money?"

Zhu Guiren closed his eyes, muttered something, and held out his hand. "There," he said. "Gold — the universal maker of friends and buyer of comfortable beds."

"Is that real?" Liu Chenguang asked skeptically.

"Of course it's real," he said indignantly. "Don't you remember how I hid gold in all those places?"

"Fine, gimme." She took the gold out of his hand and walked away. "Come on," she called, "there used to be a few places down this way. I'll get the best one for us. The one where they don't ask many questions."

The inn was dilapidated and the food poor, but at least there were beds and hot water. The owner was almost pathetically glad to have paying visitors, especially as the payment was in gold. Liu Chenguang got a suite with a large shared central area and several smaller bedrooms and alcoves since money wasn't an object and she thought they might be staying for a while. Once upstairs, she opened a window to let in fresh air, as well as a small red bird and a large black crow with an unusually long tail that had been waiting in a tree outside.

"Why did we have to do that?" asked Zhu Guiren crossly once he was transformed and standing on the wooden floor. "For the record, not having a hand translates into missing something important in my wing. Not sure what it is, exactly. I can't fly far, so let's not do that again."

Zhu Guiren massaged his handless arm until Tainu came over and started massaging it for him. "You did look a little bit like a sick chicken trying to get into the tree," Tainu remarked. "Next time I'll get up to hawk size, and if you downsize to a sparrow, I can carry you."

Zhu Guiren went from slightly flushed to bright red. "That's–that's embarrassing."

"Isn't it?" Tainu flashed him a smile. "But how can you be offended when I'm being so helpful?" He completed whatever he was doing to the muscles of Zhu Guiren's forearm. "That should make it better. Liu Chenguang can probably make some ointment for you tomorrow to help too."

"Liu Chenguang's going to be doing a lot of shopping tomorrow," she said from the table where she had watched all of this, unsmiling. "Zhu Guiren, give me your measurements. You too, Tainu, even though you're not quite as embarrassing as that one."

"What exactly is embarrassing about my robes?" Zhu Guiren demanded. "Once they're clean– Or I can get a new outfit–"

"Not like that one you can't, unless you're going to a theater and rummaging through their costumes. No one dresses like that anymore since the fall of the last dynasty, and most people well before. Not in the cities, anyway. It's Federation-style trousers and buttoned shirts and vests for you gentlemen unless you want traditional peasant wear. Cheaper that way, if you want to wear loose trousers and knotwork tunics instead." She sighed. "But I am not wearing those damn dresses. You can barely breathe or walk in them. I'll get some pants for me as well."

Tainu said, "I'll have the Federation style. Get me a hat, too."

"You're probably going to be mostly in your bird form during the day, so you don't need to worry about your accessories," she said. "You'll be highly visible. There are almost no foreigners in the Daxian Republic now with the war, and you'll immediately be taken as a Federative." If Aili came, she would have the same problem; she quashed that thought quickly. "But truthfully, given what people are going through here, I doubt most people will care much. It's just that if we want to hide in the crowd it becomes more difficult."

Tainu sat down. "I'll be glad to get new clothes, but who do we have to hide from?"

Zhu Guiren tried to comb his fingers through his hair and got stuck in tangles immediately. "I need a pincrown."

"No one wears pincrowns anymore. You need to get a haircut," Liu Chenguang said impatiently.

"No," he argued. "I like my hair long and I'm not cutting it for a bunch of mortal peasants."

Liu Chenguang snickered. "I'll get you a hairpin, Tainu can help you put it up."

Zhu Guiren glared at her and continued trying to unknot his hair.

"I'm excellent with hairpins," said Tainu solemnly. His own hair was still in the military cut, nearly-shaved to show the shape of his skull. "Anyway, who do you think might be looking for us?"

"As I mentioned, there's a war on," Liu Chenguang said, trying to keep her patience despite her complete exhaustion. Tainu was used to always being with humans. He was social that way, and interested in them — one of the many things which set him apart from most phoenixes. He would have to be more careful, this trip. "Zhu Guiren and I look like Daxians in our mortal bodies, but you definitely don't. There aren't any people here with skin as dark as yours. Most people won't care, but anyone from the Kunorese invasion force certainly will, and anyone reporting to them or spying for them will pass the word. Why would we want that kind of trouble?"

"All right," Tainu said, "I see what you're saying. We don't need additional complications. But this city is held by the Daxian army, isn't it? So it should be fine here."

"Who knows?" Liu Chenguang stood up. "There's paper and pen on the table. Leave your measurements for me, and anything else you want me to get. I'll be heading out early in the morning to the market. Bath and bed."

The inn had running water. Zai'an was a city after all; they weren't out in the villages, so she poured herself a bath and washed her hair, listening to the two talk softly in the main room, their voices — Tainu's deep voice and Zhu Guiren's lighter, quicker one — comforting probably precisely because she couldn't understand what they were saying. Sometimes, she heard Zhu Guiren's pointed laughter, or the warm tone of Tainu's voice that meant he was smiling while he talked. They seemed to enjoy one another's company, something she never would have imagined, but she remembered that when she traveled with Zhu Guiren, it really hadn't been so awful. He hadn't smiled or laughed like he did now, but as a traveling companion, he was quite pleasant aside from…well. She wondered sometimes why Zhu Guiren was doing this, but in the end, she was just grateful that they could do something to help Aili. Anything at all.

She had left Aili only a few hours ago, but across the world, on the other side of the great ocean. She had left her alone in the place that had killed her spirit, the place she called home. Aili had sent them away. Opened the phoenix gate and sent them from her.

After a thousand years of waiting, Liu Chenguang had found her person again. For nothing.

She wished that Aili had a true name so she could know it and say it to herself when she missed her, which was almost every moment that she was not fully focused on doing something else. But after everything that had happened, she was too exhausted for it to even hurt too much. It was more that the hope she had had for the last thousand years was gone now, and there wasn't any other hope to replace it.

Fully outfitted, Zhu Guiren went out after lunch the next day to "talk to some people" on his own; he didn't want anyone to know he was traveling around with two phoenixes. He returned several hours later and immediately settled down in a corner and began to scribble calculations on the walls with a pencil he'd found.

"Why do you always use walls?" asked Liu Chenguang. "We have paper." She was seated at the table, surrounded by piles of bark, roots, fungi, and herbs, making up packets and grinding things into powders.

"Paper is limited. My ideas are not," he said. It was certainly true that his diagrams were beginning to cover large portions of the wall. "What are you doing? That's a lot of powerful material you have there. What's the prescription?"

"Just making preparations. We're going to have to pay to get that cleaned."

"Who cares?" After he had scribbled a while more, he sat back on his heels and looked over what he had done. "Where's Tainu?"

"Oh, he went out to talk to some people too," she said vaguely. "He has old acquaintances."

"Why didn't he tell me?" he asked, frowning. "He doesn't know the right questions to ask."

"I have different questions." A red bird flew inside and transformed into Tainu. He smiled. "It's nice to see old friends. I've got the word out to let me know about any place where they've seen demons congregate, or anything they know about an array if they've heard demons talking."

"Who are you talking to?" Zhu Guiren asked, sitting up.

"Some fox spirits, some harmless bird and beast yao…"

"Fox spirits aren't harmless."

"To me they are," said Tainu, winking.

Liu Chenguang rolled her eyes.

Zhu Guiren shrugged. "Fine. All right, I think I've got some ideas here."

Tainu came over to stand behind his shoulder and look at what he had drawn on the wall.

"I'm pretty sure the array we're looking for is one connected to Hong Deming's birth. We know that there was one connected to Aili's birth, and one connected with Hong Deming's death, so that's the last option. Unless there was an array he was bound into as one of the perpetrators of violence…Was he ever involved in an unjust killing? That time the cultivators attacked Gunan, did anyone else set an array? I know I was too busy then…" He tapped his fingers on his handless arm. "Well, let's eliminate this option first. There are two ways for a living being to be bound into an array from birth: either you were conceived or born within an array's geographic center of influence, or your parents or ancestors were bound into the original mortal event."

From behind them, Liu Chenguang asked, "Can you remind me of what happens to a mortal who's born into an array? As opposed to the souls that you catch in it at the...event?"

"Maybe just bad luck, maybe not much, maybe a horrible life. It all depends on a lot of factors," Zhu Guiren said absently. "To be bound into an array — as opposed to just having an awful life for other reasons — means that it's more likely that bad things will happen, which leads to more bad things happening. The suffering and resentment of that person belong to the demon who set the array, as does the resentment produced by the original array event."

Liu Chenguang and Tainu were silent.

"You asked," Zhu Guiren said coolly. "Do you wish you hadn't?"

"Yes," replied Liu Chenguang.

Zhu Guiren turned to look at Tainu, who continued to study the diagram.

Eventually, Tainu said, "I don't understand all your figures here, but in general, it sounds as though the...cultivation material...produced by the array is exponential for the demon who made it? And continuously increases resentment over time throughout the population of those affected by it?"

"Correct."

Tainu said, "Let's destroy them all."

Zhu Guiren turned back to his diagrams. "As I've mentioned, I don't have the power for that. Ironically, I'd have to set more arrays to get enough cultivation to destroy just what's in Zai'an, much less the great array I made myself. We have to be strategic if we want to destroy the array here that is specifically affecting Aili. So, to get back to specifics, I've looked around and talked to some of my subordinates here–"

"You have subordinates here?" Liu Chenguang interrupted.

"I have subordinates in most of North Daxian," he said. "I haven't been physically in Daxian, in my mortal body, for several centuries. Now that I'm here, and therefore more vulnerable to attack, my subordinates are starting to move. Either toward me, to demonstrate their loyalty, which I wouldn't believe in anyway, or against me, to try to break free and take the array for themselves, for which I have to be prepared."

Liu Chenguang said, "I can now see why you enjoyed imperial court politics, actually."

"True. It felt very homey. Now back to the point of all this. Under normal circumstances, an array's power will dissipate over time as the mortal event begins to lose cogency, and particularly as living mortals are more weakly connected to the event. My subordinates have confirmed that the arrays that are in this area and are over a thousand years old are mostly just relics at this point–"

"But the mortal souls are still caught in them?" she asked.

"Yes. That's pretty much forever. Until the demon that created the array dies. I suppose I should tell you that that's one possible shortcut to destroying my array."

"Not funny," said Tainu.

Zhu Guiren risked a glance at him over his shoulder. "It's also not my preferred method. And if I'm killed by a demon stronger than I am, which I suppose it would have to be, logically speaking, that demon could set things up in advance so they take over the array. That will be the hope of at least some of the strong demons in the area, even in my own clan and certainly in others." He put his thumb against his teeth. "Where was I?"

Tainu reached over his shoulder, took his hand, and pulled it from his mouth. "Stop that. You're going to chew that thumb ragged."

Zhu Guiren took his hand back. "You can fix it. Anyway, there are very few arrays that are of the right age to be connected to Aili. There are two possibilities for the one that she is connected to: an ancient array that has been taken over by a strong demon killing a weaker one, and so it's still functioning because of that new connection, or there is one ancient array different than all the rest. It still has one living mortal bound into it. I propose we try that avenue first, because it's easiest to check for that and we can rule it out before trying to look for arrays that have been taken over. I'm hoping we don't have to do that, as I'll have to fight the owner."

"I thought you would have to fight the owner anyway," said Tainu. He was standing next to Zhu Guiren now, his expression concerned.

"True, but someone that's taken over other demons' arrays will be stronger than someone who owns a thousand-year-old thing that's barely functioning." He smiled. "And look at my secret advantage — I have a phoenix if I get hurt."

Liu Chenguang said, "You're taking a risk, for Aili."

Zhu Guiren shrugged. "I'm taking a risk. I don't know what it's for, to be honest."

"I'll…I'll forgive you. A little bit," she said. "For doing this for her."

Zhu Guiren stood very still.

She got up and walked out.

"What was that for?" Zhu Guiren asked Tainu, turning back to the diagrams.

"Why *are* you doing this?" Tainu asked quietly. "I didn't realize how risky this was for you until right now."

"I want to. I want to undo it. I'm…not sure why? Maybe there's more than one reason." He reached out with his finger and traced one of the diagrams.

Tainu watched him closely.

"Since I completed it…I haven't wanted to…" He struggled with something he couldn't quite manage to say, and shook his head at last.

"All right," Tainu said. "It's also that I didn't realize just how much your fellow demons are out for your head."

"Oh yes," he said, smiling. "Everyone wants to kill me when they get to know me."

"I don't."

"Well, you're a phoenix. You couldn't even if you wanted to, so I guess I'm safe with you." He turned and said, "Come with me. I'm going to start looking now. If I find it, I'll need you with me."

Tainu looked at the scribbles again, then followed him outside.

They began near the center of old Zai'an and walked out from there in a rough spiral as the roads allowed, which was not very well. Every so often Zhu Guiren would stop and mutter incomprehensibly to himself, or hold up two fingers as though to test the wind, or reach out and grab the air for invisible strings. Tainu amused himself by smiling in a friendly way at the citizens of Zai'an, who stopped what they were doing to watch a tall, dark foreigner and a very handsome, but very peculiar Daxian man walking down the street together.

"I wonder where Liu Chenguang got to?" he asked during one of Zhu Guiren's pauses.

"Eh," Zhu Guiren responded. "This really only needs two of us, why did you encourage her to come anyway? Back to Daxian, I mean. Aili would have been useful, but I already have a phoenix."

Tainu shrugged. If Zhu Guiren couldn't see that Liu Chenguang and Aili being together was just going to keep hurting both of them, it wasn't surprising; he couldn't have too much emotional sensitivity toward their relationship, given all that had happened. "It was better," he answered vaguely. "Any hints?"

"No," he said, annoyed. "We'll have to check the outskirts. Let's go away from the river first."

After more wandering and muttering, in a field between the edge of the city and the rise into the mountains, Zhu Guiren sat down in a lotus position and held his single hand in a seeking seal. "Again, so much would be easier with two hands. There are some seals that require them."

Tainu sat down next to him. "Can I help?"

"I don't know, set your hands into seals and see what you can find," he said grumpily.

"What am I looking for?"

"If it's a live array with a living mortal bound into it, you'll sense corrupted qi moving in a rough spiral from this spot."

After a few moments, Tainu said, "Ouch. That stings. Yes." He winced and shook his hands out. A little blood dripped from his left hand.

Zhu Guiren watched the drops fall without comment. He stood and said, "Next step." He closed his eyes and took out his sword, turning in a slow circle. "Damn."

"What?"

"Strong demon, strong array, medium strength binding," he said. "Aili's resentment is very strong right now. It's feeding into this like crazy. I can actually tell it's her."

"You can tell?"

"It's got a certain…flavor," he said, eyes still closed, "and since this array is from the time of the Wan Zhao rebellion, she's the only living mortal strongly tied to it. Previously, her resentment was probably feeding at the first level into the weak array of her birth, but now that that's destroyed, this is getting more of the resentment fed into it. It has probably already attracted the attention of the demon that owns this array, so we won't be able to do this quietly."

He opened his eyes and looked at Tainu, seeming to consider his options. "I am definitely going to have to fight," he said, "and also manage the spellcasting at the same time, with one hand. I can't also protect you. It's better if you're not visible when I start. Don't stand next to me."

"But then how will I heal you? Won't this take a lot of blood?"

He nodded, slowly. "I'll have to— I don't know. I'll call some subordinates, although I don't fully trust any of them not to turn on me, to be honest. I'll prioritize completing the spell. Once that's done, I can turn my attention to fighting the demon protecting the array. Do not under any circumstances come out while there is still another demon here." He didn't sound very hopeful, but he took a deep breath. "All right, let's get started. You transform, get over into those trees, and stay away until the other demons are gone."

Tainu stood still. "I don't want to leave you here if you're going to get hurt."

"Just go," he said impatiently. "If I have to fight more demons to rescue you, how does that help anything? Get into the trees. Set a ward." He turned his back and called his halberd, striking down onto the ground and shouting something in the demonic language.

Tainu reluctantly transformed and flew away, settling in a branch close to the edge of the copse.

From the earth, two yaoguai crawled up, one a snake and the other a beetle; from the sky, three crows flew down. All of them prostrated themselves before Zhu Guiren and listened to his instructions. Tainu saw them disperse around him in a circle, facing outward. Zhu Guiren looked very small in the middle of the circle of yaoguai and yaomo — smaller than any of them — and when he slashed his handless arm on the sword so the blood came pouring out, Tainu winced.

There was a lot of blood.

Tainu couldn't help noticing that, as the blood continued to flow and Zhu Guiren's chant began to get louder, first one and then another of the yaoguai turned to look at him, and then at one another. Uneasy, he watched from his perch as the blood continued to fill the cup, minute after minute. Zhu Guiren was beginning to look pale, even from this distance.

Suddenly, there was a rumbling noise from the trees below him and something like a boar rushed out onto the field, transforming into a huge man with a dagger-axe, hair tangled in knots down to his waist. He screamed at Zhu Guiren in the demonic language and chopped down, hard.

One of the crows flew at the demon's face, but the others remained still. The demon chopped down the crow and roared at the others. The beetle came at him, but was also crushed to the ground easily by the axe-demon. The two other crows flew away, while the snake turned to look hungrily at Zhu Guiren, still kneeling on the ground, his blood flowing into the cup of ice. The demon raced up to Zhu Guiren and swung the dagger axe again, this time slashing into the left shoulder. Zhu Guiren nearly collapsed, but then righted himself and continued to chant, bleeding now from the axe wound as well as the cut for the spell. The attacking demon reached down to grab his throat, choking him, but Zhu Guiren continued to hold his arm over the cup — half of the blood hitting the ice and half missing — chanting in a garbled, horrible voice as he tried to breathe.

Tainu couldn't stand watching this anymore. He flew straight upwards, as high as he could over the site, until Zhu Guiren was a tiny figure below him, then stooped to dive at his top speed, changing his bird shape into a falcon.

Qi spun from his wings as he dove, golden sparks that fled through the air. He beat his wings heavily in front of the yaomo with the dagger-axe, sending sparks into his eyes to distract him, then transformed next to Zhu Guiren, slamming the ground with his hand and setting a ward in the same moment. The dagger-axe caught him in his other wing as he transformed, but that actually saved him time now. He simply brushed the bleeding limb on Zhu Guiren's wounded shoulder and knelt next to him, breathing hard.

Zhu Guiren glared at him, the expression in his sharp black eyes furious, but didn't stop the chant. The yaomo began his own counterchant to undo Tainu's ward, while the snake yaoguai slithered around the edge of it, striking here and there to find a weak spot.

At last, the ice cup was full of bright blood. Zhu Guiren brought the cup to his heart, still kneeling; it seemed that he was too weak to stand, and his lips were completely without color. As the smoke began to pour out from the cup, Tainu grabbed his handless arm and healed the cut there, but giving Zhu Guiren's strength back wouldn't happen so quickly. He remained kneeling, swaying as Tainu held him upright and sometimes faltering in the chant as sweat streamed down his face. Small trickles of blood started seeping from his nostrils and ears. Tainu felt a sense of dread in the pit of his stomach. If there was a qi deviation or Zhu Guiren used too much qi and fell into a coma, there was no easy or quick way to fix it.

The smoke started pooling against the inner edge of the wards. Zhu Guiren narrowed his eyes at Tainu, still chanting.

With a sinking heart, Tainu nodded and removed the ward. He immediately transformed, flying upward and beating his wings in the face of the dagger-axe demon. From behind, the snake yaoguai grabbed one of his wings and began shaking him; Zhu Guiren's voice rose behind him, still in the chant, but with a note of panic. Tainu quickly transformed into a hummingbird and got out of the thing's mouth, then back into his human body.

He ran. He couldn't fly far until he healed from the ragged bites and the dagger-axe attack; his arm was spilling blood everywhere he went.

The dagger-axe demon roared and came for him, as did the snake. Zhu Guiren's voice took on an edge of fury as he began pouring the cup, the blood's long stream back into the earth. Tainu stumbled among the tendrils of smoke, far more complex than the ones from the array near Aili's birthplace. Hundreds of people must have died here.

The smoke burned his clothes, and then his legs where it touched his bare skin, as he dodged the strikes of the dagger-axe and the fangs of the snake; as he fell into the smoke, crying out at the burning of his body and face, he sensed someone leaping over him. The person threw something at the snake yaoguai, which hissed in rage and pain before withdrawing behind him into the woods. Then, the person grabbed him and rolled over the ground with him, wrapping him in something that seemed to protect him from the demonic smoke.

Almost as though they were flying, the person leapt away. Tainu couldn't see well out of his smoke-burned eyes yet — the healing would take longer since it was a demonic wound — but the demon with the dagger-axe had turned back to Zhu Guiren. Zhu Guiren's voice began to crescendo as the blood stream neared its end. The yaomo threw a talisman, but the person did something to make it spin away from him and tried to distract the yaomo, seemingly unable to make the attacker retreat, but constantly blocking him from Zhu Guiren. The person took the dagger-axe strikes meant for Zhu Guiren into their own body, mostly in the shoulders but occasionally a stab to the abdomen; their movements became heavier and slower, but they stubbornly remained standing between them.

The person blocked another talisman, then a strong spell that exploded with demonic qi, almost as though surrounded by a strong ward wherever they went. Tainu rubbed his eyes. Wards were not mobile that way; they were based in the earth where they were set, and in any case, whoever it was had been wounded by the dagger-axe, so it couldn't be a real ward.

Again, at the sound of the smashing ice cup, all the smoke tendrils rushed back into the last few drops of Zhu Guiren's blood, and Tainu felt the world explode around and inside him.

Tainu staggered to his feet, still unable to see well. Zhu Guiren was on the ground, collapsed and apparently unconscious, and the person defending him was lying on top, shielding him with their body as the yaomo screamed in rage, smashing into both of them with the dagger-axe. He himself wasn't healed yet, and couldn't fly again for a while, but with only one demon and the array broken, he could at least do something. He became a scarlet sparrow and hopped over to the yaomo, trailing his broken wing so it was obvious that he was vulnerable.

As he had hoped, the demon turned to follow him, growling. He dodged the creature's talismans and nets and dagger-axe as fast as he could with unpredictable little hops and flutters, baiting him back into the woods where he could duck into a little hole at the base of a tree. The demon transformed into a boar and began to dig with his tusks, finally pushing him against the roots of the tree. He couldn't dig, he couldn't get smaller, and he was beginning to be crushed and cut by the tusks. Blood poured out from his skin, feathers soaked with it.

Suddenly, the tusks disappeared. The demon roared and then screamed, a

long gurgling shriek that ended in silence. Blood seeped down into the hole —
demon's blood. Cautiously, Tainu peered outside. The boar demon was slumped
there in its mortal body, viciously impaled through the mouth by a double halberd.

Zhu Guiren knelt next to the hole. His face and clothes were striped with
blood, his hair clotted with it. His hand shook as he reached in to pick Tainu up.
"I'm going to kill you," he said, his voice also shaking.

Next to him, also drenched in blood, stood Liu Chenguang.

Tainu decided that this was as good a time as any to pass out.

CHAPTER 2
CRANE MOON

TAINU WOKE UP in his comfortable bed back at the inn and sighed with happiness. "Liu Chenguang?" he called. "Demon?"

Liu Chenguang came in. "You're better," she said. "You've been out for a couple of days. You got serious internal injuries from that boar-thing while you were being a sparrow in a hole. What were you thinking, Tainu?"

He sat up. "The same thing you were thinking, I imagine."

"Were you thinking that if Zhu Guiren dies, we have no way to break the arrays?"

He shook his head.

"I didn't think so. When we were there, he was— I've never seen him like that. He sat up, bleeding from various orifices, and said, 'Where is he?' over and over again. I wasn't in any good shape myself and could barely move, but when I told him that you'd allowed the yaomo to chase you…Well, anyway. He was frantic. He staggered over there and killed that thing and wasn't able to say any actual words again until he got you out of that hole."

She added, "And then he collapsed and you were unconscious, so we were all just sitting there in the forest until he woke up and I was healed enough to move on and heal him, and then he was frantic again because you weren't waking up, even though I explained to him that some kinds of injuries take longer for us to heal than others, and you would be fine."

Stunned, Tainu said, "He was that upset?"

"He was that upset," she replied solemnly. "And for all I know he's still that upset, but once we got back here and you transformed back into your mortal body — lucky you didn't while we were in the forest; we'd still be there — he left. I haven't seen him since the day before yesterday."

Tainu shook his head, wondering. He wouldn't have expected Zhu Guiren to be that upset, given his familiarity with phoenixes, but it must be a visceral thing. Unlike any mortal being, Tainu knew with absolute certainty through countless painful experiences and dreadful wounds, that he wouldn't die and that he would heal. In his mortal body, any injury aside from amputation or decapitation would heal; if the mortal body received a fatal wound that couldn't be healed, he would enter the rebirth fire. This endless, inescapable life was his reality, the reality of the phoenix. Perhaps nothing that had the ability to die could really understand what it meant.

He knew, also with absolute certainty, that his healing ability — unless constrained through his own weakness, qi deviation, or blood loss — would heal almost any wound in others. Yet, he had to admit that even though he knew that as long as he got there in time, the demon would always be healed, he felt very disturbed about seeing him wounded or hurt. Upset enough that he disobeyed his orders. But as long as he got there in time, always, all would be well.

But what if he hadn't gotten there in time? His mind veered away from that question. He would always get there in time. That was all. The demon would have to understand that this was an unshakable priority, whatever orders he might give before the event.

He was touched that the demon was worried about him. And happy. It made him happy. That was also the truth.

Liu Chenguang looked at him curiously. "Why do you trust him?" she asked unexpectedly.

He smiled again and shook his head. "If he doesn't come back by the time I've eaten dinner, I'm going to look for him. Oh, and Liu Chenguang," he added sternly, "I think you have some explaining to do as well."

They were sitting down at the table to eat when Zhu Guiren came back. Tainu noted that he stopped a brief moment in the doorway, looking at him, and then his face returned to its usual closed expression.

"You're awake," Zhu Guiren said, sitting down. "Good. We need to talk."

"Where have you been?" asked Liu Chenguang. "Have you eaten?"

"No." He took some rice and vegetables. "Didn't you get any meat?"

"Next time if you want meat, just say it. We didn't know you were coming back," replied Liu Chenguang.

He was silent for a minute. "I went to find and kill that snake yaoguai," he said. "That's done. But I don't know whether he told others before he died that there's a phoenix with me."

Tainu looked at him. "Is that why you were so worried about me being there?"

"*Yes,*" he said emphatically. "You have to understand how…how vulnerable you will be if they know where to find you — even where to look for you."

"You shouldn't worry so much," said Tainu, trying to reassure him. "We live all of our lives knowing that demons are looking for us, we're good at hiding–"

"Don't you understand that you are *not hiding?!*" he asked angrily, looking Tainu full in the face, his eyes narrowed. "You are with me. If they know that you are with me, they know where to look. I am going to be destroying arrays. I will be attracting the attention of every demon in North Daxian. I am leaving a path that's easy to follow, and I won't always be able to protect you. My own power– my own clan will start asking questions, and they–" His face paled.

Liu Chenguang looked down and coughed slightly. "Zhu Guiren," she said, "since when do you care about phoenixes being captured by demons?"

Zhu Guiren put down the chopsticks and walked out.

Tainu looked at her.

"What?" She looked back at him defiantly. "It's a legitimate question."

He sighed and followed Zhu Guiren outside.

The demon was pacing the yard of the inn — a rather ramshackle collection of dying bushes and a few sad sheds. When Tainu came out, he said, "You understand, don't you?" an amazing combination of plaintive and furious.

"I do," he said, leaning against the outer wall and crossing his arms. "But you can't expect her to understand that things could have been worse. I'm not even going to try to tell her that, and I suggest that you don't either."

Zhu Guiren looked at him, then nodded curtly. "All right, I'll just tell this to you. My clan has always been angry that I let her go. That I sent Liu Chenguang into rebirth and didn't recapture him. We hadn't had a phoenix for millennia before I caught him, and none since. It would have been a great source of power for us to keep her. Knowing that I'm with a phoenix now is going to– They are not going to leave me alone. They will not trust me to…keep you."

Tainu nodded. "You also have to understand that I make my own decisions about what I am willing to let you go through. I won't just let you be wounded and in danger of your life in front of me if there's anything I can do to stop it, or to help you."

Zhu Guiren stared at him.

"I can't do much. I think Liu Chenguang can do more. That's what I wanted to ask her about when you came in. But I will do what I can do to stop you from being hurt, and to ensure you can be healed." He added, "You have to understand that from our point of view, you are the most vulnerable person here. You are the only one who can die."

Zhu Guiren said, forcefully, "Yes, I can die. You can't. It's you — you and Liu Chenguang — who can spend eternity being tortured if they catch you."

"I know," said Tainu. "But we always know this. We'll be careful."

"You were not careful." He closed his eyes and took a deep breath. "You need to be more careful. We'll make a better plan for next time."

When they went back inside, Liu Chenguang made a point of being friendly to Zhu Guiren. It was completely unconvincing, but at least smoothed things over a bit. She had ordered some meat for him that the innkeeper brought up halfway through the meal: a sad bit of fried pork. Meat wasn't easy to come by now.

"So," said Tainu, after they had eaten, "Liu Chenguang, you came to the demon fight with some phoenix stuff. How did that go?"

She laughed. "Well, not as anticipated. It was these." She looked at them, nodding.

"It was…what?" asked Zhu Guiren.

"Is there something I'm looking at now?" asked Tainu.

"Don't you see them?" She stood up. "I can see them…"

Tainu came closer. "Are you saying the wings are there? That you've transformed?"

"Yes." She looked to one side, then the other. "They're right there."

Tainu put his hand out, cautiously. "Ah," he said.

Zhu Guiren also reached out.

"Don't," said Tainu, but too late.

Zhu Guiren hissed and pulled his hand back; it looked as though it had been burned. Tainu quickly bit his lip and stroked some blood on it, then turned back to Liu Chenguang.

"Pure qi," he said. "Made…semi-tangible." He reached out again and tugged hard.

"*Ouch!*"

Tainu looked down at his hand. If he narrowed his eyes in just the right way, it looked as though a small streak of light was lying in his palm. "What was that?"

"A primary," said Liu Chenguang, wincing and stroking the air. "Don't do that again, please."

"So…" he said. "I couldn't see well when you came in, but it seemed as though suddenly the smoke couldn't hurt me anymore. I would guess you wrapped me in the wings."

"Just instinct," she said. "I didn't make the decision to do that. They just… appeared. And when I was trying to defend Zhu Guiren, they blocked talismans and spells, but not the weapon itself." She winced again. "Whenever he struck my body with the dagger-axe, it went right in. But the wings blocked demonic qi."

"Hmm." Tainu walked around her, thinking. "I still can't see them, even though I know they're there…All right, so you came in not knowing this would do anything. What was your plan?"

Liu Chenguang said, "I'm taking the wings back in now." Nothing at all changed, but after a moment she said, "I learned qinggong at Crane Moon. You know that. So, I knew that I could at least leap around and be distracting, maybe block something with my body. But more than that, after I…came back…I kept thinking about Hong Deming and how I couldn't help him at all, and I wanted to…avoid that happening again. I thought a lot about how I could fight yaoguai when I can't fight with weapons or even my own body. Anything with killing intent will disintegrate if I try to use it, so what doesn't have killing intent? I can only be defensive and harmless, but maybe there were ways I could be more…I developed some…strategies." She reached into her pocket and took out a small packet. "This is one of them. I came up with some medicinal blends that are offensive to corrupted qi. They'll not do anything more than annoy a yaoguai, or for a weaker one, put it to sleep, but it's better than nothing. Back at the place where I lived for the last cycle, I have more things. If we're anticipating that we'll have to fight yaoguai, I'd like to go back there and get them."

Tainu and Zhu Guiren exchanged glances.

"I agree," said Zhu Guiren.

Tainu nodded. "Bring the wings back out again. I have another idea," he said. "Demon, touching the wings burned you, but when she was defending you, did that happen?"

"No. Not that I noticed. Although at the time, I was barely conscious."

"So, it may be that the intention to protect is important," Tainu said, thinking out loud. "Demon, do you have any demonic talismans on you? Ones meant to attack?"

Zhu Guiren rolled his eyes. "Please." He snapped his fingers and a rectangular strip of yellow paper with red characters appeared between them. "What for?"

Tainu gingerly reached out to take it in his own hand.

"Watch out," said Zhu Guiren sharply.

"I know," Tainu said, wincing. He took the talisman in his hand, and then covered it with the other, closing his eyes and drawing his hand sharply down against the length of the talisman. He said, "Now, demon, stand still," and quickly threw the talisman at him.

Zhu Guiren did not stand still.

This was a good thing, as the talisman exploded next to him. Suddenly, he was on the ground, gasping for breath and coughing blood. Tainu immediately knelt next to him and placed his own blood on Zhu Guiren's lips.

Zhu Guiren said, "What. The hell. Was that?!"

"Sorry," Tainu said sincerely. "You're the only demon we have to test things out on."

"Warn me next time!" He lay on the ground some more. "That was damaging," he said at last. "I'm still feeling it, even with the blood from you. For a weaker demon? Probably fatal."

Liu Chenguang said, "You put the feather from my wings on the talisman. And then you can use it as a weapon?"

"Because the killing action is not from you, I would guess," Tainu said. "The killing intent of the talisman is demonic. I reordered the spell to put pure qi at its center rather than demonic qi, but the attack itself, the attack function…" He shook his head. "You understand," he said to Zhu Guiren, who was now sitting up.

"Yes," he said slowly. "Well, I have a lot of those. I would feel better if each of you had some with that adjustment made. Keep them on you at all times," he said, sounding oddly formal.

"I'll go pull some feathers," Liu Chenguang said. "Better me than you, I'm going to go look in the mirror so I can pick good long ones." She headed toward her bedroom.

Tainu sat down next to him. "You're all right?"

Zhu Guiren just shook his head. "You are just…guessing about these things? Just trial and error?" he asked.

"Well, it's not like we have a manual." He picked up Zhu Guiren's hand, which was still showing blistered burns, and started putting more blood on it.

"You people are surprisingly chaotic," he said. "*We* have a manual."

"I would very much like to see this manual," replied Tainu.

They left Zai'an the next day, walking up the Cui Valley toward the gorge that led to Crane Moon. Liu Chenguang felt an ache sometimes as she saw the familiar places; the last time she had been here, she had been searching for Aili. They had to stop frequently, as there were both soldiers and refugees on the roads. Liu Chenguang and Tainu both healed surreptitiously wherever they could; done is done and pain is pain, and wherever pain could be assuaged for whomever was suffering, it must be.

Zhu Guiren watched and shook his head. "Doesn't it occur to you," he asked as they left behind one sleeping group, several children cured of dysentery, "that there's not a lot of point in healing people who are still starving and have no likelihood of getting decent food? Or healing soldiers that have just been attacking the other people you healed?"

"It doesn't matter whether there's a point," Liu Chenguang said. She remembered having the same conversation with Hong Deming, centuries before, but she had far less desire to try to explain things in any meaningful way to Zhu Guiren.

Tainu looked at her, and then said, "There's a point, demon. Think about it."

Zhu Guiren just rolled his eyes.

As they neared the village at the foot of Crane Moon's mountain, Liu Chenguang stopped and looked upward. The sunset would soon strike the place where she knew the waterfall came down, though it couldn't be seen from below; the ruins of Crane Moon were hidden from view from the bottom of the gorge. She didn't think they'd ever been found by anyone who was not a cultivator. Certainly not by the people in her village.

"Is there an array at Crane Moon?" she heard Tainu ask Zhu Guiren.

"Not that I set, or that was there when I was present," he said. "Maybe since."

"It was destroyed by violence," said Liu Chenguang, "so it's possible there's one now."

Zhu Guiren shrugged. "If so, it wouldn't affect Aili. Hong Deming was dead by that point. We have to—"

Liu Chenguang quickly walked away from him, but not quickly enough to avoid hearing Tainu say, "Demon. Can you try to be a little sensitive?"

"What do you mean?" he asked, frustrated. "Why is *she* so sensitive? She could be with Aili now. It's her choice not to be. We all know how Hong Deming died. Why does she have to get so upset? We're trying to do something to help now, but we have to be strategic…"

Behind her, she heard Tainu's expressive silence.

"*Fine.*" Zhu Guiren said. Stones rattled, probably because he was kicking them. "Fine, I don't understand anything, fine, it's all my fault, fine. Let's just keep going."

Liu Chenguang walked even faster, not wanting to be near him, especially as what he said was true. She could have stayed; she could have been with Aili now. It had been her choice to go, but it felt like…she didn't have a choice.

Because Aili didn't want her to stay.

Because Aili didn't want her.

She thrust that thought down hard and put a smile on her face as she always had when coming into the village beneath the cliffs: the pale brown wooden houses scattered on the deep green hillside, the terraced fields below.

"Doctor Liu! Doctor Liu!"

It hadn't been so long this time that the people she remembered were old or dead; only seven years or so, but still, what a difference. The children were teenagers now, the babies were children. There were some missing faces, but not many. It looked as though the war had not come here yet — neither the armies that contended for the land nor the bandits and looters that followed them. She breathed in relief.

"Doctor Liu?" Old Zhao pulled himself up short, frowning. "Is it?"

She smiled, and said, "I'm Doctor Liu's sister, Liu Chenguang. He sent me to see how you all were doing. I'm a doctor too."

"Ah!" several people said, but she knew they were looking at each other behind her back. Doctor Liu was the divine doctor. How could he have a sister?

But she just smiled and ignored it. They had never known that her first name was Chenguang; it had always only been Doctor Liu here.

Someone finally said, "Welcome! Please come, please come in, Liu Chenguang!" It was the current headman of the village — still Fang. Half the village were Fang. "Doctor Liu's house is still ready and clean if you want to go there?"

"Certainly, I will. Thank you for your hard work," she said.

One of the old women called out, "Will you introduce your husband, Liu Chenguang?"

She looked around and realized that they could only be speaking about Zhu Guiren. Tainu had transformed; he was sitting on Zhu Guiren's shoulder in his sparrow form, his head in Zhu Guiren's hair. She could almost hear him spitting with laughter.

"Ah, yes," she said. "This is my husband, Zhu Guiren."

He gave her a look of death.

She smiled. "Please, husband, go up the hill to my brother's house," she said sweetly, gesturing toward the little building set apart from the rest of the village.

He audibly hissed at her as he walked away.

"Ah, Liu Chenguang," said Grandmother Wang, hobbling up next to her as Zhu Guiren stalked away, to the disappointment of a gaggle of village girls. "Forgive me for saying so…your husband is very good-looking, but seems bad-tempered. I am sure Doctor Liu would not approve. He's such a kind man."

"You're correct to say so, grandmother," she said. "My brother does not approve at all. We'll be getting a divorce soon."

The faces of the girls brightened visibly.

"Good, good. That's best." Grandmother Wang nodded. Grandmother Wang was the oldest woman in the village, and had been when Liu Chenguang left seven years ago; clearly, she thought that her advice was welcome, necessary, and appropriate.

Liu Chenguang found it rather heartwarming.

Grandmother Wang added, "Since you've said you are a doctor also, would you be able to receive patients tomorrow? Since Doctor Liu left us, we haven't had anyone to take care of us. Some people have died. I'm sure it would make him sad."

"Certainly, certainly," she said.

"I'll send my granddaughter with a meal for you and your husband. Rest well," Headman Fang said. "We're glad to welcome Doctor Liu's sister."

Up at the house, Tainu was transformed back into his mortal body and apparently had been teasing Zhu Guiren mercilessly; he was bright red and stuttering.

This was absolutely wonderful.

Liu Chenguang smiled at the glorious sight of an embarrassed and flustered Zhu Guiren and said, "Dinner's coming soon. Tomorrow morning, I'll be seeing patients. We'll be here for a few days, most likely. We can rest and plan better than we have."

"Agreed," choked out Zhu Guiren. "Better plans are needed."

"There's hot springs at the base of the mountain, if you remember," she said. "Why don't you two relax, do whatever."

"Where are you going?" asked Tainu, looking at her as though he knew very well.

"Up to the ruins of Crane Moon," she said. "There's a place there I need to visit."

Since dinner would be coming late — the villagers had already eaten when they arrived, so close to sunset — Tainu and Zhu Guiren went up to the hot springs. The hottest spring was inside the mountain itself; it poured down into progressively cooler pools, the last few of which were outside under the stars. They chose a pool under some trees, with maple leaves swirling around in it. Tainu stripped down first and got in, gasping at the heat.

"Ah, that's better," he said, relaxing. His mortal body never really had bruises or aches for very long, but it still got tired and tense. That conversation between Zhu Guiren and Liu Chenguang had been difficult to hear; the demon really couldn't understand what the problem was, though he knew there was one, and Liu Chenguang was still in so much pain, which she wouldn't talk about or acknowledge. At least he had gotten Liu Chenguang to laugh before they came here, though he was sure that she was up at Crane Moon to cry on her own right now. Hopefully, it would do her good to let it out.

He sighed and looked up to see Zhu Guiren struggling with the buttons of his shirt. He wanted to offer to help, but was afraid the demon would be embarrassed so he looked away and busied himself ducking his head under the water a few times. When he came up, Zhu Guiren was completely naked and carefully touching the water of the pool with one toe.

Zhu Guiren naked was quite as beautiful as Zhu Guiren with clothes on, if not more so. Normally, Tainu greatly appreciated seeing beautiful naked people of his own mortal gender, whatever that happened to be at the time, but he felt differently about Zhu Guiren, so his mind didn't immediately go there. Instead, his eyes noticed that Zhu Guiren was covered with scars, large and small, strikes as though from whips, cuts from blades, old burns, pitted lumps from who knows what. It hurt to look at them. No wonder he had recognized Aili's whip scars just from touch.

Zhu Guiren noticed where he was looking and flushed from his face all the way down into his chest. "They're old," he said shortly, and got in the water.

Tainu struggled with whether to ask more; he didn't want to make Zhu Guiren feel ashamed.

But in the end, Zhu Guiren offered it on his own, after he had ducked his own head underwater a few times and was squeezing out his long hair. "Most of them are from my childhood. Or from when I was much younger, anyway. I don't even remember what most of them were from originally." He added, "None of the things that you've cured for me have scars. That's nice."

"Sometimes it scars," he said. "Even if I heal it. It depends on the person and on what caused it and other things that I don't necessarily understand. I can't always predict– The healing isn't just about the body." He didn't really know why he felt the need to explain that.

After they'd soaked for a while, Zhu Guiren said, "I've been curious. Why do you always call me demon instead of my name?"

"I can't call you your true name in front of people," he said. "And I know that you didn't really intend to tell it to me, so…"

Zhu Guiren nodded, looking at the water. "Why not call me Zhu Guiren?"

He deflected the question by asking, "What do other demons call you?"

Zhu Guiren ducked his head under the water again. "You couldn't say it, but the meaning is 'Third'."

"Third? Like…third brother?"

"No, just third. It changes. Third means that I'm the third strongest in my clan."

"Hmmm." This was interesting; he hadn't known all these things about demons. "You people really are very organized."

Zhu Guiren laughed. "Well, I don't miss it. I've been avoiding the clan since…" he waved his hand. "All this."

"So, if you're Third, there's a First and a Second?"

"Yes, and many hundreds below," he said. "The First and Second of my clan are very old. The older you are, the longer you're likely to live. Many demons die in the low ranks, in the ranking pits…I've been Third for about two thousand years now. At my rank, I can only be challenged by the demon directly below me, unless I'm directed to answer a challenge by First or Second. For those in the lower ranks, below Tenth, any of the top ten can direct anyone to fight anyone else."

"So, the demons within your clan fight each other, as well as fighting demons from other clans?" Tainu frowned. "That seems…awful."

"It is," he said shortly. "That's why I've been avoiding them for centuries. But now that I'm here, it's likely that I'll receive a challenge or directions from First or Second."

"What would happen if you lost a challenge? Would you become Fourth?"

"Ha, no. I'd be dead. I've never lost a challenge," he said casually. "Obviously."

Tainu frowned more. "I do not approve of your clan. I'd like you to be more of a free-range demon."

Zhu Guiren laughed. It was good to hear. Tainu smiled at him.

Zhu Guiren suddenly stopped laughing and looked at him, tilting his head to one side as though trying to understand something better.

"It's nice when you laugh," explained Tainu. "That's all."

Clearly self-conscious, Zhu Guiren nodded.

Feeling he should offer something personal in return, Tainu said, "You know, I didn't grow up with anyone. There are so few of us, and when I came to consciousness, I was alone. That first cycle was very strange because I didn't know what I was, or what to expect. There weren't many mortals then, and the spirit world was different too. It's gotten much more dangerous since my awakening. When I entered the rebirth fire for the first time, I was completely shocked. I didn't know that was going to happen…" He stopped.

Zhu Guiren was looking at him, and he didn't want to continue this story.

"Anyway, that's one of the reasons that when I was able, I tried to find the new phoenixes whenever they awoke. So they wouldn't be alone, so they would know what they were."

"You were always alone?" asked Zhu Guiren.

"Mostly," he said simply. "Mostly alone."

His effort at making the conversation lighter had failed miserably. The demon, of all people, looked sad for him.

He tried to change the subject. "What do you think of this place? That Liu Chenguang's been here being a doctor all this time?"

Zhu Guiren agreed to be diverted. "It makes me glad," he said. "That what I taught Liu Chenguang really meant something to him. That he was able to continue with it, too. It makes me feel as though…well."

Tainu smiled at him again. "You must have been a good teacher. I hope you get to teach someone again. What would you teach now?"

Zhu Guiren said, "I don't really know. These centuries since Liu Chenguang, have I learned anything new? Anything to pass on? It's been a strange time. Like a holding time. Like…waiting." He shook his head again. "But there are things I'd like to learn about the ancient making of the earth, about the stars…there's so much happening now in the sciences…"

Tainu noticed his eyes shining a little bit. This was good. "Maybe when this is over, you can do that," he encouraged.

Zhu Guiren looked back at him. "What would you like to learn?" he asked.

"I don't know," he said, surprised. "No one's ever asked me that before…I've just always learned whatever I needed to learn to be wherever I was, I guess."

"So you could…help people," Zhu Guiren said.

"Yes, that's why. I learned spells and such to try to defend myself and hide when necessary…how to extend my power for those who needed it as much as I could. But now, when I'm with farmers, I learn to farm. When I'm with sailors, I learn to sail…What would I want to learn, just for me, just because I'm curious?" He put his mind to it and tried to imagine. "Do you know, really, I can't…? I've never thought…"

"It's the best way to live, learning things," Zhu Guiren said, intently.

"Is it?" Tainu felt as though his whole being was smiling. Something about the demon made him feel this way; he had no idea why. "I'll have to try it."

CHAPTER 3
GRANDMOTHER WANG

Liu Chenguang came down from Crane Moon slowly, using her qinggong only when necessary. In her heart, she thought she might not return here. After so long, the pain was finally too great to even remember. But then, she lifted her body up for the next leap and she remembered so many things. Of course, most of them were from Hong Deming's lifetime. There was so much more to remember. So much more time they had had together, then. But Aili, too: that first meeting in the alley, when she had looked up at Aili's face with so much joy and excitement. Even through the confusion and bewilderment in Aili's eyes, she could see that Aili knew her, somewhere deep down, that she was drawn to her.

She remembered seeing her that very first time — sitting in the bar in Easterly, watching everyone else — and how their eyes had met, Aili's blue eyes widening as they took her in. The shock she had felt, realizing that her person was now in a female form, then dashing out into the alley to make the change of gender for her mortal body and getting caught by those annoying sailors. She had leapt out in front of Aili with her qinggong before her mind was consciously aware of it, taking the knife in her forearm. That had hurt, but she was so excited she could barely feel it. Reaching up to touch Aili's hair, dark gold, braided back in that complicated way. She could still sense Aili's heart; it was her person's heart — open and brave and kind — desiring and responding to her. She could feel it. How could she have mistaken it?

What had gone wrong?

She remembered her terror when she realized what kind of nursing Aili was training to do. She knew that her mind hadn't been clear, that she had made decisions badly. She'd been so upset, too, by discovering Aili's terrible family. At the time, she had barely known how terrible it was, but it had been enough that she was disturbed beyond sense — rejecting all of this as Aili's reality, wanting only to make reality change, make it be different. As though some blood and good intentions were enough to heal the abuse and suffering Aili bore in her soul and make it as though it hadn't happened.

But it had.

Deep night had fallen when she entered her old house to see Tainu and Zhu Guiren chatting happily at the table, both looking clean and relaxed.

"The demon wants to challenge me to a drinking bout," her sibling said to her solemnly.

"Zhu Guiren, I'm telling you now, and I'm sure Tainu has also told you, that there's no winning for you there." She sat down to eat her own dinner. "There's not enough alcohol in this village and probably the next one over to get a phoenix drunk."

"Demons are also quite capable," he said. "When we get to a town, Tainu, let's see."

Liu Chenguang looked at him, considering. At least going up to Crane Moon had helped her realize that not all her troubles were of Zhu Guiren's making. "You're a doctor too," she said. "Why don't you help me with the patients tomorrow? It will go faster that way. I guarantee everyone in the village will be in."

"Me?" To her surprise, his face lit up. "Yes, of course."

Tainu smiled.

After they had eaten, she took out the materials she'd come for: a stockpile of the anti-demonic powder, though probably it had lost strength over time, and her own talismans, which she could use to set a ward, though they were weak compared to Tainu's. She had never been as good at wards and spells.

"I'll look them over and strengthen them," Tainu said, examining them. "It'll give me something to do while you're physicking the town tomorrow."

Last were her deerhorn knives. She lifted them up — two double-crossed crescents with blunted ends.

Zhu Guiren frowned. "Show me," he said, and took out his sword.

"You have to come at me. I can only use them defensively."

When he did, though she could tell he was trying to hold back, she was able to capture the sword and disarm him effectively.

He looked at her, shocked. "Again," he said, and came at her with more force.

This time, she needed to use qi, but was still able to block and disarm.

Tainu looked on, wide-eyed. "What are those things?"

"They're designed for defense and disarming," she said. "Other people can use them offensively as well, but I can't. They're from a sect that developed about two hundred years ago. I studied with them for a while. It's a form that is well-adapted to a purely defensive, close-combat style. Of course, I can't follow up with a strike when I disarm an opponent, but I can at least run away. Or give someone else an opening."

Zhu Guiren seemed to be deep in thought. "You've been busy," he said at last. "You've used the time well."

She felt oddly proud to hear it from him.

"Can you teach Tainu?"

"Yes, of course," she said, "but it will take a while before he's proficient enough to be able to really use them in combat. I have, and I'm confident in my skill, but I also have the qinggong foundation, which he doesn't."

"I've never studied any martial art," he confessed.

"You were quick to turn that knife at my throat back in the spirit realm, remember?" asked Zhu Guiren, smiling at him. "Your reflexes are good, you're clever, you already know how to cultivate. You can learn."

Liu Chenguang noticed them looking at one another and wondered what exactly was going on between the two of them. She added, "About fifty years ago, some people decided that this sect's martial arts were good enough to deflect bullets during a major rebellion."

"Not?" asked Zhu Guiren, rolling his eyes.

"Not," she said. "They're only good against traditional weapons. Not guns. But let's practice daily. The three of us, so you'll know how you can work with us and how we can work with you. That's my first suggestion."

Zhu Guiren nodded.

"My second suggestion," she said, putting the knives back in their case, "is that we think carefully about the issue of guns. There is a major war going on, and we're walking through it. Our healing powers can't always protect against guns. Of course, your sword," she nodded at Zhu Guiren, "would easily kill mortals–"

"No," he said flatly. "It wouldn't. I don't kill mortals."

Both of them stared at him. Liu Chenguang bit down on several things she wanted to say.

"I don't. Not if there's any other way. Not if it's avoidable," he said defensively. "I only do what I do because I need the power I gain from it, and the power comes from what mortals do to each other. That's what produces the suffering and resentment we use for cultivation. There's no benefit to my power from killing with my own hand. Only from…" He flushed. "There are demons who kill mortals directly because they're just sadists or like the taste of blood, but I've never been one of them, and I don't want to start."

"You killed people when we were traveling," Liu Chenguang said. "I clearly remember it."

"That was different. We were being attacked, and I used ordinary mortal weapons, remember?" he said. "At that time, I was pretending I didn't have any spiritual power. It was an even fight."

Liu Chenguang looked at him.

"Fine, not *even*, but as even as I could make it."

She looked at him more, but this time he lifted his chin and refused to respond.

Tainu said, "Liu Chenguang, don't encourage him to do something he feels is wrong. Please."

"Well," she said at last, "you're still not a phoenix, so you may have to fight mortals if they attack you. You should think about how you want to go about it."

"As even as I can make it," he said stubbornly.

"Fine." This conversation was reminding her painfully of how upset Hong Deming used to get about how easy it was for him to kill ordinary people with En — not even a demonic weapon; how he wanted to fight yaoguai instead of cultivators. "But think about the guns, and how we can avoid them. You especially."

He nodded. "Let's focus on the arrays as much as we can, and any fighting should only be with the demons if we can manage it," he said. "That's our business. I agree that avoiding guns is also a good idea. We're not here to get involved in a mortal war."

The next morning, she and Zhu Guiren sat at first light in the open area of her little house, eating congee that Fang's granddaughter had brought up and watching the line of excited villagers form outside.

"We're the best entertainment this village has seen in years," remarked Zhu Guiren.

"Husband and wife team," Liu Chenguang snickered.

"Hush, Student Liu," he said in his old haughty tone. "Treat your teacher with proper respect."

As they began to see patients, each on opposite sides of the room, a red bird would fly in every so often, usually perching on Zhu Guiren's shoulder, though sometimes on hers. He never stayed for long, and seemed to just be checking on them, but the villagers were quite taken by his antics, of which he was well aware. Tainu had taken a form more like a swallow than a sparrow and swooped acrobatically above the people in line to keep them entertained. Liu Chenguang sometimes looked up to see Zhu Guiren watching his flight with a strange expression on his face that she couldn't read. Perhaps Zhu Guiren was not irredeemable after all.

She remembered that his theoretical understanding of medicine had been unsurpassed when she learned from him, and that was still true. As an actual doctor, though, he was awful, and his bedside manner was laughable. After she sent him a couple of warning glances while he loudly discussed his patient's yang deficiency — to the delight of the people waiting in line — she sent everyone out for a break while she tried to explain basic human interactions to him.

Tainu flew back in and joined them to eat the noon meal. He laughed out loud at the yang story while Zhu Guiren pouted at the table. "Just don't send him any of the unmarried women," he said. "They're all chattering about your gorgeous, soon-to-be-divorced husband out there."

"We're getting a divorce?" Zhu Guiren stabbed a mushroom. "I can't wait."

"Unmarried women should definitely come to me, my husband," she said. "Do not chance it. Your virtue must be protected."

Tainu snorted. "Anyway, let's finish this up today and leave by tomorrow morning at the latest. I flew up to Crane Moon just to take a look–" he said, carefully avoiding Liu Chenguang's eye, "–and from up there I could see that there is a group of men on the way. Hopefully, they mean no harm, but…better for us to not be here."

"Ordinary men?" asked Liu Chenguang, feeling a chill. "Revolutionaries or Republic? Or Kunorese?"

"Would it matter? Could I know from so far away?" he asked.

"If it's revolutionaries, they're probably just recruiting," she said. "Although the village might miss the young men and women, it won't kill them to go. At least, not right away. Army of the Republic, probably the same, but they're less likely to come to a little village like this. Kunoru…" She sighed. "Kunoru would raze this place to the ground. I have to give this some thought. Can you go out and check again when we're done eating? And see if you can get close enough to hear where they're going. Maybe they'll skip this village."

"No, do not fly close enough to listen. It's not safe," Zhu Guiren said sharply.

Tainu said, "It's all right, I'm fast."

"Not as fast as a bullet."

Tainu smiled. "I'll be fine," he said, and left.

Zhu Guiren looked at Liu Chenguang accusingly. She was not used to receiving that kind of look from him.

"You've changed," he said.

She ate some more tofu. "It's been a thousand years, Zhu Guiren," she said. "You were right when you said I wasn't paying attention, back then. If I had been, I would have realized that something was wrong much sooner. If you wanted a stable dynasty, why were you backing the most unstable and paranoid candidate for emperor?"

"It's always been amazing to me that no one noticed that at the time, but there was so much violence and paranoia built into the structure of the imperial court that people couldn't perceive how genuinely terrible Zhu Wen really was. And you're changing the subject."

"It was Tainu who taught me first," she said. "To heal people. But it was always accidental for me…not something I sought out. Most phoenixes don't. Tainu's different that way."

Zhu Guiren raised an eyebrow.

"It's important to him. But for me, it was only after…after living with Hong Deming," she said, "After that, I decided that trying to help people suffer less would take more than just healing skills. I would need to pay attention to all those things. To try to understand what was going on in the human world and intervene when I could."

"Was that for Hong Deming too?" he asked, curiously. "Like the deerhorn knives?"

"It was. And it wasn't, also. It was something we shared together — that we wanted to try to save what…to save the one that was in front of us, yes, but also…he had so much compassion. That's what drew me to him to begin with," she said. Another thing that she'd never shared with anyone before, and now it was with Zhu Guiren of all people. "He always felt people's pain and wanted to stop it. He always felt sadness for those who were suffering, even if he couldn't stop it, even if it had nothing to do with him. So, I decided to…keep going."

Zhu Guiren looked at her in silence.

Someone knocked on the door. "Liu Chenguang? Doctor Zhu?" called a man's voice. "Are you able to receive visitors now?"

Liu Chenguang stood up. "Come in," she called, and smiled in preparation. "Unmarried women should see me, please."

The last person in, close to dinnertime, was Grandmother Wang herself. She insisted on being treated only by Liu Chenguang, so Zhu Guiren was left to sit staring out the window and waiting for Tainu to return. Liu Chenguang found that Grandmother Wang was suffering from a cancer of the uterus — not something that could be fixed with traditional medicine at the stage it had already reached — so she slipped some sleeping medicine in her tea, and then quickly treated her with blood. By morning, she would be cured.

As Grandmother Wang slumbered face down on the consulting table, Liu Chenguang stretched and went over to the window.

"He's been gone a long time," Zhu Guiren said abruptly.

"He's fine. Tainu is very fast and very clever. He doesn't take undue risks without good reasons, and if he thinks it's not safe to get too close, then he won't." Privately, she admitted to herself that Tainu took undue risks all the time, especially when he thought it necessary to help people, but…a bullet wouldn't really hurt him for long, after all, and he was always very careful to avoid the notice of demons, which was the only real danger to a phoenix in the long run.

Zhu Guiren snorted and went back to staring outside. "They're bringing dinner."

Fang's granddaughter brought the meal in, accompanied by two teenagers who were all eyes for Zhu Guiren. He sat down at the table and was joyously served, but he didn't appear to notice.

"Thank you, you've worked hard," said Liu Chenguang.

One of the girls asked shyly, "Madam Liu, should Grandmother Wang stay here?"

"She's fine," she said. "She'll wake up in a little while, it's just the medicine she took, it's not unexpected."

As the three were leaving, a red bird swooped in through the open door, making them cover their hair and laugh.

Zhu Guiren looked coldly at him. "You were gone a long time," he said.

Tainu transformed and sat back down for dinner. "I waited until it was getting darker to get close. They're Daxian. Army of the Republic. They're not planning to come here. Just headed to Zai'an, and then east toward the coast."

Liu Chenguang sighed with relief.

He kept talking as he began picking out vegetables for his plate, unsmiling: "I listened to get more of a sense of what's going on. It is...extremely bad. The Kunoru are in all the eastern provinces. Hai'an is a disaster, there's scorched-earth war in the central provinces, massive flooding of the Sorrowful River...the Army of the Republic breached the levees."

"On purpose?" Liu Chenguang's eyes grew wide.

"On purpose, to block the invasion from going further inland, but you can imagine...At least four provinces are flooded. There's famine because people can't plant. They keep trying to rebuild the levees, but the Sorrowful River doesn't like being controlled. Since the Kunorese have been blocked from easy invasion by land, there've been planes bombing most of the major cities. Even Zai'an — that's why it seemed so miserable there. The soldiers were talking about it since that's where they're headed. There are refugees fleeing everywhere." He raised his head and met Liu Chenguang's eyes. "A lot of death. A lot of suffering."

Zhu Guiren tapped his fingers on the table in an irregular pattern.

Liu Chenguang and Tainu looked at him.

"We were going to travel in that direction," he said. "There are a lot of nodes in Hureng and Hai'an that I wanted to break before we attempt the central one. For the array I made."

"Where is the central one?" Tainu asked.

"Somewhere on the north side of the Sorrowful River, west of Hongye. I can't narrow it down for us more than that till we get closer. It's not geographically in the center of the array — it's central because it's the central seal."

"Well, we knew there was a war on. I'll gather as many medical supplies as I can to take with us," Liu Chenguang said. She felt the sadness of knowing what she was going to see, the hundreds of thousands of unnecessary deaths that accompanied great wars and famines.

Zhu Guiren was clearly thinking in another direction. He said, "With that level of resentment and suffering, there are going to be a lot of demons attracted. That explains why we haven't had many problems so far..."

"We haven't had problems?" asked Tainu, raising an eyebrow.

"Not really," he said bluntly. "Not as bad as I expected, to be honest. We destroyed an array and no one has come after us. Only one demon showed up to fight me. It was ridiculously easy. I've been wondering why, but this would explain it. They've all flocked east for the banquet."

Liu Chenguang winced, then thought more about that statement. "We've destroyed two out of three of the arrays," she said. "Would Aili be…better? Has it helped her?"

Zhu Guiren replied, "Her resentment was very high before we destroyed that array. At least, the destruction would have taken away something that was…exacerbating that. I can't feel her in my own array. It's too large to feel one person's resentment, but I expect that…well, it should have helped her in some way."

Liu Chenguang could tell he was trying to avoid saying something; he kept glancing over at Tainu, as though asking for help. Tainu, however, was looking down at the table, lost in thought.

Zhu Guiren finally got desperate and said, "Tainu, what do you think? How is Aili?"

Tainu started. "Aili? We won't know till we find her again, will we?" He looked at Liu Chenguang.

Liu Chenguang said, "I don't know if I'll find her again." She felt the sadness in her own voice, in her heart. "I wish I understood what went wrong. I don't understand. Not really."

Tainu looked at her and opened his mouth to say something, but suddenly, Grandmother Wang grunted and snapped upright; Tainu transformed and fluttered over to Zhu Guiren's shoulder.

Grandmother Wang seemed to have heard a little of the conversation just before she awoke. She yawned and asked, "What's that, Doctor Liu? You have someone you're looking for?"

Liu Chenguang sat down next to her. Grandmother Wang couldn't see well, she knew, but surely her voice sounded different now than when she was male? She said, "It's Doctor Liu's sister, grandmother." On an impulse, she added, "It's not me looking for someone. It's really about a friend of mine."

Zhu Guiren looked at her. "But it's—"

"Shh, you don't know this person," said Liu Chenguang, blushing. She could imagine the faces Tainu would be making at her if he wasn't currently sitting on Zhu Guiren's shoulder wearing red feathers. "Yes, this friend of mine has someone that she was in love with when they were young, and this person loved her too, and they promised to be together. But then, they were separated."

Zhu Guiren stared at her, mouth hanging open. It was worth it just for that.

"Ah, that happens so often!" said Grandmother Wang, shaking her head. "So, they married other people?"

"No, no—"

"Why not?"

"Because they didn't want to."

"What does that matter? Young people don't know what's good for them…" Grandmother Wang muttered under her breath. "So, they were alone, but they couldn't be together? Why was that? Doesn't make sense."

"You're right, grandmother, but that's how it was," she said.

"So did they miss each other?"

"One person missed the other, but the other person forgot about them."

"Eh, can you be clearer? That doesn't make sense."

"So, ah…Chenguang missed Deming, but Deming forgot about Chenguang."

"So they didn't really love each other, then?"

"Ah, there were circumstances."

Zhu Guiren left the room in evident disgust; the red bird immediately flew back in and perched on the rafters.

"*Anyway*," said Liu Chenguang loudly, "after they'd been apart all of this time, Chenguang found Deming again."

"And he was married, I'm sure."

"No, he didn't get married."

"It's fine if he did. Chenguang can still be the concubine."

"No, that's not–"

"Or is that not allowed anymore? I'm so confused with how things are changing these days. Deming's a beautiful old-fashioned name. I'm sure he's happy with his wife. If Chenguang isn't planning to be his concubine, she should stay away. How long were they apart, anyway?"

"Twenty-five years."

"Ha, that's too long. Chenguang probably can't have babies anymore. What's the point? She should just enjoy her age, I suppose. That's my advice for your friend."

The red bird deliberately flew down to the ground in front of them and started rolling around on the matting.

"Stop that," hissed Liu Chenguang.

"What's that now?" asked Grandmother Wang. "Or Chenguang could become a nun?"

"But grandmother," she tried again, "after twenty-five years apart, could they still love each other?"

Grandmother Wang considered this seriously. "Did one of them really forget the other? I forget the names now."

"They didn't really forget."

"Well, perhaps they could still love each other, then," said Grandmother Wang portentously. "But not right away."

Liu Chenguang froze. "What do you mean, not right away?"

"Well, twenty-five years…That's a lifetime, isn't it? They would have to get to know each other again." She nodded. "Really though, if Deming didn't take his chance and get married, there wouldn't be any babies for anyone, with this situation."

"No, there wouldn't be babies," she said, a little dazed. "But why do they need to get to know each other? They knew each other so well. They grew up together."

"All the more, then," said Grandmother Wang firmly. "People who grow up together…they only know the beginnings of one another. And then they've been apart, so they've missed so much. Maybe they're not the same people anymore. And maybe they do still love each other anyway, but it's not for sure. They would have to try together just like any couple does, no matter how they came together to begin with. Like me and my old husband. I didn't know him at all when we were married, but we grew to know each other." She nodded. "I tell you, there are ten thousand ways for people to fall in love at first, but loving one another past that, you have to work at it. Doesn't matter which of the ten thousand ways got you to where you are. You have to choose the way from there together." She smiled suddenly, showing her few teeth.

Liu Chenguang walked out slowly, and Tainu flew up to her shoulder.

Zhu Guiren was leaning against a wall, looking bored and beautiful. Several of the village girls ogled him as they walked by on made-up errands. "That was certainly a good use of time," he said. "Did you attain enlightenment?"

Tainu flew to his shoulder and pecked him on the ear.

"Ow! What was that for?"

Liu Chenguang walked over to the edge of her clearing, where she could look up at Crane Moon. Had it been a lifetime for Aili, truly? Only twenty-five years?

It was nothing to her, but Aili was mortal — time was different, a lifetime was different…Liu Chenguang's time with Hong Deming had only been ten years, after all, and those ten years had become the heart of her life. Aili had truly lived longer away from her than with her, and she herself had lived far longer away from her beloved person than with them. Even Zhu Guiren had said it: *she had changed.* Aili had changed also. They were not the same people that they were when they parted.

Nothing that exists is a finished thing.

She looked up at Crane Moon one last time…the old place from the old life.

"Liu Chenguang?" asked Zhu Guiren. Tainu was perched on his shoulder, his golden eyes peering out at her between the black strands of Zhu Guiren's hair.

She said, "I'll gather the medical supplies — as much as we can carry, and everything else I came for — and then let's go. We can make some good time tonight."

"East?" asked Zhu Guiren.

"East," she said.

CHAPTER 4
LITTLE DAXIAN

THE SUN WAS far too bright, and the sidewalk was far too hard. Also, there seemed to be something sticky on it.

Aili turned her head so she wasn't looking at that too-bright sun and noticed that the sticky stuff was right next to her hand. She tried to shuffle vaguely away from it and found that there were several clay jars next to her. There were also several people standing around her, but because of the bright sun, they were just painful silhouettes.

"White liquor only?" someone asked.

Someone else replied, "She drank all the golden liquor first, old Liang said. All the golden! Everything he had in stock!"

"Ahhhh!" said several others.

"More liquor," she said, and closed her eyes.

"Doctor?" whispered someone.

"Priest?" asked someone else.

Someone knelt next to her, speaking in Anglish. "What on earth happened to you? I thought you were dead."

With effort, Aili opened her eyes again to see Edna Lee's face. She started laughing. "Edna," she said, "Edna, you know what? It's so hard for me to get drunk now."

Edna's face paled. "When did you learn Daxian?"

She laughed and laughed and laughed some more. "Good liquor," she said, and passed out.

When Aili woke up again, her head was clear. She sat up and found herself on a couch in a small living room stuffed with knickknacks and decorated with Daxian landscape scrolls. There was incense burning somewhere. It reminded her sharply of Liu Chenguang.

"You're awake," came Edna's voice. She walked slowly into the room, carefully sitting down on the chair nearest the couch. "Do you know who I am? And who you are?"

"Yes," she said. "Well, mostly. Why do you ask?"

"You've been raving in Daxian and Anglish and some other languages for a few hours now," Edna said calmly.

"Well...it's hard to explain why that is."

"Can you explain why I just found you passed out on a sidewalk in Little Daxian?"

"I was trying to get drunk," she explained. "It took a while."

Edna stared at her. "I saw you get drunk on one bowl of liquor at the restaurant," she said.

"Yes. That's different. I also discovered getting drunk from here on in is going to be an expensive proposition."

"You also don't...sound like yourself."

Aili shook her head. "Well, it turns out I'm the same person all the way down...Anyway, I know. I can't explain anything to you in a way that makes any sense. But thank you for picking me up off the sidewalk." She stood up. "Also, congratulations."

"No, you're not leaving now," said Edna sternly. "Sit. You owe me an accounting."

Aili sat meekly.

"Let's just start with why you got drunk," Edna said. "And you can make it snappy. My husband will be home soon, and you'll have to start all over if he's here. Do you have a place to go, by the way?"

Aili sighed. "No," she said at last. "I lived with Nora...and Nora's..."

Edna's face grew quiet. "Were you with her?"

"I was. And she asked me to come tell her mother about it, but...I never met her family...and I don't know...what to say."

"Is that why I found you on the sidewalk?"

"One reason."

"Her mother's already gotten the telegram," she said. "You didn't come back either, so I assumed…but you survived."

Aili looked down. "In a sense."

Now that the liquor had fully worn off, everything was coming back to her. The long walk from Fallon to Easterly. Days without food because she couldn't think of how she could go into a restaurant with human beings and ask to be fed even though she had money in her pocket that she'd taken from the house before it was burned. Two days out from Fallon, wandering to find a way to cross the Tamer River without using a bridge or coming near people, she had come across a snake yaoguai and fought it and killed it, then staggered on. Nothing felt real except pain, but Little Daxian felt familiar and homey to her — hearing Daxian, even in a dialect different from the one she'd spoken with Liu Chenguang.

"Ah," she said out loud. "Oh, it hurts." She bent over, feeling the hot spike in her heart again, and the ache in her head. When the pain had passed, she remembered Nora again. "I thought it would be a good thing I could do," she tried to explain. "It didn't seem like…like there was much point in me…existing, though. Besides that." It had been easier in the spirit realm, being flayed nightly by the soul-devourers. It had taken her mind off of all of the pain that couldn't be healed, ever. After she had destroyed Fallon, what else was there to do?

Edna stood up, her pregnant belly visible in her dress. "Do you need a doc-tor?"

The pain in her head was unbelievable. "Needles."

She heard Edna call someone on the telephone in the other room, speaking in a rapid southern Daxian dialect. "My husband will be here soon. He's trained in both styles. Although he can only practice among Daxian," she added with a little bitterness. "His office is just down the street."

"Your husband," Aili said, trying to act like a civilized human being instead of a lump of quivering demands. "Can you remind me his name?"

"David Lee. He's happy to have me home, obviously," she added, patting her belly. "The generals decided married women couldn't be pilots, so here we are…"

Edna's husband was her height exactly, a neatly dressed man in glasses, with a kind face and a gentle voice. Unlike Edna, he spoke Anglish with an accent.

Aili said, "We can speak Daxian."

"Either is fine," he replied, his expression not showing any surprise at all. He took her pulse and asked her symptoms, then had her lie flat as he began to insert the needles and burn incense.

The pain disappeared almost immediately. She lay there with her eyes closed, enjoying the sense of being free from it. Then, she wondered where it was coming from; after all, with her situation…as it was, should she be having these repetitive bouts of pain and weakness? She remembered Liu Chenguang checking her pulse at the barn in Fallon. Her face had been worried…her expression when she turned into the phoenix gate to cross into the spirit realm, she had been so determined, and in so much pain. Aili could see it in her eyes.

Ah, there it was again.

"What's that?" muttered Doctor Lee; he started moving needles around. "There's something…"

"Chenguang," she said. The pain in her head subsided.

"Who's Chenguang?" he asked in his quiet voice.

"A friend," she said. Then she added, "Chenguang's a doctor too. She used to do this for me." Because they were speaking Daxian, she knew, he wouldn't be able to tell whether Chenguang was male or female. Just as well, though probably Edna would tell him later.

"Did you often have this kind of complaint in the past?"

"No, it's recent…"

He nodded and finished resetting the needles. "Wait here."

When he came back in, Edna was with him. He said, "My wife and I are concerned about you. Since you're a friend of Nora's and you have nowhere to go, would you consider staying with us tonight?"

"I couldn't trouble you."

"It's no trouble," Edna said. "When you're better, we'll go see Nora's mother together, all right? So you can keep your promise to her."

Aili nodded under the needles. "Thank you," she said. "I hope I can repay you someday."

Doctor Lee said, "No worries. I'm going to leave the needles for a while. Sleep if you can."

Edna sat down next to her one afternoon a week later and said, "I need to talk to you before we go see Nora's mother." She looked a little uncomfortable. "I know that you and Nora both had…interests in women. I've known that about Nora since we were kids together. And you and that woman had…well, whatever that was. She's gone now, right?"

"She's gone now," she said. "Yes."

"It doesn't bother me. You know, when we were growing up, there weren't a lot of places for me, as a Daxian girl. There weren't a lot of other Daxian kids. My parents weren't born here…Nora was kind to me ever since we were little. She protected me from bullies…" She wiped her eyes.

Aili felt her eyes tearing up as well. "Nora was like that," she said. "To me too."

Edna took a deep breath. "It's still not real to me. So, I want to hear what you have to tell her mother, too…and it's fine for me to be there. Her mom really likes me. She'll like me even more now since I'm married and pregnant." She rolled her eyes. "But what I wanted to say is that the reason Nora's been living on her own since she was seventeen is that her parents kicked her out when they found out that Nora had a girlfriend. They were able to accept her back into the family when she was older only because she never mentioned it to them, and they never asked, and she always wore dresses when she visited. So, don't bring it up…don't mention it, all right? And…I'm going to come right out and say it. Aili, I'm going to need to get you into some more…Nora would say *femmey* clothing."

Aili snickered, hearing Nora's vocabulary from Edna, and Edna giggled too.

Aili said. "I don't think we need to go that far. I can just dress the way I did when we were on the base. We had regulations for dresses and stuff like that, remember?" Aili had arrived in Little Daxian wearing the old clothes she'd gotten from the house in Fallon, which at least weren't the bloodstained rags she'd worn out of the spirit realm but were definitely more farm*boy* than farm*girl*.

Edna nodded, relieved. "That's right, like that." After a while, she said, "That person— What was her real name again?"

"Liu Chenguang," she said steadily.

"And you really liked her, didn't you?"

"Yes," she said. "I really liked her a lot."

Edna rocked in her chair, her hand over her belly protectively. "So, what happened? Can I ask?"

Aili sighed. "You wouldn't believe it…"

"Not any unbelievable stuff, please." She held up one hand. "Just the love stuff. That's all I'm interested in."

Aili thought for a moment. "It…it can't really be explained without the unbelievable stuff…But it comes down to— I love her, and she used to love me, but I don't think she can love me now."

"Didn't you only know each other for a few weeks?" Edna asked, frowning.

"I told you, there's unbelievable stuff."

"Love is a strong word," she said sternly, "for someone you've known so briefly."

Aili shook her head and started laughing — laughing in a good way for the first time in ages. "Edna, you are so right. Can you take it as given that we haven't known each other briefly, but for a long time? But...the version of me that she knew and that she loved– That's not who I am anymore. So..."

Edna rocked her chair a little more. "Ok," she said firmly. "You know what? I'm going to go for it. Tell me the unbelievable stuff."

That evening, they went to visit Nora's mother. Aili wore a dress and told her that her daughter had been brave up until the very end; that she had been trying to help wounded soldiers on the battlefield, under fire; that she had been the best of friends and cared for all those around her; that her death had been quick and painless.

Nora's mother cried, but said she was glad to know, glad that she hadn't been alone. Aili found that she couldn't cry herself, though she wished she could.

When they left, Edna eyed Aili carefully. "All right, now come on. My parents live down this way."

Aili found the dress to be incredibly constricting, thanks to the foundation garments she had to wear beneath it. "Ugh," she said. "Clothing in ancient Daxian beats this by a long shot."

"From what you told me, you didn't wear women's clothes in ancient Daxian, so you have no basis for comparison."

"True."

They walked down along the seawall of the bay, then turned a corner back into Little Daxian. Edna stopped in front of an old house with a large collection of orchids on a rack on the porch, alongside a lot of drying laundry.

"I can't believe I'm doing this," she muttered. "Promise you won't tell David."

Aili sighed. She felt no anxiety about this at all. "If I was Liu Chenguang, I could diagnose and probably do this much more effectively," she said. "But all I know how to do is put blood on his tongue, ok?"

"Don't tell David," Edna muttered again, "or my mother."

"I think she's going to notice when I slash my hand in front of her and start dripping blood on him."

"I'll bring her out of the room. I'll– I'll tell her I need her to feel the baby–"

An old man was lying in bed, deeply asleep or unconscious. The room smelled like incense burning and bitter medicine. Aili closed her eyes at the scent. Edna, as promised, hustled her mother out of the room with some excuse, saying that Aili was a visitor from the worship house; she discreetly stuck a sacred book in Aili's hand to make this a little more believable. Her father had lung cancer, but it didn't matter. After all that training with the Navy, in the end, Aili knew only one cure.

Two days later, Edna sat down next to her again. Aili was lying still, covered with needles; David insisted that she needed regular treatment to ensure that the terrible headaches wouldn't come back.

"He's cured," she said. "He's up, puttering around with his plants again. Can breathe normally, eat, sleep…No pain, no coughing."

"Yes," said Aili, unsurprised.

"So, you told the truth."

She nodded.

"So," Edna said. She leaned forward and took Aili's hand. "Now, you have to tell me the rest of the truth. Why you were drunk in Little Daxian, and why you are in so much pain."

Aili didn't want to keep depending on the Lees, but she didn't have enough money to rent an actual apartment of her own. She found a room just outside Little Daxian and mostly sat in it, alone. Edna, she knew, was worried about her, but what could she say to make her feel better, when she herself felt…as she did?

She began wandering around Easterly at night, remembering how Liu Chenguang had been able to help people by doing this. Like Liu Chenguang, she found quite a few people lying in the alleys who needed help. More importantly, she started to see the people who were hurting them and thought that she should probably put a stop to that. One night, she found herself standing in front of an old house with wooden shingles rotting off, hearing the rowdy customers inside it, and a girl screaming in pain and fear. Of course, she had always known these places were here. These were the places where runaway girls who trusted friendly men were taken. Luckily for her, she never did trust friendly men, so she was still lying on a bench at the bus station when Nora had found her. She never told Nora that she had had to fight off two men before she showed up; Nora probably thought the bruises were from her dad.

Aili didn't bother bringing En out for this. Qinggong and bare hands were enough. One by one, she threw all the men out into the street. The women followed, some of them wailing that she was interfering with their business, others silently running for whatever safety they could find.

Well, she couldn't give them safety. But she could give them this.

The rage was sunlight and lightning inside her, washing away the pain of Liu Chenguang, all the shame and humiliation of her two lives, her cowardice, and her utter and complete failure at protecting the people she loved. She lifted her hand, shouted, and lashed down, the whip of phoenix fire striking her anger on the world.

The remaining women also screamed and ran away.

Aili stood there, breathing deeply, eyes closed, enjoying the feeling of the flames on her skin. When the fire department arrived, she used qinggong to leap away — back to her lonely, dark room — and fell asleep soundly for the first time in weeks.

She did it again the next night.

And the next.

And the next.

This time, to her surprise, a few of the prostitutes were young boys. Like the girls, most of them ran away, but not all of them.

A teenager walked out after his customer and looked at her, frowning. "What are you doing?"

"What does it look like I'm doing?" She pulled the phoenix whip out of the air and showed it to him. "I'm burning this place down."

"Why are you burning down my home?" he asked evenly. "You think people like me don't deserve a roof?"

"You should have a better home than this," she said. For some reason she felt herself tearing up. "A better life than this."

He laughed bitterly. "Well, go ahead and burn it down," he said, walking away. "But all that happens is I don't have a place to sleep."

The night after that, there were patrols organized by the brothelkeepers and the organizations that profited from them. Someone shot her. She burned him, as well as the house he was guarding. The night after that, there were large groups patrolling and almost no customers. She was pleased with this situation, but there was nothing to burn. No one to hate. She needed someone to hate, so she went looking across the bay in San Toma and found some places there to destroy.

The seventh night, she went back to the bar where she had met Liu Chenguang and drank. Beer wasn't nearly as effective as white liquor, but she did recognize one of the sailors who had attacked Liu Chenguang. She followed him out into the alley and broke both his arms. When he fled, begging for mercy and help, she laughed out loud and looked up to see a crow watching her. She threw her whip at the crow, and almost caught it.

On the eighth, she went down to the waterfront and waited silently at the water's edge until the quietest part of the night. A drunk man slept on a rock next to her, covered in tidal slime and deeply unconscious: perfect bait. When the yaoguai arose from the water, one yellow eye still dimmed, she leapt in and tore it to pieces with En and the demon-quelling seal. The drunk man was still sleeping as she staggered back to her apartment.

The following night, she went to San Toma again, taking the ferry from Easterly. As the boat crossed the bay, she watched the waves sheet over the water and wondered who else in the world she might usefully hate. She found that she couldn't really hate the Kunorese, even though they were the ones who had killed Nora; those had already been punished. Who else was there, besides her father and grandfather and great-grandfather — murderers, men who abused women and children?

She stood in front of a pleasure house she had found in San Toma — a large one, not far from San Tomas Little Daxian neighborhood, which was decorated for tourists with red lanterns and dragons. Even though it was completely false, the red lanterns made her feel homesick. She looked at them for a while. Someone somewhere in that street was playing a qin. The sadness and the rage were fighting with one another inside her; it seemed that there was nothing else left in the world but those two things to choose between.

She sighed and looked back at the house. At least with the rage, she was doing something. Something that would help people. Being sad was just…nothing.

As usual, she went in and used her hands and feet to knock down and drag out the customers, one by one. Someone hit her with a knife this time, which she blocked casually and then grabbed, stabbing the person in the shoulder before she remembered that she was trying not to kill people, then realized this person was a woman, not even a customer; this was someone she was trying to protect. Aili quickly slashed her hand and healed the wound. The woman spat in her face. She ignored this, and went back outside when she was sure the house was empty, ready to burn.

As she lifted up the hand with the whip, she felt someone grab her wrist.

Doctor Lee. "No," he said sternly. "Stop it."

She stared at him, uncomprehending.

"Edna sent me," he said. "Edna. My wife. Sent me. Stop it."

She raised her empty hand for a palm strike to his chest, ready to send him flying down the street.

"No," he said. He looked at her calmly.

She couldn't kill Edna's husband. She slowly lowered her hand, looking at him, though the whip was still burning.

He glanced at the whip, and she realized that he wasn't as calm as she had thought; he was trembling a little bit. This was an ordinary person, after all — not a cultivator.

She flicked the whip out of her hand, out of existence.

He brought her over to sit on the curb across the street from the unburned house. The prostitutes and their customers started to stealthily sneak back in.

In his quiet voice, Doctor Lee said, "Edna sent me. She's worried about you. So am I. Someone told me you got on the ferry tonight, so I came too."

"Aren't you also afraid of me?" she asked.

"Well, yes, since you're burning things down with your hands," he said calmly. "You didn't mention to Edna that you can do that."

"There were a lot of things I didn't mention," she said. She hadn't told Edna anything about being a cultivator, or En, or the yaoguai and the soul-devourers, or burning down Fallon.

Doctor Lee thought for a minute. "Edna would be here herself, but I didn't want her to risk it in her condition," he said. "In case things got out of hand. But if she were here, I know what she would say to you. She'd ask you to think about the people you love, and who love you, and ask yourself if they would want you to do this. You shouldn't only be doing things out of hatred and anger."

"That's all I have left," she said, almost in a whisper. "The people I love are dead, or don't love me."

"I doubt that," he said. "I'm here for you, Edna's here for you, and we hardly know you. That doesn't even begin to count as love. Just the beginning of friendship, and look at us. There are people who know you better, who love you more." He paused. "Even if they're dead, they still love you. You can still question if they would be happy with this — with you becoming like this."

"Can I not burn all the pain out of the world?" she asked, wondering aloud. "If I destroy all the evil, will all the pain go away?"

Doctor Lee said, "What do you think?"

Aili sighed. She reached out and pulled En into her hand, looking at its blade. David's eyes widened slightly. "My sword. I named it En. Isn't it funny to have a sword named for gratitude and benevolence, owing a debt to the one who saved me? Can a sword also be like that?"

Doctor Lee looked at her. "I…don't even know how to think about that question. My guess is that gratitude comes from life, not from death." He was silent for a little bit. "I also know that death and life are not easily separated, neither is good from evil. They're too deeply intertwined. How can you cut one without also cutting the other? Better to grow the good than cut the evil."

She shook her head. "I don't know. We didn't go to worship growing up." The only sacred book in the house had been in Sammish. It was somewhere on a base in the islands now, unless they had shipped it back with her belongings.

"It seems to me, as long as good is growing, that's the important thing. So, the question would be, can this sword be something that helps what is good to grow? Can you be something like that? Can your life be something like that?" He looked at her, very earnestly. "There's a lot in my life that I am angry about, I'd like you to know. Not as much as you have, you might think, but everyone has their own pain. It's not that I'm not angry, but there's good in my life. There are people I love. We're going to have a child — making a good life for them so they can live well, doing whatever good thing is in my power…isn't that better than seeking revenge and destroying what has hurt me, even if it's in my power to destroy it completely?" He nodded at her sword. "It's in your power to destroy. More than most, I would guess, so you need to think about it, very carefully."

She was silent, staring at her hand wrapped around En's hilt and remembering Liu Chenguang in the caverns, his hair brushing his wrist. Liu Chenguang would not want this, she knew. More for her to be ashamed of.

As though hearing her thoughts, David said, "There was something Edna specifically wanted me to tell you, and I'm sorry if this is getting into too much of your personal business, but Edna's very perceptive, and we share our thoughts a lot. I'm a doctor, too, so don't think that…well, there are lots of confidences I keep."

After a while, Aili said, "All right, what is it?"

"Edna wanted to tell you not to be ashamed of anything. That you've never done anything to be ashamed of, and whatever's been done to you, that's nothing to be ashamed of either. She wanted me to tell you that you can't blame yourself because of things that other people have done."

Aili was silent.

He continued, "She also wanted me to tell you, if I found you, which I have, and if it seemed important, which it does, that whatever happened to you as a child or in your past, that's not your whole life. Just because bad things happened to you before doesn't mean that good things can't also happen. Just because someone you trusted betrayed your trust doesn't mean that everyone will. Just because love wasn't enough to protect you when you were young doesn't mean that love is nothing."

Aili looked over at the red lanterns hanging outside the stores in Little Daxian and listened to the qin music. "I've done things I'm ashamed of," she said at last.

"It's better to do something different, I think," he said thoughtfully. "To do something to make amends. Just being ashamed…it doesn't make anything better."

When she didn't respond, he stood up, brushing his pants off where the dirt of the curb had stuck to them. "That's all I had to say. I know it probably is just words to you, but I wouldn't have said them, and I wouldn't have come all this way, and Edna and I wouldn't have spent so much time talking about you if you weren't a person worth all of this and more. I hope you know that."

"Thank you," she said. She looked at him seriously. "I'm…I'm grateful."

He nodded and stood nearby as she sat there a while more, watching the prostitutes and their customers go in and out of the house. Aili thought of Wu Fan and wondered what had happened to him. Maybe she would light an incense stick for him if there was a place in Little Daxian, even if it only was a place for tourists and not a real shrine. She decided to go ahead and do it, and stood.

For the first time, she realized that she had been wearing Liu Chenguang's jade pendant around her neck through everything: the spirit realm, the destruction of the array, the madness. She put her hand on it, feeling its shape and the warmth of the jade, the wings of the crane from so long ago. She should give it back. It had always been meant for her — for Liu Chenguang — but perhaps she had needed to be reminded, too.

"Will you come back to Easterly?" he asked.

"Not tonight."

She took a late-night bus from San Toma and reached the hotel outside of Fallon the next day. As she had thought, her mother was staying with Mrs. Mitchell, helping out around the bar and hotel for room and board. After she had gotten over her joy that Aili was still alive, they sat in a room together, Aili's mother's eyes constantly filling with tears.

"You look tired," she said to Aili. Her Anglish had improved a great deal, but being able to talk to her in Sammish made her even happier. She completely bought Aili's story that she had learned Sammish on the ship to the base.

"A lot has happened," she said. "Mama, I can't stay. There's somewhere I need to go."

She nodded. "That girl."

Aili started. "How did you know?"

Her mother smiled. "I didn't have enough Anglish to tell you what I knew. I always knew that you liked girls. I'm not a fool or blind. It was obvious that you liked her, and she liked you. She liked you very much, I could tell." She smiled again. "As she should, my beautiful Aili. You deserve to be loved very much."

Aili looked down. "Her name is Liu Chenguang," she said. "Or Tairei, that's her…nickname."

Her mother said, "Your father died, of course you knew."

"Of course."

"I'm glad," said her mother. "The best day in my life, the day they told me he was dead."

"Why didn't you leave sooner, Mama?"

"I was afraid," she said. "First it was for you, because if I wasn't there, I thought it would be…even worse. After you left, he said…he said he knew where you were. You were in Easterly. And that's where you were, wasn't it? Even now, I don't know if he really knew or was just guessing to threaten me, but he said he would kill you if I left, and then he would find me and kill me."

She looked at her hands. It was not necessary for either of them to say that they believed he would do exactly that.

"I couldn't think of anything to do to be free, to free you." She sighed. "So many times, I thought about killing him, but I didn't dare."

After they were quiet for a while, she added, "I wish I could have protected you better, my Aili. That's the great sadness of my life. It wasn't because I didn't want to. Only because I was too weak to do it."

Aili said, "You're like a phoenix, Mama."

Quizzically, her mother looked at her with blue-gray eyes that were the same as her own. "I don't understand. What is that?"

Aili hugged her, feeling the scars on her mother's back through the thin fabric. "You didn't have any weapons, but you tried to stand between us anyway."

Aili slept that night in the hotel and had a good breakfast with her mother and Mrs. Mitchell before starting west. She didn't want to walk through the burned remnants of Fallon, but she thought she would need to hike along the coast itself to see what she needed. As Zhu Guiren had said, she didn't have to go for many miles; by mid afternoon, as she walked north along the high cliffs above the boulders and the foaming waves, she saw a huge arched rock about half a mile out. She'd known it since she was a child, and she was fairly sure that this was the dragon gate. There was no point in her trying to take the phoenix gate into the spirit world, since she couldn't enter a demonic gate to go to Daxian and would just end up fighting yaoguai endlessly.

Just to be sure that she was doing what was necessary, she stood at the very edge of the cliff and whispered. "Eftahede."

In her mind's eye, she saw a brilliant line of white-gold light leading from her own heart outwards, straight across the ocean.

So it was necessary, then.

She settled into a lotus position, first to cultivate, then, as the sun drifted toward the west, to consider how Zhu Guiren would call a dragon. She held En in front of her for confidence and tried to send out some sort of intention into the ocean, asking for a response. It was enormously difficult, probably because she was doing it wrong, somehow, and it took nearly two hours. As the sun began to shine blindingly across the water, as it did near sunset, she saw something break the surface near the rock. Several somethings.

She moved toward the edge of the cliff again, shading her eyes with her hand. Yes, there it was. At first, it was like dolphins — regular curves clearing the surface again and again — but she knew that this wasn't dolphins.

From far below came a clear, thin voice that cut through the sound of the waves. "What is it?"

Aili cleared her throat. "Lord Dragon, I need to cross the ocean. I beg the favor that you take me through the dragon gate with you."

"My gate requires a sacrifice. A mortal life."

She had been pretty sure that would be it, since Zhu Guiren had decided that Tainu wouldn't agree. "I am amenable."

"Send the sacrifice to me and come to the shore."

She walked back from the edge of the cliff several steps, then several steps more, then again. The cliff here was at least three hundred feet tall, at least; "very high" in her childhood's recollection, and still more now that she was doing this. She felt that things would go better if she missed the rocks at the very edge and at least got into the water. When she turned around, she took several deep breaths and closed her eyes, digging her toes into the earth. She bounced up and down a few times, like a runner at the beginning of a race, then put her head down and

flew forward with all the qinggong she had.
    When that ran out, she fell like a stone.

CHAPTER 5
REFUGE

THE ROAD EAST was brutal.

Mostly, the crowds of refugees were headed west, inland, away from the Kunoru-held provinces. Many of them were sick or wounded, and since Tainu and Liu Chenguang kept stopping, blending with crowds — Tainu usually in his bird form, as his tall, dark-skinned figure was very noticeable — and finding ways to surreptitiously heal people, sometimes they would travel less than three miles in a day.

"It's so much easier when they're sleeping or unconscious," sighed Tainu after several days of this.

They were seated around a campfire a mile or so off the main road, in the ruins of a nameless village. It had been burned and broken, but the corpses at least were buried in a recent line of mounds.

Zhu Guiren looked around and said, "No one even bothered to set an array here after it was attacked. The pickings must be very good to just ignore something like this."

Liu Chenguang just put her head in her hands and sighed. "I'm so tired. There's so much...so many people."

After some dispirited silence, Zhu Guiren said, "Why do you two have to do this? Can you just...stop? We're not making any progress on our actual goal of destroying arrays because I have to constantly watch the two of you mingle with crowds of sick and suspicious mortals and keep an eye out for demons."

Tainu and Liu Chenguang looked at each other. Tainu finally said, "We could stop, but we don't want to."

Zhu Guiren moodily poked the fire with a stick. "If anyone has been wondering how I spent my day, I've been off fighting with random demons that are stalking the refugees."

Tainu said, "Well, that explains why you look like that." He reached over and took the stick out of Zhu Guiren's hand, then laid his own against Zhu Guiren's forehead. "Why didn't you tell me? Where's the wound?"

Zhu Guiren unbuttoned his shirt, feeling slightly embarrassed; unbuttoning and buttoning were difficult. How had Tainu even known he was wounded? There was nothing visible until his shirt was peeled away to show a large patch of burned skin oozing a viscous dark liquid.

"Talisman," he explained.

Tainu looked closer, bit his hand, and gently brushed the wound. He held up his hand and closed his eyes, whispering. A gentle golden glow surrounded his fingers as he laid his hand against Zhu Guiren's chest. It felt warm; Zhu Guiren realized that the wound on his body had been leeching a freezing cold inside him. He hadn't even noticed.

"You've never done that before," Zhu Guiren said, watching Tainu's face. He didn't wince when his wound was touched, but Tainu did.

"You've never had a wound like this before. At least, not since we've been with you," Tainu replied, eyes still closed. His hand trembled slightly. "This couldn't have come from an ordinary demon. It's eating away at you. The true wound is inside. This is just the mark of where it's poisoning your meridians…" He took a deep breath and removed his hand.

Zhu Guiren's skin was smooth and unwounded.

"I've never seen anything like that before. What was it?" Tainu met his eyes, but Zhu Guiren looked away.

"I told you," Zhu Guiren said brusquely. "Talisman strike. I've had wounds like that before. It's not that different."

He worked on buttoning his shirt with his single hand. He did not want to tell them who had given him this wound, but eventually, he decided he had to. They were partners now. He had never had partners before — people that he needed to trust and coordinate things with. It was something new to consider. But every morning, they practiced together for an hour, and of the three of them, he was the only one who could really propose strategy. Neither of the phoenixes understood what they were facing, and Tainu still had no martial arts to speak of. It made his skin crawl to imagine demons coming after Tainu if he wasn't there to protect him. He looked up and saw that Liu Chenguang had slumped over, asleep already, but Tainu's dark eyes were watching him. Belatedly, he realized that Tainu was concerned he couldn't button his shirt.

"I'm fine," he said. "I can do it."

Tainu replied, "Of course. But I'm wondering where that wound really came from. It's not from a normal demonic weapon."

He nodded. "It's a weapon sent by the First of my clan. His special talisman. It's not something he would send out lightly or give to just anyone. It carries a good amount of his power. He doesn't have many of those."

Tainu frowned. "You fought First? Does that mean you're now the head of your clan?"

Zhu Guiren snorted. "No, if I fought First…I don't think I'd survive that. Probably, I couldn't beat Second either. I fought Seventh."

Tainu gave him a quizzical look.

"She would never have tried against me without a direct order from First, and he had given her weapons that would be effective against me."

"She's dead?" asked Tainu.

"I'm alive," he said shortly, "therefore she's dead."

Tainu was quiet for a moment. "Tell me, though. You're Third, she was Seventh…There was no way she was likely to win against you, given that she's not your nearest ranked demon, from what you've told me. What was the point of sending her, even with a powerful talisman? What would have happened to you with that wound if I hadn't been here?"

"Those talismans are used for punishment. If Seventh didn't kill me, I would have eventually been paralyzed until First could send demons to pick me up and bring me back to him for discipline." He would also have been in atrocious, mind-breaking pain, but he didn't feel the need to mention this. "It didn't affect me immediately. It would have taken a while to work, so I…forgot about it."

In a very level tone of voice, Tainu said, "You should not wait for me to ask you before showing me a wound. Do not do that again."

Zhu Guiren looked up, surprised. He had never heard Tainu angry in quite this way before. Annoyed, yes, but actually, truly, angry? No. Well, wounds were wounds; sometimes he didn't notice them.

"I'll do my best," he said. "I didn't mean to hide it from you. I was just concerned about what this means for us. First is looking for me, and clearly is not sending me a polite invitation to come chat. His assumption is that I will not obey discipline unless I'm forced to, which means that he is currently treating me as an enemy and finds me suspicious. If Seventh was out looking for me, certainly I can assume other top-ranked demons are also out there looking, and we haven't even destroyed any arrays yet."

Tainu stirred the fire with the stick, saying nothing.

"I'm not sure what to do," Zhu Guiren said. "We're moving very slowly, and I am now a visible target. I am wondering if there's a safe place you can wait while I…deal with this."

"What do you mean, deal with this?" Tainu asked quietly.

"Demons only solve problems in one way," Zhu Guiren said, annoyed that he had to explain obvious things. "I need to go kill ten or twenty or so of my clan."

"How do you propose to do this?" he asked, still in that quiet voice.

"It's not an unfamiliar exercise for me, or for them, for that matter. All of us know what we're doing and have done it before or we wouldn't be alive and where we are. I'm not exactly sure what kind of details you want from me." He felt oddly defensive, as well as strangely…sad? Sad. Had he ever felt sad before? He imagined poking the feeling like Tainu was poking the fire.

"That fight was draining. I need to cultivate," he said, and stood up to go over to the new cemetery — a convenient little store of resentment for him.

He settled in a lotus position on one of the graves, the dust on it still loose; this village hadn't been destroyed long ago. The souls of the dead — except those held to earth by strong obsessions — would mostly have gone already since they weren't caught in an array, but the resentment of the dead was still here for demonic cultivation.

As he closed his eyes and focused, resentment poured into him, sharp-edged and bitter like the wind filling the sail of a broken ship, a drink like sweet soy milk hiding shards of glass. He remembered the first time he had cultivated, long before he was able to form a mortal body: how much it had hurt, how the teaching demon had to force him and the others to settle to it, to learn to drink the pain and find it good. Not all of the others could. He remembered the examples made of those who failed or gave up. It was all a lesson learned.

The glassy edges smoothed as the flood of resentment became thicker; now, instead of sharp slashes it was a river of heat — acid, burning and blistering — the layered resentment of war and destruction, far beyond a few mortal bodies lying in the soil and their wasted lives. This was the resentment of death multiplied ten thousand times, the breaking of all dreams, the loss of all hopes, the burning of the earth and the wasting of the waters, the betrayal of trust and the futility of love.

He took a deep breath, as close to truly drunk as he had been since he first set his own array — since Liu Chenguang's blood and destruction had sealed the array that held two million mortal souls. This was why demons were here, flocking to the eastern provinces. So much thick, rich resentment. So much power, so close at hand, ready for anyone who would take it.

He would have to cultivate more regularly if he was going to fight so many in such short succession. Others would be gathering power, setting arrays even now. If he really wanted to survive, to win, he should also be setting his own… He should be in among the mortals — spreading lies, fomenting more cruelty, more betrayal — increasing the flood of power that could be his own, as he once had done. Once his power was great enough, he wouldn't need to fear any other demon, allied or enemy. His life would be his own, then. Why was he wasting his time here?

Zhu Guiren opened his eyes to see Tainu sitting in his own lotus position, the light of the fire on his face. He looked very tired. Liu Chenguang had lain down from her slumped posture earlier, not visible behind the flames except for one out-flung hand and her shoulder-length black hair hiding her face. Tainu had covered her with a blanket.

Suddenly, Tainu seemed to feel Zhu Guiren's gaze and turned his dark eyes toward him. Zhu Guiren closed his own eyes again, embarrassed, though he didn't know why. He couldn't quite get the flow of cultivation again either. Something seemed to be interfering with his focus, though he tried for what felt like hours.

Could he really leave the phoenixes? They were good at hiding. They had said so themselves many times. He wasn't a monster. They had been friendly to him; he didn't need to capture them or betray them. They had their things to do and he had his. That was all. It wasn't his job to protect phoenixes or to destroy his array. He was a demon. His life was what it was.

"Demon?" Tainu's voice was very close to him.

When Zhu Guiren opened his eyes, he saw Tainu had come up to him silently, and was kneeling in front of him. The light was very poor, and the fire had died down low.

He felt something trickling down his face and froze in shock. Why was his face wet?

"Demon," said Tainu quietly, "you're tired. Come to sleep."

He felt Tainu's hand take his, pull him up, walk with him back toward the remains of the fire. There was a blanket ready for him; Tainu helped him lie down and put another one over him.

"I'm tired," Zhu Guiren said at last.

Tainu put a hand on his forehead again, then gently on the blanket lying over his chest where the wound had been. "You're very tired," he said. "Sleep now. Tomorrow's another day."

He seemed to be hesitating, thinking about saying something else. Zhu Guiren watched him, his mind in a fog. Truly, he was tired. It must be the effects of the talisman. He had never heard of anyone escaping the punishment talisman before; there was no knowing what Tainu had saved him from.

"Thank you," he mumbled, and closed his eyes, sinking further into the misty world of sleep. As it enveloped him completely, pulling him down into unconsciousness, he dreamed that Tainu kissed him on the forehead, very softly.

The next morning dawned gray and sad. The ruined village surrounded them as they wearily ate some stale oilcakes together.

"Demon, do you need to leave?" Tainu asked.

Zhu Guiren shook his head. Let them come find him, he thought. With all the resentment around, he should have an easy time cultivating enough power to deal with them. "I shouldn't stay too close to you, though. I'll be off to the sides as much as possible."

Liu Chenguang yawned. Zhu Guiren decided he'd let Tainu fill her in; he didn't want to talk about it anymore. He had never liked Seventh much — who did he like? Who was likable among demons? — but he had known her for millennia. They were close in age. At one point, three or four thousand years ago, before either of them had reached their advanced ranks, Second had ordered them to bear offspring together. This idea had so infuriated him that he had immediately left the clan home to wander for several centuries. He wondered how Seventh had felt about that. If perhaps she had wanted offspring; if she had borne any before she died.

Why was he thinking about these things? It was none of his business. Seventh knew what she was getting into when she came for him.

"Should we practice this morning?" Liu Chenguang asked.

"Every morning," Zhu Guiren said firmly.

He brought out the sword. First, he attacked Liu Chenguang, then Tainu practiced diving at him to block his eyes. Liu Chenguang practiced disarming him. Then, the two of them drilled in ways that they could work together to defend him during those crucial moments when he was weak and unable to fight while spellcasting: warding, diving, disarming, blocking, Liu Chenguang's wings. Zhu Guiren's role at this point was to watch and suggest ways they could coordinate more effectively, to show Tainu how to block without getting injured, and occasionally to play the demonic attacker. They didn't practice using the phoenix-infused talismans; they were too painful for Zhu Guiren to receive and too valuable to waste. Zhu Guiren privately considered them for emergency use only — if the phoenixes were attacked and he wasn't able to protect them.

Zhu Guiren finally called a halt. "Your energy is low. Do you need another day to rest?" he asked. "Do you need to cultivate? I've been taking it easy on you but no other demon will."

Tainu and Liu Chenguang looked at each other again, just like last night.

"We should cultivate," Tainu said reluctantly. "We really are…too weak now. Liu Chenguang, I don't think I could heal anything serious right now. How about you?"

She said, "You seem worse off than me."

Zhu Guiren remembered the talisman wound last night and wondered if this was why Tainu was so tired. He opened his mouth to ask, but Tainu spoke first.

"This place isn't a good place for us to rest," he said. "This whole landscape isn't good for our cultivation. It's full of death. We would need to get somewhere else — somewhere better…but I can't just leave all these people."

Liu Chenguang nodded, and wearily sat down next to him.

Zhu Guiren couldn't stand it anymore. "Are you two literally the only people in the world that can help others?" he asked sharply. "Why is it all your responsibility alone?"

Tainu smiled at him, which made him feel a little confused. He was so frustrated with these damn phoenixes.

"Even with everything we can do," Tainu said, "it's nothing compared to the flood, you're right. But there are things that only we can do, so we have to do them."

Liu Chenguang asked, "Isn't there anyone else, though?"

Tainu whispered softly under his breath for a while, and then shook his head. "Kunoru, Innam, Tomasines, the great plateau," he counted off. "We're the only ones in North Daxian."

"No, we're not."

Tainu's head came up sharply. "Yes. We are."

"There's that–"

"Don't be ridiculous. They haven't come down from their mountain in what, three thousand years?" His eyes narrowed. "Did you know I went to her and begged her to let you come to Mount Shi, back then? She refused. Even if you had made it there, she would have warded you out."

Zhu Guiren looked back and forth between them, intrigued. "Are you saying there's someone who can help that's at Mount Shi? That's not so far, if it's just me going. I can be faster than you. I could go get them, and you could stay here and rest and wait for me…cultivate for a while. Although, it's not very nice for you. It's really more my kind of place," he added, looking around at the burned buildings and the cemetery.

Tainu said, "Don't bother. She won't come, the shameless coward."

Zhu Guiren smiled, "I've never heard you swear about someone before. You must really dislike this person."

Liu Chenguang poked Tainu in the shoulder. "Don't let him fool you," she whispered very loudly to Zhu Guiren. "Beneath his kind attitude is boiling rage."

"It must be difficult to be a phoenix with an anger management problem."

"Oh, you're not wrong," said Liu Chenguang sincerely.

Tainu just glared at them. "This is just a distraction. Liu Chenguang, it's just us. Let's cultivate a few hours and head out."

"Oh no, I want to meet this person," Zhu Guiren said. And, he thought privately, this would be a good opportunity to get away from the phoenixes for a few days. Fight some demons perhaps…get them off their trail. The phoenixes could hide and rest, and he would draw attention from them. And perhaps, if he got someone else to take care of all the mortals, they would remember the reason they were here at all and get back to work.

"I'm telling you, she won't come," said Tainu through gritted teeth.

"I wasn't planning to *ask* her," Zhu Guiren replied, smiling. "This is a phoenix, correct?"

"It's warded. Heavily warded. She never goes out." Tainu frowned at Zhu Guiren, clearly seeing through his ruse to get away from them.

He shrugged. "Nothing ventured, nothing gained. Where?"

Liu Chenguang smiled. "I would love to see this if you can get her to come."

"Don't encourage him," Tainu said. "Demon, don't try it. You'll be injured at best, maybe seriously. Her wards are strong."

"As strong as yours?"

Tainu was silent.

"No," said Liu Chenguang.

Tainu glared at her again.

Liu Chenguang continued, "Tainu, what can it hurt? He can at least ask.

Look at all of this — all of these people. At some point, she has to have some compassion."

"No. Do not." He stalked away, his shoulders stiff and furious. Over his shoulder, he yelled, "Liu Chenguang, come on, let's go. Demon, don't do it. I'm telling you."

Zhu Guiren leaned down to Liu Chenguang. "Tell me where she hides, how to find her," he whispered, "and you two go back down the path a little bit. Where we camped night before last was better than this for you, probably. Those trees, remember? I'll meet you there in three days. Rest and cultivate."

Liu Chenguang looked after Tainu, irresolute, but finally she told him.

A week later, Zhu Guiren marched into their camp and tossed a woman bound with glowing, blue-black chains on her ankles and wrists in front of Tainu. Tainu looked at her in horror, then at Zhu Guiren in fury.

"Fix me!" Zhu Guiren crowed, holding out his arms wide. He was covered in blood, burns, and bruises, and his clothes hung off him in rags.

"Liu Chenguang," gritted Tainu, "you do it."

"Oh no," said Zhu Guiren. "I get to pick. You do it. I want you."

Liu Chenguang shrugged.

Tainu stiffly moved over to Zhu Guiren and began dabbing blood on wound after wound.

Zhu Guiren felt almost giddy with blood loss and success. He'd killed Eighth, Sixth, and Fourteenth, in addition to several other demons from other clans. No one else had gotten a talisman on him, and he'd broken the wards to capture this annoying phoenix after she insulted him and told him that all the mortals could die and the two busybody phoenixes could rot in their self-righteousness as far as she was concerned. While he appreciated her point of view, no one spoke to him that way. She wasn't particularly strong — not nearly as powerful as Tainu or as clever at self-defense as Liu Chenguang — so it hadn't been difficult once he had gotten a spellchain on her so she couldn't transform and fly away.

"You have a lot of internal damage from her wards, didn't you notice?" Tainu said. His voice finally lost a little bit of its edge of anger, which made Zhu Guiren feel secretly relieved.

"No," he said honestly, "I was busy with all the other damage. I might have cared if I didn't have a phoenix to come back to." He smiled guilelessly up at Tainu.

Liu Chenguang laughed. "Zhu Guiren, let her go. I didn't really mean you should chain her up and force her to come. What good is that? She can only help if she wants to."

He snapped his fingers and the spellchains disappeared.

Tainu finished by touching his mouth with his bloody fingers, which felt rather odd; Tainu had only done that twice before — in the spirit realm when he had lost his hand, and after he was attacked with the phoenix talisman — and he supposed those times, he'd been in too much pain to really feel it. Tainu's fingers pressed inside his lips, parting his teeth and brushing his tongue lightly with blood. He didn't remember that part. He raised an eyebrow, but Tainu was already walking away from him, looking grim, to sit by the strange phoenix.

She sat up and tossed back her long, unbound black hair, rubbing her ankles where the chain had been. "How dare you, sibling," she hissed at Tainu. "Both of you. How dare you partner with a demon to insult and abuse me in this way."

"I apologize," Tainu said tightly. "We didn't intend this. We only wanted him to ask you if you could come down and help the people. There's a lot of suffering, war, flood, famine–"

"Why should I care about this? Let nature take its course. Let the mortals do what they need to do. Why do you need to interfere? You've insulted me, inconvenienced me, and set me back in my cultivation. Look at the two of you — what's the effect of constantly interfering with mortal lives? You are only increasing suffering, and you are covered with the world's filth. You," she said coldly to Liu Chenguang, "are barely a phoenix anymore, and you," she glared at Tainu, "eldest, century after century you keep trying to fix what can't be fixed, cure what can't be cured, and you wander the world in pain. For what? Stupid. Let the dying die. You're only prolonging the inevitable."

Tainu clenched his fists and closed his eyes.

Zhu Guiren stared at the phoenix, then back at Tainu. He leaned over by Tainu's ear and whispered very loudly, "You want to hit her, don't you? Do you want me to hit her for you?"

Tainu snorted, and then laughed out loud. His fists relaxed. He looked away from the phoenix and smiled at Zhu Guiren.

Zhu Guiren grinned back. Tainu laughing was the best sound. Also, he would very happily hit this phoenix if she called Tainu stupid again. He shot her a nasty look to make sure she understood that.

Despite being glared at by a demon, the phoenix opened her mouth again, but Liu Chenguang spoke first. In a reasonable voice, she said, "We're sorry for the inconvenience, but after all, you're already here. Why not walk with us and heal for a while? You've been alone a long time. Surely it would be good to be out in the world for a bit. There are so many—"

"No," said the phoenix coldly. "I'm leaving now." She held out her arms in preparation to transform, then suddenly stopped. She looked consideringly at Tainu, then at Zhu Guiren. Abruptly she said, "Those wards were the strongest I could devise, but this demon barged in with no problem."

Zhu Guiren lazily examined his fingernails. "Your wards were pathetic. I'm sure you're the weakest phoenix I've ever met. Probably you couldn't heal people even if you wanted to."

The phoenix ignored this and turned to Tainu. "Did you give him a talisman or spell to break the wards?"

"No," he said. "He did it himself. While they damaged him internally, they didn't kill him, obviously."

"And now you've healed him, for no reason I can see other than to annoy me. Well, I have a bargain for you, eldest sibling. Make me a refuge. As strong as the ones in the spirit world. A refuge that's only for me. If you promise to do that, I'll walk back to the sacred mountain with you and heal along the way. I want it just like the refuges in the spirit world. Just as strong, a cultivational focus, but one that won't let any other being enter but me. Do that, and I'll help."

Tainu looked at her very seriously. Liu Chenguang looked at Tainu. Liu Chenguang's face was shocked, but for Zhu Guiren, it was as though he had always known; of course Tainu had made the refuges. Who else could it ever have been? But with a trickle of unease in his stomach, he saw that Tainu looked… not afraid, exactly, but as though he was carefully considering whether he could accomplish something. As though he was bracing himself.

Tainu turned to Liu Chenguang and Zhu Guiren first. "If I agree to this," he said, "I'll be incapacitated for a while. I don't know how long. Weeks, most likely, if not more. Completely incapacitated. I won't even be conscious."

"I don't want you to do it," Liu Chenguang said.

Zhu Guiren nodded. "No. To hell with her. Why should you do anything for that piece of garbage?" He felt suddenly that this was his fault — his fault for bringing her here, even though he meant it all to help. He glared at her, but she ignored him. Stubborn like all phoenixes.

Tainu was quiet, thinking, then he said to Liu Chenguang. "There's no one else. And she's been cultivating nonstop for more than three cycles. There are so many thousands. We can't help them all, but she'll be able to do…a lot."

"I will," the phoenix said. "I'll heal as many mortals as you like between here and Mount Shi. It's a waste of my time and my power, of course, but I'll have a refuge to cultivate in afterward, so it's a good bargain."

"Isn't it." Tainu's voice was flat. "Sibling, your selfishness will eat you from the inside out in your dark prison."

Zhu Guiren was stunned. He had never imagined Tainu condemning anyone in this way, his face cold with disgust.

The phoenix, however, was unimpressed. "Sibling, your wasted compassion is dissolving you in despair," she said just as coldly. "I desire solitude and peace. You walk in pain wherever you can find it to step in. No thank you."

"I'm tempted to build it without a door," Tainu said, "but since my wasted compassion isn't quite dissolved in despair yet, I'll make sure it's possible for you to leave whenever your heart wakes up and realizes it's alive."

"Don't," said Liu Chenguang.

"Will you stay with me afterward?" he asked, looking at Liu Chenguang, and not at Zhu Guiren.

"Of course," she said.

"*I* won't," Zhu Guiren said, feeling irrationally angry. "This is stupid. Don't do it."

Tainu smiled at him. "I'm doing it," he said, his voice composed and determined, "and I hope I'll see you when I wake up. Let's go." He started walking.

Zhu Guiren stood still, watching him walk away, followed by the other two phoenixes. Finally, he walked in the same direction.

Later that morning, Tainu found him walking alongside the column of refugees and fluttered to his shoulder. "It's because she's never been with people enough. She doesn't have a real name — either a true name or one that others call her."

Zhu Guiren didn't answer.

"Demon?" Tainu asked, his tone a little uncertain, but Zhu Guiren kept walking.

"I don't want to talk to a stupid bird," he said, although of course he knew that Tainu couldn't be in his mortal form among all the Daxians; he was far too visible. He could feel Tainu's little claws clutching at his shoulder and his feathers brushing against his skin and it annoyed him immensely.

"It will be worth it, demon. It's good you brought her. It's only been a few hours and she's already healed dozens of people. She's awful at self-protection, but she has enormous stored power for healing because she's almost never used it. And for the other thing, truthfully, I don't mind doing it. Now that I see how frightened she is and how weak her wards are...When we're done with this, she'll be completely drained as well. She'll need protection."

Zhu Guiren felt that unreasoning fury again. "Waste of time. Get off my shoulder. I have things to do." He barely restrained himself from pushing the little bird off by force. As Tainu fluttered upward, Zhu Guiren raced away toward the hills above the roadside, looking for yaoguai, wanting to feel something die.

At evening, he looked down and saw the red bird — still hovering, still swooping down to touch people. That night, he didn't come back to the camp.

Several nights later, Zhu Guiren stalked into the firelight to see that Liu Chenguang was already wrapped in a blanket and passed out. He didn't look for Tainu. The strange phoenix, who he had mockingly named Feng Huang, cultivated neatly to one side. He walked over and kicked her. "Heal me."

She opened her eyes and glared at him in disgust. "Ask Liu Chenguang."

"She's asleep."

"I was cultivating. It's more important than sleeping."

"Sword cut to thigh, calf, left shoulder. Stab wound in upper left chest. Talisman strike."

"Ask eldest sibling. He's the one that'll cure anything that crawls out of the mud."

Zhu Guiren said, "No. You."

"What if I refuse? It's not like you'd attack me."

He snorted. "How is it possible you don't think so?"

She finally snarled, stood up, and bit her fingers to get to work.

While she healed him, his eyes slipped against his will around the fire. "Where's Tainu?"

"How should I know? With the refugees most likely."

"Alone?"

"He's always alone. I'm done." She went back into her cultivational pose and ignored him.

Zhu Guiren wavered a bit, but then went to look. It was very late; mostly the refugees were asleep, scattered along the side of the road for miles. There were thousands of people. He couldn't be sure. Perhaps Tainu was there somewhere, but he couldn't find him among all the moaning masses. Such a waste of energy.

Infuriated, he ran back down the road looking for yaoguai preying on the stragglers. Now that he was healed, he felt very much like killing something again.

He tracked a yaoguai through the woods — a centipede — and killed it. He hadn't been wounded by that scum, so no need to go back to the phoenixes yet, but the slime had gotten on him and he didn't like the feeling of it, so when he found a stream, he knelt by it to wash his face.

"Getting the blood off?"

He whirled around to see Tainu, sitting on the ground with his back to a tree. He must have walked right past him. There was a child asleep with its head on his lap, a little girl holding onto Tainu's hand.

"What are you doing here?" Zhu Guiren asked, and turned back to the stream to splash the water on his skin. He hadn't realized he was covered in blood. Somehow, he had gotten used to it.

"This one was left for dead," Tainu said. "I found her on the road. I can't leave her alone." He added, "I must have fallen asleep myself."

Zhu Guiren flicked the water off his arm and bit it back as long as he could. Then he said, "What are you doing, Tainu?" He turned to face him. "Why are you wasting our time and energy for this? We've lost weeks, and we're just flailing around getting nowhere with arrays. That girl's going to die no matter what you do. It's only temporary. She's still starving to death. No one is going to give that child food when you leave her behind. Were you planning to take her with you and feed her?"

"No," he said. He stroked the girl's hair gently. "I can't take her with us. I know that. A child couldn't be safe with us. I can't fix anything. The world is what it is. It's only temporary. I know." Looking at his hand on the girl's head, he said, "You have to understand, demon. Everything is temporary for me. Nothing lasts, everything dies. Except this one thing."

"What, feeling sorry for people?" Suddenly enraged, Zhu Guiren said, "You must feel sorry for me too."

"No. I don't feel sorry for you. Why would I?" He shook his head and said, "Do you want to understand? No one really understands…It's tiring sometimes."

"I don't want to understand. I want you to stop doing this. Look at you. You're exhausted. We have so much else to do. There's a reason we're here and this isn't it. These people are all going to die. Or if they live for a little bit longer, that's beyond your control too–"

"I *know*," Tainu said, as though trying to emphasize something. "I know it's beyond my control. I'm not trying to control it. It's just that they are beautiful, demon. Can you see? Every one of them. Beautiful and temporary and suffering and I want them to– I want them to know that they matter, however short it is, however temporary. It is the most amazing and beautiful and true thing in the universe that they exist, that this little girl exists, and I don't–" He struggled for a moment, then continued. "I don't know her name, but it matters that she is here, and her suffering matters, and her love and yearning matter."

"So, these people," Zhu Guiren said furiously, his fist clenched so the nails cut his skin, not understanding why he was so angry at Tainu, at his gentleness and kindness. Why was he so angry? "These little, short-lived vermin whose names you don't even know…they matter more than the whole reason we're here? More than Aili? More than Liu Chenguang?"

"What are you talking about?" Tainu asked, confused. "Why is there a measurement? Of course, if I had Aili in front of me or someone I don't personally know, I would– But it's never like that, or almost never. I can do both."

"No, you can't! You can't do everything! You have to– Even if you decide you want to care so much, you still need to– It's so–" He took a deep breath and calmed himself. "Whatever, I don't know why I'm trying to talk to you. You have limits too. You're not inexhaustible."

Tainu raised his eyebrow. "Well, to be fair, I'm pretty close to inexhaustible, in certain circumstances." He gave an exaggerated leer.

"Are you– What– Are you bragging to me?" Zhu Guiren spluttered. Why was Tainu always going in the direction he least expected? "Really? What are you even–"

Tainu laughed until he choked. "It's so fun to tease you," he said, coughing.

"How can you still be laughing?" demanded Zhu Guiren. "You can barely stand up. You just fell asleep, unwarded, with a hunting yaoguai ten feet away. Did you even know? I just killed it! It was probably stalking you."

"I'm not that foolish," he said, clearly a bit stung. "I did have a ward set."

"Why–" Zhu Guiren stopped mid-sentence, appalled at the implications.

Tainu said it anyway. "My wards recognize you now."

"That's…permanent?"

"More or less," Tainu said. "I can revoke it, but I don't really see the need."

Zhu Guiren bit out, "The yaoguai didn't trip your wards because I was with it."

"All right, I see your point. But I'm still not going to revoke you."

"You. Are. An. Idiot."

"Thank you," Tainu said, serious again. "I know. You're right. I'll do what I can do. I know I can't do everything. But I won't revoke you. And I can't ignore a dying child in front of me."

Zhu Guiren stared at him, his heart roiling for some reason. How could Tainu bear to live this way, seeing every being he encountered as beautiful and worthy of his attention and sacrifice? Tainu's eyes were locked with his, pleading for understanding that he had no desire to give.

"Ignore it," he said, finally. "And don't do whatever it was you promised that trash phoenix."

Tainu laughed again and broke the lock of his gaze. After a moment he said, "She's also my sibling. There's a lot of people who owe their lives to her, and even if they never know it, even if she doesn't care, still she did it. It still matters." Tainu stood up, carefully lifting the child in his arms. "There's some people that take in lost and orphaned children. I'll bring her to them, leave her there before she wakes up. It's the best I can think of. Do you have any other ideas?"

Zhu Guiren said, "The one thing that doesn't matter to you is, apparently, my opinion. It doesn't matter, does it, what I say."

"It matters," Tainu said. "It matters a lot, because you wouldn't say it if you didn't care about me." He held the child against his shoulder and met Zhu Guiren's eyes, smiling at him as though he were something that could be trusted.

Zhu Guiren laughed out loud. Even to himself, the laugh sounded strange and brittle. What was wrong with him? "Do you have some misunderstanding of me," he asked harshly, and walked away from him, looking for something to kill.

Three weeks and uncountable hundreds of people healed later, they stood on Mount Shi, at the entrance to the hidden cavern where Zhu Guiren had found the phoenix.

Zhu Guiren wished more and more that he had never come. He hadn't spoken to Tainu since that day; had only followed behind and to the side, watching as they healed, and healed, and healed, and healed — never thanked, never noticed, always hiding. Even Feng Huang had found ordinary mortal clothes to replace her cultivator's robes, braided up her long hair, smeared dirt on her face, and blended in, dabbing blood here, there, everywhere among the thousands and thousands of refugees flooding the roads, huddled in the makeshift camps, hiding in the cities, starving, wounded, sick. Every day, he saw Tainu in his bird form, hovering above the crowd, choosing a person that was weak or faltering, looking for his opportunity to claw himself and drip blood on their wounds and then swooping down, or waiting until they slept when he might be able to approach in his human form and put blood between their lips.

He remembered Tainu's fingers between his lips. The taste of his blood. Zhu Guiren clenched his fist in disgust. Every time Tainu did that, he became weaker. Why did he have to do it? Why did they all have to do it? For what benefit?

What goal?

Every night, he found a graveyard or unburied corpses — there was no shortage — and cultivated, drinking in the pain of the people, alive and dead. Tainu's efforts made no dent in this flood of delicious resentment. He felt it pouring, pounding through his meridians, almost too much to hold, tearing him with its bitter edges, sensuously exciting in its turbulence. There was no point to what Tainu did. It didn't stop death or suffering. It didn't change anything. Night after night, he took in resentment till he was gasping trying to contain it all, and then he would leap out, seeking death; seeking other demons to kill, and finding them.

When he was wounded again, he went to Liu Chenguang. She asked him once why he was avoiding Tainu.

He just stared at her and said, "Fix it."

Tainu must have heard; he hadn't kept his voice down in response to Liu Chenguang's whisper. He was cultivating nearby, though really almost falling asleep — his head was tipping toward his chest. He looked up at Zhu Guiren, his eyes tired and bruised underneath, but didn't say anything.

Zhu Guiren hated seeing him like that. When Liu Chenguang was done healing, he left again.

He didn't know why he was here, looking into this damn cavern, standing next to the three most annoying creatures in the world. Maybe just to see it end. Tainu wrapped his arms around himself as though trying to reassure himself that he could do something. Liu Chenguang just looked at the ground. The strange phoenix stripped off the mortal clothes with complete disinhibition until she was naked. She had a perfect body, silken hair falling past her waist, but Zhu Guiren mostly looked at her and wanted to kick her. Hard.

"Do it," she said coldly.

Did none of these people consider going back on a promise? Zhu Guiren could kill them all just for being such idiots.

"Don't do it," he said to Tainu, the first thing he had said to him in half a month.

Tainu looked at him and smiled. "It's all right. It's not a bad thing to do."

Zhu Guiren turned his back on him.

Tainu kept talking. To Liu Chenguang, probably, since he himself was very obviously not listening, but of course he could hear it as though Tainu was speaking to him too. "I've only ever done this in the spirit realm before," he said, "and normally I would go into a refuge immediately on completing it to cultivate and heal. I have no idea how long it will take me to heal after this, since I'll be creating a refuge I can't stay in. Once the work is complete, I think it will bring me outside since the wards will only recognize that one and repel all others. But I will heal, you know I will, so don't be worried."

Liu Chenguang said, "I'm worried, Tainu."

He continued as though he hadn't heard. "I don't want you to watch. You stay outside. Both of you," he said, as though Zhu Guiren was actively listening, which he was not. "I'll be unconscious at the end, remember I told you. You'll have to bring me somewhere to stay. Somewhere safe, all right? Where we can stay for a few weeks, at least."

Liu Chenguang said, "Zhu Guiren, please. I won't be able to carry him."

Zhu Guiren nodded curtly, still not turning around.

"Demon," said Tainu, "thank you."

He finally turned and said, again, "Don't."

Tainu smiled at him, a smile that blazed like sunshine through the clouds. "You know, I can remember anything I've seen. I only need to see it once."

Zhu Guiren watched him turn and walk into the cavern, frozen in place. That smile like sunlight…there was something inside him, something that was locked, and the sunlight fell on it and warmed it.

He shook off Liu Chenguang's hand on his arm, pushed the naked phoenix out of the way, unseeing, and followed Tainu into the cavern.

Tainu stood inside it, on an even part of the floor, his arms outstretched like wings with his hands in seals, and he was murmuring words that Zhu Guiren knew — words in the demonic language.

"No," Zhu Guiren said sharply. "No, what are you doing?"

But Tainu was already deep in trance, working the spell. If he tried to physically touch him now, he might hurt him — hurt both of them — seriously. The qi was gathering into the shape he was calling it, but Zhu Guiren knew no phoenix could speak the demonic words without pain. And there was pain. He could see it in Tainu's posture, throughout his body, holding himself upright by sheer will. That was a posture Zhu Guiren was familiar with. He had experienced pain like this many times, but this person had never let anyone see him in pain, had always hidden it so well.

"Stop it," he whispered, but helplessly. It was too late now.

What Tainu had begun, he would have to complete.

The demonic words were ripping Tainu's mouth and throat. Zhu Guiren could see the blood dripping from his lips as he chanted, moving his hands into a new seal. The golden qi was spiraling around him, surrounding him as he was held by it in midair, slowly expanding into a perfect sphere with him at the center.

Zhu Guiren narrowed his eyes. It was hard to see through the golden net, but he thought— There was something happening to Tainu's body.

To his shock, he saw…rips…begin to open in Tainu's skin, small tears, then larger ones, as though many, many old scars had simultaneously ruptured, spilling out his blood, so many that it looked as though he had been flayed, more wounds than whole skin, everywhere, all over him. He couldn't imagine the pain.

"No," he said. "No."

Even knowing it was impossible, he reached forward, trying to grab him, trying to stop it, but the qi blocked him; the anti-demonic spell was already working, throwing him backward to the floor. Inside that net of gold, he could see Tainu still chanting, the words even louder now, though his eyes were closed tight. Suddenly, as he reached the crescendo, the blood dripping and trailing from him burst out in a mist, following the curve of the golden sphere so that its inner wall was a delicate membrane of blood.

The golden sphere suddenly solidified, became opaque, and faded into blue-gray stone.

Tainu appeared on the floor next to him, not breathing, covered in blood.

"Liu Chenguang!" Zhu Guiren screamed, kneeling next to him. "Liu Chenguang, come! Come now!"

The other phoenix came first — naked and beautiful as a creature from before the mortal world was made — running gracefully past them and diving into the place Tainu had made for her with his blood. Zhu Guiren heard himself growl like an animal, reaching out his hand to grab her and tear her apart, but too late. She was gone.

Liu Chenguang was there, kneeling next to him, calling him.

"Zhu Guiren," he heard her say at last. "Zhu Guiren."

He looked at her, stunned past bearing. The rips in Tainu's skin, his sunlit smile, those two things did not belong together, but they did, they went together, somewhere in his heart there was a place these two things had lived together a very long time, behind a door that was locked and the lock had been broken so the door couldn't be opened anymore except by force, and now the force had come, but it hurt, it hurt to open it.

He looked at Liu Chenguang without seeing her.

"Zhu Guiren," she said, her voice quavering, "I can't heal him with my blood. Phoenixes can't heal one another. We need to get him to somewhere safe and clean, and treat him as best we can with mortal remedies, and beyond that we need to let his body heal itself. Our bodies will always heal. This is why he reminded us. He knew that it would be like this. We just have to– to follow his instructions."

He didn't respond.

"Please, Zhu Guiren," she said, sounding desperate, "I need you to carry him. I'm not big or strong enough."

He finally understood this part. His mortal body was not as tall or heavy as Tainu's, but he was a demon with a demon's strength. He could do this, except that Tainu's blood was everywhere. It was so slippery. "Get the cloth."

Liu Chenguang handed him the white cultivator's robe that the other phoenix had discarded. He carefully and gently wiped off the blood as well as he could. The cuts were still bleeding, but this was all he could do for now. He put his handless arm under Tainu's knees and his other arm beneath his back, holding him cradled against his chest. Tainu's head lolled against his shoulder.

"I have him," he said.

CHAPTER 6
AFTER THE REFUGE

ZHU GUIREN SAT next to Tainu, watching him sleep.

So much of his past wasn't clear to him — it had been very long, and he had done many things, and many things had been done to him by others — but this he remembered. Sitting by this person and watching them sleep. Worrying about them.

He seemed to recall that it would be better to be closer. Tainu's skin was dark, his eyes closed. Underneath his eyes were darker bruises. He remembered the bruises under his eyes.

"Tainu?" he asked, quietly.

Tainu didn't respond, except for a little wrinkle in his eyelids.

"It's me," he tried. He didn't know why it seemed so important to tell Tainu that it was him speaking. Who else would it be? Obviously not Liu Chenguang. Who else was even here? Why did he think that Tainu would be comforted by knowing he was close? Why did he even care about whether Tainu was comforted or not?

Why was he doing this at all — undermining his own cultivation, undoing what he'd spent thousands of years preparing to accomplish?

The question came and went in his mind without any answer. He slowly reached out with his single hand and interlaced his fingers with Tainu's, their pale and dark skin making a pattern together.

He had never held hands with anyone like this before, trying to give them comfort. He remembered how Liu Chenguang had asked to hold Hong Deming's hand after he died and squeezed his eyes shut so he wouldn't see that anymore. Something about it made him hurt inside. Every time he saw it, every time he saw Liu Chenguang reach for Aili's hand while Aili slept in the spirit world, it ached. Even when it happened — when Hong Deming's dead body lay next to Liu Chenguang and he knew that Liu Chenguang would soon be destroyed and reborn. Even though he would never change his mind about any of it. He had come so far, done so much; he wouldn't stop so close to the end. Even then, even so, at that moment, he felt something he had no name for, something both sharp and sad. Liu Chenguang's eyes, his voice saying, "Please."

As he watched, Tainu's eyelids wrinkled a little bit. Was he in pain? Should he come closer? Would that help him?

Zhu Guiren laid down on his side on the edge of the bed and carefully reached out across Tainu to hold him. His head rested on Tainu's shoulder, so he could still see his face. He closed his eyes after a while, feeling Tainu's breathing calm, his heartbeat become peaceful. "It's me," he whispered, hardly moving his lips. "It's me. It's Arciniang. I'm with you."

"What are you doing?" came a hissed whisper from behind him. "Get away from him."

He raised his head to see Liu Chenguang, eyes wide with shock, holding a bowl with water and herbs and a clean cloth to wipe Tainu's wounds. "I want to be close to him," he explained, although it should have been perfectly obvious. He wasn't really his usual self right now, unable to destroy those who would block his will; he felt very soft inside.

"What? I don't care. Does he want to be close to you?" Liu Chenguang replied. "I don't want you close to him like that. Let him go. Get away."

Reluctantly, he untangled himself and sat up, careful not to wake him. "Now he'll be cold," he said accusingly, still in that strange, unknown space in his heart.

"That's what blankets are for." She covered him up, trying to push Zhu Guiren aside.

He wouldn't go.

"What is going on with you?" she asked, exasperated. "This isn't like you at all. What's happening? Are you having some kind of qi deviation?"

He reached out to take Tainu's hand again, interlacing their fingers.

Liu Chenguang firmly reached out and took Tainu's hand away from him.

He looked at her, confused. "Please?" he asked.

Her face was filled with a mix of disgust and resignation. "I can't deal with this right now," she said, and left the room.

That was perfectly fine. He held Tainu's hand again and watched him sleep.

Liu Chenguang had found an inn close to the road near the base of Mount Shi, probably once one of the finer accommodations in Shi'an; under war conditions, everything was shabby and poor, but the room was still a decent one, and it had a window looking toward the mountains. Zhu Guiren vaguely felt that this was good for the phoenixes; much better than the landscape full of resentment they had been walking through, a good place for Tainu to heal.

But week after week, it didn't seem that Tainu was healing beyond the superficial closing of the wounds. He didn't wake for more than brief intervals during which he didn't speak or seem to perceive where he was, his eyes clouded and quickly closing. Liu Chenguang was worried, and he himself felt a sense of deep distress whenever he couldn't be near Tainu. Liu Chenguang had finally accepted that she would have to let Zhu Guiren do some of the watching. There wasn't much to do, other than sit there, but he always felt a sense of relief when she would let him in, so he could hold his hand, and look at him. Zhu Guiren would try to go cultivate, or do something, *anything*, but all he wanted to do was sit near as Liu Chenguang would let him. He knew, as though watching himself from a distance, that his behavior was ridiculous, but his sense of dignity had fled completely, and settling into cultivating resentment had become impossible, some block in his spiritual body resisting it.

Some four weeks after Tainu had set up the refuge, Zhu Guiren noticed that his hand suddenly felt warm. Much warmer than usual. At almost that same moment, Tainu opened his eyes and looked over at him, his gaze clear and serene, and smiled.

He looked so happy.

Zhu Guiren felt something inside him opening up at that smile and those warm, dark eyes on him. "Tainu?" he asked cautiously.

"I feel a little unbalanced," he said. "Can you help me get out of bed? I want to look out the window."

Zhu Guiren helped him up, wishing for the millionth time that he still had two hands. "Come on. Do you need a chair?"

"No, I'm fine, I want to stand…" At the window he looked out at the sea of green running up into the mountains. "It's beautiful here. Are we in Daxian?

That looks like Mount Shi."

Zhu Guiren looked at him in shock. "Yes…Are you all right?"

"I feel good. When do I ever not?" Tainu looked at him and smiled again. "And you're here."

Zhu Guiren felt that strangeness again, somewhere inside him, when Tainu looked into his eyes and smiled that way. He didn't have words for this feeling; he hadn't felt it before. "I'm…I'm here."

"Are you worried about something? Don't be worried." Tainu reached out and pulled him closer. His balance really wasn't good. When he pulled on Zhu Guiren's arm, he stumbled backward to lean against the wall next to the window.

Surprised, Zhu Guiren fell forward, so their bodies were fully against one another. He felt Tainu's arms around him, enclosing him with warmth.

Tainu laughed. "Arciniang," he said, very softly, and Zhu Guiren felt Tainu's lips gently covering his.

Zhu Guiren realized that his entire mortal body was trembling, and every inch of it was filled with light.

"I'm so happy you're here," said Tainu, murmuring against his lips. "Arciniang."

Then he fell over to the side and landed on the floor.

"Liu Chenguang!" shouted Zhu Guiren, panicked. "Liu Chenguang!" He picked Tainu up to put him back into bed and realized, not distracted by his lips and his smile, that his skin felt like it was burning up. "What's happening?"

Liu Chenguang rushed in and took his pulse.

I could have done that, Zhu Guiren thought, too late, I'm the one that trained her after all. But it seemed that any sensible thought in his brain had gone long ago and far away.

"Qi deviation," she said brusquely. "Stand back."

"But he was fine! He said he was happy! He wanted to get out of bed–" Zhu Guiren flailed inwardly, desperate to get Tainu back to that now-desirable state of simply sleeping all day.

Liu Chenguang didn't even spare him a glance. "His qi is very strange. Maybe it's a backlash from using the demonic spell?" She started to transfer qi to him, moving from one meridian to another.

"I can– I can help," he said, reaching out his hand.

She pushed it away. "No," she said, "you can't give him demonic qi. It would make it far worse than it is."

Zhu Guiren's eyes widened, and he took a step back, then fled the room.

Outside, he covered his face with his shaking hand. But Tainu had been strange before he touched him, before…kissing him. That hadn't been what caused this…Had it?

He took several deep breaths, trying to calm himself down, and found he couldn't.

He attempted to put his thoughts in order, kneeling next to the wall and scribbling frantically with the pencil he kept in his pocket. Tainu had used a demonic spell and the demonic language to create the refuge, combined with his own blood; that could only have worked if he was somehow manipulating demonic qi, resentment that he had gathered from the surrounding environment. Had there been some kind of reverse connection, where his blood had not only entered the spell, but the spell had also entered his blood? There had been those hundreds of cuts all over his body…

He closed his eyes and reordered his thoughts from that sense of horror. Tainu's skin tearing and bleeding in front of him, again…why did he think *again*, as though that had happened before?

If the demonic qi had entered him at that point, the pure qi would be attempting to overcome it and purify it. Perhaps this was a crisis point and it would resolve on its own. The heat and loss of cognitive focus would be ways in which the spiritual body was attempting to purify itself — removing various internal barriers to an increase of qi beyond what the mortal body could normally tolerate and attempting to make the spirit well inhospitable to the demonic qi — just as a fever in a mortal illness was a way in which the body overcame…

How was kissing him part of this process?

With great effort, he stopped himself from thinking about Tainu's lips on his and returned to the main point.

But perhaps it was part of the process, after all? He scribbled more, a quick diagram; was the phoenix's mortal body attempting to expel the demonic qi through connecting physically with a demonic mortal body? The demonic body would act like a magnet for the demonic qi…

This possibility made him feel somewhat sad, but at least it was a solution.

Would it have to be kissing?

He felt, truthfully, that he was a little biased about this question. Would holding hands also do? He decided that, purely objectively speaking, kissing would probably be more effective. Because they'd been holding hands for weeks already. Tainu said that in the past he'd only ever done this in the spirit realm and had entered each refuge to cultivate immediately on completing it. The refuges were anti-demonic; they would have done the work for him. Tainu probably hadn't realized that in the mortal realm, with a mortal body, he couldn't do it on his own.

Lucky he was here, really.

"Oh no. Hell no. You get away from him!" Liu Chenguang shouted. "Are you insane?"

He tried to explain his theory.

Liu Chenguang stared at him. "He kissed you?"

He nodded, blushing.

"You're blushing."

He blushed more.

"Anything else?" she asked, shaking her head and visibly retreating into *I'm a professional physician, nothing shocks me* mode.

"He called my true name."

"He knows your true name?!" she asked, professionalism immediately lost.

"Yes, so, he knew who I was, and what he was doing," he said. "You can stay here, and if it doesn't seem like it's helping, just…jump in and do more of whatever you're doing. You can tell me to stop."

She looked at Tainu, who was now lying in a pool of sweat on the bed, shivering. "What I'm doing isn't helping," she said, finally. "I can't get it under control and he's getting worse. All right. I'm going to keep my fingers on his heart meridian while you…do this."

She sat on the edge of the bed with her fingers on Tainu's wrist, then looked at him. "If you don't mind I'm going to close my eyes. I don't want to have to remember this image later."

He nodded nervously, then sat next to Tainu and tried to prepare himself.

After a few minutes Liu Chenguang opened her eyes. "Why aren't you doing it?"

He cleared his throat. "I don't really know how."

Liu Chenguang appeared to mentally count to twenty backward. "All right. Just lean over and put your lips on his. If your theory is correct you won't have to do more than that. The demonic qi will be attracted to you without any effort, right?" She squeezed her eyes shut. "Ugh, just do it. I'm never getting this picture out of my mind."

He took a deep breath, leaned over, and brushed Tainu's lips with his.

It was definitely working; he could feel the corrupted qi leaping toward him. He pressed a little harder. He hadn't cultivated much for weeks now. It was actually quite helpful—

Tainu's arms came up around him, pulling him closer, kissing him harder.

Liu Chenguang said "Ow!" and fell off the bed.

Zhu Guiren couldn't feel the demonic qi anymore, only Tainu holding him, kissing him back, it felt, it felt— Zhu Guiren kissed him back too, lips moving against his, lightly and then with more pressure, feeling the different parts of Tainu's lips, the corners and the fullness in the middle, sometimes separating a bit, then coming closer together—

Tainu sighed. His hands dropped to the bed, leaving him, and he turned his head to the side, asleep.

Zhu Guiren sat up, shaking slightly.

Liu Chenguang grabbed Tainu's dangling hand and checked the pulse. She breathed a sigh of relief. "Well, as bizarre as it was, your theory was correct. The corrupted qi is completely gone. He should probably wake up tomorrow or the next day and be pretty much finished with this. So, we can expect some awkward conversations at that point, I guess." She looked at Zhu Guiren. "Are you crying?"

"No."

"You are," she said. She sat up and looked at him more fully. "What's wrong?"

"Nothing's wrong," he said. "I don't think he'll remember this, so we probably won't have to have any…conversations."

"Zhu Guiren," she said seriously, "he should know what had to be done to heal him. This can't be kept a secret from him."

"Of course. You can tell him. He should certainly know that he can't do this again unless there's a demon ready to help heal him. He should know that the demonic qi gets into him during the spell. He may not really understand that."

"Then why are you crying?"

"I told you," he said, standing to leave. "He won't remember."

Zhu Guiren was sitting on the grass under some neglected trees at the outskirts of Shi'an, looking toward the summits of the mountains, when Tainu found him a few days later. Tainu stood looking at Zhu Guiren from a distance for a while; his shoulders were a little hunched, and his expression was very dull. Was something…was he upset about what he had had to do to save him? About kissing him? It must have felt very uncomfortable for him. Tainu winced.

Finally, Tainu walked to him and said, "Where have you been? I've been looking for you." He sat down next to him without being invited and noticed how Zhu Guiren inched away from him. Well, that was to be expected, probably. Tainu let his body experience the 'sitting on the ground' feeling, his muscles aching; he really wasn't fully recovered.

Out loud, he said, "I never realized exactly how much it took out of me, to build a refuge. I always had the refuge to cultivate in before, and even though it hurt, I healed on my own eventually."

After a while, Zhu Guiren said, "The way you built the refuge…You've been captured before."

"Yes." So this was why the demon looked so unhappy. "At the beginning of my second cycle. My first rebirth. There weren't any refuges then…That's why I'm the oldest. I'm really just the oldest surviving phoenix. There were others before me, but once the demons realized what they could do with phoenix blood… Well, you know. We were always captured as soon as we were reborn — when we were at our weakest. And since that was happening in the spirit realm, where we can truly die, all the oldest ones were killed before you figured out that if you brought us into the mortal world we would just have to…keep surviving it, over and over."

Zhu Guiren was silent. With a single finger, he drew a pattern on the ground. "How did you get away?" he eventually asked.

"My people skills, of course," he said. "There was a demon assigned to watch me. I think he didn't like to be doing what he was doing, so he started talking to me."

"Probably he was just bored," Zhu Guiren said.

"Probably. But also, he had a good heart. He didn't want to be hurting me. And he was brave, and clever."

"How can a demon have a good heart? It's not our nature."

"It wasn't his nature to be cruel," he replied. "They would have to make him into that." When Zhu Guiren didn't respond, he continued, "So he let me go, and I watched him carefully — saw what he did. I designed the refuges from what I saw him do. I turned the spell he created inside out to mimic the original spell that captured me, and then I changed its ordering and mixed it with my blood instead of a demon's blood, so instead of being a prison for a phoenix, it would repel demons. In a sense, the world outside the refuge becomes the prison for demons; the wall of their prison is the wall of the refuge, and they can't pass. There were some other pieces I designed into it, of course, to make it suitable for cultivation…"

Zhu Guiren had raised his head and was staring at him, unblinking. "What happened to the demon who let you go?"

"I've always wondered," he said. And he always had. "I've always wanted to see him again, and make sure he was all right."

Zhu Guiren just kept looking at him.

It seemed like the appropriate time to say it, so he finally did, although his heart was afraid to know. He looked in Zhu Guiren's eyes, the expression always the same, as he knew it would be, essentially always himself no matter what shape he took. "What happened to you?" he asked gently.

Zhu Guiren looked away. His voice even, he said, "I am sure I was punished. It must have been a very severe punishment. Enough that I don't…remember the details. I don't really remember you. Just…bits and pieces."

"Oh," he said, not knowing what else to say to that. But after all, even if Zhu Guiren remembered, what could he possibly say? He closed his eyes, remembering Zhu Guiren's cold, triumphant expression when Liu Chenguang's mortal body was destroyed, when Hong Deming lay dead. He breathed deeply, trying to release that image, the worst of all his long life.

"I'm glad I let you go," Zhu Guiren said suddenly.

Tainu opened his eyes to find Zhu Guiren looking at him intently, clearly wanting to see how he would respond, as though he needed some kind of reassurance. He smiled, impulsively reaching over to tousle his hair. "Look at you now, grown up all big and evil."

"Stop that. It's so undignified," said Zhu Guiren, batting at his hand.

"I know." Tainu grinned.

Then, he looked at Zhu Guiren's hair again. It was a tangled mess with a hairpin stuck in it at a strange angle. He realized that there was no possible way the demon could have put his hair up properly with one hand. Thinking of him trying to do it and never asking anyone to help him made his heart hurt. "Let me," he said, reaching forward. "Why didn't you ask me to help you? All these days."

He took the hairpin out and laid it down carefully, then stroked the mess of the demon's hair into a smoother fall. He couldn't get the knots out without a comb; that would have to wait. "Do you want it all up, or some down?" he asked.

"All up," Zhu Guiren said, looking at him again with that unblinking stare.

He knelt to get closer and reached back behind his head to gather it all. With a few quick twists, he made it into a topknot and smoothly slid the hairpin in. "There, that should last the day. I told you I'm good with a hairpin. Is it good?"

"Very good," Zhu Guiren said.

"Let me help you do it in the mornings," he said. Then he closed his eyes and drew a quick, harsh breath, suddenly assaulted by sensations: holding Zhu Guiren, kissing him, feeling his body moving against him—

"Tainu?" came Zhu Guiren's voice, "are you all right?"

Zhu Guiren grabbed his wrist to feel for his pulse. At that very moment, Tainu's imagination was overwhelmed with the feeling of his lips blended with what it had felt like to stroke his hair, the weight and warmth of it, and the heat of the nape of his neck under his hand—

"Your pulse is fast, but your qi seems all right…Tainu?"

"I– I–" He breathed himself back to normal. "It– it must be an aftereffect. That's all."

He was shocked by those images, those feelings. He had never thought of the demon in that way. It wasn't that he was inexperienced with such matters, but never with those few who were truly important to him — only those who could come and go and leave no mark in his heart.

An aftereffect of the demonic qi. That was all. Surely it hadn't been like that, kissing him. Surely the demon wouldn't have…it wouldn't have been like that. It would never be like that. It was just something still healing in his mind. He could calm himself. It would fade.

Without opening his eyes, he said, "Liu Chenguang told me what you had to do to save me. Thank you. I never knew that the demonic qi was entering me when I built a refuge. If you hadn't figured it out I'm not sure what would have happened to me. I'm sure it was very awkward for you."

"Do you remember it?" Zhu Guiren asked.

"No," he said, attention still on trying to get himself under control. "It's all just a blur since I started the refuge spell." At last he felt himself enough to open his eyes. He smiled again at him, wanting to convey his gratitude. "Really, now you've saved me twice."

Zhu Guiren shook his head, his eyes focused on the distant mountains. "It's nothing."

That night, after Tainu and Liu Chenguang were asleep, Zhu Guiren prowled through their rooms at the inn, unable to settle. He opened the door to Tainu's room and went in to watch him sleep; it felt strange to not do it, to not be close to him every day and night. Instinctively, he reached out with his hand to interlace it with Tainu's fingers, but then drew back. He was healed now. He didn't remember anything. He didn't remember calling his true name. He didn't remember that he said how happy he was to have him there. He didn't remember holding him or…anything else. He was peaceful and easy in his sleep. He didn't need anyone to be there for him now.

Zhu Guiren thought, I want to be close to him. Why do I want it so much?

Whatever had happened between them when they met, it was gone. Cut and burned out of his mind. Only those bits and pieces remained. Only his smile, and his blood.

Leaving Tainu's room, he returned to his own, the walls covered with his scribbles and diagrams. Viciously, he struck out the diagram of the phoenix and the demon together.

The other diagrams — the arrays, his notes, trying to recall exactly which nodes were where, which were strongest, which he should break first…He looked at them coldly. He didn't have the patience for this now.

Shi'an wasn't as full of resentment as the refugee roads, but there was more than enough. He ran through the dark streets, hunting for a good place, until he found a cemetery. There was another demon already there, cultivating; he drew his sword silently and the other demon wisely fled. He longed for his true body, for claws and fangs. This mortal body remembered too much and yearned to have more.

Zhu Guiren settled down among the graves and closed his eyes, welcoming in the familiar pain.

CHAPTER 7
YISUE

THE SOUND OF the waves was lulling, crashing nearby, spraying on her face. Every bit of her skin felt sticky and crusted with salt. Aili sat up and reflexively put her hand on her forehead, just to make sure her head was still attached given the level of pain she was feeling all over her body.

"That was funny," said a voice off to one side.

"Was it?" she said. "What was it?"

"You jumped off the cliff to be a sacrifice for your own passage through my gate." The voice's owner wasn't visible; wherever they were was very dark. "It was hilarious. You're not dead though, so it doesn't count."

She remembered that now. "You're mistaken," she said. "I did die. At least, my mortal body would have been dead if I didn't have some special medicine."

"True," said the voice. "You certainly did look dead when I fished you out of the water. You were all floppy and bloody and your limbs were in different positions."

Aili decided to let that go.

"Did it hurt?" the voice asked, a bit salaciously.

"Yes," she said. "So it should count as a sacrifice. Definitely."

The voice was quiet. Then it asked, very suddenly, "Are you a starfish? I've never met a starfish that cultivated a mortal body before."

Aili considered this. "Yes," she said. "Yes. I'm a starfish."

There was a softly-growing light that illuminated their surroundings: a wet cavern dripping with seaweed and lined with mussels and barnacles, and, closer to her than she had expected, the dragon.

It didn't look quite like she had imagined. It was smaller, for one thing — only ten feet long or so — and it had webbed feet along with its claws. It was pure white, lithe and serpentine, without wings, with delicate tendrils dangling from its jaw and temples. Its claws seemed to be like hands, and one of them held something that looked like a very large pearl; it was this that was the source of the light, shining through the webbing.

"Greetings, master dragon," she said formally. She tried to consciously ascertain what language they were speaking and realized that it was Anglish.

The dragon brought its head closer to her; she could now see that its eyes were a blue-green color. "All right," it said, "I don't really think it counts as a full sacrifice, but it was funny, so I'll accept it. My gate is here. Where did you want to go?"

"Can you take me to Zhashan?"

"I don't know where that is."

"It's a city in Daxian."

"Is it next to the ocean?"

She shook her head.

The dragon explained, "I can take you anywhere else in the world that there is a dragon gate, but dragon gates are only on ocean coasts or deep under the sea."

Aili thought about this, trying to recall the geography she knew of Daxian. Unfortunately, in her lifetime as Hong Deming, she had never crossed into the coastal provinces at all. "Can you bring me to a gate that's close to the mouth of the Sorrowful River?" she asked, finally.

"I've always wanted to go to Daxian," the dragon said; it sounded more excited. "I have relatives there, but I've never been, so I don't really know exactly where to go. I can just aim for a gate on the north coast. That will get us close, right?"

"Ummm…I actually have no idea."

"Let's go!" the dragon said happily. It held the pearl high, and it glowed fiercely: white, blue, green, purple.

Before she knew what was happening, the dragon had bitten down on the collar of her shirt and leapt forward into the light.

In no more than a moment of swirling confusion, the dragon dropped her and spat. "Ugh," it said, "your clothes taste terrible. We're here!"

'Here' was a small, flat cleared area covered in barnacles and seaweed under an arched rock, surrounded by surging water and waves. The mainland was about a half mile away.

Aili stood shakily. She still didn't feel completely herself physically; the battering of her leap into the ocean had been serious. "I don't think I can swim there," she said, holding one hand over her eyes.

The dragon looked at her. "You're going to the *land?* Really? I want to come with you."

"Ah, why?"

"I told you, I've never been! Hold on to me." This time, it threw her on its back and leapt into the water. The dragon was an excellent swimmer — faster than a dolphin and just as graceful. Moments later, it pulled the two of them onto the rocky shore and shook itself, apparently delighted with the exercise.

Aili coughed, wondering where they were. Looking around, she didn't see any obvious place where people lived, but the northern coast of the Federation was like that too, after all, if you were looking from the ocean at the shore. People lived inland, mostly. They seemed to be near the tip of a rocky peninsula, surrounded by the ocean on three sides.

The dragon looked at her expectantly. "Where are we going now? Are we going to see human people? Are we going to see dragons?" It wiggled in excitement.

Aili was beginning to develop a suspicion about this dragon. "How old are you?"

"Oh, five hundred, maybe? I haven't left the ocean much before…just near the coast where you jumped off," it said casually. "I haven't seen a lot of people. Do you want to see my other form? My name is Yisue. My parents live in the deep ocean but I like the coast, so they let me stay there by myself." Its long white body shimmered and transformed into a light-skinned boy of around ten years old, with long white hair and blue-green eyes. "This is my other body! I haven't used it much. Let's go!" He turned to walk and immediately tripped over a rock and fell down.

"Ah, you should get some clothes," she suggested.

"Why? Ow! This hurts." He rubbed his bleeding knee. "Scales don't rip like this. Are we going to the Sorrowful River? My parents told me I have an uncle there."

Aili whispered Liu Chenguang's true name. The white-gold line went inland to the southwest. "All right," she said. "Yisue, listen. Thank you for bringing me, but you should stay here, or go back to the ocean right away. It's really not a good idea for you to come with me. I'm probably going inland and not coming back, and truthfully, I don't know how long it will be before I find the Sorrowful River. And there's a war happening. Mortals will be attacking each other. This isn't a safe place for you and I'm sure your parents wouldn't want you to stay here–"

"Look! There's a little starfish like you in this one. It's eating something…Do you have relatives here?" Yisue was ignoring her in favor of tide pools.

She turned and walked in the direction of the light — toward Liu Chenguang. She didn't have any sense of how close or distant Liu Chenguang might be, but the light had gone straight over the horizon; certainly several hours' worth of walking, if not a full day.

Behind her, Yisue yelled, "Hey, wait for me!"

The little dragon boy didn't stay close to her, wandering and exploring and occasionally jumping in the water, but gradually, they came closer to signs of human habitation: garbage, cemeteries, old buildings. It looked as though war had passed through here, more than once. Yisue drew closer to her and more silent, looking around. When they first saw actual people, they gathered and pointed, whispering in Daxian about Yisue, who certainly caught the eye.

"Can you become a bird or something?" she asked, a little worried about how much attention they were drawing.

"Can you?"

"No, I only have one body," she said.

"I'm a dragon. This is my real body, just like my dragon body. We have two true bodies — not just one and a mortal body — but obviously I can't become a *bird*," he explained. He picked something up off the ground. "What's this? Can you eat it?" He stuffed it in his mouth before she could respond, then immediately spit it out, choking and grabbing his tongue.

"No," she said dryly. "Are you hungry? You should probably go back to the ocean then."

"No. I don't want to. The ocean is boring."

The occasional houses and outlying villages coalesced into a city, which she soon learned was called Zhaishou; Aili didn't remember this city from her life as Hong Deming, but she'd never entered Hai'an in that time. There were a surprising number of foreign people — soldiers and merchants of the Twin Empire — scattered among the Daxian in the streets, and many, many Kunorese in imperial military uniforms. They looked curiously at her and Yisue, making her very nervous about how to keep the boy safe.

The sound of spoken Kunorese made her shiver; she still hadn't forgotten Nora.

"All right," she said at last. "Put these on."

Aili handed him a shirt and pants she had stolen, unnoticed, from a rooftop string of laundry using her qinggong. She felt awful about this, but she had no money that would be accepted here. She would have to find some somewhere; she had no idea how they could survive otherwise for a long journey unless Yisue proved more willing to eat rabbits than Liu Chenguang had ever been. Of course, she would then also need a bow. Could she create a spirit weapon that would shoot rabbits? Were there even rabbits in Hai'an? Many of the people looked starved and beaten, most likely anything edible had long ago been eaten.

Yisue was holding the pants and shirt as though he had no idea what to do with them.

"If you put these on, I'll feed you," she said, a little desperately.

"I don't know what these are," he said, dignified. "Also, they stink."

"They've just been washed. Don't be so picky…" She helped him put them on, remembering helping her little brother when they had been growing up. They'd only been three years apart, but he hadn't always wanted to wear clothes properly either. As she looped together the knotwork buttons around Yisue's neck, she stopped suddenly, surprised. That had been…For the first time since his death, that had been a happy memory of her little brother, Eddie. She had… happy memories. There had been more to their life together than coming home the day he died. Why had she never been able to realize this before? To remember him as he lived — the good things, and not only the bad ones?

"What?" Yisue said. "These are itchy."

Aili tried to think of what she could do to earn some money, or at least a meal, with what she had to offer: strength, cooking, swimming, healing…Healing, yes — people would be willing to pay for that…Of course, she would do it for free, but she needed to get them something to eat. Surely it would be a fair trade.

She found a woman running a noodle stall who was suffering from a toothache; she cured it easily with a bloody finger for a few bowls of noodles. Yisue put them away in shocking fashion. The stall owner watched in resignation.

"These…They are so…Amazing…" he mumbled through his full mouth. "Never going back. Noodles."

Well, that was a bit of a misfire, then. She tried one last time: "Yisue, I am really afraid this will be dangerous for you, and I can't get you back to the ocean anytime soon once we leave the coast. I don't know when we will be at the Sorrowful River. The cook says it's on the other side of the province, and I'm not going in that direction. And she said there's flooding, too. The dikes were broken inland, so the Sorrowful River is probably a mess anyway. I would really, truly, feel much better if you went back to the ocean now."

He slurped his last noodles and looked at her with his blue-green eyes. "No," he said. "More noodles."

Conversation with the stall owner led to a deal: the stall owner would spread the word that a healer was available, and people would come pay Aili; the owner would get a cut and let them eat and sleep in the stall until they had enough money to move on.

"You've got a good deal with me if he's going to eat like that every day," the noodle-seller said, but she didn't sound too angry. The tooth had been giving her a great deal of pain. "Excuse me for asking, but why does he look that way? Does he have an illness?"

"He was born like that," Aili said. "Don't mention it, he's sensitive."

"Ah, yes," the woman said. "I remember, my sister's husband's cousin had a child like that. Couldn't bear the sunlight. Well, I have an extra hat. I'll give it to you for him."

Aili was grateful for it, and when she had a little money, she decided to buy another for herself — one of the large conical woven hats that she could tuck her hair beneath to try to look a little less unusual. She braided Yisue's hair as well, warning him to try to keep out of the sight of the Kunorese soldiers while she worked.

Earning the money to leave took a good number of days.

Aili's plan was to stock up on Federation-style medicine as much as possible, since she knew how to use that in addition to blood healing, but in the end, she had to be satisfied with some anti-diarrheal medications, some bandages, and a curved needle and thread for sewing stitches; truthfully, she doubted she'd ever bother with this, since blood healing was so fast and easy, but it was part of the kit. All other medical supplies, like almost everything else, were tightly rationed. At least it gave her some kind of cover for what she was really doing, and in any case, she couldn't help but notice that most of the ordinary Daxian people she met simply assumed that as a Federative she knew all kinds of powerful medical secrets. She bought additional clothes for herself and Yisue and considered buying a riding animal, but decided it was likely to just get eaten. That left all the rest of her savings to buy food along the way.

Three weeks later, she asked Yisue if he would return to the ocean, and as she had anticipated, he refused. She whispered again; they took a ferry across the bay of Zhaishou, and then began walking due west.

Aili stood still, frowning.

Yisue said, "What are you looking at?" He tilted his head to one side, looking at the road in front of them, which looked very much like the road behind: pitted with ruts, with groups of people who tried not to talk to one another as they hurried along.

"So many," she said, dazed.

"So many people?" Yisue sat down on the ground, dissatisfied. "There are so many people always. Soldiers and people who are sick and scared. That's all we see."

"Ocean is due south. Just turn left and go home," she said, something she said several times a day at this point.

"No," he said, equally automatically. Really, he was just stubborn.

There were so many people on the roads, always, but there was something else too. People speaking without sound, being speared, impaled, cut apart, dying in front of her. Silently. Unnoticed by the plodding groups of ordinary people.

"Don't you see them?" she asked. She moved forward and tried to touch one — a young man wearing the armor of the Feng dynasty, shot by multiple arrows, lying gasping with his eyes staring upward. Her hand tingled, but she couldn't touch him.

With that one, tingling sense, something rushed through her body and she could hear: the screams, the yells, the clanging, and that nameless sound of flesh being parted by sharp metal. Her head snapped up, flooded with memories from her life as Hong Deming, from the Western Sea.

"What is it?" Yisue asked, sitting up. "What's wrong?"

The young man she had tried to touch looked at her and said, "Sister, tell my mother, tell my mother–"

And then, he died.

Aili calmed her shaking mind and body and settled into a lotus position, out of the way of the road. She waited. And waited. Yisue curled up and fell asleep, then woke up and asked for food; she absently pointed to the travel container, continuing to watch.

She watched several thousand people die violently over approximately eight hours. After that point, the remaining living — those who had killed but not been killed — wavered and disappeared. The bodies remained.

Another person appeared, a man she recognized. Zhu Guiren.

But he had two hands.

He knelt on the ground near the center of the corpse-laden field, refugees walking through his figure as they used the road west. In his hand, there was a glimmering container made of some substance she couldn't name. From it, he poured a liquid out on the earth, chanting, and then knelt and struck the earth with his hand.

Something raced out from where he touched the earth — a spider made of smoke, leaping from corpse to corpse, shooting out into the air to fasten onto things she couldn't see that went beyond the field's boundaries. The refugees stumbled through, unfeeling, unaffected, but the corpses all shivered and then disappeared. Zhu Guiren also stood, his hand held in a seal as the smoke spider returned to him. Then he, too, evaporated.

Aili took a deep breath and stood up. "Yisue–" she said, and then stopped.

The field was full again of screams, metal, blood.

Yisue yawned. "Are we going anywhere today?"

Aili sat down again, chin in hand, then switched back to a lotus position to cultivate. "No. Get out the sleeping things. We're staying here."

Eight hours later, she attacked Zhu Guiren. He didn't notice. Nothing changed.

The sun came up.

"Now?" asked Yisue. "I'm *bored.*"

"Eat," she said, handing him the bag. "Go climb some trees or something. Go exploring, but don't go far. I'll be here."

Every so often, she jumped into the battle just to see if she could change anything, first with En, then with the phoenix whip. No one noticed; nothing changed.

Eight more hours later, she stood next to Zhu Guiren and tried to take the container away from him with her hands, then with En. He didn't notice. Nothing changed.

She tried to catch the stream of what she was now sure was Liu Chenguang's blood, glimmering in its thin waterfall. It went through her hands. Nothing changed.

She brought out the phoenix fire and let the blood pour through it. She felt the heat of Chenguang's blood against her skin and closed her eyes.

"Eftahede," she whispered, and the world exploded around her.

It seemed that she was always being knocked unconscious and being woken up, which was annoying; but after all, most of these times she probably should have been dead, so, overall a win. Aili laughed out loud.

Yisue was staring at her, as were a good number of the refugees walking past, giving them a wide berth. Whatever she had done, she had done it in the middle of the road. She sat up and wiped blood from her mouth.

"How long have I been out?"

"A day," he said, eyes wide. "I've been sitting here, keeping people from trampling you."

"Thank you."

While she hadn't been paying attention, Yisue had apparently decided that his hair would look especially attractive in a blend of braids and knots with some random pieces of metal, cloth, and shell stuck into it. "Isn't that piece of glass in your hair a little close to your throat?" she asked diplomatically.

He silently took it out and handed it to her, staring. "Your mouth is bleeding," he said.

She nodded.

"Also your ears. And your nose. And a little bit out of your eyes."

"Ah," She tried to stand up and found she couldn't. "What happened?"

"You were standing in the middle of the road and you took out your sword. You never told me you had a sword," he said accusingly.

"Sorry about that. Do you want to see it?" She tried to call En, but it wouldn't come. "Sorry...I must really not have anything left..." She felt very vulnerable knowing that. "I need to cultivate..."

"And then," he continued, "you were moving your hands around, and kind of muttering to yourself, and then there was a big flash of light, and almost like an earthquake, and a wind that blew everything around. Everyone was very scared. When the light went away, you were lying in the road. All the people who were nearby ran away, and since then, people have just been ignoring you, and no one would help me move you somewhere safe," he added, glaring at the people who continued to walk by without paying them any attention except looks from the corners of their eyes. "I was thinking about transforming and picking you up in my mouth when you finally woke up."

"Don't do that," she said, and stood up, dizzy. "We're not near the ocean. I don't know if it's safe for you."

Yisue reached out and took her hand. Surprised, she looked down at his face and realized that he was frightened and trying not to show it. "Don't worry," she said, "I'm fine. I think...I think I did something that's good. Can we wait here just till it gets dark, to be sure?"

They waited all night. Yisue curled up to sleep next to her, and Aili alternated between sleep and cultivation. The battle and Zhu Guiren did not reappear.

They worked their way across Hai'an slowly and with greater and greater horror. Yisue sank into silence, eyes wide at the mortal word in an endless death throe: flooding, corpses, orphaned children, famished families, shattered cities, soldiers marching, soldiers killing.

Aili was aware of the host of demons that followed the suffering as well — both yaoguai and the more powerful yaomo that, like Zhu Guiren, had cultivated human forms and hid among the human beings. She fought them when she found them. They were almost in a frenzy, an ecstasy of resentment; they rarely chose to hide or run, and some of them had started preying directly on the mortal beings, murdering and torturing the stragglers. No doubt, others had blended into the flood of humanity, encouraging more brutality, betrayal, and cruelty as Zhu Guiren had at the imperial court.

Because of all this, and because Aili needed to cultivate regularly to manage the drain on her powers, they moved very slowly through the misery of Hai'an in wartime. The people on the road had gone through too much to easily befriend strangers. They were suspicious of one another, and of possible collaborators and informers — afraid of being robbed of their meager belongings and keeping others at a safe distance — so despite the crowds, Aili most often felt they were alone. There was hardly any wood to be had for a fire, so their nights were cold as well. Yisue curled up shivering close to her, and she wrapped him in the blanket to keep them warm together.

"This can't be good for you, little dragon," she said eventually. "Go back home. I'll walk with you to the ocean."

He was quiet for a while. "But that's not where you're going," he said. "Where are you going?"

"Did I never tell you?" Aili shook her head. "I should have told you. It's just been so…well, we didn't get time, I guess. I'm looking for someone."

"You know their true name." he said astutely. "I hear you whispering sometimes."

"You don't actually hear it, do you?" she asked, flustered. "I don't think anybody is supposed to hear it."

"No, I hum so I won't hear. It would be very bad manners," he said, sounding very prim. "But you should probably be quieter. But, if you know their true name, you must be very important to each other. That person must be waiting for you to come."

"I hope so."

"I don't have a true name yet," Yisue said. "I'm too young."

"Me too," said Aili.

"What are you?" asked Yisue seriously. "You can heal like a phoenix, but you can also fight and do other things, so you're not a phoenix. What are you?"

"You guessed it already," she said, bopping his nose with her finger. "I'm a starfish."

After a while, Yisue said, "Well, I don't want to go back to the ocean. It's lonely there. My parents live very deep and if I'm with them, I don't see anybody. They don't like mortals. They hardly ever even come to the surface. But I like mortals. I like them and I'm sad that they're sad now."

Aili nodded. "Me too," she said again.

"Also, noodles are good," he added sleepily.

That night, airplanes flew low over the refugees camped along the road, sending people into a panic as they tried to cram into whatever little shelters they could find. Aili had heard of the terror of the air raids from many people. Though this whole province now was Kunorese-occupied, and therefore not bombed anymore, too many people had lost their homes and loved ones to planes to be able to think about that clearly; the panic started and flowed everywhere, and people were crushed and trampled.

Aili moved from place to place, doing her best to heal surreptitiously when people were desperate enough to let a stranger come close. These were the kinds of wounds that really required blood healing — bandages weren't going to do anything for crushed internal organs — but it was starting to become obvious, as she was so physically visible, that people were miraculously healed wherever she went. She wasn't the only foreigner among the refugees. There were missionaries, journalists, and others, but far from enough for her to blend in, especially with Yisue at her side.

Two nights after the panic, Aili was cultivating when she heard a quiet voice murmur, "Not quite a phoenix, but something interesting. An experiment, he said."

Another voice coolly said, "Well, take her alive, then. We can experiment some more. Kill the dragon."

Aili swore and rolled to one side, getting space between her and Yisue. "Run!" she yelled at the boy, and jumped up, calling out En as well as the phoenix whip.

A woman like her — though much more beautiful, light-skinned with golden hair — stood off to one side while a man with black hair and dark eyes in a Kunorese imperial uniform came racing at her. He was using a ranged weapon she was unfamiliar with, small disks he threw with vicious sharp edges, incredibly fast and unpredictable in the air. She knocked several of these out of the air with En, but one caught her in the thigh and immediately she felt something cold and sharp climb through her veins from the wound, damaging her spiritual power more than her body.

Now that she was moving more slowly, the woman came from the other side so she had to deal with two at once. She released En and took out a second phoenix whip. She needed something more powerful and unpredictable than the sword for this, and started whipping out, aiming primarily at the man to begin with, then quickly switching when the woman came close. Both the man and the woman were also fighting with double weapons: the woman with a sword and spear, the man alternating the throwing weapons with two swords.

Aili used her qinggong to leap up onto a ruined wall, trying to think.

She couldn't see Yisue. Hopefully he was hiding.

She needed a ranged weapon too. She attempted to form the phoenix fire into a bow, but it was too unstable, so she let it go and tried to summon a spiritual bow. It didn't work. I should have practiced this kind of thing, she thought, annoyed with herself. She gave up and called the whips back.

The woman jabbed at her with the spear. Aili wrapped a whip around it and pulled it out of her hand, but she immediately summoned it back to herself.

They had reached a stalemate, neither of them able to get close enough to her, and she was unable to do enough damage to would end this.

The woman said, "We want to take you alive, creature. Come with us, or we'll hunt down the dragon child instead. He's far less able to fight or hide than you — it won't take us long."

"Not a very attractive offer," Aili said, breathing hard and trying to think.

The man spoke to the woman in the demonic language, and she nodded.

"Where is Zhu Guiren?" she asked. "Tell us where he is, and we'll let you go. For now."

"I don't know where he is. Why would I know?" Aili jumped down with the whip, aiming for the woman's arm. She seemed to be suffering there from an old wound that limited her mobility, and when the phoenix fire wrapped around it she gave a muffled scream and jerked away.

The man laughed, as though he found this amusing.

The woman snapped, "Shut up. Just get her. She must know how to find him."

Aili was starting to feel the effect of the wound in her thigh; the physical wound had closed, but the spiritual damage continued to grow. She didn't have any other ranged weapons in her training but the bow and arrow, and she couldn't seem to make one, but maybe…She switched the phoenix fire to a looped rope. She had learned this as a child for fun — how to lasso the calves and horses — although they'd not been armed or quite this fast and the phoenix fire didn't have the true weight of a rope, but she could try…

It did confuse the man, at least; he backed up quickly when she threw the rope at his feet, and then at his arms or his head, while attacking with the phoenix whip in the other hand. Clearly, this was a fighting style he was unprepared for. He finally became frustrated and came close to her with his two swords, blocking the whip and letting the rope hit him in an effort to get inside her guard. The rope didn't catch him, but the phoenix fire burned him. He leapt back, yelling in shock.

She followed up quickly, striking with the whip again and again. His upper body was starting to catch fire, and with one final scream of rage he turned into a hawk and fled, dripping sparks across the sky.

The woman swore and backed away. Aili moved toward her, switching one hand back to sword, and then started to run. The woman backed up more quickly, then feinted to one side and came at her with the spear again. The spear took her under the ribs; she hacked down with En to break it, then lashed with the whip, catching the woman around the neck. She screamed and scrabbled at her burning skin, then she also fled.

Aili sat down, bleeding, and closed her eyes. She had been healing so much and not cultivating enough; it was taking a while for her own body to heal — longer than it should. That spiritual damage was also still there. She settled into cultivation and attempted to purify it, but she was so tired.

"Aili?" Yisue stood, uncertain, a little space away.

"Stay away for now," she said, "in case they come back tonight. Just stay where you are so they can't get both of us at once, ok? If they come for me again, you need to run."

He nodded and settled down, his white form dim in the darkness.

Aili sighed and closed her eyes. She whispered again. They had crossed most of Hai'an already and were nearing the mountains. It would be good to see the eastern sacred mountain at last.

CHAPTER 8
REUNION

Tainu was still weak, so for days on end, they remained at the inn in Shi'an. Zhu Guiren mostly disappeared, either in his room scribbling or out cultivating at night. When Tainu went looking for him, he was never to be found.

"Is the demon upset about something?" he asked Liu Chenguang one day.

Liu Chenguang looked at him. "Did you two talk about what happened?"

"That he had to kiss me? Of course we did."

"And that was…fine? He was ok?"

"Why would he not be ok?"

Liu Chenguang leaned her chin on her hand; she was working at the table over some maps. "Tainu, I don't want to interfere if he didn't want to talk to you about it, but he was…upset. At the time."

"Oh." Zhu Guiren had to kiss someone he didn't want to after all, so it was to be expected, but Tainu felt a little hurt. He had thought it was all settled. "Well, I'm sorry he was upset."

Liu Chenguang was still looking at him. "Are you worried about him? Why don't you just ask him?"

"I can't find him," he said, frustrated.

"Oh." She looked back down at the table.

Tainu sat down. "Let me guess," he said, "it's only me he's avoiding."

"I'm afraid so. What can you do, Tainu? Let it be — he'll get over whatever it is eventually. He's off cultivating resentment and killing other demons. I'm sure that is his medicine for all ills. Meanwhile, he has me trying to draw up accurate maps that compare the landscape during the Feng dynasty with the landscape now, and it's difficult, as you can imagine. The bed of the Sorrowful River has shifted at least three times, and of course now it's flooded all over. Current, accurate maps are classified material. If I keep trying to buy one I'm eventually going to get targeted by either Daxian guerrillas or Kunorese spies."

Tainu looked over the papers on the table. "Do you want me to go survey?"

"Are you strong enough?"

"For flying? Of course."

"All right then. Can you fly over to Hongye and check where the Sorrowful River is compared to this map?"

He looked, memorized the map and nodded. "Probably three hours," he said, and left.

It took far more than three hours. He had to go to ground repeatedly to avoid gunshots and planes, and really he didn't have enough energy for this; he was still weaker than usual. By the time he returned, exhausted to the bone and very much in need of a bath, it was well after dark.

As a reward, though, Zhu Guiren was sitting at the table with Liu Chenguang. He looked very pale, and a little shaken.

Tainu stopped in the doorway for a moment to look at him. "Is something wrong?" he asked, concerned, as he walked in.

Zhu Guiren growled, "Where have you been? You were supposed to be back hours ago. Don't do that again."

"I've been to Hongye. It took longer than I expected because I was being careful and safe," he said, soothingly. "Liu Chenguang, show me the map." He went to stand next to Zhu Guiren, who edged himself away.

Ignoring his own sense of hurt, he traced his finger down the line of the Sorrowful River to just west of Hongye, then skewed north. "Here," he said. "It's moved far closer to Hongye than in this map. Hongye is right on the bank now, at least of the actual bed. Water is low, though, since the levees were broken upstream."

Liu Chenguang nodded and made the corrections, then bundled the maps off to her room for further work. "You should eat," she said over her shoulder. "We already have."

"Well, that's important to know," Zhu Guiren grumbled. "Some of my contributing arrays might be underwater."

"Would that break them?" Tainu asked curiously, sitting down with a bowl of cold noodles. It wasn't lost on him that Liu Chenguang was trying to give them some space to talk; he was grateful, but also very hungry.

"I don't know," Zhu Guiren said shortly as Tainu slurped his noodles. "But something is breaking them. Something other than me, since I haven't done anything at all about arrays for months on end at this point."

"What do you mean?" Tainu frowned. "Do you think it's another demon?"

"I don't know. It could be someone trying to weaken me, I suppose," he said. "But as I said before, demons would want to keep the array and just take ownership — not destroy it. And I don't know any other way of destroying an array than the one I came up with."

Tainu ate more noodles, then asked, "Are you all right?"

"I'm fine. But I feel it, when an array is destroyed. The larger, the more…The arrays are part of my internal cultivational structure now. They've been there a long time, feeding me resentment. I feel something…rip…when it's destroyed." He paled and put his hand on his abdomen, just above his hip.

Tainu touched his arm, a little uncertain. "Do you want– Can I help you? Are you in pain?"

"I think I just have to adapt. That's all," he said, shaking off Tainu's hand on his arm. "You don't have to touch me."

"Ah," he said, taking his hand back as quickly as he could. "All right." That really did hurt, but he let it go, and ate some noodles, avoiding Zhu Guiren's eyes.

"I'm sorry," the demon said eventually. "I didn't mean that…that way. Just, you can't heal me."

"Will it get worse?" Tainu asked. "What will it do to you when we start destroying more? When they're all destroyed?"

He shrugged. "I don't know."

They sat in silence for a while, Tainu still smarting inwardly from Zhu Guiren's rebuke. When his noodles were finished, he stood to retreat to his room, dispirited.

"I'm sorry," Zhu Guiren said again, with more force. "I didn't mean it that way, I told you."

Tainu nodded — he really must be very tired; he felt close to tears — and turned to go, unspeaking.

Suddenly, Zhu Guiren stood up and grabbed him, hugging him fiercely.

"I'm sorry. I didn't mean you can't touch me."

Tainu froze in shock. Zhu Guiren's embrace was so strong it was almost painful, imprisoning him, yet not at all as though he was angry. Not angry at all. Just…desperate. For something. For what, exactly? At least Zhu Guiren didn't hate him after all, wasn't disgusted by touching him. Tainu was relieved, his heart felt light.

"Thank you," he said, and hugged him back more gently. "It's all right. I'm just tired, you are too. I'm just going to sleep. I'm not angry with you."

Zhu Guiren's face was hidden on his shoulder, invisible to him, but Tainu could feel him take a deep breath and sigh it out, his body relaxing.

"Is there anything I can do to help you, Tainu?" the demon asked, still holding on to him.

Another wave of shock. Tainu tried to count on his mental fingers how many times in his life people had asked him if he needed help, if he wanted it, if they *could* help him. It was so rare. He couldn't remember the last time; he was always the one other people came to. So this was a question that required a serious and honest answer, and he gave it thought — forgetting that he was still in Zhu Guiren's arms — long enough that Zhu Guiren raised his head to look at him, questioning.

At last he said, "Just don't go away from me again. Don't hide from me. I've missed you, these days."

Zhu Guiren put his head down again and held him a moment longer. "Yes, of course," he said. "I'll be around."

Tainu reached out and touched his hair. "You promised you'd let me help with your hair every morning," he said, half-stern.

"Did I promise that?" Zhu Guiren smiled at him as he let go and stepped away, seeming more himself. "Well, I will."

Liu Chenguang went out shopping again the next morning, fortified with some of Zhu Guiren's never-ending fortune. The markets in Shi'an were as impoverished as anywhere else, from famine and war and occupation, but at least she could buy what was available in them. She paid the innkeeper for their food, so what they needed tended to be things like clothing, and paper and ink, and information, and of the three of them, she was best suited to find information. Zhu Guiren was too imperious — although he insisted that he could be very convincing, she seriously doubted he could ever pass as a poor or even common person — and frankly, too good-looking. People would remember him. Similarly, Tainu was too noticeable in his mortal body; for brief flyovers or for quick dips into enemy territory, she'd ask him. Not as far as Hongye again until he was fully recovered, though. He had looked half-dead last night, so it had probably set him back in healing. She herself looked ordinary enough: Daxian, perhaps a little more tanned than a city woman, wearing ordinary peasant clothing, which she found much more comfortable than western-style dresses, attractive but not too much so, her hair roughly cut to her shoulders. She could be friendly, but not too friendly. She could sit and eat and listen to others, unnoticed.

Today, she looked in the bookstore, where she was well-known at this point. Not a lot of people were buying books under the circumstances, and the owner was eager to please her. He went into his back storage area, looking for any old maps he might not already have sold her or books on the history of Hongye. She needed a better map of the district around Hongye — Zhu Guiren thought that the seal of the great array would be somewhere to the west of that area and wanted maps to remember where that final battle where Hong Deming had died had been held — but she would buy almost anything even remotely relevant to her request, though she knew most of it probably wouldn't be very useful. Zhu Guiren's gold would have a good purpose if it was supporting a family here.

With the maps and books in a package under her arm, she went back out and wandered toward the apothecary to pick up some additional medicines for strengthening Tainu's vital energy. Of course, he would heal on his own eventually, but it didn't hurt to add support. After some thought, she devised a prescription for Zhu Guiren as well. While they were waiting for Tainu to return last night, she had had to listen to several hours of Zhu Guiren's anxious sniping, and had taken the opportunity to check his pulse. There was definitely something off about his qi circulation. It was very ragged and turbulent, as though he'd sustained some kind of injury. She tried to adapt the remedy she would normally use for natural qi to take consideration of what corrupted qi would require, avoiding purifying substances since that might hurt a demon's cultivation, but she'd have to see if it would work for him or not.

Next, she went to her favorite noodle shop, where she was well-known as someone who would sit, reading quietly and eating noodles, for a few hours at a time. It had been destroyed in the original bombardment of Shi'an, the owner had told her, but the reputation of his noodles was such that he was able to open again immediately, even just under a ragged cloth, as soon as he could get flour and oil to cook with.

She sat and listened, trying to gather news about the war, and the road ahead. The official newspapers, everyone agreed, were full of lies, but the gossip in the market was not necessarily any more accurate. Zhu Guiren had said there was a major sub-array in Hai'an that he wanted to tackle first, so it would be good to know how the roads were and whether the Kunorese were setting up roadblocks. The roads were broken, and the railways had long been cut, so transportation now was by walking. She'd have to plan to bring food with them; it didn't sound as though there was anything to be had on the roads east of Shi'an and Zhu Guiren was never to be bothered with that kind of planning, as she well remembered.

"I'm so *hungry*," whined a little boy's voice.

"All right, all right, I know you want noodles," said another voice, tolerant and amused.

"It's been so *long* since we had noodles."

"Look, see that character? Can you read it? That means this shop sells noodles."

Liu Chenguang sat with her noodles halfway to her mouth, her body shocked into complete stillness. Then, she very carefully put the noodles back in the bowl, placed her chopsticks at a polite angle, and stood. There was no way.

There was no way.

She turned around to look out the doorway to the street. There was a little boy with tangled white hair beneath a straw hat, blue-green eyes staring up at the sign, looking bored. Next to him stood a tall woman, her thick, dark blonde braid lying over one shoulder and ending just down past her collarbone. She was pointing at the sign above their heads and outlining the order of the strokes to the little boy, who was rolling his eyes and following her movements with his hand. When he drew the character in the air on his own, she nodded and laughed, and walked into the store with him. She met Liu Chenguang's eyes.

They both stood still as statues, staring at one another, but it didn't last long. The boy grabbed Aili's hand and dragged her over to the counter, talking about everything he would get on his noodles. Aili looked back over her shoulder, and Liu Chenguang continued to stare at her, but neither of them said anything.

Liu Chenguang sat heavily in her seat, still watching them. Her heart was pounding so hard she thought she might faint. *Aili, Aili. Aili was here.* Her mouth was dry, her eyes unable to look away. She could see — could tell, because she knew this person — that now Aili was feeling self-conscious; her easy posture and open smile were gone as she bought noodles for the little boy and then brought him over to sit with her.

"Aili," she said finally, hurriedly making room by shoving all of her books and medicines onto the floor. "You're here."

"Liu Chenguang," Aili said, her voice thin and tight. "Are you, how are you?"

The boy slurped noodles and ignored them for a while. When he was getting near the bottom of the bowl, he looked up and said, "I'm Yisue. Are you the person Aili was looking for?"

"Yes, she is," said Aili.

Liu Chenguang flushed all over.

Yisue looked at her doubtfully. "Aili knows your true name?" he asked, as though this seemed very uncertain.

"Yes," Liu Chenguang said. "I told it to her so she could find me."

"Oh," he said. He held up his bowl. "More noodles please."

Liu Chenguang gestured to the owner. "Just, just go up to him and tell him it's my treat, then tell him what you want."

His eyes lit up and he ran off, leaving her alone with Aili.

"I'm so glad to see you," Liu Chenguang said, the words so weak for what she was feeling.

Aili nodded, then said, "You are– you're well?"

"I'm fine. We've been busy. A lot has happened…" She felt as though she was staring too intently at Aili's face but she couldn't stop herself; her eyes were very blue today — they sometimes looked more gray, but now they were a deep, multi-layered blue — and Aili looked tired — very tired, but not tormented, not in that horrible, endless pain that she remembered from leaving her through the phoenix gate. Was that because they had broken arrays? Had that helped her? She hoped so much that it had.

"Tainu and Zhu Guiren are here too. We're staying in an inn. Will you come there with us?" she babbled, still staring.

Aili smiled. "Of course."

"How did you get here, anyway?" Liu Chenguang asked, realizing there was no obvious way. Then, she looked at the tangled white hair of the boy at the noodle counter; he had bits and pieces of metal and cloth woven into it. "Oh, no, Aili, is he– What did you do? Did you–"

"She did," said the boy, bringing his bowl over. "She made a sacrifice to come through my gate." Yisue settled down and began slurping. "This is really good. She was all bloody and floppy," he confided.

Liu Chenguang's initial horror evaporated because Aili covered her face in her hands, but was clearly laughing.

Sternly, Liu Chenguang said, "Aili, I do not want you to do things that make you bloody and floppy again under any circumstances, please."

"She's a starfish," Yisue added.

Aili seemed to be dissolving into helpless giggles behind her hands.

"That's really good to know," Liu Chenguang replied very seriously. "I'm glad we cleared that up."

Since this conversation clearly wasn't going anywhere fast, she started eating her noodles again.

Aili looked up from her hands, her eyes a brilliant blue and filled with laughter, and Liu Chenguang smiled.

"Eat," she said.

Tainu was asleep and Zhu Guiren was in his room, scribbling or whatever he did, when she brought Aili in. He came out quickly for the map she had gone to buy, and Aili and Zhu Guiren stared at each other. Aili's eyes went to his missing left hand. Neither of them said hello. Liu Chenguang had forgotten that, of course, they still hated each other. Or Zhu Guiren was indifferent, as he put it, but Aili had not spent the last months with Zhu Guiren, as she and Tainu had, and she realized that she now saw Zhu Guiren very differently.

How was that? she wondered. *No matter what he does now, he still did what he did then. He's the same person that ruined our lives and so many others. He's still a demon, still cultivates resentment.*

But somehow, it had changed.

She handed him the prescription. "I came up with something for you. Try it out. It's for your meridians — your circulation is very strange now." She added, "Aili's back."

"I see," he said stiffly.

Aili nodded at him, but Liu Chenguang thought she saw a glint of laughter in her eyes.

She was sure of it.

She added, "And this is Yisue."

Yisue looked at Zhu Guiren and yawned. "Demon," he said in acknowledgment. "Where am I sleeping? Are there beds? I want to sleep in a bed."

"I don't care," Zhu Guiren said, and turned around to go back to his room.

"Zhu Guiren," called Aili. "Come back. I have something to ask you." She had noticed the maps on the table and said, "Look here," as she traced back east into Hai'an. "Here. Did you set an array here?"

He came over and looked where she pointed. "It's hard to say," he replied. "The maps don't give enough detail for me to remember the locations of all the arrays. I'm trying to devise a way to sense them magically, which is what I need to get back to right now."

"A large battle," she pressed.

He shrugged. "There was an array in western Hai'an that I created using a significant battle, yes. I don't remember who fought in it, if that's your next question."

"With Liu Chenguang's blood?"

He hesitated, just slightly. "Yes."

"I broke it."

Zhu Guiren's eyes widened, and he sat down heavily.

Tainu came out of his room, yawning. "Sorry, I fell asleep again after lunch. What's going on?"

Zhu Guiren looked at him and said, "Aili's back, and she can break arrays. And you owe me a drinking bout."

Later that night, Tainu let Zhu Guiren lean on him back to his room, then carefully helped him lie down on the bed. "Do you need to throw up?"

"No, no," he said, eyes half closed. "I'm fine."

"All right, then." Tainu carefully laid the blanket over him. "Sleep it off. I'll decide what you owe me as the winner tomorrow."

"Ha, you're not the winner. I'm not done yet..." Zhu Guiren suddenly reached out and grabbed his hand. "Don't go."

Tainu tried, unsuccessfully, to disentangle his hand, even attempting to peel Zhu Guiren off him finger by finger. He seemed to be falling asleep but was holding Tainu's hand as though his life depended upon it. "Demon?"

When nothing happened, he gave up and sat on the edge of the bed, waiting until full unconsciousness hit in the hopes that Zhu Guiren would loosen his death grip then. Since there was nothing else to look at, he looked at the demon's face and thought he looked very beautiful, as always — maybe even a little bit more so because he was a little sweaty and flushed from the alcohol. There were little strands of hair sticking to his face, which he reached over and carefully peeled off.

"Kiss me," mumbled Zhu Guiren.

Tainu froze. "What?" he asked.

Zhu Guiren opened his eyes, seemingly with a great effort. "Can you say my name?"

Helplessly, Tainu said, "Arciniang."

Zhu Guiren smiled and closed his eyes again, still not letting go of his hand; Tainu tugged a little bit to see if he could escape, to no avail.

"Have you ever kissed me?" the demon asked. "Will you kiss me?"

Tainu laughed, uncomfortably. "I've never kissed you, and I won't kiss you now. You are extremely drunk. You won't remember this in the morning."

"I will. Kiss me. Just kiss me on the forehead, if that's all you want to do," he said as though throwing down a challenge, his eyes still closed.

Tainu leaned over and pecked him on the forehead. "There."

Zhu Guiren opened his eyes and said, "That wasn't good. You can do better than that."

Tainu pulled his hand harder. "Demon," he said, trying to appeal to any bit of sobriety that remained in the mortal body lying in front of him, "I'm not trying to impress you with my skills, believe me. I don't want to kiss you."

"You don't?" Zhu Guiren sounded sad. "Oh."

"Can you let go of my hand?"

"No," he said. "I won't let go. Stay with me." He closed his eyes again and seemed to fall deeply asleep this time.

Tainu stretched as far as Zhu Guiren's steel trap of a hand would let him and hooked a chair with his foot so he'd at least have somewhere to sit beside the edge of the bed, and sat there, looking at Zhu Guiren sleeping. His mind wandered after a while, wondering where all this was coming from. He wondered if demons fell in love with people. They had children, certainly, not like phoenixes. From the hints he'd gotten from Zhu Guiren, it didn't sound as though demonic society was very pleasant. Probably, their relationships were fairly awful as well, although he really had no idea what demons got up to in their intimate lives. Maybe even if Zhu Guiren didn't have a relationship with other demons, there was someone else — some other spirit or yao or even a mortal. Who knew? He started snickering imagining Zhu Guiren trying to court someone; he would probably insult them all day long. Certainly Zhu Guiren wasn't courting *him*, this was just alcohol, but maybe there was someone he loved, or someone he wanted, or someone he had loved once and lost.

He himself had had no shortage of experience with physical intimacy. Sexual pleasure was just that: pleasant and comforting, one of the few genuine pleasures of the mortal world, and not threatening or dangerous at all. He had never fallen in love with anyone, though he had watched human beings love one another, shaping their lives by their desires to be with one another, growing old together, sacrificing for one another. It was so different from the solitary and endless existence of the phoenix.

What would it be like to love someone fully, mind and heart and body and soul, to give oneself completely to someone, and then lose them? He would always, in time, lose everyone except other phoenixes. If he were to love anyone the way that Liu Chenguang loved Aili, and then watch them die as everyone died, he thought he would very likely lose his mind, yet he would still live forever with the pain of it. He had always thought that mortals were so courageous to do such things when their loss was so certain, so inescapable, so inevitable. He thought a thousand years ago, and still thought, that Liu Chenguang was brave beyond belief.

Zhu Guiren's eyes had smoothed out with true sleep, although his hand hadn't loosened at all. He looked at his sleeping face, their entwined fingers, and the thought came: *what if? What if…if I did want to kiss him…*

He took a deep, long breath and closed his eyes, trying to imagine, then shook his head. That would never be. Not with this beautiful, strange, brave person. There was no one like him in the world. It was good as it was, just to be together.

"Tainu?" Zhu Guiren opened his eyes, just a little. "Your hand feels very warm."

He pulled, helplessly, as Zhu Guiren tightened his grasp and fell back to sleep.

Aili came back from checking on Yisue in the other room. "He's sleeping," she said, and sat back down. "Where did Tainu and Zhu Guiren go?"

"Zhu Guiren passed out and Tainu basically carried him away," said Liu Chenguang. Before Aili could change her mind and go back to her bedroom, she pushed over another bowl of liquor. "So, who do you think would win between the two of us?"

Aili looked up, smiling, her blue eyes very slightly unfocused. "Well, I'm bigger. That should make a difference, right? The last time I was really drunk in Easterly — it was an entire store's worth of golden liquor plus six or seven jars of white liquor…"

"You got drunk in Easterly?" Liu Chenguang asked. "Which store?"

"Old Liang's."

Impressed, Liu Chenguang nodded. "That is not a small store. What happened afterward?"

"I passed out on the sidewalk, Edna Lee found me."

"Edna," Liu Chenguang echoed, remembering. She felt a little jealous. Aili had so clearly admired Edna for being a pilot. She drank her bowl, refilled it, and reached out to refill Aili's. When she looked up, Aili's eyes were on her, but she quickly looked down at the table.

Liu Chenguang had completely run out of things to say. She didn't want to reminisce about Crane Moon, or talk about the war, or stupid Zhu Guiren and whatever he was up to, or arrays. She racked her brain for some topic that wasn't painful in Aili's life, because she wanted to know about Aili's life, but everything she could think of went right to the worst places and what good was that? The silence drew out between them, becoming more and more awkward.

She looked up again, and Aili was looking at her again. And she looked away. Again.

Liu Chenguang suddenly recalled Aili sitting in that bar in Easterly when they first met. Alone. Watching other people, as though from the outside, and realized…

Aili was shy.

Had Hong Deming been shy? Would she have even known? She'd never cared about how Hong Deming was with anyone else. In their years together, he had almost never spent time with Hong Deming among other people; it had far more often than not been just the two of them. As she had told Grandmother Wang, there were circumstances, and she herself had no ability to make friends with others, but it also had never occurred to her to wonder, except with jealousy, about whether Hong Deming had other people in his life and whether they made him happy too. She hadn't known better then, but now she'd spent a thousand years living in a village full of people who were family and friends to one another. She could understand now how important it was, but back then, she had never paid attention to whether Hong Deming had friends, or made them easily. Probably not. She'd only ever heard Deming talk about his martial brothers, and one time about Mo Xiang, who he had to fight. Maybe he…hadn't been easy with people, really. And now, since they'd lost the ease they had together in that life, Aili wasn't easy with her either.

But Aili wanted to be with her. Aili was here — had come all this way on her own, to sit with her at this table and drink with her — even though it was obvious that she was terribly uncomfortable about it. Liu Chenguang tasted the liquor, smooth and sweet and biting on her tongue, and thought, *my person is so very brave.* She felt warm all over, not only from the liquor.

"What are you thinking about?" Aili's voice broke into her reverie. Her eyes were on Liu Chenguang again, and she smiled.

She picked up her bowl and drank it, then poured a new one for both of them. *I'm so happy that you are here,* she thought, but that was too soon to say. She was sure Grandmother Wang would advise against it. She said, "Friends. I was wondering about your friends, your friends in Easterly. Edna, and Nora."

Aili's face lit up. "They're both such good people. Nora was really...well, she was so much fun to be with. And so kind. She was the one who helped me find a job when I first got to Easterly and gave me a place to stay. We went everywhere together."

"Really?" Liu Chenguang poured another bowl, sweet and stinging, one for each of them, and reached for a full jar. It was so wonderful to be with Aili, to see Aili happy; it warmed her inside, more than the liquor, more than anything that could be. "Tell me more."

CHAPTER 9
FOX SPIRIT

"At some point, we have to do it," said Zhu Guiren. "We have to go find an array and start breaking it." He pointed to the map. "I've triangulated four arrays within a few days' journey of Shi'an that would be worth breaking. We don't have to expect that the owner of the array will attack, since that's me, but we need to be prepared for other demons attacking. We just have to get started."

Liu Chenguang asked, "Tainu, are you strong enough?"

"I'm fine," he said. "I'm more worried about the demon."

Zhu Guiren impatiently waved his hand. "I'm fine, or as fine as I'm going to be. We have to do it. I haven't broken one of my own arrays yet and we need to see how it works."

"I can do it," said Aili, sitting in the corner of the settee, legs stretched out in front of her.

"Not all of them," Zhu Guiren replied impatiently. "From what you told me, the crucial point where you can intervene is when I'm pouring Liu Chenguang's blood. I made hundreds of arrays without doing that before Hong Deming was even born. You won't have an intervention point for any of them, and some of those would definitely need to be destroyed for us to have any chance at the great array."

"At what point, exactly, did you start using my blood?" asked Liu Chenguang, raising an eyebrow. "Not just that last year?"

"No. Why would I wait? I took blood from you once a year at least, since the first year you came to Crane Moon. While you were in seclusion, Taiqian would bring you the drink and he was always the person cutting–"

Aili turned pale, stood, grabbed Liu Chenguang's elbow, and pulled her out of the room.

"Well played," said Tainu.

Zhu Guiren put his head on the table. "Why? Why is everyone so sensitive? Everyone knows this happened! Everyone knows! It's important to be precise. Why is it always such a shock to these people?"

Tainu wasn't feeling very sympathetic, so he wandered out after Aili and Liu Chenguang. He saw them walking, talking together; it seemed that Liu Chenguang was trying to calm Aili down. He suspected that Aili had been about to go for Zhu Guiren with whatever weapons she carried around these days. Thank the heavens for Liu Chenguang, although rightfully, she should have been just as upset. The little dragon boy, Yisue, was shooting marbles in the yard with some of the local children. Tainu had taken charge of his hair, combing and braiding it decently, but he'd let him keep a few of the beads.

"Hello, Tainu," said Yisue. "Aili's upset."

"I know," he said, squatting down next to them. "She has a good reason."

After watching the game for a while, he went back inside.

Zhu Guiren was back in his room, scribbling. The demon looked up at him. "I want to undo it. I'm trying."

"I know," Tainu replied. Done is done — that was the basic way the phoenix approached the world — and pain is pain. "I know you're trying." He found he really couldn't say much else, but he came over and put his hand on Zhu Guiren's shoulder. Zhu Guiren didn't look up, though he stopped scribbling and stared at the floor.

"Come on," Tainu said. "Show me the maps. Your plan is to find an array that didn't use Liu Chenguang's blood and test what happens when you break it yourself?"

Zhu Guiren nodded. "There are four possibilities that would be good…test sites. The arrays that Aili already destroyed were not strong for the most part, there was only one strong one, but it has affected me significantly. When I made my initial calculations, I didn't realize that the loss of the sub-arrays would also damage my cultivation, or my ability to cultivate at all, in this way. That's going to change some of the calculations. I need to know if it's different if I do it my-self."

They had walked back over to the map table to examine it. Cautiously, Tainu asked, "Does it matter that much? If Aili can break an array that was made with Liu Chenguang's blood, then she can break the great array, can't she? Why don't we go right there?"

Zhu Guiren said, "Well, it's good I didn't bring this up given how emotional she is over the whole thing, but I'm not at all sure she can break that one. I didn't exactly pour Liu Chenguang's blood for the final seal. It was…a different situation."

Tainu closed his eyes.

"You see," Zhu Guiren hurried on, "I don't think that there's an intervention point for her in the same way. At the moment the great array was sealed, the moment Liu Chenguang entered rebirth, I was already miles away in my crow form. Also, I'm not sure…"

"You're not sure Aili can actually watch it happen without trying to kill you?"

"Correct. That's it."

"I agree," Tainu said. "I would not be surprised, and frankly couldn't blame her. Could you?"

"No," he admitted. "To be honest, when we get to the point where we are breaking the central seal, I don't think she should be there at all if we can avoid it. Or Liu Chenguang, either."

Tainu nodded. He felt very conflicted about this entire conversation, but whatever the reasons, he could fully agree that Liu Chenguang and Aili shouldn't be put through that.

"The other thing…it's not directly relevant," Zhu Guiren said. "It's not about the arrays, but just about safety. We have a child with us, and this is not going to be a safe situation. Aili told me that the little boy wanted to go to the Sorrowful River. Some of these sites are close, or on the other side. I think we should bring him and let him stay in the river, instead of with us."

Tainu looked at him, surprised.

"You're surprised I would think of things like that," said Zhu Guiren, straightening and looking at him.

"I am, honestly," Tainu replied. "You're usually so…" He cast about for a word that wouldn't be too insulting. "Utilitarian."

"Well, then think of it in terms of efficiency, if that makes more sense to you," Zhu Guiren said. He sounded a little bitter.

Liu Chenguang and Aili sat together under one of the trees near the inn, watching Yisue play. Aili's face was still pale with shock. "I can't believe it," she kept saying. "All that time, he was doing that to you and no one knew. No one cared." Her eyes were a little unfocused, as though she was seeing something else.

Aili was almost visibly burning with fury; Liu Chenguang didn't dare hold her hand or touch her, as though touching her would scald the skin. She knew that Aili had been within a dust mote's width of attacking Zhu Guiren. When the demon had said that Taiqian had been cutting her since she arrived at Crane Moon, she had seen Aili's hand move in the air to call En, then had just as quickly twisted back before grabbing her and leaving.

"Aili," Liu Chenguang said at last. "Aili, it's done now. It's long done, and there's no undoing it. I don't want to remember it." But of course, that was unfair. The truth was that she didn't remember it. It was Aili who had seen it; it was Hong Deming who had rescued her and brought her out. She sighed, and finally laid her hand carefully next to Aili, open, in case she wanted to take it.

She was surprised to suddenly be engulfed completely in Aili's arms, to have Aili hold her tightly — almost too tightly for comfort — gulping air as though she had just come up from a deep dive without oxygen.

"Aili?"

"You're all right," she said, muffled, her face in Liu Chenguang's neck. "You're all right now."

"Yes." She carefully reached up to touch Aili's hair. "Yes, I'm all right now, Aili. I'm…I'm fine." Which was actually true, she realized. "I'm fine, and you're here. I don't want to spend all my life remembering the horrible things Zhu Guiren did. Zhu Guiren is not worth that much of my attention."

Aili laughed, shakily, and let her go. "Yes, I see that now…But how can you not hate him? How can you be…with him all the time like this?"

"I don't know. If I think about it, I know it makes no sense. He's still a demon. He hasn't changed. I had my time of hating and raging at him, but then it was just…done. We had other things to do. And other than coming out with little tidbits like that every so often, he's really…not awful." She added, "Tainu likes him, for some reason I can't comprehend, so I have to put up with it. And you know, Zhu Guiren and I had a decent time together, back then. He was boring and stuffy and bossy, but he did teach me a lot."

"That doesn't make up for any of it," Aili said, her expression darkening again.

"No, it doesn't," she agreed. "In some ways, it makes it worse. But it is what it is. I don't hate him anymore, that's all. I have other things to do."

Aili nodded. "All right. Well, I'll put up with him for Tainu, I guess."

"And because he can break arrays," Liu Chenguang said. She stood and reached down to pull Aili to her feet. This didn't work at all; she nearly fell into Aili's lap, laughing. Aili laughed too, and pulled both of them upright as she stood.

Liu Chenguang looked up at her, feeling…something. Like a little shock of electricity — as though their bodies were touching one another even though they weren't; aware of Aili's body near hers, like a bell's thrumming after a strike.

Ever since her interrupted regeneration when she had met Hong Deming, she had always been small in her mortal body. Hong Deming had been taller than her, as had most adult men in her previous life, but Aili was taller than Hong Deming. Standing so close, Liu Chenguang was suddenly very aware of how far back she needed to tip her head to see Aili's face, and how much that felt like she was asking to be kissed, and maybe she was.

She stepped back quickly, unsure whether Aili had noticed anything.

Aili just smiled. "All right, let's go back to the demon." On the way back, she patted Yisue on the head and said, "Yisue, dinner in an hour, don't go far."

"Yes," he said, staring at the marbles in the dust. "But Bai Chao says that his parents don't have much food for him. They have to save it for the little brother and the grandmother. Can he share our dinner?"

From behind Aili, Liu Chenguang said, "You can bring some bowls down to share with him, but he can't come up." It would just be too awkward trying to explain Zhu Guiren and Tainu and the maps all over the room. Yisue had already been told to be discreet, but he knew how to be discreet the way a fish knows how to walk.

Later, they settled around the table for dinner; Yisue came up and got his two bowls, and said, "There's someone downstairs looking for Tainu."

"Who?" Tainu frowned and stood.

As Yisue slipped out the door, his hands full, someone else came in without knocking. He was almost as tall as Tainu, his face as beautiful as Zhu Guiren's, but somehow more magnetic —attracting the attention of everyone in the room. Once noticed, it was almost impossible to look away. He stood just inside the door, his dark eyes focused on Tainu from under his thick lashes, and smiled slowly. His lips were beautifully shaped, and when he smiled a small, sharp tooth was visible, pressing into the pink skin.

"Who are you?" asked Zhu Guiren sharply. "Who told you to come in here?"

The man ignored him, looking only at Tainu. "It's good to see you," he said.

Tainu suddenly seemed to become a different person. He leaned back against the wall in a way that emphasized the long lines of his body, languidly hinting at its capabilities, graceful as a leopard, matching the man's gaze with half-lidded eyes and a lazy smile of his own. "You too. Who told you I was here?"

The man shrugged. "I heard that you were looking for information on the arrays and demons here. I thought you might like my help." He took a step inside the room, like an entranced wild animal, as though he couldn't resist coming closer to Tainu.

"We don't need your help," said Zhu Guiren loudly, looking at Tainu and trying to catch his eye.

Liu Chenguang began to feel as though she'd like to either start laughing or leave the room — one or the other of those things would need to happen soon — while Aili looked back and forth, clearly confused.

"Shall we talk in private?" asked the man, leaning forward. The very tip of his pink tongue brushed across his upper lip.

Tainu smiled.

"Don't," said Zhu Guiren, standing up so abruptly that his chair fell over with a clatter, his eyes glittering. "You, get out."

The man ignored him, as though he didn't exist, and took Tainu's hand, leading him out the door. Tainu looked back at them and winked before disappearing.

Zhu Guiren was breathing hard and fast, his eyes narrowed to slits. "That was a fox spirit," he hissed.

"Obviously," said Liu Chenguang. She picked up her chopsticks and kept eating. "That's why he's better looking than you."

Aili snickered. Zhu Guiren looked as though he was considering how many ways he could kill them both with a chopstick.

Then, Aili said, "Oh! I remember now, I met a fox spirit once."

"Did you?" Liu Chenguang frowned. "Were you…?"

"It wasn't a friendly encounter," she said. Her humor disappeared. "I wasn't in the mood, believe me."

Liu Chenguang glanced at her, then at Zhu Guiren, then at Aili again, meeting her eyes. She covered her mouth to stop herself from laughing, and Aili managed to smile too. "But Zhu Guiren," she said innocently, "I do want you to know that except for that fox spirit, you're really the most handsome man I've ever seen."

"Absolutely," agreed Aili. "You shouldn't feel bad."

"He does wear the clothes nicely," mused Liu Chenguang.

"True," said Aili. "Zhu Guiren, you should ask him where he shops."

Zhu Guiren went and sat down in the corner to scribble furiously on the wall, ignoring them. Soon, he said, "He's been gone a long time."

"He's been gone five minutes," said Liu Chenguang.

"Too long," said Zhu Guiren. He stood up. "I'm going to go get him. Probably he needs to be rescued."

Liu Chenguang laughed out loud. "Zhu Guiren, I promise you, my sibling does not need to be rescued from a fox spirit. He's very capable–"

"Shut up!" Zhu Guiren turned bright red. He ran out of the room, clattering down the stairs.

Liu Chenguang and Aili looked at each other and laughed hysterically.

"Oh, that was so worth it," said Liu Chenguang, wiping tears from her eyes, "I'm going to invite fox spirits in regularly. I've never seen Zhu Guiren upset like that, ever, even in our other life–"

"But he must be familiar with fox spirits," said Aili. "He sent the one I met, I'm sure." She prodded a piece of tofu, then said, "To be fair, I think I lived… as long as I did, because that fox spirit didn't want to kill me. So, I suppose I should be a little grateful…" Then she shook her head. "You know what, no. No I'm not."

Liu Chenguang laughed. "Well, I'm glad you're not grateful to a fox spirit. That wouldn't be a good favor to owe as far as I'm concerned." She looked at Aili, considering. "Also, if that fox spirit laid a hand or any other part of its body on you, I have some things I'd like to say to it."

Aili flushed. "Liu Chenguang, have you ever…"

"What?" Liu Chenguang smiled at her.

Aili opened and closed her mouth a few times, as though not sure what to say, then went back to eating.

Eventually Tainu returned, still smiling. "Well, that was worth it."

Liu Chenguang smirked at him. "Was it indeed?"

He laughed. "I meant he actually did have information–"

Zhu Guiren burst back into the room after him, panting. "Tainu!"

Tainu looked at him, "Yes?"

"Are you all right?"

"Yes…?"

"That was a fox spirit!"

"Of course he was a fox spirit. I'm well aware, demon."

"But fox spirits always– They always want…something!"

"I know what they want. I'm ten thousand years old, demon. I've met fox spirits before." Tainu looked at Zhu Guiren, smiling. "Come on, you've got to be near my age. You must have some experiences too?"

Zhu Guiren turned red, and then completely pale, as though he was going to faint. "Did he– did he–"

"Did he what?" Tainu started to laugh uncontrollably. "Oh no...oh no, demon, do you really not– Oh my goodness, how old are you?"

"Shut up!" Zhu Guiren shouted. "Did he kiss you? Did he– did he do other things?"

"A gentleman never tells," Tainu said primly.

Zhu Guiren ran out of the room again.

Zhu Guiren was knocking down trees with some kind of demonic unarmed combat skill when Aili found him, his beautiful face twisted in fury. She looked at him, feeling sympathetic; it didn't matter to her if Liu Chenguang had been with fox spirits or who knows what else for seven thousand years before they met, but obviously it bothered Zhu Guiren to think about Tainu...

Why would Zhu Guiren care about Tainu...

In fact, she really did care that Liu Chenguang had been with fox spirits.

She took out En and prepared to deal death to some innocent nature.

"You!" said Zhu Guiren, turning toward her. "Why didn't you stop him?"

"Me?" She pointed at her chest. "Me? What right do I have to stop him? Anyway, he said that the fox spirit had information. That's why he went," she said, trying to soften the blow.

"He didn't listen to me." Another tree met its splintery end. "I asked him not to go. Didn't you hear me? Do you think maybe he didn't hear me?" he asked, suddenly hopeful.

"I'm pretty sure he heard you," she said. "But really, I'm sure it was just to get...the information."

Zhu Guiren spun in the air and took out two trees at once.

Aili watched him for a moment. "Want to spar?" she asked suddenly.

Zhu Guiren looked at her. "You really think you're qualified?" he asked, sounding more like himself. "Hmph."

She called the phoenix whip and flicked it at him. He yelped. "Please, show me your skills," she said, smiling.

His halberd appeared. "Don't hold back because I've only got one hand."

"Oh, not a problem," she replied, and they launched at one another.

Zhu Guiren didn't come back until the next day. Aili returned after a few hours, covered in dust and splinters, and said that they'd been sparring and Zhu Guiren needed to go cultivate to recover. She herself, she said, just wanted a bath, but also disappeared till the next day's breakfast. Tainu and Liu Chenguang exchanged glances, Tainu trying not to snicker out loud at Liu Chenguang's overly-innocent smile. It was so typical of Aili's personality to be jealous, though he couldn't understand why Zhu Guiren was so upset. Probably he just didn't like fox spirits. Plenty of people didn't.

When Zhu Guiren did return, Tainu shared what the fox spirit had told him: there were a great many powerful demons in the area, and that there had been several battles between demon clans recently. Many of the less powerful or harmless yao were fleeing west to avoid being caught in the demon wars, including him. He had asked Tainu to go with him.

Zhu Guiren clearly wanted to kill something, preferably the fox spirit, on hearing this.

In a clear bid to distract him, Aili said, "Oh, I just remembered — I fought a demon who was looking for you, Zhu Guiren. She thought I'd know where you were. There were two of them, a woman with blonde hair and a man who might have been Kunorese. At least, he was in a Kunorese uniform."

Zhu Guiren sat up immediately. "Did they transform? What weapons did they use? How did you get away?"

After she had described it all, and much to Liu Chenguang's evident discomfort at imagining Aili having to fight two demons at once, Zhu Guiren nodded and began scribbling on the table.

"Stop that," said Liu Chenguang. "At least use a wall or something. I don't want to have to replace all the furniture in here too."

He shook his head. "My clan, two other clans. Those are not allies to one another, although the woman's clan is allied to mine, or at least used to be. The woman was probably the one I fought on the way to the refuge, Liu Chenguang. I wounded her in the arm."

"Did you tell her I was an experiment?" Aili asked, looking at the ceiling.

"Well, technically you are," said Zhu Guiren. "In the literal definition of experiment–"

Tainu covered his eyes and said, "Demon, I beg you, please just stop."

Zhu Guiren stopped. Then, he said, "There's so much going on right now. I need…I need to work this out. We're leaving tomorrow. Here." He put his finger down into the mostly empty map space due west of Shi'an. "Aili and Tainu, prepare the boy. We're bringing him to the Sorrowful River first. Liu Chenguang, get your supplies together. Food for four days in case we're delayed. Tell the innkeeper we'll come back here afterward. We need to have a safe place to return to. We leave in the morning." He turned and went into his bedroom.

Everyone else stared at each other blankly. At last Liu Chenguang stood up. "That's a lot to get together by tomorrow morning. I need to get to work."

Aili said, "All right, I'll talk to Yisue," and went downstairs.

Tainu stared at the closed door to Zhu Guiren's room, and finally walked over to push it open.

Zhu Guiren was kneeling against the wall, scribbling in his system of symbols and diagrams that no one else could understand. His hair was messy, Tainu noticed. He hadn't slept in his room, and Tainu hadn't seen him before this impromptu meeting; before that, it was Zhu Guiren running out of the room with all of them laughing at him about the fox spirit.

No wonder he was upset.

He went and knelt beside him. "I'm sorry."

"For what?" Zhu Guiren wouldn't look at him.

"For teasing you."

The pencil stopped moving for a brief moment, then continued. "Why did that fox spirit want you to go with him?"

Tainu tried very hard to answer this question without making a joke out of it. "We knew each other a long time ago," he said. "He remembers it fondly, I guess."

This time the pencil stopped completely. Zhu Guiren's body froze for a moment.

This truly upsets him, Tainu realized, feeling a deep unease about this situation. Why does it upset him so much?

"It's not that he was special to me," he tried. "Just…it was a nice time we had together, back then. Probably, fox spirits don't often get to see their partners again."

This definitely was not going well. Zhu Guiren began scribbling again, even more furiously than before.

"I didn't go with him," Tainu pointed out, a little desperate. "I didn't want to." When there was no response, he said, "Demon, won't you look at me?"

Zhu Guiren finally looked at him. To his shock, he saw that the demon's eyes were red around the edges.

"Demon?" he asked, panicking a little bit. He reached out for him, but Zhu

Guiren drew back, shaking his head.

"No," he said. "Not…not now."

"What's wrong? Why are you so upset?" He sat and waited in silence, determined to get a response out of him and unwilling to leave without one. Something was very wrong; something needed to be dealt with. "I'm not leaving until this is better," Tainu said at last. "I'm sorry. If anything I've said or done has hurt you, please tell me. I'm worried about you. I really–"

"You always look sad," Zhu Guiren said suddenly. He was still writing feverishly on the wall.

"Do I?" Tainu asked, surprised. "I don't feel sad. Just like usual."

"What would make you happy?"

"I told you, I'm not sad."

"Do you miss your family?"

"Where are all these questions coming from?" he asked uncomfortably. "What do you mean? You know my family's long dead. Now I have my little sibling. That's all. She's right here, I don't miss her."

Zhu Guiren scribbled even more furiously. At last, he sat back to look at what he'd written. "Tainu," he said.

"What?"

"What do you think you will do when we're done with this? When I've broken the arrays? Will Liu Chenguang stay with you?"

Tainu's heart fell a little bit. "Probably not. We're usually solitary. Maybe she'll be with Aili if that works out."

"Is Aili your family too?"

"I'd like her to be, one day."

"Where will you go?"

"Wherever the suffering is."

Zhu Guiren looked away from the wall, at last meeting his eyes fully.

Still a little red, but better, Tainu thought in relief.

"Tainu," he said.

"Yes?" Tainu frowned in confusion.

"What if I went with you? Would that make you happy?"

"You mean, you would be my family too?" Tainu smiled, warmed inside. "Would you?"

Zhu Guiren looked at him, unspeaking.

"No?" Tainu felt his smile disappear, a sense of loss. He shouldn't have asked; it was too much to hope for.

Zhu Guiren took a deep breath. "I don't want to be your family."

Tainu nodded, automatically accepting this even though he was still trying to understand what was happening. "Well, that's all right then. It's fine–"

"I want you to be in love with me."

Tainu's heart plummeted into the earth. He stared, his mouth hanging open. Then he closed it.

Zhu Guiren stared back, still except for the fingers of his one hand, which trembled.

"I don't do that," Tainu said at last, weakly.

"You've never done that," Zhu Guiren corrected. "That doesn't mean you can't."

When Tainu didn't respond, he said, "I want to make you happy. I want you to be happy with me. I want–" He breathed deeply. "I want you. I want us to love one another. Not as my family."

Tainu stared at him, unable to move or think or feel anything except that *this can't be happening.* This couldn't be. His mind could make no sense of what he was hearing.

"Why do you always have to be alone?" Zhu Guiren asked, almost pleading. "Why do you always have to suffer, and take care of everyone in the world, and never have any happiness for yourself? I want to be with you, I want to go where you go, I want to–" He closed his eyes. "So many things."

Tainu stood up, awkwardly. "I'll go now."

He stumbled once, as he walked out of the room in a trance. When he looked back, Zhu Guiren still knelt, his eyes closed, but he had leaned forward so his forehead was against the wall, as though he couldn't support his own weight. He ached to see him like that; he wanted to go back, to put his arms around him and say *it's all right, I'm here,* but he couldn't. He couldn't do it. His heart was beating so fast he thought he might faint. What if Zhu Guiren— what if— if that happened, if he let himself— He hadn't known, he hadn't imagined. He had thought only of friendship, only of being together, and now, everything was torn open. Everything was possible: the things he had never wanted, things he hadn't dreamed that he could want—

Tainu half-fell downstairs to the door outside, flung it open, and transformed to fly away.

CHAPTER 10
ZHU GUIREN'S ARRAY

THE NEXT MORNING, Tainu left before dawn without waking anyone up. On the table was a note that he was going ahead with Yisue to the Sorrowful River, Liu Chenguang would be able to find him.

Aili slapped her forehead and said, "No, I should be there, Yisue will want me," then asked Liu Chenguang to tell her Tainu's direction and ran out the door at top speed. Yisue wasn't a fast walker; she could catch up.

Liu Chenguang stood with Zhu Guiren by the supplies she had gathered and asked, "What is going on?"

Zhu Guiren just shrugged. "Can you find him when you need him? Can he find you?"

"Yes, of course," she said. "I know his true name, he knows mine."

"Well, he can find me. If he wants to. Let's go." He started walking.

Liu Chenguang yelled, "Someone has to help me carry this, Zhu Guiren, and you're the only one here."

Zhu Guiren turned around silently, chose the two heaviest bags, and then started walking again. Liu Chenguang made annoyed noises under her breath and followed. This was far too much like following Zhu Guiren around in her previous life; no one told her what was going on, and she wasn't going to put up with it.

She ran to catch up so she could walk next to him. "Zhu Guiren. Tell me what is happening."

"Nothing is happening. If you want to know why Tainu ran off before the sun came up, you'll have to ask him," he said. He looked straight ahead, not meeting her eyes, as they walked out of Shi'an and into the countryside. "Aili, same. Neither of them consulted me about their plans. We have about a day's journey to the site. It's not necessary for either of them to be there. I only need a phoenix." A little bitterly, he said, "Since you can also help defend me if necessary, you're better than Tainu for this. It's just as well."

"You're worried about him?" she asked.

He shrugged. "He's more vulnerable," he said flatly.

He refused to say anything else about what had happened between him and Tainu. Liu Chenguang knew that just a few nights ago they had been very friendly with one another — that they had been drinking, and that Tainu hadn't come back to them after he'd brought Zhu Guiren to his room. And then Zhu Guiren had been so upset about that fox spirit. *Had they…?*

She looked at his closed expression with horror and decided she really, really didn't want to know the answer to this question. Instead, she said, "Go over with me exactly what we'll do. Aili can find me. We can wait for her if you want real protection, but if you want to begin with only me, let's lay it out."

He nodded, and they discussed strategies as they walked. Liu Chenguang inwardly considered — as Zhu Guiren explained the timing of the blood and when he would need healing as opposed to blocking, assuming other demons showed up, which he was sure they would — Zhu Guiren and her sibling together. What a horrible thought. Surely Tainu hadn't been *that* drunk.

Aili caught up with Tainu and Yisue on a back road out of Shi'an, headed northwest rather than due north. Tainu was in his bird form, riding on Yisue's shoulder, which was stupid. It's not as though Yisue isn't already visible enough, she fumed, there should be an adult standing near him at all times so no one will try anything.

"Yisue!" she called.

Yisue turned, his face very glad. "Aili! You came!"

Tainu fluttered around but didn't say anything. Aili tried to give him a dirty look, but this didn't work so well with a bird.

She gave Yisue a hug, then said, "You're going to need to walk faster than this if you want to make it to the Sorrowful River today."

"Tainu said that we'll stop when we're tired and then keep walking until we get there," he said. "He said it's hard to tell, comparing flying to walking, but he thinks it would be about a full day if we didn't stop at all. So if we stop and rest and then walk more, we'll get there in the nighttime, but that would be ok. It doesn't matter to me."

She held his hand as they walked. Tainu sat on her shoulder now, which annoyed her; she wasn't pleased with Tainu at all. How could he just leave with Yisue like that, not even consulting with her? Didn't he think that they might want to say goodbye to one another?

"Did Tainu explain why you need to go?" she asked.

"You said last night," he replied. "I understand. You're going to do dangerous things, and so it's better for me to be with my relatives."

"That's it," she said, relieved. It was good he was going willingly. She had been afraid that he would refuse, in the end. "Will you have problems finding them in the river?"

"I don't know," he said lightly. "I haven't been in rivers much. There's no river dragon close to my coast. But I think that once I'm in the river, my uncle will know and he'll come look for me."

"You'll be safe there," she said, comforted. "And when you're finished visiting, you can go back down to the ocean and go home."

"No," he said, just as lightly. "When I'm done visiting I'm going to come out of the river and find you."

Ah, here it was. Aili coughed. "Yisue, how will you find us?"

"You can tell me your true name?"

"I don't have one, remember?"

"Oh." His face fell. "I could come back to that city. Shi'an."

"We may not be there. I don't know where we will be."

He thought about this for a while. "Will you be near the Sorrowful River at all?"

"I don't know, Yisue," she said gently. "That's one of the reasons we want to take you there now — so you can be in a safe place."

"Well, you can find me, then. When you're done with the dangerous things. Come to the Sorrowful River and throw this in." He twisted his hand and a small pearl appeared in it — not the large one that he had used to create the dragon gate, but a small one, like those she had seen on earrings. "I'll know. I'll come to you. Promise," he said plaintively. "Promise you will."

Aili took it. "I promise," she said, and put the pearl in her pocket. "Yisue, you're a good friend."

He beamed at her and ran ahead.

"Tainu," Aili muttered, "what's going on, why did you run off with him?"

Tainu didn't reply, but flew off above Yisue as though keeping watch.

The landscape was terrible — flooded repeatedly, full of ruined houses and empty fields. There were no people left here. They had all fled long ago. Aili had never seen anything emptier than this place, except the ocean from the deck of the troop carrier. Only birds flew above them, waterfowl especially. At last, Tainu decided that he might as well take his mortal form again, since there was no one here to see.

"Well, the ducks are happy, at least," Tainu said after Aili had ignored him for several miles.

"Why did you leave without telling me?" Aili asked. Yisue was jumping up and down in a flooded field ahead of them.

Tainu didn't reply at once. Finally he said, "There was something difficult with the demon. I just needed to get away."

Aili frowned at him. "Zhu Guiren? But what?" The sadness underneath Zhu Guiren's anger about the fox spirit when she was with him the other day was so clear to her. "Zhu Guiren wouldn't do anything to hurt you," she said, oddly certain. "For whatever reason he seems very…attached to you."

"I know," he said. "That's what's difficult."

"Oh," she said awkwardly. "Well. You don't feel the same for him? You seemed to…like him quite a bit too?" She'd only been there for a few days, but this had been almost painfully obvious. She tried to think what advice Nora would give, what questions she would ask.

Tainu kicked a puddle, splashing them both with mud. "I like him. I like him a lot."

"All right," said Aili, secretly thinking there was no accounting for taste, "then what's the problem?"

Tainu just shook his head. "I don't– I don't…have relationships like that."

This was extremely confusing and starting to get quite embarrassing, but she pressed on bravely. "Do you mean…not with men? But that fox spirit?"

Tainu turned back into a bird and flew away again. Aili gave it up as a lost cause.

It turned out that they didn't have to go all the way to the main channel of the Sorrowful River. A few hours later, Tainu landed and said that Yisue would be able to swim from a flooded area just ahead and Aili, at least, probably couldn't go any further than that.

Yisue turned to her and said, "Goodbye, but only for now. You promise!"

"I promise," she said. "Be good for your relatives."

"I will! You be safe. Watch out for demons." He hugged her fiercely, then turned around and ran splashing into the water. When it was up to his chest, he shimmered and transformed — a white dragon who soon turned a muddy yellow color from the silty water. He turned back and nodded his head, then dove beneath. Aili watched the track of his wake until he entered the deeper channels and it disappeared.

Tainu watched, the smile falling off his face as soon as Yisue was underwater. "Let's go. We'll have to find them now. I'll look for Liu Chenguang." He whispered and then said, "They've made better time than us. I'll fly ahead and tell them to wait until you come, so the demon has more protection." He transformed before she could say anything; clearly, he was avoiding any possible further conversation.

Aili looked one more time to where Yisue had disappeared and silently wished him well. If they didn't come back, he would surely give up eventually and go back down to the ocean, or perhaps stay in North Daxian with relatives who had more time with mortals; either way, he would be safe. He was so fascinated by the mortal world. She smiled, then settled into a more combative frame of mind. Time to get to work.

"Eftahede," she whispered, and started running down the white-gold path.

Liu Chenguang was glad Zhu Guiren was carrying the heavy bags. The countryside was sodden and often flooded, but Zhu Guiren walked quickly and by late evening, they had found the place he thought the array had been set. He settled into a lotus position and concentrated, then stood up and walked around, feeling in the air with his single hand, until he stopped with his feet in several inches of water. "Problem. I need to be able to pour the blood into earth. Pouring into water will just dissipate my own spell."

Liu Chenguang said, "I'm sad to say that shovels weren't part of my supply planning."

Zhu Guiren glared at her, clearly in no mood for joking. He stalked over to a ruined farmhouse and started digging through the detritus piled against the walls. He threw her a spade and took a rake himself. Together, they piled up enough dirt in the spot he selected so that there was a little island, just a handsbreadth wide and a finger's width above the water. He wiped his face, striping himself with dirt. Liu Chenguang stood up and stretched.

"Are you ready?" he asked, looking at her as though he hated her and everything else in the world.

"Is there something wrong with you? This probably isn't the kind of thing you should be doing if you're distracted." Under her breath she whispered Tainu's true name to gauge the distance. "Tainu isn't far away. Let's wait. It would be safer if Aili's here too."

"No," he said, even more bitterly than before. He turned his back on her, slashed his handless arm before she could say anything more, and started chanting.

Stunned that he began something so dangerous with so little notice, Liu Chenguang brought out her wings, invisible though they were, and readied herself, balancing her deerhorn knives in her hands.

The attackers showed up almost immediately: four yaoguai and three demons. Liu Chenguang swore to herself. Zhu Guiren was on his knees, still chanting. The cup of blood was nowhere near full.

The demons attacked first, evidently considering this their privilege. One of them shouted something at Zhu Guiren in the demonic language and threw a talisman, which she blocked with her wings. It was enormously strong, unlike anything she had felt before; it felt as though her wing had been broken by it, and the shock from the qi almost knocked her unconscious. Luckily, it did not, as she then had to block a sword stroke and disarm one of the demons — a man with blue eyes and short, ash-blonde hair.

"Little one," he said, "that was quite clever, but not enough." His other hand held a mace, which smashed down toward Zhu Guiren.

She could only desperately try to block. The force of the blow nearly broke one of the deerhorn knives as she dodged and circled behind him. If only she were able to actually fight...But this was all, and she couldn't even use all of her defensive skills of circling and avoidance because she needed to stay between them and Zhu Guiren.

The smoke of the spell was now curling outwards from Zhu Guiren's hand, moving over the ground in a complex woven pattern. The demons brushed through it, unconcerned. Behind the three demons were the yaoguai, misshapen creatures, circling hungrily. Liu Chenguang risked a look at Zhu Guiren. His face was contorted as though in pain and his voice was shaking, but he didn't stop chanting. One of the other demons took advantage of the fact that she couldn't protect him from all sides and circled behind him, stabbing him in the back with a short sword. Zhu Guiren grunted, but somehow managed to work it into the chant.

Liu Chenguang put more effort into her qinggong, giving up on the deer-horn knives to simply use herself as a shield — wings against talismans and spells, body against weapons — flipping and circling around and above Zhu Guiren as rapidly as she could. But now, there was a fourth opponent: a snake yaoguai who had circled in under her guard. She hadn't even had time to heal the cut on Zhu Guiren's arm as they had planned, and so even though now the cup was full and he was pouring it on the little pile of earth, his blood still sluiced from his arm into the water. His face was deathly pale. The snake yaoguai bit him in the lower back, its mouth nearly encircling his entire waist; he screamed, then continued the chant. His voice tried to crescendo, but he seemed to have nothing left. The blonde demon got through her guard and smashed Zhu Guiren with the mace, slashing his face with its spikes and breaking his left shoulder into meaty pulp. He screamed again and broke the cup on the ground, or tried to; the little island was too sodden with water and blood for it to actually break, but the smoke rushed back into the last drop of blood anyway. The spell was complete.

A violent ripple passed through earth, air, water, and all their bodies, shaking everything. Zhu Guiren screamed one more time — a long, drawn-out cry, as though something was being torn from him — and fell face forward into the water.

The surrounding demons didn't disperse. One of them laughed. The snake yaoguai slithered forward again. Liu Chenguang's wounds had almost all healed, but the talisman she had blocked was still affecting her qi. She didn't think she would be able to heal Zhu Guiren, but she leapt over to him and continued to block, taking the wounds in her body. She wasn't immune to pain by any means, and it was agonizing, but she would heal, if only she could stay conscious soon Zhu Guiren could fight, or Aili would come—

Suddenly, Tainu was there in his falcon form, sending qi into the eyes of the demons and beating his wings. He landed next to them and tried to set a ward, but the earth was covered with water and the ward wouldn't take. He shouted something she couldn't understand and turned Zhu Guiren over in the water.

She left Zhu Guiren to him. Once he was healed, they would have a fighter; meanwhile, all she could do was block, and block, and block. The demons and yaoguai circled continuously, stabbing and slashing at her. She gave up trying not to scream.

Behind her, she heard Tainu talking endlessly to Zhu Guiren, nothing she could understand under the circumstances; Tainu had taken several wounds as well, acting as a secondary shield over the demon. So far, the demons were satisfied with simply attacking them, knowing that if they refused to fly their capture was inevitable, but this would last only until the two of them could no longer heal themselves, she knew.

"Where's Aili?" she yelled at Tainu, spinning, blocking, being raked and stabbed, feeling talismans burst against her wings like burning embers. "And why isn't he getting up? We need him!"

"I don't know!" he yelled back at her. "I don't know!"

From the other side of the field, there was a splashing sound and a shout. Aili raced toward them at last — phoenix whips in each hand — so quickly that her footsteps seemed to not pierce the surface of the water. She lashed out at the circle of yaoguai and destroyed them one by one, almost in passing, then leapt up with qinggong and twisted to land in front of Liu Chenguang.

"Get back!" she ordered, her voice raw. "Behind me!" The phoenix whip lashed out again and again.

Liu Chenguang collapsed into the cold, bloody water, sobbing for breath. She and Tainu covered Zhu Guiren's body as shields, and she spread her wings over all of them, still blocking talismans. "Aili," she murmured.

She could hear Aili's wordless cries of rage over the demons and yaoguai howling and screaming at her and at one another, could smell burning flesh where the phoenix whip found a target, but all she could see was the bloody water under her.

Tainu was cradling Zhu Guiren's head, keeping it out of the water so he wouldn't drown — unless he already had? She frowned. No, she could feel a heartbeat. What was wrong with him? Tainu had clearly given him blood, and plenty of it, since he was wounded himself. The two of them were practically bathing the demon in phoenix blood, why wasn't he getting up?

At last, Aili collapsed into the water next to them with a loud, "What the hell?"

Liu Chenguang sat up with great effort and looked at her; she'd never heard Aili swear quite like that before. Her face was flushed and speckled with blood and she had a few small wounds, but there were two dead demons and four dead yaoguai in front of her. The blonde demon had apparently fled.

"Aili, are you all right? Can I heal you?" she asked, forgetting that Aili could now heal herself.

Aili was yelling again. "What the- what the hell were you two doing, starting without me?"

Liu Chenguang timidly reached out to her shoulder.

Aili shook it off, her blue eyes flashing. "What if I came later?" she demanded. "I ran as fast as I could! The two of you were being slashed into mincemeat

— how long could you have held out? This was just luck, you understand?"

"Aili–"

"Damn it!" She got up and staggered away from them, splashing through the muddy water. From a distance she turned around. "Zhu Guiren!" she yelled. "Zhu Guiren, get the hell up. I have things to say to you!"

Tainu had ignored all of this. Finally he managed to stand, holding Zhu Guiren in his arms. He walked slowly through the water and mud and blood, carefully so as not to trip. "He's not waking," he said at last when they reached drier ground. His face was drawn with anxiety. "Liu Chenguang, help me check what's wrong. I don't understand…"

Liu Chenguang tore her eyes away from Aili and helped Tainu lay Zhu Guiren carefully down in a place without visible water, though every inch of earth here was really just mud. His wounds were mostly closed already, and he was breathing. Liu Chenguang listened to his lungs. "He has some water in them," she said, "but trying to get the water out here would be counterproductive, I think. As soon as we reach somewhere warm and dry…" She went into her physician mind and began to check his meridians. "Ah, Tainu, feel this."

Aili came back over. Liu Chenguang risked a look at her and realized that she had been crying.

"What's wrong with him?" Aili asked, still not quite in a normal tone of voice.

Liu Chenguang said, "We're trying to find out. Tainu, do you feel it?"

He nodded. "All his meridians are irritated, and some are torn," he said. "Severed."

Liu Chenguang sat back on her heels and looked at him. "It's just as well he's unconscious," she said at last. "The pain must be very intense. Let's move him while we can."

Aili said, "It's a long walk back to Shi'an."

"We didn't pass anywhere better. To go forward instead of back, we would need to cross the river, and there's nothing there either," said Liu Chenguang, standing. "This whole area is just a giant floodplain now. The villages are deserted or ruined. Tainu, can you carry him?"

Tainu silently bent down again, and carefully picked him up.

"We'll take turns," said Aili.

When they reached Shi'an, muddy, bloody, and bedraggled, it was luckily well after dark. Tainu flew ahead to warn them of Kunorese patrols since it was after curfew and the last thing they needed was to be dragged in for questioning. Their rooms were waiting for them.

"Tainu," Liu Chenguang said, looking at Zhu Guiren's muddy figure on Aili's shoulder, "I can't put him to bed like this. Can you bathe him or do you want me to?"

Aili and Tainu both looked at her.

Liu Chenguang sighed. "He's filthy," she said. "We're trying to heal him, not give him amoebic dysentery or who knows what else from lying in that water with open wounds and getting it in his mouth and lungs."

"But I gave him blood," said Tainu meekly. "He won't get any of that."

"You people are ridiculous," Aili snapped. "I'll do it. It's part of my training, Liu Chenguang."

Now Tainu and Liu Chenguang both stared at her.

"What? I'm already carrying him anyway." She turned her back on the two ridiculous phoenixes and brought him into the bathroom.

Zhu Guiren was still very much unconscious; Tainu's treatment should have taken care of all his wounds, internal and external, but Liu Chenguang had said he was probably in pain from the meridians, so she was still careful with him as she cut off what remained of his clothing, wiped him down, and put him in the bathtub. She frowned at his long hair. It was a good thing that they cut hair short in the military, she thought, because it added quite a bit of complexity to getting him fully clean while he was unconscious; she had to be sure that he wasn't aspirating water while she rinsed him.

As she cleaned his body, she saw the scars of his old wounds and stopped briefly. "Zhu Guiren," she said quietly, "I'm sorry, I didn't know." At least she'd been able to spare him the embarrassment of having Tainu do this for him. She had a sense that his feelings for Tainu actually ran quite deep, as bizarre as that seemed.

Stupid demon, stupid phoenixes, she thought as her mind went back to what she had seen, running across that flooded field: the two of them being attacked, defenseless, bloody, stabbed and slashed again and again, not moving, not trying to get away; Liu Chenguang lying face down, half in the bloodstained water—

She finished drying him, wrapped him in a robe she found, and carefully laid him in the bed, then went back to her own room to get clean herself.

Aili stalked coldly from Zhu Guiren's room into her own without speaking to them.

"She's so angry," Liu Chenguang whispered, but Tainu couldn't respond; he was too worried.

He went directly into Zhu Guiren's room as soon as Aili had left. He was lying in his bed, completely clean, his hair still damp. Tainu touched his hair, his hand shaking a little bit. *Demon,* he thought, *demon, I'm so sorry.* He wanted to gather him up and hold him again. What was he thinking? Why was he so confused?

"What's wrong with you?" Liu Chenguang asked, following him in.

He shook his head. "His meridians– Check again."

"You too," she said. "Feel here…and here…"

The tearing was, if anything, increasing in severity.

"There must be some kind of chain reaction through his whole cultivation structure," Tainu murmured. "From the destruction of the array. It's become a part of him through the centuries."

"Did he expect this?" she asked, frowning.

"He told me it was a possibility."

"Then why did he refuse to wait for you?"

Tainu winced. He sat next to Zhu Guiren and took his hand, his face bowed.

"Tainu. Focus," Liu Chenguang said sharply. "Whatever happened between you two can wait. His condition is deteriorating. I've done what I can do. Trying to give him qi through the meridians isn't helpful. It's just becoming more turbulent. I can keep coming up with prescriptions for him, but until he's able to drink it's not going to do much. What ideas do you have?"

Tainu laid his hand on Zhu Guiren's side, where the damage was worst, and tried to feel it echo in his own cultivational structure. He winced again. "I'd have more to offer if he didn't cultivate resentment," he said at last. "Anything you or I could give him, it will feel to him like resentment does to us. It will hurt him."

"Hurt him as in painful, or hurt him as to worsening the injury?"

"Definitely painful, at least if he were conscious. It may not worsen the injury, it may stop the damage, but I don't think I can heal it. It's as though the resentment has left the meridian system and is simply rampant in his body now. Like internal bleeding. I can…" He closed his eyes and felt more deeply, intuiting as he did when going into a trance or creating a spell. "I can reconnect the meridians to others so that the system is closed again, and I can take the loose resentment into myself to remove it. That will hurt me, but I'll get over it. It's not much compared to…other things. But his cultivational structure — the damage will be permanent. He can still cultivate, but it will be more difficult for him… more painful, from now on. I can't think of anything more I could do."

Liu Chenguang nodded. "Tainu, if there's nothing more you can do, there's nothing more anyone could do."

"Maybe another demon could help him more. Another cultivator of resentment," he said, wavering. "I don't want to do this to him if there are other options. It can't be undone."

"Do you know of any demon who's ever done anything but try to kill him?" she asked. "Don't make up imaginary solutions, Tainu. If this is all there is, it's all there is. Unless this can be stopped, I think he's going to sink further into unconsciousness, then coma, then death, within two days at most. He won't wake up for us to ask him about it."

Tainu jerked. "No!" Then he said reluctantly, "Yes. That's also…what I foresee. Without doing this."

"Go ahead," Liu Chenguang said. "Do it now. He's only getting worse as we wait."

Tainu sighed, closed his eyes, and held his hand lightly against Zhu Guiren's bare skin, whispering in the phoenix language, calling healing for him. *Arciniang.*

A soft, golden glow bathed Zhu Guiren's side and began to travel through his body, veins of light spinning out from where Tainu touched him, connecting and reconnecting but avoiding the place where his hand lay, which he had shielded to cut off from the network. Tainu grieved inwardly for him — losing this piece of himself — but the demon had known that it might happen. They should have talked more, Tainu thought, about what to do if it did. Why had they not talked? Why had Zhu Guiren not waited for him to be there when he broke the array? Had he hurt the demon so much?

He reversed the flow, drawing the loose resentment bleeding through Zhu Guiren into his own cultivational system, feeling its sharp edges, the bitterness and pain, and wondered if it felt this way for the demon, too, or if it was just because the demonic qi was incompatible with his own. Gasping, he let go, a bit of blood coming from his own lips.

"It's all right," he said, holding up his hand as Liu Chenguang frowned. "It's done. I just need to cultivate and purify now."

He settled himself down to cultivate.

"Here?" asked Liu Chenguang, still frowning.

"Here," he said. "I'll stay with him."

"He won't wake up tonight, or probably tomorrow either."

"I know. He shouldn't be alone." He found that he didn't want to meet her eyes.

Liu Chenguang sat down next to him, wrapping her arms around her knees, and finally said, "Tainu, he can't hear us now. What is happening between you? Why did you run away this morning? Why didn't he wait for you if he knew something like this might happen to him? I didn't know it. He never said anything to me. He just said he wouldn't wait for you, and started right away."

"Was he angry?" he asked. "Or sad?"

"How should I know? I think you know, though."

Tainu considered a cowardly plea that he needed to cultivate and get rid of the resentment he'd taken in, but of all the beings in the world, who could he possibly talk to about this aside from his little sibling? "I ran away from him last night, not just this morning. I was avoiding him."

Liu Chenguang raised her eyebrows. "Did something happen last night?"

Tainu twiddled his fingers for a while, and finally said, "He told me something."

"That's all? He's told you lots of things — most of them incredibly insulting or deeply pathological. What did he finally say that got you to run away from him?"

Tainu cleared his throat. "He– he said," he coughed more. "He said…"

Liu Chenguang turned her whole body toward him. "Spit it out, Tainu. What on earth could it have been?"

"He said…" He took a deep breath. "He wants me to be in love with him."

Liu Chenguang stared at him, wide-eyed. "What?"

"He– he said that," Tainu said weakly.

"What does that even mean? It's not like you can make a decision about it," she said. "It's either something that is, or it isn't. Aside from whether it's a good idea, which obviously it's not, you can't control if you have that feeling for him."

Tainu was silent.

"You…do?" she asked, astonished.

"I don't know," he mumbled. "I don't know how."

"Tainu," she said, smirking a little bit, "come on. You surely do know *how*."

"Not like that," he said. "Of course I've had a lot of…pleasant experiences. But I think this is…not the same?"

"It's not the same. If you are asking me, no, it's not the same at all." She leaned forward, seriously. "Tainu, I'm sure there's nothing I could say to you about falling in love with a demon that you haven't already thought of."

He snorted. "I'm sure you could say lots of things because I have never in my life thought of this happening." He shook his head. "It does feel like falling…I'm so afraid."

"What are you afraid of?" she asked gently. "Of losing him?"

"Yes. Liu Chenguang, I don't know how you could bear it. Losing him."

"Is that all?"

"Isn't it enough?" He looked down at the ground, his eyes unexpectedly filled with tears. "I can't– I can't."

Liu Chenguang reached out and took his hands. "Tainu, there's no knowing what will happen. He's a demon, after all, not a mortal."

"That means he lives until he's killed," he said. "We live forever. Someday he'll leave me. Someday– If I let myself love him so much, how can I–"

His little sibling looked him, steady and serious. "Tainu," she said, "if you love him so much, what are you doing wasting time like this? Do you think that somehow, if you don't…well, have him as your lover–" Her face turned bright red. "Do you think that somehow that protects you from being heartbroken if something happens to him? You already have these feelings for him. How would you feel if you lost him and had never taken this chance to love him as much as you could?"

He closed his eyes.

"How long has it been like this for you? I think it's been much longer than you've ever told me."

He nodded.

She asked, "If you let yourself think about it — if you try to put the fear away just for a few minutes and let yourself know what you want — what is it?"

They sat quietly together beside the bed for a while, watching as Zhu Guiren breathed; Tainu lifted up his head to look at his sleeping face and tried to be without fear. Finally, he asked, "Liu Chenguang, if you had it to do over…knowing how it would end…would you still do it?"

"I would," she said. "Even knowing what I know now, I would still have tried."

CHAPTER 11
TALKING

THE NEXT SEVERAL days, everyone seemed to tread carefully around one another: Aili avoided Liu Chenguang, Zhu Guiren mostly slept, Tainu obsessively watched him while he was sleeping and avoided him while he was awake, and Liu Chenguang decided they were all ridiculous and went out to eat noodles and heal refugees in the shanty camps.

A week or so later, when she came back exhausted from a day in the camps, sneaking blood to people who thought they were getting traditional Daxian medicine, she found Aili waiting by the door of the inn for her. Passerby were staring at the tall foreigner in Daxian peasant clothes.

"Do you want to walk with me?" Aili asked.

"I'm tired," she said, and started upstairs. They would have to leave this inn soon. Both Aili and Tainu were far too visible. The Kunorese puppet government of the city would start paying attention soon if they weren't already. She was feeling pretty thoroughly done with Shi'an anyway.

"I know," Aili said. "I'm sorry."

Liu Chenguang shook her head. "I can't right now. Do whatever."

"Tonight?" Aili asked cautiously. "After you've rested? I really want to talk with you."

Liu Chenguang turned around on the stairs, already up several of them so she was a little taller than Aili — certainly an unusual point of view — so she could look down and see Aili's upturned face, serious and determined. Well, they would have to have this out at some point.

"All right," she said. "Were you planning to take me to a moon viewing platform? I don't think there's much to see tonight."

Aili's mouth quirked up a little bit. "That's an excellent idea. I'll look into it."

She turned and walked away, so Liu Chenguang continued up the stairs into the land of Tainu's personal drama, which she was also feeling very done with.

Just sleep with him already, she thought to herself uncharitably, the world has enough problems. His cultivational system is practically destroyed and he's pining after you on top of it? I feel sorry for him at this point, and I don't even like him. You're clearly in love with that person, who knows why, but it's obvious to anyone watching you two together. You're ten thousand years old. Put it in perspective; mortals love and lose each other every day — thousands of them, sibling…

She threw cold water on her face and fell down into her bed. "I am not able to talk to anything with any emotional issues for the next three hours," she announced to her pillow. She felt no anticipation whatsoever about seeing Aili later and thrashing out whatever was going on there. "There's a war going on. Has no one else noticed?" she said, also out loud.

"I'm here and I have noticed," Tainu said from the other room.

"Oh," she said after a moment.

He knocked on the door and stuck his head around it. "I saw you in the camps today," he said.

"You were there too?"

"Yes," he said. "Just so you don't think I'm only avoiding someone, I am actually doing things."

"Whatever. But good, that's good. How's Zhu Guiren?"

"He's been trying to cultivate, and as anticipated, it's very painful," he reported. "He's gone to find someplace with lots of resentment to cultivate in, so, for all I know, he's in the camps as well. Other than that, he's totally recovered."

"Good," she said. "And you?"

He hesitated. "We haven't talked," he said. "But we will, I promise."

"All right."

"You and Aili?"

"Tonight."

"Ah," he said. "Well, good luck."

"Ergh," she groaned, her face back in the pillow. "I'm going to sleep now."

Tainu laughed and closed the door.

She woke up several hours later, feeling refreshed, and went downstairs to find Aili waiting for her outside.

"It's almost midnight," Liu Chenguang said, yawning. "Have you been here all this time?"

"No, I thought if you were napping, I might as well too. I've just been here for a little while, thinking about what we should do."

"And?"

"I didn't find a moon viewing platform," Aili said seriously, "and there's no moon tonight anyway. So, it's just…" She smiled. "How tired are you?"

"Why?" she asked, suspicious.

"I've never been to the summit," Aili said.

Liu Chenguang laughed out loud. "Are you joking? If I could transform, maybe, but I'm not walking to the summit of Mount Shi tonight."

"Even with qinggong? Even if I carried you?" Aili asked persuasively.

"Really?" Liu Chenguang shook her head, still laughing. "All right, you can give it a try."

Aili knelt in front of her. "On my back, arms around neck, legs around waist," she said.

Liu Chenguang couldn't see her face, but she could tell that she was still smiling.

"I'll probably need to use my arms sometimes, so hold tight."

"Do you even know the way?" she asked, laying her weight on Aili's back and wrapping legs and arms around her as directed.

"Nope," she said in Anglish, sounding quite satisfied. "Assuming that going up will get us there eventually."

"Not exact–"

Aili laughed and started racing up the road toward Mount Shi, making her laugh out loud as well. Aili's qinggong was powerful and graceful; she took great leaps from boulder to boulder, up cliffs, dancing between the established paths and the peaks above and to either side of them. Liu Chenguang could feel the strength and sureness of Aili's moving body beneath her — and even more than that, Aili's sheer delight in what she was doing, in feeling life run through her in this way — and how Aili wanted to share this with her.

Every so often, Aili would stop and put her down, breathing steadily, so they could look out at the growing panorama beneath them and the stars above their heads. In the dark, the terror of the war wasn't obvious; occasionally planes flew past, but there were no bombs tonight, and the flooded Sorrowful River was simply a glint in the starlight. Once, Aili reached out and held her hand, and she let that happen. She had flown over Mount Shi so many times, and for thousands of years she had lived in mountains. She was familiar with the peaks and cliffs of the world, but it was different to share it with someone.

Aili smiled at her, her face nearly invisible in the dark, limned only slightly by the starlight, like the river below. "Come on," she said, kneeling again. "Let's go."

Slowly, the edge of the eastern world grew lighter, sharpening the shapes of things. Liu Chenguang had lost track of time. Delighted, she asked, "Will we be there at sunrise?"

"That's the plan," Aili said, breathing deeply but easily and continuing to leap up the cliffs. "Actually, we've been faster than I thought we would. I took some detours so it would work out for dawn."

Liu Chenguang rapped her gently on the back of her head. "Trickery," she said. "You didn't tell my brother you were planning to keep me out all night. My reputation will be ruined."

Aili laughed. "Could you have done this yourself?" she asked.

"Yes, but not with as much style, I admit," she said, and before she knew it, she bent her head to kiss the back of Aili's neck where her braid left it bare. Aili's skin was warm beneath her lips, tasting slightly of salt.

Aili stumbled, but then continued without saying anything.

Liu Chenguang said, "Sorry,"

Aili stopped and put her down.

"Are we there?"

"Not yet. I just lost my breathing rhythm for a minute. I have to get it back."

"Oh," she said, looking up at her.

Aili looked down, seeming very tall against the stars and the beginning of the dawn. "Liu Chenguang–" She shook her head. "I wanted to say to you that I'm sorry I was so upset at you. About the array. I just want to protect you so much."

Liu Chenguang sat down, and pulled at Aili's hand so she would sit down too. "I know," she said. "We all want to protect each other. But you can't always protect me from everything. There are things I'm going to choose to do because I need to do them."

How many times had she had this conversation in her mind, over the past thousand years? This time, it went somewhere she had never anticipated, as she blurted out, "Do you think I loved you just because you were good with a sword?"

Aili looked at her for a moment and then said, very seriously, "As I recall, I was indeed *very good* with a sword, so I think you did take it into consideration."

It took Liu Chenguang a full minute to realize what she was saying, and then she turned bright red. "Aili!" she yelled, laughing uncontrollably.

Aili just watched her, smiling.

"All right," Liu Chenguang said at last, wiping her tears. "You were good with a sword, I confess it."

"My work here is done," said Aili portentously.

"Behold, the dawn!" Liu Chenguang collapsed into laughter again.

"Really? In that case, I've failed. We're not at the summit yet." Aili looked up. "But I feel like this is a good place."

"It is." After a moment, Liu Chenguang said, "I'm really not saying this to trick you into hugging me, but I'm honestly very cold."

Aili reached out and pulled her into an embrace, holding her from behind so they could watch the sunrise together. "Sorry," she said. "I'm warm from the exercise. I didn't think about how cold it would be. If I was really good at this, I would have brought something warm for you to drink."

Liu Chenguang tapped her hand. "How would you have carried it?"

"True." As the sun started peeking above the horizon, Aili said, "Thank you for coming up here with me."

Liu Chenguang pulled Aili's arms around her more tightly and pressed back against her chest for warmth, shivering a little. "Someday," she said, "I'll take you to the place where I used to live, these past years. There are a lot of good people there. Although they'll be very confused about you. I'll have to tell them you're a missionary or something. Can you pull that off?"

Aili snorted. "Highly unlikely. Tell them I'm a nurse."

"Done."

She felt Aili nuzzle the back of her head gently — her lips brushing against her hair and her breath warm on the tips of her ears — and she felt a little shivery for reasons that had nothing to do with the cold.

"Chenguang," Aili said, her voice a little bit strange.

Liu Chenguang's heartbeat suddenly raced and her body lit up, but she didn't say anything else.

Aili's arms tightened around her, and then let go. "The sun's up. Should we go check on those two? What exactly is going on between them?"

Liu Chenguang laughed, and although she was tempted, she didn't want to gossip about her sibling. "Who knows," she said.

Aili hugged her one more time. "Let's go. Going down will be quicker. Let's get back for breakfast."

After Liu Chenguang left with Aili, Tainu sat at the table, looking aimlessly at Liu Chenguang's map projects. None of them had talked about how to continue breaking the arrays since Zhu Guiren's collapse. Probably, Liu Chenguang and Aili didn't really care, but Tainu was very worried; this hadn't even been the great array, and without Tainu's healing, the demon almost certainly would have died.

What would happen to him if they kept doing this? Did they even need to? Aili seemed fine enough now. Maybe just breaking those two arrays was enough to make her well. Maybe Liu Chenguang's binding protected her from Zhu Guiren's array…

Two million mortal souls.

The time passed slowly. Zhu Guiren didn't return.

He decided to go look for Zhu Guiren accidentally; really, he was just going for a walk because he was bored, and who knew — maybe Aili and Liu Chenguang would come back and want some privacy.

The streets of Shi'an were devoid of mortal life except for the government patrols and Kunorese guards stationed here and there, but there were many yao. As his fox spirit friend had said, the harmless and less powerful yao were fleeing from wars of demons and mortals, and Shi'an had become a resting place for those going west, since they preferred to stay near mountains. He saw mouse and rabbit yao, foxes and dogs snapping at one another, cat yao leaping from roof to roof, and even two deer yao, male and female, delicate and frightened, under the eaves of a building destroyed in the bombardment. Among them stalked the demons in mortal bodies, and the smaller yao drew back where they passed. Tainu took his bird form and fluttered among the sparrows.

He knew that Zhu Guiren would have sought a place of strong resentment — a cemetery, or perhaps a bombed building; a place where many people had died violently or were buried — but there were so many such places in Shi'an that he wasn't sure where to begin. Finally, he closed his eyes and tried to intuit where his own revulsion was strongest and headed in that direction.

It was a cemetery next to the refugee camp, or rather, a morgue where unclaimed bodies were placed until they were buried, graves unmarked, in the field next to it. He had been near here that morning, trying to heal a little boy. It was very difficult when he couldn't get blood directly into people's mouths — blood that didn't come from his own physical touch generally wouldn't work for healing, so putting it into tea or food was ineffective — and he hadn't been able to do it in time. The little boy's body was here somewhere, probably.

Zhu Guiren was in his lotus position on a recent grave, but as soon as he heard the rustle of Tainu's clothing he was up, sword against his throat. "Oh," he said awkwardly when he saw who it was. He immediately stepped back, releasing his sword. "Sorry."

"It's all right," Tainu said. "I was just worried about you. That's all. How are you doing?"

The demon shrugged and turned away, returning to his cultivation spot. "It hurts," he said, laconic, and closed his eyes again.

Tainu went and sat on a grave near him. He had already explained what they had had to do to heal him — the permanent damage to his cultivation system — and the demon had listened to that, nodded, and said nothing.

Nothing between them had been addressed; nothing had been discussed.

Tainu wondered if, some day, he simply would go out and not come back at all. It seemed that he was withdrawing from them all so much. "I don't want you to leave," he said aloud, surprising himself.

"Who said I was leaving?" The demon opened his eyes and looked at him.

"Aren't you?"

He considered it. "I suppose, maybe. If there's nothing else I can do about the arrays, then what's the point? If I can't cultivate, eventually I'm just going to have to run for my life anyway."

Tainu said, "I don't want you to leave. Even if we can't break the array."

The demon just stared at him.

"Please."

Zhu Guiren said, "I'm trying to cultivate. Can you leave me alone?"

He swallowed. "No."

Zhu Guiren ignored him.

"If you can't cultivate," Tainu improvised, "you should stay so Aili can protect you. And I can heal you if you're hurt."

After a long silence, the demon replied, "Do you think that I could stay with you and draw other demons to attack you just because I'm afraid of being hurt? Do you think I would risk you just in case it would buy me a little more safety, a little more time to live? If that's what my end will be, that's what it will be."

Zhu Guiren lifted his eyes to meet his and Tainu realized that he was genuinely angry. He also realized that he had never really seen Zhu Guiren angry before. Not at him.

"Do you think that I'm that kind of coward?"

"No, not at all, that's not what I–"

"I'm trying to cultivate so I don't have to go," he said flatly, still staring at him. "If I can continue to gather power and fight and defend you, I will stay. Otherwise, I'm not going to put a target on your back. Aili's good, but she can't keep you safe against my whole clan *and* everyone else who is looking to kill me and get a phoenix out of it."

Tainu was silent, trying to think what to say, what to do. At last, after Zhu Guiren had already closed his eyes and settled back into cultivation, he said, "Is it very selfish to say I– I would want you to stay with me anyway? Even if…"

He couldn't bring himself to say, *even if you aren't as strong as you were, even if you can't defend me*; he was sure the demon wouldn't accept those words from him, and they wouldn't be helpful.

He couldn't say, *if you're going to be attacked and hurt and maybe even, even die, I want to be with you for that. I don't want you to be alone. I don't want to lose you again. I don't want…I want…*

He couldn't figure out how to say any of those things.

Zhu Guiren's closed eyes wrinkled a little bit at the corners.

"Or," Tainu said, getting braver, "I'll go with you. If you leave, I'll just follow you. I know your name. I can do it."

Zhu Guiren shook his head. "I'll tie you up and bring you back."

"Then I'll just go again," he replied. This strategy seemed to be working; he felt quite light in his heart now. "You won't be able to get away from me, no matter what you do."

Zhu Guiren looked at him at last. "You are an idiot."

Tainu smiled. "I am," he said comfortably. "I am an idiot you are never getting away from."

Zhu Guiren's eyes followed him as he came over to sit on the same grave, next to him.

"I don't like this place," Tainu said conversationally.

"Of course you don't. You're a phoenix, and it's full of resentment," the demon responded. "Which, as I mentioned, I'm trying to cultivate right now."

"You said it hurts. Can I help you?"

"How could you possibly help?"

Tainu gave this very serious thought. He looked at Zhu Guiren; he couldn't see much of him in the dark, but he could see his eyes in the light of the stars, and that gave him a sense of where to place his hands on either side of his face. Before he could let himself think about this any more deeply, he leaned over and kissed him, lightly, on the lips.

Zhu Guiren's entire body jumped as though he had been hit by a talisman.

Tainu felt such happiness, he laughed and kissed him again.

"What are you doing?" the demon asked. "I don't understand."

"I don't know," Tainu said, because he really, truly didn't. "I wanted to kiss you. Is that all right?" He still felt very light inside. It felt good to be touching his face like this, looking into his eyes, to be so close to him, to not let him go.

Zhu Guiren continued to look into his eyes with that little frown he got when he was very confused. At last he said, "This doesn't really help me with my cultivation."

"Does it help with anything else, though?" Tainu leaned over to kiss him one more time. Zhu Guiren's lips were very firm and narrow, Tainu brushed his own against them and tried to see if he could feel their shape better, trying to learn how he felt in the dark, feeling little dangerous shivers inside.

"Yes. It helps me know that you really are an idiot." Very cautiously and lightly, Zhu Guiren leaned over to kiss him back.

They looked at each other in silence. Tainu felt as though he couldn't stop smiling. The demon looked very serious.

At last Tainu said, "I am an idiot. Is that all right with you? Will you stay?"

The demon nodded slowly. "I still need to cultivate," he said. "Go back. This isn't a good place for you to be."

Tainu reached out and touched his hair. "Promise you'll come back soon," he said, "and I'll go."

"I promise."

When Tainu woke up the next morning, he heard the three others in the main room having breakfast. He stretched and went to join them.

Zhu Guiren looked up immediately to meet his eyes, but didn't smile. Tainu sat next to him and reached for a simple steamed bun — all there was, since the rationing was getting worse even for people with Zhu Guiren's endless amounts of gold.

Aili and Liu Chenguang both looked very happy, though, as well as windswept and tangle-haired.

"What have you two been up to?" he asked.

"Mount Shi," Liu Chenguang laughed. Her eyes sparkled in a way he hadn't seen in ages; it was a weight off his heart.

Tainu caught her eye and winked, wondering just how far up Mount Shi the two of them had gone.

Zhu Guiren looked at Liu Chenguang and Aili and frowned a little bit, but didn't say anything. He didn't look at Tainu, either, which bothered him a little.

"Demon?" he asked.

To the table as a whole, Zhu Guiren said, "I'm able to cultivate now, but it's slow compared to what I'm used to. I don't know if it will get better over time."

Aili said, "That's good? Not good?"

"Good, as far as it goes," Zhu Guiren said.

Tainu noticed he wasn't eating anything and placed a steamed bun in his hand, but he just put it down on the table, still without looking at him. This was honestly getting a bit disturbing.

"The one thing we found out for sure when we broke that array was that it doesn't make a difference whether I break the array myself or whether Aili does it. It's going to damage me either way."

They were all silent.

"Sorry for the bad news," he added. "If it is bad news."

Tainu wanted to touch him but was uncertain whether that was all right to do now; Zhu Guiren had never acted like this before, ignoring him as though he wasn't there, and so he had never imagined that such a thing would be this upsetting.

Finally, Aili said, "Zhu Guiren, it is bad news. Did you really think we wouldn't care whether you're hurt?"

Silently, he got up and left the table, still without speaking or looking at Tainu.

After a few minutes of the three of them looking at one another, confused, Tainu followed him into his room with another steamed bun. "Demon?" he asked, cautiously.

"Why did you kiss me?" he asked. For once, he wasn't scribbling on the wall, but lying on his side on the bed, his back to the door so Tainu couldn't see his face.

Had he misunderstood all along? Was that not…what he had meant, when he said he wanted to be in love, to be together? He felt his skin getting hot with embarrassment. Feeling greatly ashamed, Tainu said, "I thought you wanted it. I thought that's what you wanted."

"Is it what you wanted?" Zhu Guiren asked. "Or did you just do it because you thought– For me?"

Tainu thought, if I did it just to make you happy, isn't that also good? But the truth was… "I wanted to kiss you. I just…I don't…"

"What about that fox spirit? Did you want to kiss him?"

"What about the fox spirit?" Tainu asked, a little angry. "It was literally centuries ago, demon. Probably I wanted to kiss him, but not in the same way. It's not the same at all. Why do you keep going on about that fox spirit?" He decided it probably wasn't the time to mention that in ten thousand years there had been a lot more than one fox spirit.

"Why is it not the same?"

"Ugh, demon, why are you asking these questions?" Leaving the bun on the side table, he sat down on the bed leaning over him to see his face at that strange angle, nearly upside down. "Because I told you– because I've never done this. It's new for me. It's all different."

"Being in love? Will you be in love with me, then?" He turned over and now Tainu could see him properly. His eyes were rimmed with red. "Do you want me?"

"What's wrong?" he asked, alarmed. Tainu lay down next to him, laying a hand on the side of his face. "Are you all right?"

Zhu Guiren looked at him with those clear, dark, serious eyes, still full of pain.

Why so much pain? Tainu stroked his hair gently, and looked at his eyes, and then kissed him again.

At last, his demon sighed and allowed himself to be soothed, but he said, "You don't look at me the way you looked at that fox spirit. You're still touching me and kissing me like I'm a child who hurt his knee. Someone you're trying to heal. Is that the kind of love you have for me?"

Tainu's hand froze on his hair.

"That's what I thought," Zhu Guiren said, and rolled himself over, away from him, to sit up.

"That's not..." Tainu protested weakly, still lying there, looking up at in him shock, his hand still frozen where he had been touching his hair. "I don't– I didn't mean– demon, please..."

"That's not how I love you," the demon said. "That's not what I meant."

So quickly that Tainu wasn't at all sure how it happened, Zhu Guiren was on top of him. Tainu's two hands were captured in his one and pulled up over his head, and then Zhu Guiren was kissing him with a rhythmic, desperate force, his tongue entering into his mouth and his leg pressing between Tainu's so there was no doubt whatsoever about exactly what Zhu Guiren wanted. Tainu's body was responding eagerly and he heard the demon groan softly in his ear as they moved against one another, but his mind was somewhere else completely; when the demon finally looked up into his eyes, Tainu knew that all he saw there was absolute shock and panic.

Zhu Guiren let go of his hands immediately and sat up. "I'm sorry. That's not what you want, is it?"

Tainu just stared at him — still lying down, still aroused, and still shaking all over.

"But that's what I meant," the demon said. "That's how I want to love you. Like that. Not like a child."

When Tainu still couldn't respond, his mouth unable to make words out of anything, he continued, very formally, "I'm sorry I frightened you. If this isn't what you want, truly, Tainu, you need to…stop touching me. Because I want to touch you like this. I want to love you like this. I don't want you to only love me like something you need to take care of — like everyone else in the world."

Tainu closed his eyes, still lying in Zhu Guiren's bed as he heard him walk out, and felt in his body how much he did want him.

How had this all gone so wrong? Somehow, it had, and he couldn't figure out what to say to make it better because it was very true of him; he took care of everyone, and he wanted to take care of the demon too. Wasn't that love? Didn't that count? He didn't love that fox spirit — he didn't even know his name — and that fox spirit didn't love him either. That's why things were easy with fox spirits.

When he came out of the room at last, not knowing what he could possibly say to any of them, only Liu Chenguang was there. She said, "Aili and Zhu Guiren went to go break another array. Aili will do this one and Zhu Guiren will protect her, but I guess it takes longer when Aili does it, so they'll probably be gone for a few days."

"Who will heal him?" he asked, confused. "Why did he go without us? Why with only Aili?"

"Aili can do it, remember?"

There was something about this idea that felt dangerous to him, but he couldn't think of what it was; his brain had stopped functioning completely and his body was still tingling all over, so he just nodded, and sat down. "Did you hear?" he asked. It wasn't a large space, and the walls were thin.

"Not the conversation," she said diplomatically. Then, she added, "We heard the part that wasn't really a conversation. If you and Zhu Guiren intend to do more of that sort of thing, we should probably make sure we're not here. Just, you know, give me a hint."

"Thanks," he said, putting his head down on the table. "I think it's unlikely to happen again."

"Oh…I don't understand. It was pretty confusing to us. Zhu Guiren came out looking as though he had not had a good time at all, which frankly was kind of surprising, all things considered, and told Aili his plan, and since I already had the supplies set up from last time they just went."

"Confusing to me too." Without anything else to do, he said, "I'm going to the camps."

"All right," she said. "I'll come too."

CHAPTER 12
ZHU GUIREN IS MISTAKEN

ZHU GUIREN AND Aili walked together in silence across the empty, flooded countryside. Neither of them were very talkative even under normal circumstances, and Zhu Guiren was feeling very much not normal. He could still feel Tainu's body beneath him, feel his own intense need for more; he could still see Tainu's eyes, begging him to go away. Tainu didn't want his love, not the way he wanted to give it. Only as someone to take care of, just like he took care of everyone else.

Zhu Guiren suddenly spun around and threw some qi toward an inoffensive wall, which had clearly already endured much in its life. It obediently crumbled to the ground.

"Fuck," he said loudly. He hadn't said that word since living in the Federation. It felt good.

Aili looked at him, probingly. "Zhu Guiren?" she asked. "What's wrong?"

He shook his head.

To his surprise, Aili continued to press him. "Zhu Guiren, you and Tainu. What's happening?"

He ran ahead of her, fast, wishing he could still turn into a crow. Unfortunately, Aili was also fast. She jogged up to him easily, not even breathing hard, and said, "Come on, I'll tell you a secret."

"What is it?"

"The secret is that you don't really have any secrets," she said solemnly. "Those walls are thin."

"FUCK!" He threw more qi toward a ruined farmhouse almost half a mile away.

"Impressive," said Aili, her mouth twitching.

"Did you hear everything?"

"Only the part that didn't involve words."

Zhu Guiren started walking much faster. "Well, nothing happened, so I don't know what you think you heard."

Aili didn't say anything.

Zhu Guiren oriented himself and tried to get his anger under control. "None of this matters," he said. "The array is southwest."

After they had walked for a while, Aili very seriously said, "It does matter, Zhu Guiren. It's not a distraction from important things to love someone. It is the important thing."

Zhu Guiren replied, "You're a mortal, that's why you think so. Also because– because you have been able to love someone, and they love you back, so you can say that." He didn't speak again for about two miles. Then, he said, "Not everyone has what you have, so we have to have other important things. Like surviving."

"There's a tree up ahead," said Aili. "Let's take a break there. It's around dinnertime."

When they had settled down, Aili handed over a cold bun left over from breakfast. "This is dangerous for you," she said. "Are you sure you want to be out here without either of them to help you? It's not too late to go back and get them. I can smear blood all over you, but it's not going to do what Tainu did to get you out of the coma. I don't know how to do that. Neither does Liu Chenguang, actually, she said."

"It's fine," he said, stubbornly, and ate some bread. He knew he was taking a stupid and unnecessary risk, but he couldn't bear having Tainu take care of him again, as though that was their whole relationship. Although apparently, it was. "Just…" He waved the bun in the air. "Just carry me back. If you need to. It might not be that bad this time."

"Why not?"

He shrugged. There was no reason why not at all. The sub-arrays they were breaking were all strong ones. These were the ones that might weaken the central seal enough for him to break it. He truthfully wasn't sure he would survive breaking it, but he was determined to do it now. He wanted it to be gone. He hadn't told anyone this; not even Tainu, though he was sure Tainu was beginning to guess. Those pitying eyes looking at him… He threw the bun on the ground.

"Don't," Aili said sharply. "People are starving. Don't just waste it like that." She picked it up and tried to brush it off.

Sometimes, he wondered how much of the incredible suffering he saw around him — this three-sided war, the mortals killing one another unendingly, the children dying, the famine and starvation — was from his array lying like a curse over this whole area, resentment built on resentment, a chain reaction of suffering. The sheer scale of death and devastation was beyond imagination. Of course, mortals were just like this. That was true. And of course, there were other demons encouraging things to get worse. That was true too. But what was absolutely undeniable to him was that he was benefiting from it. The net of his array had grown exponentially since it was set a thousand years ago, encompassing and binding millions of descendants. The resentment of the people dying all around him didn't all just bleed into the air. Some of it came directly to him, directly into his cultivational body, feeding his own powers, and he didn't want it there anymore. He just hadn't thought it would be so painful to remove, or that he wouldn't be able to replace it with more normally-cultivated resentment.

He was tired of drinking suffering and death. He didn't want to live this way anymore.

He wanted to live another way, but that wasn't working out either.

Aili was nibbling her bun thoughtfully while looking up at the gray sky through the branches of the tree. He felt incredibly envious of her.

"You and Liu Chenguang," he said. "You two love each other. I could see it, back then."

She nodded. "I'm told it was very obvious," she said with a little smile, looking up at the sky as though remembering.

"I could see it even though I didn't know what it was," he said. "Only that he wanted to be with you. It was annoying."

"No doubt." Aili looked at him, then smiled. "You know, I was very jealous of you. At the time."

"Those rumors…I never had those kinds of feelings for Liu Chenguang, but the rumors were useful in their way. It kept importunate people away from me. It used to happen pretty often, back then, that someone would throw themselves at me."

Aili raised an eyebrow like she wanted to laugh, but didn't.

"I knew about these things," he insisted. "From observation of others. I needed to understand those feelings because that's one way mortals were motivated to do or not do things, and that was my business then. Manipulating them. But I never…had those feelings myself."

Aili handed him his bun back. "You still need to eat," she said. "When you say never, you really mean…never? Aren't you as old as Tainu? And Liu Chenguang?" She added, clearly not happy to say it, "I wasn't the first person Liu Chenguang was with, by any means."

Zhu Guiren looked at her, stunned. "But you…but he…"

"I know," she said. "Not thrilled with the idea."

"I'm younger than Tainu. I'm around nine thousand, maybe nine thousand and a half…I don't really keep close count."

"That is a lot of never," Aili said.

"Well, you know…among demons…why would we voluntarily be with each other like that? It's pretty much all rape, or because we're forced to by the clan leaders. We don't trust each other at all, for very good reasons. Who could let down their guard that way? And unlike some people, fox spirits never–" Fox spirits had never even approached him, thinking, correctly, that he was far too dangerous to risk. "Anyway."

"Anyway. But you were able to avoid being forced, at least. That's good," Aili said, her tone odd.

"Some demons do it with mortals, but it's just more…it's no different, not really. A demon's relationship with a mortal is always to get something for the demon. Pleasure or power — that's all. I never did. I never wanted to."

She nodded.

"But I know what it is. I know from watching. I know that I want it now. And he doesn't." He savagely bit into the bun. There, he'd said it.

Aili finished her food, but she didn't stand up. "Zhu Guiren, this is important for you to know before we go ahead and do what we're going to do today. Last time, Liu Chenguang said you went into it all half-assed–"

"What does that even mean?" he said, repulsed.

"It's a technical term that means you didn't think clearly about what you were doing," she said seriously, "and you started before you were really prepared."

"Oh." He felt that this was a sadly accurate description.

"And that didn't end well. You shouldn't be going into something as dangerous as this is for you with your heart bitter and angry," she said. "I don't know much about resentment, but that must resonate with what you're trying to destroy, right? Maybe it causes you more damage because of it."

He nodded slowly. This did make sense. When Aili had broken arrays in Hai'an, it hadn't damaged him as much as it had during the last time, when he had felt so bitter and hopeless after Tainu had rejected him. The first time. Now, again.

"So, you should know that you can't know about it from watching. Not from watching others, not from study, or looking at books, or whatever exactly you think you know," she said. "You have to find what you want, and what your partner wants." She seemed to be trying very hard not to look embarrassed, but it wasn't going very well; her skin had more pink in it than a Daxian's, and she looked very red now.

Zhu Guiren stared at her, wide-eyed.

"If you're going off what you saw happening in the imperial court during Great Feng, I'm telling you right now that you know exactly nothing about any-thing meaningful between you and Tainu."

Zhu Guiren frowned. "Really? Nothing?"

"Well, maybe in terms of pure mechanics," she allowed. "Maybe."

"Oh." Zhu Guiren was finding this conversation incredibly illuminating. "Because those people didn't love each other. Is that why?"

"A good number of them, probably not," she said. "Most of the people you saw didn't have a choice about being there at all, or who their partners were. Or their partners were just there for their pleasure. Or power. It's not that different, is it, from what you said about the demons?"

Zhu Guiren nodded. It was true. It was certainly very true, what she was saying. He looked at her with new respect. "For someone who's lived less than fifty years, you know a lot of things," he said.

Aili smiled at him. "Mortals have to learn fast. We don't have long."

He thought about this for a while. "But he doesn't look at me that way. He doesn't want me that way."

"Why do you think so?"

"That fox spirit," he said, with difficulty. "Did you see how he was? How he…stood for him, and looked at him? He doesn't look at me like that."

"Zhu Guiren, you are not a fox spirit to him. Tainu cares about you very much."

He shook his head. "Not the way I want him to," he said. "Not like you and Liu Chenguang."

Aili laughed out loud. "Do you think that we just…like fox spirits?" She smiled at him. "It wasn't like that at all. I've only ever been with Liu Chenguang, so I'm not speaking from vast experience of this subject. But I think that just because two people love one another, it doesn't mean that suddenly you just," she waved her arm around awkwardly, "roll into bed with each other and everything's fine and easy."

Zhu Guiren decided this would probably be the only chance he'd ever get to say this to someone who could give him advice. Who else could? He steeled himself to say it. "I tried with him, and he just wanted it to stop. He didn't like it at all."

Aili coughed. "All right, the truth is that as soon as we heard you two doing more than talking, we left the room. It was too embarrassing. But it didn't sound as though he wasn't liking it."

"He was afraid," he said, looking down. "He was afraid of me."

"Maybe it was too fast for him. Maybe he wasn't ready. But Zhu Guiren, think about it. He loves to be with you, he loves talking with you, he loves to touch you and be close to you. Do either of you even know how much of the time you spend just looking at each other and ignoring everyone else around you? He is so sensitive to you, wherever you are, whatever you are doing." She smiled. "It's really rather sickening."

"Oh. Is it unusual?" He hadn't thought of this before. Then, he said his greatest fear. "Don't you think that he sees me just as one more person to take care of? Just a...healing project?"

"No, I don't think he sees you that way at all" she said, very seriously. She shook her head. "Zhu Guiren, do you feel less resentment now?"

He took stock. "Yes," he said, rather surprised. "I feel different now."

"Good." She stood up and stretched. "Let's run for a while. I want to get this done. I don't like leaving them alone without one of us."

Aili felt rather satisfied with that conversation, which was mostly drawn from her memories of Nora's advice. She smiled to herself, remembering Nora's long and fairly explicit lectures in the apartment before they went to the bar or out on double dates which had never worked out for her personally but nonetheless were, in Nora's opinion, important experiences for a young woman learning the ways of the world. Poor Zhu Guiren. Nine thousand and something years old and no one to teach him anything important at all.

"To the right," called Zhu Guiren from where he ran behind her as they came to a fork in the road.

She ran in that direction. The flooding now was quite serious, and after a while she was wading to her knees even in the higher ground next to the roadway.

Suddenly, she saw a body lying in the water in front of her — the body of a child. She sloshed over to it to turn it face-up, but her hand passed through, tingling, and then she could hear the screams. She stood still.

"We're here," she said to Zhu Guiren without turning around. Beneath the cries and the metal and the weeping and wailing of women, she could hear him wading up next to her.

"What do you see?" he asked.

"It's a village. Bandits. The men are already dead. The women–" She covered her eyes.

"Ah," he said calmly.

The water on the ground of the present was not visible when she looked at the people dying, just a film laid over reality, though which was the film and which was reality, she couldn't quite tell anymore.

Aili put her hand over her mouth. "The children," she said.

He nodded. "These weren't really bandits," he said. "It was a splinter group from a foray by the Emperor's forces to punish an upstart general who was trying to govern this territory separately. They had been given orders to take no prisoners, although as things were going, those orders weren't even necessary. It had become common practice."

"Who gave them those orders?" she asked quietly.

He didn't respond.

"Why do I see them?" she asked. "You don't see them. No one else sees them. Why do I?"

"I've given it some thought," he said.

His calmness disgusted her, but of course he couldn't see; all he was looking at was muddy water in a field, she had to remind herself. But he knew it. He knew what had happened. How could he be like this? She continued to watch the slaughter and rape of the women and children.

"Truthfully, I can't completely explain what has happened to you — the combination of the array and Liu Chenguang's binding. But you are a mortal soul caught in the array. I think you can see these things because they are connected to you. You are also part of this reality, though not completely, since you're alive."

"I saw Nora and others after they died," she said. "They weren't in an array."

"You must have been connected to them in some way," he replied. "Certainly there has to be some limiting factor, otherwise you'd be wading through ghosts every moment."

She nodded. "The attackers have disappeared," she reported after another hour of watching the horror. "There's only corpses now. So soon–" She started forward.

"What?" he asked.

"Chenguang," she said, her heart in her mouth.

She walked forward, the muddy water around her knees, but not feeling it. Liu Chenguang was there, moving among the corpses, bending down to check each one.

The scholar's robe he wore had only a gourd at its sash; he hadn't yet been given the jade ornament. It was before they had found each other again, before Hong Deming had met him that night in the yard of the Delicate Orchid. His eyes were sad but calm as he knelt next to a woman and closed her eyes.

Aili called, "Chenguang, Chenguang," tears falling down her face. It was so good to see him again.

"Aili," Zhu Guiren said. "Aili. Liu Chenguang can't hear you. He's not dead. His soul isn't here. This is just an echo of him in the event."

She had reached him, reached out to touch him. He ignored her and stood up, turning to look in another direction.

"Teacher Zhu," he called, "there are no survivors." His hair was falling forward over one shoulder and he pushed it back, annoyed.

Aili reached out shaking to touch his hair; he didn't have a pincrown yet. "Chenguang," she said, "Chenguang, it's me." He didn't look very different; Liu Chenguang male or female was very much the same person — small and lightly made, the beautiful eyes shining even through his sadness at all the death around him. She tried to touch his hair again, but her hand moved through his body. He didn't see her or feel her or hear her. He was not truly even a ghost.

The corpses around them lay still. Liu Chenguang stepped over them, going back over to another person: Zhu Guiren in his traveling robes; Zhu Guiren with two hands and a cold, haughty expression.

"I didn't think there would be," he said. "Go back to our camp. I will follow you in a few minutes, after I examine the field to report to the Emperor's forces."

Liu Chenguang bowed, and as he walked past the last corpse before the edge of the field, he disappeared.

Zhu Guiren watched him go. Aili clenched her fists and found that a phoenix whip had appeared in one of them.

The ancient Zhu Guiren walked to a spot near the center of the field.

"What's happening?" asked the Zhu Guiren who had come with her.

She restrained herself from lashing out with the whip at him, but it was difficult, very difficult. "You're here," she said. She forced herself to walk away from him, to not kill him, fighting the image in her mind — striking him down, avenging Liu Chenguang and the obscenity he had made of Liu Chenguang's trust, his healing lifeblood.

He didn't respond. Aili walked out to the center of the field to meet the other Zhu Guiren, who had taken a small container out of his sleeve and began to pour a dark liquid out onto the ground, chanting.

Aili knelt and placed her hands beneath that stream of blood, feeling its heat like the tears on her cheeks, calling the phoenix fire. "Eftahede," she whispered.

She woke up feeling that she was being bumped around quite a bit. "Put me down," she said.

Zhu Guiren carefully set her down on the ground. "You've been out for about twelve hours," he said. "It's nighttime now. There was no good place to rest near where you did it, so I've just been carrying you back toward Shi'an. We should get there in the early evening tomorrow, but truthfully, I need to sleep a bit if you can keep watch."

She nodded. "No demons came?"

"No," he said. "This is a clear advantage of having you do this. You're just a mortal and your presence isn't alerting them. We should have you do it as much as we can manage in the future. Assuming it's not damaging you?"

"I don't think so. When we get back Liu Chenguang can check," she said wearily. "It's just a lot of power, I think."

He nodded.

"You?"

He didn't respond.

Zhu Guiren held his body as straight as he could as he walked into the inn's courtyard, not wanting to let anyone see how much pain he was in. This was something he was quite good at; Aili had had no idea all the way back.

But Tainu came directly up to him and said, "What's wrong? How is it?" then reached immediately for his arm to check his meridians.

"I'm fine," he said, pushing his hand away. "Is that all you ever have to say to me when you see me?"

Tainu looked down at him from his slightly greater height and said, "Yes. Under the circumstances, that goddamn well is what I have to say to you. Sit the hell down."

Zhu Guiren sat down.

Tainu silently checked his pulse, then moved his hand over his abdomen.

"Are you angry?" he asked.

"Can't you tell?" Tainu's eyes were narrowed, and the movements of his hands over Zhu Guiren's body were jerky and sharp. "Yes, I'm angry. You went by yourself. With Aili. You knew she would see Liu Chenguang. You experimented to see if she would attack you–"

He nodded.

"You didn't ask me, you didn't bring me…" He took a deep breath. "The damage is severe. Not as bad as last time. But still."

Zhu Guiren nodded again. Tainu was kneeling next to him to check his meridians, and Zhu Guiren was stunned to see that there were tears in his eyes. "Tainu?" he asked, uncertainly.

Tainu got up, turned around, and walked away.

Zhu Guiren followed him inside. Liu Chenguang and Aili were over in the other part of the yard, holding each other and talking. Shouldn't they also be doing that? He was in so much pain that he couldn't think very clearly, but he knew he didn't want Tainu to yell at him; he didn't want to be angry with Tainu either. "Tainu–"

"Shut up." Tainu went into his room and shut the door.

Zhu Guiren pushed the door open and followed him. "Tainu, I'm sorry–"

"For which thing?" Tainu asked, turning around to face him. "For throwing yourself on top of me and then just leaving me there? For telling me I don't love you? Telling me not to touch you anymore? Or for running away and getting yourself hurt, or for not talking to me about what you're doing, or that you're risking your life and not letting anyone know? Which of those things are you sorry for right now?" His voice had gotten louder and louder, and by the end of it he was shouting.

"All of it," he said, shaken. "I'm sorry for all of it."

Tainu shook his head and fell silent, sitting on the bed.

Zhu Guiren sat next to him, heavily.

"You're in pain," Tainu said at last. "Do you want me to try to do something for you?"

"Not yet," he said.

"Why, do you enjoy being in pain?" Tainu pushed his shoulders down to make him lie flat. "Let me do it. It needs to be done before the damage spreads."

"Wait." Zhu Guiren grabbed his hand and tried to put his thoughts in order. "I wanted to tell you I'm sorry," he said finally, unable to remember anything else he wanted to say. "I'm sorry." Then, he remembered. "I don't want to just always be healed by you. That's not why I love you. That's not what I want."

"You've made that pretty clear," said Tainu, and put his hand against his side, murmuring as he began the healing.

Zhu Guiren heard him say his true name, and that made him feel warm, though the qi hurt him.

He winced, and Tainu said, "Sorry, I have to…" He removed his hand and sighed. "Not as bad as last time."

"Do you love me?" Zhu Guiren asked.

"*Yes,*" Tainu said. "For the love of heaven, how many times do I have to say it? How many ways?"

Tainu leaned over to him and kissed him, fierce and rough, jolting him inwardly so he gasped, trying to follow Tainu's lips as he pulled away.

"There, is that good enough, do you believe me now?"

Zhu Guiren just looked at him. "I'm sorry," he said again. "I'm an idiot."

"You are," Tainu said. "You are my idiot, and I am yours."

He reached his hand up to tug Tainu down to lie next to him; his face was still stained with tears, though he wasn't crying anymore, and Zhu Guiren laid his single hand on his cheek. Tainu just looked at him.

Zhu Guiren said, "Your eyes are so beautiful. I could look at your eyes forever." When Tainu still didn't speak, he said, out of bone-deep weariness and an inability to say anything that wasn't completely true, "I want to make you happy."

Tainu covered his hand with his own, turned his face to kiss it, and said, "Shhh. Go to sleep."

When he woke again, it was still dark, and Tainu was gently shaking him. "Demon," he whispered softly in his ear, "we need to go. Don't make a light, don't make a noise. There's a Kunorese patrol talking to the innkeeper. They're here to arrest Liu Chenguang. The bookstore owner that sold her maps has been taken into custody already. Liu Chenguang and Aili have already gone. They have all the maps and Liu Chenguang's fighting materials and medicines. We're going to split up and find each other later. Into the mountains at first. We need to go now."

Zhu Guiren sat up. "You should have woken me sooner," he whispered. "You transform now. Go, I'll go on my own."

"No—"

"Fly above me if you're worried," he said shortly. This was not the first time he had awakened and immediately needed to run for his life, but it was more dangerous now; he knew he wasn't as strong as he'd been, and he had a phoenix to worry about. "Go."

Tainu transformed and flew out the window. Zhu Guiren shook himself so his limbs felt loose and ready and threw himself out as well with a flip for momentum, leaping up to the courtyard wall and over it with his qinggong, then running toward the mountain. Shouts in Kunorese and Daxian came from behind him.

Just as he had reached the edge of the road, ready to move for the cliffs, he heard a gunshot behind him and felt a hot pain in his shoulder. He coughed a little bit, but kept going; Tainu would heal him. It would be fine. It was nothing to a demonic wound—

There was a second gunshot, and he felt it smash through his side where his internal cultivational structure had been nearly destroyed. He fell to his knees, putting his hand on the wound. It was very surprising. This must be how it felt to mortals to take a wound, to have their flesh torn and destroyed, unsupported by the strength of the spiritual body. Truly, it was more painful than he had thought it would be.

Then Zhu Guiren slowly toppled over, bleeding onto the dirt and mud of the road to Mount Shi.

CHAPTER 13
ESCAPE

Zhu Guiren woke up not dead. The gunshot wounds in his shoulder and side were healed. These were the good things.

The less good things were that he was in a cell, tied to a chair, freezing, aching, and tired.

The good thing, again, was that these bad things had been done to him by mortals, not demons, so he would be able to leave more or less at will, at which point he expected to more or less demolish this place entirely, because he was not pleased.

The bad thing was that since he wasn't dead, and his wounds were healed, Tainu must have come down to heal him when he was shot. There had been guns and people very close to him when he collapsed. He couldn't imagine how Tainu could have gotten to him without getting seriously injured or captured, or both.

There was someone else in the cell with him; he spoke in Kunorese, asking where the Federative woman had gone. Zhu Guiren pretended he couldn't understand it.

A Daxian man entered and smiled at him pleasantly. Things immediately became much worse. This man was a demon, though luckily not one from his own clan; he might try to destroy him, but he wouldn't be carrying First's punishment talisman.

The demon spoke in Daxian. "We have already interrogated the innkeeper.

The Kunorese want to know where the blonde Federative woman and her Daxian assistant have gone, what your plans were, all such things." He smiled again and continued, "And other parties would like to know where the second phoenix is. The first one, we have."

Zhu Guiren said, "Make up whatever you want to tell him. I have no idea and no interest in these games." He kept his expression fixed and showed no concern, but his heart plummeted and his skin crawled. *Tainu.*

The man bowed and said, "I should introduce myself. I am Third of my clan. You and I are clearly destined to meet. The First of your clan is looking for you, we have heard. Perhaps you would like to challenge our Fourth and join ours instead? We are not allied to your clan and our First and Second have extended an invitation to you."

"If I was interested," he replied calmly, "I would of course challenge you. Why would I want to be Fourth?"

The demon bowed again. "That could be considered, but since I would kill you, my clan would not benefit from your joining us in that case. Challenging our Fourth is better, in my opinion, but the decision would belong to my clan leaders if you wish to make this request?"

"Why are your clan leaders extending this invitation?"

"It's not for me to ask." He raised his eyebrows. "Surely your First and Second don't share their thoughts with you? If so, no wonder your clan is such a disaster. I've heard that you've killed twelve of your own high-ranking clansfolk since returning to Daxian. For myself, I would keep you far away from us, but the choice isn't mine." He smiled, and turned to the Kunorese officer to translate something that would excuse the length of their exchange.

Zhu Guiren fell into the rhythms of thought that had kept him alive for nine thousand years. His near panic about Tainu disappeared, as though he had cut it off. He would kill this demon at the first opportunity. He would then find and take the phoenix, because the phoenix was his and no one took what was his. The first thing, before killing the other demon, would be to find where Tainu was held. The demon didn't know the phoenix's true name; a thread of worry came back, as he remembered there were others who did, that Liu Chenguang might be looking for him as well. He let that go. He breathed deeply and considered. The Kunorese thought Tainu was a Federative spy, thus he must have appeared in his human form rather than his bird form. This demon clan was pretending to work with the Kunorese, so the phoenix was likely held in an ordinary cell, but in order to hold him and ensure he didn't transform they would have had to place a strong demonic shackle on him, or else be bleeding him continually. It occurred to him that the phoenix might be undergoing interrogation already, and that this would be painful. This made him angry.

"Make the request of your clan leaders," he said suddenly. "I require an answer within twenty minutes. Otherwise, I will simply kill you, but will not join your clan afterward and the phoenix goes with me."

The Daxian man broke off his interchange with the Kunorese officer, nodded briefly to him, and said, "I am confirming the offer you are making: if you kill me, you will join our clan and will bring the phoenix voluntarily?"

Zhu Guiren nodded.

"And if I kill you," the other demon said comfortably, "we will take the phoenix, and I'll have had an entertaining hour or so. It's boring here." To the guard, the demon said, "He says that he needs a map to think about where the Federative woman has gone. I will go get one," and he bowed and left the cell.

The Kunorese officer remained, staring at him. Zhu Guiren considered his options, then decided to muddy the waters. In Kunorese, he said, "That man was lying to you."

The officer jumped. "What? What did you say?"

Zhu Guiren made his voice small and frightened. Hopefully the man wouldn't be alerted by the change in tone. "I didn't want to speak to you before. I didn't want the Daxian here to know I speak Kunorese, because some of them are spies. They kill people like me. My mother was Kunorese. My father brought me to Zhaishou when I was a child during the first glorious conquest." His mind quickly flashed back through the recent history Liu Chenguang had explained to him. "I didn't tell him what I knew. I tested him by telling him something that was true to see if he would tell you, but he didn't. I never asked him for maps. I told him that the Federative woman was from Zhaishou. He's a spy. Please save me from him. I was tricked by the Federative woman, she came to Zhaishou and hired me as an interpreter, that's all I know!"

"Our intelligence tells us the Federative woman speaks fluent Daxian," the man said. "Why would she need an interpreter?"

"I don't know! I don't know!" He cowered in the chair as though afraid of being hit. "I know she could speak Daxian, but she wanted me anyway. I don't understand her plans. The other Daxian woman too — she was just a servant. She was sent out to the market to buy things, but she didn't understand why. But the Federative man, he's the one that really knew everything."

The man said, "Tell me more." He shouted behind him for someone else to come. "If your information is accurate, we'll consider helping you to return to Kunoru."

"Thank you! Thank you!" He attempted to bow in the ropes. "You can see my hand," he said, "the Federative man is the one who healed it. He's a doctor of some kind, but he's here for other reasons. They go out in the countryside to look for things. I don't understand what."

A second Kunorese officer arrived, and they conferred just outside the door; he couldn't quite understand what they were saying. Time was getting short. If the other demon returned first, it was back to the original plan, but if this one worked, he could get the phoenix before fighting instead of after. That would be better.

As though he was suddenly seized by inspiration, he shouted, "I know! They must be going out into the countryside to make contact with the guerrillas! They must know where to meet with them, how to send messages to them! That's why that man lied to you. I knew it!"

The two Kunorese remained in the corridor, looking at him contemptuously, but as he hoped, they were unconsciously encouraged by his shouting to speak just slightly more loudly —still whispering, but his ears could catch it now. He closed his eyes to concentrate better.

One of them muttered, "Traitorous scum. Why would you trust anything that comes out of his mouth?"

The other replied under his breath, "He's the least valuable, but also the weakest. It doesn't hurt to check the story. It's the Federatives we need, but catching rebels is also a mandate if we can get information on that as well. He does speak Kunorese fluently. That's something unusual."

"Where's the one that was caught with him, the Federative man? We should see if we can test any of this with him before acting on it."

"The lowest floor. The commander is observing the interrogation."

That was enough to go on, and time was running short. Zhu Guiren smiled and twisted his wrist to call his sword of ice and smoke.

He ran down the corridor lightly and without anxiety. The two Kunorese officers and several other people that crossed his path were dead. He had not needed to use the sword for this; he disdained using a demonic weapon on mortals, and in any case, it was not necessary. His hand and his feet were more than enough.

He heard a delighted laugh from behind him and the other demon leapt and flipped over his head to face him.

"Finally," the other man said, his black eyes glinting. "*So* boring here."

Zhu Guiren said, "Do you really think you're qualified?"

"My clan leaders have permitted you to challenge me," he said. "If you kill me, you'll need to go to my clan, or else my own clan leaders will hunt you down for breaking your contract with them."

"What contract?" He called his halberd. "I have no contract with you. You're ten minutes late."

The other demon leapt for him, and Zhu Guiren jumped aside.

"That's your own fault. You weren't in the room anymore when I came back," the other demon said conversationally.

"Don't blame me for your failures. There is no contract. I'll kill you because I feel like it."

Two mortals came running around the corner; they were caught in the crossing waves of weapon energy and qi and more or less exploded into blood and flesh. The other demon laughed. Zhu Guiren threw a talisman at him, but he dodged.

This was wasting time. The other demon was Third in his own clan. He might be close enough to Zhu Guiren's normal level to delay him only slightly under normal circumstances, but he was not currently at his own full strength. He would need to hide this; he couldn't afford a drawn out fight that would display his weaknesses. The other demon held a sword and a close combat weapon he was unfamiliar with — a circle of metal with razored blades on one side. He himself could only hold one weapon at a time; with that bladed circle, close combat would not be to his advantage, and he could no longer use a bow and arrow.

As always when fighting, his mind was extremely clear and focused. While switching between spear and halberd to keep the combat at a distance, he considered what ranged weapons he could still use with one hand. He didn't even consider lowering himself to use a gun; that was far beneath any self-respecting demon. He could only think of the spear thrower, a weapon so ancient that even he could barely remember when it had still been in regular use, but he had once been quite good with it.

He threw a talisman in the air and switched to spear thrower, casting a spear of demonic qi so quickly that the spear impaled the talisman on its way to the other demon. Spear throwers were fast; it caught him in the throat. The combination of the talisman and weapon strike disabled him enough that Zhu Guiren was able to leap over and decapitate him. He laughed watching the blood spill out. What an arrogant fool. Who would want to join a clan that had that travesty as Third? His clan leaders were well rid of him.

Two more appeared around the corner. Demons, not mortals. One of them opened their mouth to say something to him. Lest it be something along the lines of honoring that dubious contract, he took one out with the spear thrower as well, then disemboweled the other one with his halberd.

And then he took *another* gunshot, this one luckily to his back, which was still protected by his demonic cultivation system. It hurt nonetheless. He turned and ran toward the unlucky mortal at the other end of the corridor, who trembled but aimed again. He released his sword and took the man by the throat just as the man shot him at close range, also in the throat. Luckily, the bullet missed his jugular, his brain, and his spinal cord, any of which would have been quite serious, even for him. He coughed and spat blood in the man's face.

"Where?" he said in Kunorese. "Prisoner. Federative. Show me."

The man nodded, eyes wide with terror. "The stairs. That way, three floors down."

Zhu Guiren noticed that he had pissed himself. *Disgusting.* He threw the man against the wall, which most likely killed him, and then ran for the stairs. He was bleeding heavily now; he needed his phoenix. His phoenix — no one else's. If there was anyone hurting his phoenix, he would kill them. The phoenix was only his.

The stairs were behind a locked door, which he blasted to smithereens. He didn't hear anything. Would he hear anything? That sense of anxiety started to return whenever he thought of Tainu being hurt, so he immediately stopped thinking of him and systematically began to check doors. He needed a phoenix to heal him. That was all. There was a phoenix here that he would find.

Behind one of the doors, he smelled blood and heard someone speaking in Anglish. There were several people behind the door. Because the phoenix might be there, he didn't destroy the door, but simply killed the two mortal guards outside. They screamed, and someone helpfully opened the door for him.

Tainu was shackled to a chair. One of the shackles was a demonic ward, the difference from the others visible to him, though the mortals wouldn't be able to see it. They had surely searched him, but not stripped him; he was still wearing what he had worn when they went to sleep the night before, his loose pants and shirt torn and bloody. He was not unconscious, but very close to it, and hadn't been disabled yet, though there was a great deal of his blood on the floor. His wounds were still healing very quickly, but they had injured him severely enough at some point that he didn't seem to realize Zhu Guiren was there.

Zhu Guiren felt as though something had struck him in the heart — so strongly that he actually looked down to see if he was wounded — but no, there was nothing, except seeing Tainu like that. He put it out of his mind. It was a distraction. He needed to focus.

"Hello, my dear," said a woman's voice in Anglish. "How nice to see you, Third."

Zhu Guiren froze, then turned and bowed. "Second," he said.

"Kill the mortals," she said.

He immediately released his sword and leapt to strike them one by one with his hand, so quickly that they were dead before they fell to the floor.

"Very good," she said. "Little Third, I take it this is your phoenix?"

"It is."

Second looked at him, smiling. He knew this middle-aged Daxian woman with a kind face was not the true appearance of her mortal body; First and Second rarely walked in the world without an illusion enchantment. In fact, they almost never left clan home at all.

"You're surprised to see me here," she said. "We're all out enjoying the banquet, of course, and all the entertainment that goes with it. I heard they had captured you. I had intended to come retrieve you myself from those insolent yokels when I was done here, but I see that you've saved me the trouble. Did they ask you to defect?"

He bowed in acknowledgment.

"Well," she said, turning back to Tainu, "I was only staying here to ensure that our new phoenix is well cared for. The other clan had at least put a shackle on him, but look how they've treated him, the idiots." She made a *tsk*ing noise. "I killed the mortal interpreter and took her appearance an hour or so ago so I could intervene. What a waste of phoenix blood…Look at it, all over the floor."

She walked over to Tainu and slapped his face. Zhu Guiren felt his fist clench at his side.

As though knowing what he was feeling, as almost certainly she did, Second whirled and threw a punishment talisman at him. It brushed his shoulder as he dodged, which was all it needed to do to start its work. He shuddered as the cold began to work its way through his meridians.

"Why have you ignored our summons?" Second asked. She simply dodged his attacks as he went for her with his entire range of weapons; she was incredibly fast as well as strong. "I don't want to hurt you, dear. You just need to come home and reflect a bit on your choices. We have the phoenix now. All will be well."

He could feel himself slowing. Before he could lose the power to do it, he slashed each of the mortal shackles on the phoenix, then slicked the demonic shackle with his own blood and began chanting.

Second laughed. "Really, dear! What good will that do anyone?" She threw a demonic talisman. Not at him, but at the phoenix; the phoenix screamed in pain, and the sound drove Zhu Guiren nearly out of his mind.

He attacked in a frenzy, coming at Second's face again and again using his sword — his favorite weapon. She had stopped smiling, and had finally called her own preferred weapon, a saber.

The phoenix was free. His chant had worked. He hadn't been sure it would since his own power was so diminished. Luckily, it hadn't been Second who set the shackle herself; he wouldn't have been able to break it.

"Go!" he heard himself yell. Why had he done that? Didn't he need the phoenix to stay with him, to heal him?

But instead, he shouted, "Get away!" and drove Second back from the phoenix so she couldn't hurt him.

Second hissed and threw another talisman.

He jumped in front of it so it couldn't hit the phoenix, but it was strong. Very strong. He fell down to one knee, choking on his own blood. The talisman had opened all the recent wounds in his body — the gunshot wounds in his side and throat particularly — and blood poured out everywhere.

The phoenix hadn't left. The phoenix stood behind him, putting his own blood on the wounds and saying something he couldn't understand. He turned. The phoenix seemed upset.

"Go away," Zhu Guiren said, and fell over.

Second ran toward the phoenix, another shackle in her hand, chanting the spell as she leaped toward him.

The phoenix took something out of his ragged clothing, something folded very small, and slapped it hard on her forehead. A bright white-gold light exploded silently in the room.

Second screamed as the talisman burned into her skin and hair. The false appearance collapsed into ashes and her mortal body showed: a tall, black-haired woman with deep blue eyes. Her golden skin was blistering and running, bleeding and burning, and she screamed again. She threw one last qi javelin and fled.

Zhu Guiren felt the phoenix roll him onto his back and continue applying blood to his wounds. He was talking feverishly. Zhu Guiren realized that the phoenix was crying. "Don't die," the phoenix was saying. "Don't, please, stay with me, don't go."

"Won't go," he said. "Not dying."

The phoenix laughed a little. Tainu laughed. He remembered now. All the terror he felt for him, all the rage at how he had been hurt, came back at once.

Zhu Guiren closed his eyes and shoved it back down. He couldn't afford this; they still had to get out. Tainu bent over and kissed him with his blood-stained lips, and he kept his eyes closed to feel Tainu's tongue flicker inside, a quick caress. He let Tainu's lips stay on his just for a moment.

"My shoulder," he said, as soon as his mind had recovered enough to start working again. "Punishment talisman."

Tainu used Zhu Guiren's sword to cut off the shirt — it wasn't worth saving anyway, just bloody rags now — and Zhu Guiren saw his face turn very serious as he laid his hand on the talisman mark. "Bad," was all he said before he closed his eyes to concentrate.

"Ah," said Zhu Guiren as heat poured into his body from Tainu's hand, clearing the bitter cold of the punishment talisman from his meridians and warming all the places that were hurt and aching that he hadn't even known about. When he opened his eyes again, his mind felt clear and his body was able to move. "Help me up."

Tainu pulled him upright, then to his feet. Zhu Guiren looked at him silently. There were no marks on him. Not anymore.

Tainu said, "I know you're angry at me. Can you tell me about it later?"

"I'm not angry. Not at you, anyway." He looked at the carnage in the room. "Can you transform?"

Tainu shook his head. "Not yet. That punishment talisman is very hard to deal with. I don't have much left. I need time to recover." He didn't say anything about all his blood on the floor from whatever they had done to him before Zhu Guiren arrived.

"All right," Zhu Guiren said. "There are at least two clans of demons here, one of them mine, in addition to the mortals. The mortals aren't a problem except for the guns, and the guns aren't a problem as long as I have you. And you are staying with me unless I tell you to run. You have to do exactly what I tell you, when I tell you to do it."

Tainu nodded.

He tried to think. "How long till you can transform?" He could carry Tainu if necessary, but not endless distances. "Once we're out, will you be able to fly?"

"I don't know," Tainu said. "It's not good for me, right now." He was swaying where he stood, as though his balance was affected.

"Damn." He no longer had time for nuanced decisions. "All right, just follow me as fast as you can. Warn me if you're falling behind or need to be carried. I can't always be watching." He called his sword and ran for the door. Tainu followed.

Zhu Guiren didn't bother trying to get out at ground level; instead, he ran up the stairs to the top floor of the three story building, killing all along the way. He looked out the window and realized that they had been taken to the south of Shi'an — the side of the city farthest from the mountains — and shook his head. "We should run west into the countryside first. We'll be caught if we try to circle Shi'an for the mountains from here. If we can get away, we can cross the river and circle back toward Hongye from the other side. Although Hongye is also Kunorese territory…" He gave it up. One thing at a time.

Tainu nodded. "Demon, I'm sorry. I'm keeping you here."

"Shh," he said absently, thinking. Well, it was what it was, though not ideal. "Get on my back. I'll take you down with qinggong through the streets, then you'll need to get off and start running with me."

Tainu nodded, looking determined, and put his arms around Zhu Guiren's neck to be carried.

"Hold on," Zhu Guiren said, grimacing a little. Tainu outweighed him, and of course he had the strength to carry him, but it wasn't something he could do without effort. He considered his path, then jumped out the window toward a neighboring rooftop and began running along it.

The yao of nighttime Shi'an scattered before him as he raced and leapt down and down, holding Tainu, focusing on the next step, the next jump, where to cross to avoid patrols, how to get out without using a guarded gate. Finally, he reached the ground to the southwest of the city and began racing forward to use as much of his momentum as possible before he needed to stop. They would hit the flooded areas soon; he had no idea what they would do then, but they needed to find somewhere safe and hidden where no one would look for them. They would need to rest, and he would need to cultivate. He would need it desperately if he was going to get them through this.

He let Tainu off and ran with him for a while, both of them slowing more and more with exhaustion. They waded through the empty, flooded fields in the dark until they found themselves on a low, wooded rise. There was a little house, mostly ruined, completely empty. It didn't seem to be a farmhouse. Belatedly, Zhu Guiren realized it was an old shrine. At least it had a roof.

He went inside and fell down. "What god is it?" he asked, rolling over on his back. There was still a very faint scent of incense along with mildew.

Tainu said, "There's no knowing now. It's all long gone. Just an altar cloth." He bowed before the altar and then went out.

"Tainu?"

He came back carrying an armful of small branches with dried leaves. "I'll make something to be a bed," he said. "You rest. We can't risk a fire here."

Zhu Guiren said, "I'll help you. You need rest as much as I do."

Together they piled up the branches and leaves, then Tainu went outside and brought back some long grass from the edge of the flooded area to soften it.

He bowed again and took the altar cloth. "We're going to freeze otherwise," he explained. "We both barely have clothes at this point."

Zhu Guiren shook his head. "I can keep us warm," he said sleepily, then realized what that sounded like and immediately amended it. "With qi. That's what I meant."

Tainu laughed and laid down next to him. "Keep us warm, then, demon," he said, spreading the altar cloth over them.

Zhu Guiren pulled him closer into his arms, wanting to feel that he was really there, but didn't say anything. He didn't know what to say. Falling back into the demonic world had made him feel very strange. Which was real? The blood and hatred, or this person and the months they had spent together, talking and laughing? Had that been the dream?

He could feel Tainu's eyes on him. It was so very dark that everything was by touch, or by guess: the warmth and weight of Tainu's body, his breathing and heartbeat, only an occasional glint of his eyes, a line of his face. The darkness made everything important — every little thing that he could glean of him, Tainu's warm, quiet voice when finally he spoke.

"That was one of your clan leaders?"

Zhu Guiren nodded.

Tainu reached out, fingers gently stroking his face. "Can I tell you something?"

"Yes," he said.

"I looked for you."

"What do you mean?" He frowned, then felt Tainu trace the fold between his eyebrows.

"You always frown when you're thinking hard."

"What do you mean, you looked for me?"

"After you set me free from that terrible place I found you," Tainu said. "I wanted to tell you this a long time ago, but I didn't know how. I was so young, I told you. That was my first rebirth, I didn't even know what had happened to me before I was in a child's body again, shackled to the stone couch and tortured every day for however many years it was."

Zhu Guiren closed his eyes; it didn't matter in the dark, but he couldn't bear to know. "Don't tell me this," he said.

"You have to know this," Tainu insisted, "because I met you there, and you were so beautiful to me. You were brave and kind and strong. Your heart was so innocent and you were so full of life and joy and everything about you was beautiful. And I loved you. Even then, I loved you."

Zhu Guiren felt his eyes grow hot. "I don't remember it," he said. "They took that from me."

"You were the best memory for me in that worst time. Your heart was so beautiful to me. I never forgot. You were so brave. You took such a risk for me — to set me free." Tainu leaned closer and kissed his lips, gently. "I have never regretted anything in my life as much as not being able to bring you with me. You stayed behind. To accept punishment. Can you forgive me?"

"I don't remember it," Zhu Guiren said, honestly, "but if I chose to stay, that was my choice."

"I looked for you. As soon as I was able. I established the first few refuges, and then I started looking. I went back to the clan home where I had been held, where you had freed me, but you weren't there. I looked and looked."

"How long?" he asked. "How long did you look?" It felt important to know.

Tainu caressed his face again. "I never stopped looking. I always hoped I would find you. I went all over the world, in the spirit world too. And about a thousand years ago, I started finding traces in North Daxian. A demon hiding among mortals, someone who loved to learn things, and study the stars."

Zhu Guiren's heart pounded hard. "Don't say it. Don't say it," he whispered.

"I went to Crane Moon," he said softly, "and I found you at last, torturing my little sibling."

Zhu Guiren flinched. The branches beneath him crackled.

"I didn't want it to be you, but I knew that it was. I would never not recognize you. Even when I didn't want to. Even when I wished so much that I had never found you." After some silence, he continued, "I helped Hong Deming get Liu Chenguang away from you. Did you know it was me?"

Zhu Guiren shook his head slowly. "I didn't know you were there."

"Would it have mattered if you knew?"

"No." This was the truth. It would not have mattered. It would not have stopped him.

"You chased them and persecuted them, engineered Hong Deming's death. You destroyed the life they could have had together. Then you...you cut my sibling into pieces."

"You were there." Suddenly, as he never had before, he felt shame. That Tainu had seen him, seen him doing that...

"I was there."

Zhu Guiren was silent. His heart was silent and despairing. "Tainu," he said at last, but he couldn't say anything else.

"And all this time since…Liu Chenguang." Tainu took a deep breath. "I followed you afterward, to see what you would do."

"And what did you see me do?" Zhu Guiren asked, his heart empty because he knew.

"I saw you go where the suffering was and cultivate from it," Tainu said bluntly. "You followed the Mitang invasion to the west. You followed the Imperial conquest of the southern continents. You were in the Common Federation for the past three centuries."

"Yes," he whispered. "That's where I was. That's what I did." He had been a crow following the path of carrion and cruelty and death, eager to feed on anything that suffered.

Tainu had seen him, all those centuries.

Tainu was still here, still looking at his face in the darkness. He knew because his cold fingers suddenly felt warmth, Tainu's fingers, interlacing with his. "Arciniang, it's all right," he said softly. "You always want to know why I won't call you by the name everyone else calls you…I don't call you Zhu Guiren because I don't think you are really Zhu Guiren anymore. To me, that name is a thousand years old, and I don't think you are the person that I watched do those things a thousand years ago."

Zhu Guiren looked at him. "How can you know that?" he asked, at last.

Tainu said, "Arciniang, I know…I know that you haven't built an array since this one. You have not made anything worse in the world. You haven't caused anything that wasn't already happening. I saw you try, sometimes. To be kind. I know that you wish you hadn't done this."

"If I hadn't done this," he said, "I'd be dead."

"But you still wish you hadn't done it."

"Yes," Zhu Guiren said. "But wishing doesn't change what I've done."

Tainu said, softly, "I love you, Arciniang."

Zhu Guiren felt something he still had no name for — a warmth and a desire and a pain — inside him. He bent his head to Tainu's face, finding him in the dark. "Tainu. I want to kiss you. Can I kiss you?"

"Yes."

He leaned over and put his arms around him, feeling him come closer, the leaves and branches underneath crackling under their weight. "I need you so much," Zhu Guiren said helplessly, "I don't even understand what this is. Do you understand it?"

Tainu lay on his side with one leg thrown over him. His hand gently traced the lines of his jaw, his throat, his shoulders, as though he was curious to explore his body even though he had touched it so many times to heal so many wounds.

"Tainu, I want you to kiss me," Zhu Guiren said again. "I want you to touch me. Do you want to?"

Tainu closed his eyes and whispered, "Yes, I want to. I'm just so afraid."

He was tired but still strong enough for this — to pull Tainu closer and press him into the leaves and branches, feeling the shape of him in the dark, stroking him, kissing his mouth and his throat, feeling his heart begin to race and his breath to quicken. He heard himself say, "Don't ever be afraid, not of me. I will always love you. I will always keep you safe. I want you to be happy with me, always. Always."

He kissed Tainu's throat so hard that it almost became a bite; Tainu gasped and pulled him closer, entwining their bodies against one another to reach him better, touch him more intimately.

Zhu Guiren said fiercely, "You're mine. No one else can touch you."

Tainu laughed softly, which was the best sound in the world.

"Yes," Tainu said. He traced Zhu Guiren's lips with his fingers, softly pressing in to touch his teeth and tongue.

Zhu Guiren caught his fingers in his mouth and teased them with his tongue, delighting in how Tainu cried out softly and arched his body to press hard against him. He shivered, at the edge of a deep need in himself, uncontrollable as gravity when he would let it take him.

"I want you," Tainu said. "I want you to be the one who touches me." His beloved one began kissing his mouth again, deeply, longingly.

Breathing hard and fast, Tainu's breath warm against his skin, Zhu Guiren said, "Tell me– Show me how to touch you. I don't know what to do. I want you to like it–"

And so, Tainu did.

CHAPTER 14
MORNINGS AFTER

THE NEXT MORNING, Zhu Guiren got out of their makeshift bed and began trying to cultivate. At least he did this after several times of beginning to get out of bed and then changing his mind because there were very important things to do in bed, so it was really lunchtime by the time he got up.

"It's not as though we have food anyway," he protested when Tainu told him this.

Tainu kissed his ear and told him to get up, which was also counterproductive. Then Tainu said, "Fine," and got up first.

He went out to cultivate, so Zhu Guiren followed him.

But he couldn't cultivate.

This was only partly because he was distracted and teasing Tainu. The pain was incredible, and he felt no more than a trickle of resentment flowing in, like ground glass flowing through his eyes. After an hour or so of this, he realized that he must have been making a noise because Tainu came to sit opposite him, looking serious.

"Demon," he said, "let me check you." Tainu ran his hand gently over Zhu Guiren's abdomen — not quite touching him, but close enough so he could feel the warmth of his hand — then closed his eyes and asked, "Can you cultivate while I'm observing?"

"All right."

After a few moments, Tainu said, his eyes still closed, "That is not helping your cultivation."

"But it's helping me with other things."

"Get your lips back where they belong and concentrate."

Zhu Guiren sighed and concentrated.

"Ah," said Tainu. After a while, he said, "Demon, I'm going to try something. Keep cultivating, but put your hand out, palm flat."

Zhu Guiren felt Tainu's hand extend just above his, not actually touching, but close enough to feel the energy of his skin.

Tainu said, "Now keep cultivating. Let me know if you feel something new." Then, after several minutes, "Stop that."

"You realize that you're sitting only a few inches away from me practically naked and holding my hand," he protested.

"Tomorrow, we leave and buy clothes. Concentrate."

Zhu Guiren concentrated. Surprised, he said, "Yes." There was something — something gentle, buffering the pain of the resentment as it flowed into him. As the pain lessened, his meridians were able to accept more and gradually, the trickle increased to a more normal volume.

Tainu carefully removed his hand. "Is it still working?" he asked. His voice was strained.

"Yes." Zhu Guiren stopped cultivating, then began again. "It still works." He opened his eyes. "Tainu?" he asked, concerned. Tainu was swaying where he sat; just in time he leaned over to catch him and hold him upright.

"Did it work? Did you feel it?"

"Yes. What was it?"

"Natural qi, purifying resentment," Tainu said, leaning against him. "Did it hurt you?"

His eyes widened. "No, not at all."

"I thought, since we've been doing…what we've been doing, you might not be so sensitive to pure qi anymore," he said, "so I could try to cultivate with you to strengthen your meridians."

Zhu Guiren kissed him gently. "What exactly have we been doing?"

"Shut up, demon."

"But you're hurt?" Zhu Guiren pulled him closer, so he was sitting in his lap.

"The resentment still hurts me," he said. "I haven't gotten less sensitive to it."

"But it always hurts. That's just how it is."

Tainu stirred. "Always? Every time you cultivate, it feels like that? Like something sharp is tearing you up inside?"

He nodded. "It's probably worse for you because it's new," he said. "When I first learned, it was very intense. I'm used to it now. It's just the injury that's making it hard."

Tainu just looked at him.

"Well," he said defensively, "wasn't it hard when you learned to cultivate?"

"I'm probably not a good example. My whole existence is based in pure qi, but I'm sure if you ask Aili, she'll tell you that it didn't hurt her to learn cultivation as a child."

Zhu Guiren frowned.

Tainu made himself more comfortable in his lap, sitting facing him with his legs wrapped loosely around his hips. Zhu Guiren decided he approved of this, but before he could take advantage of it Tainu spoke in a serious voice: "Arciniang, what will happen when we keep destroying arrays? When we destroy the final array?"

He said, honestly, "I don't know."

Tainu kissed him softly. "Arciniang, if you survive it at all, and I'm not sure you will, your cultivational structure will probably be completely destroyed."

"I've thought of that," he said, reluctantly. He knew that if he admitted this Tainu wouldn't let him go forward. "But I don't…I don't want it anymore, Tainu. I don't want to have an existence that depends on…that."

Tainu nodded, touching their foreheads together. Zhu Guiren said, "Last night you said that I hadn't made anything worse in the world. But I haven't made it better either. You know that. If you have been near me in the past five hundred years I have drunk your suffering too, the suffering of mortals you cared about. I don't want it anymore."

Tainu kissed him and said, "Yes, I know."

Zhu Guiren said, "Tainu. I don't want to benefit from that. I can't…go looking for it. Not anymore."

"But I want you to survive," Tainu said. "I know you don't want it, but I want you to do what you need to do. Promise me."

"I'll do what I need to do," he promised. "Also to protect you. But I want the array to be broken."

Tainu said, shyly, "Let me try something again." He closed his eyes and leaned in to kiss him, keeping one hand on Zhu Guiren's side where the cultivational structure was ruined.

Zhu Guiren gasped. An enormous amount of fiery heat passed through his body. A different kind of burning than the futile, lifeless acid of resentment — like a sun inside him, settling somewhere beyond his ability to feel it, nowhere and everywhere, as intangible as light. He felt Tainu collapse a little bit against him, breathing deeply. Zhu Guiren held him close and asked, "What is it?"

"I did something preventative," Tainu said. "For your meridians, so you will have a better chance of surviving the shock when the array is destroyed. I don't know what will happen with it. But cultivate with me, sometimes. That will strengthen what I've done. Can you try to cultivate natural qi in addition to resentment? Just to see what it feels like?"

"How do I do it?" he asked, frowning.

"Instead of seeking out resentment, seek out joy," he said. "Life, energy, movement, love, desire…It's better if you're in a place full of life, but even here, you could cultivate. There's trees, there's life in the water, the birds are flying…"

"You're here," Zhu Guiren said. "Can I cultivate by seeking out you?"

Tainu smiled, his eyes still closed. "Technically, yes. I am an endless fountain of spiritual energy."

"Excellent," said Zhu Guiren, and kissed him.

Tainu said, "Arciniang, my true name—"

"No," he said, very quickly. "Don't say it."

Tainu opened his eyes, surprised and clearly a little hurt.

Zhu Guiren said, "If I know it, and I'm captured, they will also know it. I won't be able to hide it from them. They'll be able to use it to find you." He put his arms around again and could feel Tainu's disappointment. Encouragingly, he said, "Someday. Someday, you can tell me."

In his heart, he didn't think that day would come; he didn't think he would survive the breaking of the great array, no matter what Tainu did to try to prevent it, but he felt no anxiety about it. All was well. All was *very* well. He kissed Tainu again and lifted him up to carry him back inside.

They really couldn't stay in this place longer than one day; they had no food, largely symbolic clothing, and while mortals would probably lose their path in the floodwaters, pursuing demons would not. Zhu Guiren let Tainu sleep through the afternoon and cultivated. He really couldn't feel anything when he tried to cultivate natural qi, but was successful in cultivating resentment, and by sundown, he felt much more confident that he could get them through the next stage. He went back inside and gently shook Tainu awake.

"It's dark," he said softly, "let's go."

Tainu nodded and whispered "Liu Chenguang has left the mountains. I think they are worried, and coming to find us. If we head northeast, we'll intersect them sometime in the next few days. From there, we can cross the Sorrowful River. You're sure the final array is there?"

"It's…somewhere," he said, not encouragingly. "The bed of the river has shifted and the topography is all different. We'll have to search. If Aili is with, us that will help. She's tied to it."

The stars came out as they walked, but the sky was cloudy, so the light was very intermittent — glinting off the water everywhere, the same off deceptively deep channels with strong currents and the shared surface of the shallow puddles on the roads. Zhu Guiren began to feel a sense of unreality in the landscape, full of trickery and shadows.

Tainu seemed to feel it as well. "This is a very yin landscape now…"

"Does that mean your powers are weaker?" Zhu Guiren asked, interested. He had always wondered about how things worked, being a phoenix. "Phoenixes are yang energy, aren't they?

"Not exactly. I have yin aspects too," he said. "Every phoenix is different. My yang aspect is stronger, so I need to consciously balance with yin, or I'll burn myself out and be forced to do it."

"I've seen you do that," Zhu Guiren said.

Tainu smiled. "You help me," he said simply. "You help me be more balanced."

Zhu Guiren felt that as a warmth in his heart — that he could be helpful to Tainu.

"I was just thinking about that as we're walking through all of this…Liu Chenguang naturally is more yin than I am. Whether she's in a male or female mortal body, that's just her personality." Tainu smiled fondly. "It's been good to be with her again, these months. We haven't spent this much time together in centuries."

"Why are you thinking about this?" Zhu Guiren asked. He stepped slightly to one side and got wet up to his knees, which didn't matter much as they were both already wet and muddy. "How are we going to get clothes, by the way?"

"You'll have to take care of that part when we get to a town…" After a while, Tainu said, "I was just thinking of the difference between yin and resentment, that's all. Yin energy has associations with death, isn't resentment death also? I was thinking about how it hurts you to cultivate resentment. It doesn't seem right. If it was part of the natural world, like yang and yin, it shouldn't be painful to cultivate."

Zhu Guiren shook his head. "I haven't thought about the pain part, but I've thought about resentment a great deal at times in my life, because I needed to understand how to create it and capture it for my array. The resentment is spiritual, beyond the cycles of the natural world. Resentment is suffering, loss, bitterness…Only spiritual beings produce it. The natural world dies and is reborn without resentment."

He continued, "Spiritual beings — mortals and yao — we produce resentment at death because our spirits long for what we can now never have, for what's been taken from us, for what we left unfinished and unsaid, for the debts owed to us and the debts unpaid, for what we've suffered in life and in dying. At death, our spirits know that there is nothing more we can do. Any failure is final, any loss is irrevocable, any suffering will not be healed, and our spirits release that into the world as the souls go wherever souls go. Or else, if the resentment is obsessive or it's caught in an array, the soul remains as a resentful ghost."

Tainu took his hand.

After they had walked for a while more, Zhu Guiren spoke again. "I spent two hundred years creating the great array by doing all I could to ensure that the suffering of the people was as great as it could be. None of it was by my hand, but all by my design, so that each person who died would produce resentment at the highest possible level. Those I caught in the array — they still feel it. Their descendants belong to me too, drawn into as much resentment as the array can produce in the circumstances of their lives. Every day, they relive it for me, and it feeds into me to strengthen me. I don't even have to cultivate it. It's like my heart pumping blood."

Tainu sighed. "Arciniang–"

"That's why," Zhu Guiren said. He knew Tainu wanted to say something comforting, but there was nothing to say. "That's why I need to destroy it."

Tainu nodded, and they continued to walk in silence through the dark watery land, hand in hand.

They came to a little village after sunrise, still with people in it. Zhu Guiren went in to buy some clothes for them, as well as a blanket and some food; no one commented on the bloodstained clothing he was already wearing. The villagers here had been through much. There were only a few younger men remaining. Most had gone to join the army, willing or unwilling, but their parents and grandparents sold their extra clothing to Zhu Guiren at a steep markup.

Tainu tore off his remaining rags, used them to wash himself as best he could in the silty floodwaters where he had waited outside the village bounds, and gratefully put them on. "Much better," he said. "Demon, the only problem is I have none of those talismans left. I wanted to tell you. I only had the one sewn into those sleeping clothes."

Zhu Guiren nodded, though his heart sank a bit. "How far is Liu Chenguang?" he asked.

Tainu closed his eyes and whispered, then he said, "About two day's journey walking, if we're all walking at the same pace toward one another."

"How long if you were to fly to her?" he asked. "Just to rendezvous, and to get some of the talismans from her? I don't like you being completely defenseless except for me."

Tainu shook his head. "Still several hours each way. I don't want us to be separated for that long."

Zhu Guiren smiled at him.

"Not because of that! My goodness." Tainu laughed as he came over and put his arms around him, looking down at him with his beautiful eyes. "I have clothes on now," he added. "So there."

"Clothes are removable," said Zhu Guiren.

"Not till tonight." Tainu started walking. "Let's go."

Zhu Guiren hurried to catch up. "Let's find a nice place to stop for tonight."

"I don't think there are any nice places here."

"A nice, abandoned house."

Tainu looked at him sideways, smiling. "Walk faster, then."

As they came closer to the Sorrowful River, the landscape became more and more dangerous. There were no landmarks left — no visible roads, only occasional rises above the level of the floods — and the walls of ruined houses sticking up from the yellow waters. Both of them were soon soaked and muddy again, tricked repeatedly into stepping into deep channels carved into the soil beneath them. Before sunset, they stopped at a treeless rise by common, unspoken consent, exhausted. There had been no usable shelters on the way, nor anywhere in front of them.

Zhu Guiren looked consideringly at Tainu. "Go," he said. "Fly to Liu Chenguang. You shouldn't have to slog through this for me. Find a safe, dry place with them and wait for me."

Tainu shook his head stubbornly.

"Tainu, even the food we bought this morning is wet. I want you to go somewhere better than this. I'm strong enough to defend myself well. There's nothing you need to concern yourself about."

"No," he said. "Arciniang, you know you can't find me if I leave. We'll have to come to you anyway and slog it out regardless."

"Tainu," Zhu Guiren laughed, "are you just using this so you can tell me your true name?"

He nodded. "If you're confident that you'll be safe, you'll let me tell you. Otherwise, I won't go."

"Tainu, just because I'm safe for a few days somewhere in wherever this is doesn't mean I'm safe forever," he tried. "You just go. I'll meet you somewhere."

"Where?" Tainu sat down in the mud. "You don't have a map. I don't even know where we are. No, I'm not leaving you like this. You don't know anyone's true name, and I'm the only one who knows yours. If something happens to either of us–"

Zhu Guiren said, "Fine. Stay with me in the mud, then."

"I will." Tainu yawned. "It's not so comfortable that I feel the need to stay here all night, though. Just…let's rest."

Zhu Guiren came to sit behind him so he could lean back and sleep. There was nothing else to lean on, not even a rock or a tree stump. The evening slowly drew down to a muddy, uncertain darkness. Something fluttered down from the sky to land next to them.

A bird.

A crow.

"Tainu." Zhu Guiren stood, bringing Tainu upright with him. "Tainu, wake up."

Another crow came down, and another.

Tainu shook himself awake. "What?" he asked, confused.

"Transform now, and go," Zhu Guiren said, his sword appearing in his hand.

Four more crows landed on the rise, surrounding them.

Tainu shook his head.

"Go!" Zhu Guiren shouted. "Now!"

The crows all transformed at once. He didn't recognize all of them — some must have been from the other clan he had met in the jail — but Tenth was there, and Fourth, and Fifth. All would be carrying punishment talismans, he knew.

He begged one last time, "Tainu, fly. Fly now."

"Demon, do you think I can outfly all of these?" Tainu asked. He knelt down and slapped the earth to set a ward.

It wouldn't last long. The earth was too saturated to hold it; the water would move its foundations, seeping through.

Zhu Guiren said, "I love you. Fly now, please," and leapt out of the wards to take the offensive.

He took down two of the strange demons immediately, but the first punishment talisman had already brushed his thigh. Tenth followed up with a strike with his favored weapon — a bladed whip that cut him heavily in the arm — but he paid for it by being impaled and then disemboweled by Zhu Guiren's double halberd. Fourth would be more problematic; he could see her eagerness to kill him personally. To take his place. Her preferred weapon was a bow, hard to defend against with only a sword. She sent arrow after arrow at him, and he blocked and blocked, but the second punishment talisman took him square in the back, and he fell to his knees.

Tainu rushed out of the wards to him.

"No, no," he gasped, but it was too late. Tainu was next to him, had set a new ward around them and was trying to heal the damage from the talismans so he could keep fighting, but the ward was weak. Another of the strange demons forced his way through it and grabbed Tainu around the neck with a garrote of demonic qi. Tainu gurgled in pain as it burned and cut the skin of his throat, and the other demon dragged him bodily away.

Zhu Guiren screamed in rage. He forced himself upright, chasing after the other demon, but already his reflexes were slow. Running was as though he was fighting his way through deep, cold snow; every movement was five times more difficult than usual, his striking ability taken as his meridians froze.

With relief, he saw Tainu transform into a hummingbird and dash upwards, but then there were two crows pounding up into the air after him, less maneuverable, but larger and much more powerful. A third crow rose up to herd the small red bird from every side, until at last one of them managed to pierce the little bird with its claws and it went limp, bleeding. Zhu Guiren screamed again and cast a spear, but it fell far short. The crow flew away to the west.

Zhu Guiren turned back to Fourth. "You're dead," he managed to say, and took her through the upper chest with a javelin. She pulled it out contemptuously and stood with the remaining demons, watching him flail, more and more slowly, against the muddy ground where he lay as the two punishment talismans took bitterly quick effect. They were so very strong, and he couldn't resist. The pain increased as his mobility lessened. All he could do was lie still and scream, and eventually, he couldn't even scream, trapped in frozen silence as his body and mind were torn apart by the talisman.

Fourth said, "First said to leave you here with the punishment talisman if we didn't kill you. He'll send someone to pick you up later." She viciously kicked his head, and he passed out.

He came to sometime the next day, being dragged bodily along the ground into an old farmhouse surrounded by the floods. The people dragging him talked over his head, laughing; he couldn't understand their words. The humiliation was worse than the pain, and he knew this was part of the punishment. His heart was nothing but hot, panicked terror. *Tainu.*

A paunchy middle-aged man sat behind the desk in an army uniform. "Brother," he said, winking. Then, "Dismissed."

The men holding Zhu Guiren threw him on the floor and left.

When they had gone, the man stood up. "Did you know I sent ordinary men to pick you up?" he asked. "You've damaged your own cultivation to the point I didn't even need to send demons once the punishment talisman had done its work." He strolled over, casually removing the illusion enchantment that had hidden his true appearance: tall, handsome, dead white skin, black eyes with a hint of red in them, white hair cut rough like a mane to the top of his shoulder blades. He moved his hand sharply, and Zhu Guiren's paralysis lessened, though the pain remained.

"First," Zhu Guiren managed, pulling himself up to a kneeling posture and bowing his head. "Instruct this person, what has he done to earn discipline?"

"Little Third," First chortled, "such a charming child. Do you have to ask?" He tipped up Zhu Guiren's chin to look at him better.

Zhu Guiren stared back at him, unblinking, his heart hammering so loudly that he knew quite well that First could feel it. He felt nothing for himself, but Tainu, Tainu — how could he save him now? He felt anger too; if only he had left when he was told, if only he had flown away, then he'd be safe. Then, he would have nothing to fear, if only Tainu was not also captured. They would be doing things to him already...

He knew what they would do. He thought he might go mad thinking about it.

First smiled down at him, stroking the line of his jaw, pressing his fingers into the soft place under his chin.

Zhu Guiren swallowed, against his will.

"Let us review. You let a phoenix go. Back then, we had a long discussion, similar to this one. Don't you remember it?"

Zhu Guiren shook his head.

"Ah, you wouldn't," said First. "It broke your mind a bit, as I recall, but you were quite good after that, for a long time. Quite good. Only a little bit of disobedience here and there, and that doesn't bother me. Our strongest children are always like that, needing a little freedom. But then…" He tapped Zhu Guiren hard in the forehead acupoint; it echoed through all his frozen meridians and he screamed out loud with the pain of it. "You let another phoenix go. You took what you wanted, set your own array, and let the phoenix go into rebirth. And then, we had another conversation. You wouldn't remember that one either. When we were finished, I let you go again. So many chances! You were supposed to find another phoenix to make up for it. And you did."

First knelt down, smiling, to look in his eyes. "You didn't bring the phoenix to me, as you were supposed to. You refused my summons. But all that is done now." He reached out and kissed Zhu Guiren softly on the lips. "My dear little Third…This phoenix is rather special to you, is he not? It's so good to know my little Third has finally grown up."

He shook his head and closed his eyes, his heart hammering with terror.

"Oh, my dear," First said, not unkindly, "do you think that if you don't intend to tell me, you won't? We will have such a good talk." First caressed his face with his long, white fingers, and then kissed him again, long and hard.

Zhu Guiren tried to make his mind blank in preparation — tried to empty it of all thoughts of Tainu, of everything he knew and felt — though he knew in the end, everything in his mind and heart would be spread out bloody for this being's entertainment.

"Let's begin, little one."

Tainu felt himself tied down to the stone couch again. He struggled weakly, panicking, tried to use everything he had, but it wasn't enough. It was nothing. The demons binding him barely noticed. It was the same, the same place; they had brought him to the clan home.

Because he had chosen, for millennia, to live his life in the riskiest possible ways, there was very little abuse that could be heaped upon a mortal body that he had not already experienced at some point; he had long ago lost the illusion that there was some limit to cruelty, or any saving grace in it. He did not trust these people, so trust was not broken. He knew what to expect, so he was not surprised. Thus, what the demons had already done to him did not injure his mind or his heart — only his mortal body, and that healed. They had done things to him in ways he would not choose to remember, but that was nothing compared to seeing his demon there, his Arciniang, looking at him indifferently, as though he didn't know him. His hair had been cut brutally short, and his face was calm and unconcerned.

When he had been fully shackled at the neck, ankles, and wrists, his demon came over to him, looking down. Tainu met his eyes, knowing what would happen now if they had done so much to him that his demon could see him shackled to the stone couch without his expression even changing, without his eyes looking the least bit distressed. His single hand held a knife of ice and smoke. With his hair cut short, his face looked colder and more distant — a harsher beauty, each line of his face clear and unhidden.

"Bleed the phoenix," called the ancient demon, sitting in a comfortable chair some distance away to observe with visible delight.

Tainu knew that this must be First. He could sense the cold, murderous aura radiating from him.

Without hesitating, Zhu Guiren reached out and sliced deep into Tainu's left bicep. Blood poured out.

"Demon," he whispered desperately, "it's me. Please, don't you remember?"

Zhu Guiren's dark, clear eyes met his. "I remember," he said. "I remember everything."

He sliced again.

"No," Tainu said. "No." He felt his eyes filling with tears — from the pain of the deep cuts, from the pain of knowing his demon's hand was wielding the knife, from imagining what his demon must have suffered from them to now be like this.

First, sitting with his chin in his hand, smiled and said, "He does indeed remember everything, and his will is free. He's no puppet. He chooses to do this to you."

Zhu Guiren looked back at First. "I'm choosing it now. I may not always choose it. Don't push me."

First laughed. "Do you see? He's still himself."

Zhu Guiren cut him again.

Tainu looked into his face, trying to find a trace of him, the one that he knew. "Demon," he said, softly, "you still have your heart. Don't you feel it? Please. You don't want to do this. This isn't what you want. Why are you obeying him?"

First had heard him, despite his efforts to speak quietly, and replied, "His heart is still there. I've made some adaptations. But he remembers everything there once was between you. He's told me all about it. Did you know that? He remembers it even now, while he's cutting you." He laughed out loud. "Third!

Make him say your true name."

Zhu Guiren turned to him. "Why would I do that? My true name's not for you to hear."

"You see?" First laughed. "He's still himself."

The cuts were closing immediately. Tainu hadn't lost much blood yet. It would take much, much more damage before his wounds would cease to heal; he remembered that, as well. He stared up at his demon, the tears streaking his face despite himself, and said, uncertain, "Demon?"

Zhu Guiren knelt down next to him, and met his eyes, his expression earnest. "I remember what happened," he said quietly, his face close to Tainu's. "I remember that there were feelings between us, but I don't feel them anymore. I don't have any animosity toward you. I just see no reason for my life to be governed by what I once felt, and do not feel anymore. It's…inconvenient for me. And you are a phoenix, after all. We need the power your blood gives us. This is just how it has to be." He struggled for a moment.

Tainu watched him, his heart breaking.

"I'm not being cruel," he said at last. "This is how it is. This is just what's necessary, no more."

Tainu looked at him — his beautiful face, his eyes trying to communicate something to him that he understood well enough. "Even now," he said, "you are still who you are. You don't want to do this. Even now. Don't let him make you do it."

Zhu Guiren touched his cheek, frowning. "It is what it is," he said at last, and stood up again, and cut him, again.

"Leave us," First said, suddenly. "I have things to say to the phoenix."

Zhu Guiren bowed and left without a backward glance. The other demons followed.

First came over to Tainu and stared down at him for a while. Then, he said, "Second should be the one explaining this to you, but she's out doing other things." He sat down in a chair next to the head of the stone couch so Tainu could turn his head and look at him. "You are the eldest living phoenix," he said. "The one who created the refuges. Third has told me."

Tainu didn't respond.

First nodded. "But I am far, far older than you are. Older than you can comprehend. You, Third — both of you are only children to me, and Second, and the leaders of other clans. Children only just learning to walk. You should know that we eldest demons don't cultivate from mortals at all. We cultivate from the resentment of other demons. All we do is meant to cultivate the suffering and resentment of the demonic people so we can drink it, and it is far, far more powerful than mortal resentment."

Tainu began to understand, and looked away.

"We are not people who need our children to grow up and replace us, after all. Our children exist only to feed us. Third is now ready for harvesting. Thus," he waved his hand over Tainu's body, "I have cut the connections between his heart and his conscious awareness. This was rather pleasurable for me, although not for him. I'd like you to know that he's suffered a great deal since he's come back to me. As much as I could contrive without killing him outright or rendering him into useless meat, and it is probably something of a relief to him that he can't feel at the moment. You should also know that his heart is still very much there, and that insofar as I can comprehend such things, he still loves you. He is actually *feeling* in his heart everything he is doing to you. I imagine that inwardly, he is screaming without cease. It's only that he is not aware of what he is feeling, as though I had given him an anesthetic, kind and thoughtful as I am, for his current condition."

He steepled his fingers together. "At some point, I will heal those connections, and he will know his own heart again. He will feel it all, all at once. I anticipate that at that point, he is likely to kill himself. If he does not, I will kill him. There is no path here that does not end with his death, but the longer he doesn't feel, the longer he will live. You should understand this, as I believe it matters to you in some way."

Tainu's eyes were closed, but he could hear in First's voice that he was smiling as he mused, "I've never cultivated the resentment of a phoenix. Perhaps I'll try, this time around."

CHAPTER 15
THE GREAT ARRAY

It came so fast, when it came. Aili and Liu Chenguang were still awake, drowsy but talking and drinking in the main room, when Liu Chenguang held up a hand and said, "We need to go."

"What?" Aili asked. She was feeling a bit odd after breaking the array earlier and seeing Chenguang. She hadn't wanted to talk to her about it — it was too strange — but she suspected that Liu Chenguang had figured it out anyway.

Liu Chenguang got up and said, "My supplies for a journey are already packed, luckily. Just let me roll up the maps."

"What is it?" Aili stood and started rolling the maps with her.

"Give me that one." She stuffed them all in a bag that was ready near the door. "There's someone speaking Kunorese outside. I heard them go past. They may not be here for us right now, but if they are here at all, they'll come for us sometime tonight. My medicine and talismans are already packed…Tainu?" she whispered loudly.

Tainu came to the door of his room, wearing his sleeping clothes.

"Wake up the demon, we need to run," she said. "We'll split up, head into the mountains, and meet there. Me and Aili, you and him. Do you have the phoenix talismans?"

He patted the seam of his shirt. "Always," he said. "You?"

She nodded. "Go."

Aili knelt. "Hold tight," she said brusquely. "This will be faster than before."

She felt Liu Chenguang clambering onto her back and set herself into her breathing to prepare. *Thank goodness we got Yisue out*, she thought. She bent her head and listened carefully for talking, for footsteps, and decided that the stairs were clear for the moment.

"Now." Aili stood up and began racing for the mountains.

There were people in the yard; someone shot at her, someone yelled in Kunorese. Her heart was in her throat, not so much for herself and Liu Chenguang — she knew she could survive a gunshot and could probably even still keep running through it — but for Tainu and Zhu Guiren. They were still in the room, and the demon was far more vulnerable to injury.

Liu Chenguang had the same thought, Aili could tell, but she bent her head and said, "Keep going, we can help them by drawing some of them away."

Aili didn't spend breath responding. Her previous visit to Mount Shi with Liu Chenguang had been a pleasure jaunt, but this was a race and she was very, very fast. She didn't take the main road, but ran off to the side immediately and started leaping for the cliffs, looking to get away from the places that were easy for mortals to reach.

"How far?" she asked after three hours or so of qinggong, when they were deep into the craggy hills. She had gone slightly west along the edge of the highest peaks, avoiding the temples and the well-known roads.

Liu Chenguang said, "This should be good. I need a rest anyway, even if you don't." She got herself off Aili's back and stretched out. "I know you're faster and stronger than I am, but from here on in, I can manage with my own qinggong."

Aili felt her way around the rocks. "I thought so," she said, "there's a good place here to get under cover."

It wasn't quite a cave, but a deep depression within the rock face that created a small, dark room, invisible from above, below, or the side. Liu Chenguang brought the bags in and took out a blanket to lie on and another to cover them.

"So prepared," said Aili, smiling.

Liu Chenguang laid the blanket down. "Come over here," she said, and made Aili lie down first. "If I knew we would be doing this tonight, I would have made you rest more. I know I said your meridians aren't damaged, not like Zhu Guiren's situation, but whatever you did was exhausting for you and now you've been doing this." She settled down next to her and pulled the second blanket over both of them.

"I'm fine," Aili said. In fact, she didn't feel tired at all, and better than when she had been sitting in the room resting; qinggong was invigorating for her, though she knew it was much more challenging for Liu Chenguang. She was very aware of Liu Chenguang's body next to her beneath the blanket, and the rhythm of her breathing and heartbeat. Out loud she said, "What should we do now? Should we aim for Hongye?"

Liu Chenguang snuggled up against her for warmth, and Aili automatically put her arms around her to draw her in; she didn't think about it until it was already done, and her face was buried in Liu Chenguang's hair. She still had that scent about her — incense and bitter medicine, uniquely Liu Chenguang's scent — and she breathed it in deeply. Her hair was so soft and smooth. As natural as holding her or breathing her scent was to kiss her hair, so she did that too. She could feel Liu Chenguang's breathing quicken and her body, seemingly as instinctively, press back against her, molding to hers.

Aili stopped immediately. "Sorry," she said.

Liu Chenguang was silent, and then she said, "Don't be sorry." She turned over in Aili's arms and looked up at her, as though wondering about something.

Aili said, "Your eyes are so beautiful, Chenguang."

Liu Chenguang smiled. "I like to hear you call me Chenguang." The silence drew out between them for a while, but at last, she said, "Aili, we haven't really talked. Not about the important things."

Aili felt her heart drop and drew back a little bit, but Liu Chenguang shook her head.

"No, I didn't mean that. I want you close to me. Do you remember, back in Fallon?" She sounded a little nervous. "You asked me what I wanted?"

Aili remembered that, very well. "I was…in a very strange place, then," she said. "When I asked you that, I was…a little…not completely in my right mind."

"You never told me about it," she said. "About Edna Lee and Little Daxian, but not about what really happened to you when we left you."

"I know. It's very hard…" When she trailed off, she felt Liu Chenguang's hand close around hers encouragingly. Finally, she said, "Something snapped in me, or something that was hidden came out. All the things that were hidden, I think. All the things that had always been hidden, in both my lives."

Liu Chenguang looked at her with her beautiful eyes — dark and quiet, like the depthless, still water that received everything given to it — so Aili continued, "I destroyed Fallon with the phoenix fire, and a lot of other places, too. I was so angry, and I couldn't hurt the ones that I was angry at, so I hurt the ones that I could reach."

"Ah," said Liu Chenguang. She picked up Aili's hand, gently unfolding her fingers to kiss her palm.

"I killed some people," she said, because it seemed important that nothing she had done be secret. "Not many, not on purpose, but there were people who sometimes got in my way, and I wasn't clear enough in my mind to control what I was doing."

Liu Chenguang nodded.

"I'll be honest with you, Liu Chenguang. It felt…it felt very good to do it. But it also felt pointless, in the end. The rage never would go away. It was like a fire that would never stop. The more I fed it, the more there was. Each time I felt better, and then it would be gone, and I would need to do it again just for that small relief of the burning." She shook her head.

"Were you angry at me?" Liu Chenguang asked quietly.

"You were part of it," she said. "Because…"

"Because?"

"Because I loved you, and you…you loved Hong Deming. How could you love me instead?" She felt the tears come to her eyes unexpectedly, hot and aching.

Liu Chenguang closed her eyes. "Aili," she said. She reached up and pulled Aili down close to her.

"Aili," she said again, and kissed her eyebrows and her nose and lips, lightly, softly. "What I want– What I wanted then, and what I want now…We are who we are. We're not like other people who have only met once, who have only one life together, long or short. It's not only you who's not the same person you were a thousand years ago. We have two lives, and this is our second time to know one another and love one another. So that's what I want." She smiled at Aili, her eyes shining again. "I want you to be happy. If you decide that you don't love me in this life after all, then I want your happiness however you will find it, but my selfish hope is that you will love me again. That I can make you happy."

Aili nodded, unconvinced, but sighed a kiss back onto her lips.

Liu Chenguang said, "I bound you to me when you died, but that's not a magic talisman that makes you love me. I know that."

"Who says I don't? That's not–" Aili said, flustered. Liu Chenguang's body was so warm and welcoming in her arms; it felt so very different than her memories and yet the same. Of its own accord, her hand began to lightly stroke Liu Chenguang's waist, her smooth skin beneath the loose jacket, and then tease a little higher. Liu Chenguang gasped a little bit, and she stopped herself, embarrassed that that had happened. *What was she thinking?*

Liu Chenguang laughed and put her head down. "Aili," she said, teasing, "you don't need to stop."

Aili shook her head, and Liu Chenguang kissed her lightly, accepting.

"Why did you love me, that first life we had?" Liu Chenguang asked. "Why would you love such a strange person that caused you such problems? I know I wasn't your only option."

After some thought, Aili said at last, "I just always loved you. Since I first met you. Before I knew what it was." Because they were being very honest with one another, she added, "There could have been others. I could have chosen someone else. Maybe I would have loved them too, but it was you. It was you I loved, it was you that I wanted, and so that was my choice."

Liu Chenguang said, "Do you know why I loved you? Because you picked me up and held me, and I had never had kindness like that before. And then I came to you, and I saw who you were. Who you are. And so, I made all my choices because I loved you, and then I loved you because I had made those choices."

They held each other in silence for a while. The tension in Aili's body, the heat and yearning, slowly faded; she wasn't ready for that. Not yet. Aili felt Liu Chenguang's breathing even out, her body relaxing, felt her own body drifting off to sleep, her heart deeply peaceful. It was a feeling she hadn't had in a thousand years, since the inn at Gunan, before they had lost one another: kissing Liu Chenguang's lips, trusting there would be time for them, time for everything.

Aili woke first the next morning, just after dawn. The shadows of the peaks still hung heavy to the west, where they loomed out over the lower hills and the Sorrowful River valley. She went to the edge of the cliff and settled to cultivate, watching the bars of the morning sunlight slowly slip over the world in the cold clear air. When Liu Chenguang came out, stretching her arms wide, Aili surreptitiously watched to see the shape of her body, and then mentally slapped herself and tried to focus on cultivation again.

Liu Chenguang, uncaring, sat next to her and looked out over the world. "It's a beautiful morning," she said quietly. "I love the dawn time."

Aili nodded, "Yes," she said. "It reminds me of you," which just slipped out.

Liu Chenguang brushed against her shoulder, smiling. She whispered, then frowned. "Tainu isn't in the mountains. They're south of us. Not far from Shi'an."

"What do you think? Are they all right? Should we go find them?"

Liu Chenguang looked irresolute. "I don't know," she said at last. "Tainu can transform and should have been able to get to the mountains easily. If he didn't, it's because something happened to Zhu Guiren."

Aili stood. "We should go."

"Let me think," Liu Chenguang said. "It's broad daylight and you're a tall, blonde Federative for whom I'm sure they've put out alerts. If only one of us could transform…" She looked at Aili, obviously frustrated. "If they've found a safe place to hide, it would only make things more dangerous for us to go stomping close to them."

"Show me on the map," Aili suggested. "The direction you think he's in, and the distance if you have any sense of it."

Liu Chenguang chose one of her maps of the Shi'an countryside, whispered again, and then drew with her finger toward the southwest. "This is a flooded area," she said. "They won't be able to go much further in that direction unless they find a boat. They'll have to turn either north, toward us, or west to get into the next province."

Aili examined the map and Liu Chenguang's notes on it. "There's literally nothing in that area. If we go there and the Kunorese are searching for them, we'll certainly draw attention." She stood straight and looked out toward the south. "Does it matter, though? Not to brag about it, but even before I had the phoenix whip and near-immunity to gunshots, I could handle ordinary people fairly well."

Liu Chenguang snorted. "Do you really think you can just wade in there and take on the whole Kunorese army?"

Aili considered. "Barring artillery or air support."

"You are really quite full of yourself, Aili Fallon," said Liu Chenguang, her eyes narrowed in mock disapproval. "Well, while that is technically a solution, it's not a good one in my opinion. Let's call that our last option. A better one would be finding them without alerting the people that we have to assume are looking for them."

Aili looked at the map again. "Then we have to come from the other direction," she said. "We can course correct as we need to if they start moving, but if we go make a circle northwest and then back south, I don't think we can possibly make things worse for them. Tainu will also be looking for you, won't he?"

They used qinggong to get back down to the plains west of the mountains and began picking their way west and slightly north. The ground was sodden and flooded in places, and mostly very empty. They walked in silence, listening to the sound of waterfowl splashing and calling to one another. There was almost nothing else to hear.

Liu Chenguang whispered under her breath every few hours and confirmed that Tainu was still in the previous location. "I'm worried that he hasn't set out to look for me yet," she said. "He's not moving at all. He could certainly fly to us from where he is now."

"Zhu Guiren could be hurt?"

"But then he would surely have healed him…"

Aili said, "I think that Tainu wouldn't leave Zhu Guiren alone for that long to fly to us, and Zhu Guiren wouldn't want him to go on his own either. We'll have to get closer."

Liu Chenguang whispered again, late that night. "They've started moving," she said, relieved. "Or Tainu has, anyway. He's free to move as he wills, so it must be all right. He must just be moving slowly for Zhu Guiren's sake."

"He does a lot for Zhu Guiren's sake," Aili remarked.

Liu Chenguang rolled her eyes. "I know. Not at all who I anticipated as a brother-in-law."

"I will admit, he has somewhat grown on me," Aili said. "I think he's a very lonely person."

"I don't think he can really blame anyone but himself and his charming personality for that," Liu Chenguang said wryly, but then added, "it's true, though. Tainu's always been very lonely too. I never realized until I saw how happy he was to have someone he could talk to, even if it was Zhu Guiren. It's…it's nice that they have each other. If that's what's happening."

Despite knowing that Tainu was on the move, getting closer to him wasn't easy, since neither of them could fly. A flooded area lay between them and where Liu Chenguang thought Tainu was.

"There's just, just nothing," said Liu Chenguang, days later, as they retraced their steps trying to find a place where it became shallow enough to cross. Already, they had had to turn back three times at sudden channels, one of which nearly swept Liu Chenguang away before Aili swam over to catch her and bring her back.

Aili shook her head. "I'd suggest swimming, but these currents and the depth are so unpredictable." She thought she could probably make it herself, but Liu Chenguang didn't seem to be a strong swimmer. She wrung out her clothes and Liu Chenguang carefully patted all the talismans dry.

Finally, Aili said, "Let's look at this another way. Our real destination is across the Sorrowful River, isn't it? Why don't we just look for the main channel and a way to cross? There must be bridges somewhere. They can follow and meet us there, or we can try to walk along the north side and find another bridge closer to them. Didn't you say that the flooding was only south, not north? They didn't break the northern levees."

Liu Chenguang nodded slowly. "All right."

They worked their way along the side of the flood channel, going more directly north toward the great barrier of the river itself, the dike rising high above the land where it hadn't been breached against the Kunorese. Because the original breach of the dike had been further southwest, the river level was relatively low within the levees here, and they were able to find a usable bridge without much difficulty within four days, though they had to keep a watch out for Kunorese patrols. By the time they crossed, it was almost night, and Liu Chenguang found them a room at an inn near the edge of a mid-size town. Aili jumped up into the window after she was inside.

Liu Chenguang pulled clean clothes out of one of the bags. "I'm sorry. They're all kind of wet, but maybe less filthy?" she said helplessly, then sighed.

Aili took them from her silently and laid them out in front of the room's brazier. "Let's hope for the best for tomorrow. Go have a bath, I'll go next."

While Liu Chenguang took the bathing room, Aili stood at the window, musing. There was something strange about the night, or the place. Something about having crossed the Sorrowful River. She could no longer remember where she had crossed as Hong Deming, during those last days of his life; he had been more or less delirious with infection, she realized, looking back. The river itself had moved, and the floods had changed everything, but there was something here. Her mind drifted, as though the river had its currents, and she were on it, beyond her own volition.

When Liu Chenguang came out in her nightclothes, toweling her hair dry, she came over to where Aili stood staring out the window, arms behind her back. "What is it?" she asked softly.

"Don't you feel it?" Aili asked.

Liu Chenguang closed her eyes. "No," she said, "but I don't know what I would feel."

"When I find an array," Aili said, dreamily, "it repeats over and over in front of me. I wonder what I'll see in the great array?"

"Aili," said Liu Chenguang next to her. She put herself in front of her, blocking the view of the window. "Aili," she said more sharply.

Aili shook her head. "What?" she asked in a more normal tone of voice. "Chenguang? Are you done in the bath?"

Liu Chenguang looked up at her.

"Chenguang? Are you all right?"

Liu Chenguang asked slowly, "Who are you?"

"Hong Deming," Aili said, smiling.

Liu Chenguang felt all the hair on her skin rise. "Aili," she said. "Aili."

Aili's blue eyes focused. "Yes," she said a little impatiently, "I'm here."

"Aili," said Liu Chenguang, very seriously, "come away from the window." She put her hands on Aili's shoulders and deliberately turned her around so that she was facing into the room. "Come with me." She walked backward, pulling her away from the window. "Look at my face," she said. "Look at my eyes, don't look back there."

"Liu Chenguang?" Aili asked as Liu Chenguang made her sit on the bed. "What's happening?"

Liu Chenguang sat firmly on her lap, putting her knees on either side of Aili's hips so she couldn't get up again and she couldn't see anything but her.

"Liu Chenguang?"

"Aili, listen. You became very strange when you went to the window. Are you sensing the great array is somewhere near here?"

Aili closed her eyes. "Yes. It's near."

"Is it having an effect on you?"

"I don't know...Chenguang?"

"I'm here."

Aili's eyes were still closed, but she reached her hands up into Liu Chenguang's hair and pulled her down into a kiss.

Liu Chenguang sat still in shock, feeling Aili's hand on the nape of her neck, the pressure of her lips and tongue entwining hers in the way she remembered so well, but was so different now.

"Chenguang," she murmured, "you're all right. I found you. I've been so afraid..."

She struggled to pull herself away, but Aili was much stronger and pulled her in more tightly. "Aili," she said helplessly, "No, not like this– please–"

Aili shook her head and let go of her. "What? Liu Chenguang, what's happening?" She seemed to suddenly realize what she had been doing and tried to back away from Liu Chenguang on the bed.

Liu Chenguang said, "Tell me who you are."

"I'm Aili," she said, looking at her, hurt.

"Where are we?"

"Somewhere in the Daxian Republic, north of the Sorrowful River. We just crossed..." Aili's eyes lost focus.

"Who are you?"

"I'm Hong Deming. Chenguang, don't you know me?" The exact same hurt expression crossed her face. It would have been funny if it wasn't so horrifying.

"Where are we?" Liu Chenguang asked, keeping her voice calm. "Why are we here?"

"I came looking for you," Aili said. "You've been gone so long. I've been looking for such a long time…I've checked all the battlefields. I always have to check the bodies to see if you're there. I've been so afraid that I'll find you that way…"

An expression of such pain crossed her face that Liu Chenguang's heart clenched inside her. Panicking, Liu Chenguang tried to think what was best to do. She said, "Deming, you've already found me. It's all finished now. It's been finished for a long, long time."

Was it a ghost? was Aili possessed? But Hong Deming could have no ghost, he was alive, just as she was.

But they must be near the place that Hong Deming had died.

Liu Chenguang hid her face behind her hands; Aili's hands gently covered them and removed them.

"Liu Chenguang?" she asked, looking at her. "Liu Chenguang, there's something wrong, isn't there? Because we're near the array. That's why you're asking all these questions. Am I–" she swallowed. "Am I forgetting who I am?"

Liu Chenguang nodded, putting her hands on either side of Aili's face and leaning forward so their foreheads touched. She felt, suddenly, a huge and unexpected fury that this was happening to Aili. "Let's destroy it. Let's just go do it now. But you have to always look at me. Promise that you'll always look at me. Think of what you'll see on the battlefield — of what you're going to see — get it all into your mind now, and then remember that I'm real. That it's me you need to look at. Remember that I'll always tell you what is real and true."

Aili took a deep breath and nodded. "Chenguang, I don't know how long the battle went on before I got there, or how long after I died," she said at last. "We may have to wait for hours, or even a day before we get to…where it happened. Where Taiqian did what he did to you."

Liu Chenguang nodded.

"When I do these things…when I break arrays," Aili continued, "I've been… what happens is…"

Liu Chenguang took her hands. "Look at me," she said gently. "Look at me, Aili." She leaned down and kissed her. "I'm real. You're real. We're real together. What is in the past is only a memory of what happened. You don't have to be afraid of it. You don't have to be afraid of talking about it with me or describing it."

Her kiss had been only for comfort, to help Aili focus, but she unexpectedly felt a rush of arousal, sitting straddling Aili's hips like this, and closed her eyes. This was obviously not the time. Aili also seemed to feel it and come to the same conclusion, drawing back very slightly. Neither of them mentioned it.

She cleared her throat and kept her eyes on Liu Chenguang's. "What happens is at a certain point, when the event is done and the victors or survivors have left the area, Zhu Guiren appears and pours your blood. The way I'm able to stop it is by placing my hands into your blood, catching it in my hand with the phoenix fire, and calling your true name."

Liu Chenguang's eyes widened. "How did you figure out that would break an array?"

"Trial and error," Aili said, with a little of her familiar half-smile. She reached up to Liu Chenguang's nape and pulled her down to kiss her, again, even more thoroughly.

This time, Liu Chenguang felt almost dizzy with excitement as their mouths met — as Aili's hand caressed her jawline and throat, feeling the outline of her ear — and then they parted again, both breathing quickly.

Liu Chenguang said, "What...I..."

Aili shook her head, confused. "That was me," she said, and took a deep breath. "Not Hong Deming."

Liu Chenguang nodded, shaking a little bit. "What's happening? I don't want– I don't want us to...just because of the array," she choked out.

"I know. This isn't right," Aili said. She put her arms around her and held her for a moment. "Not that I don't also want to kiss you," she added, "but it's as though the world is fragmenting. Things aren't holding together the way they should..."

Liu Chenguang felt it now too — the sense that there were too many realities overlying each other in this place, conflicting and opposing powers, something trying to tear down, something else building up, a net across the world that was being realigned, pulling everything in a different direction — and suddenly she realized what it was. "There's another demon," she said. "Another demon is trying to take over the array. Zhu Guiren said that might happen. It's– it's undoing things, and then re-doing them in a different direction."

"I wish Zhu Guiren and Tainu were here," Aili hugged Liu Chenguang one more time, firmly, and said, "But I think it's going to have to be just us."

Liu Chenguang nodded.

"Can you transform?" Aili asked. "Your wings might help keep us focused — protect us from whatever's flying around, at least a little bit."

She nodded again.

"Get your talismans and your weapons…Something to tie our hands together, in case we get disoriented by whatever is happening out there…And something to blindfold me."

They felt their way out past the last buildings in the town toward some low hills. Houses had been built on them, but not many, and most of them were unlit, unoccupied. Crows flew and cawed in the dark above them as Aili, blindfolded, directed Liu Chenguang toward where she felt the center was. The illusions had become dizzying for her, the ghosts disappearing and reappearing, changing direction around her as though north was now south, everything rearranging like iron filings shifting their shapes in response. Aili tried to find the magnetic pole that drew everything to it, and said, "There's two centers — the old one and the new one. The old one is straight ahead. The new one is to our right."

Quietly, Liu Chenguang said, "Straight ahead is a low place between hills. To our right is a hillside."

Aili nodded. "The old center is what we need. Take me straight in. On that hillside, there's probably the demon that's trying to take the array. Try to stay away from it. Once I tell you to stop, sit down and don't move till I tell you."

Liu Chenguang led her in, grass brushing against her legs. There was no other sound until she felt a tingling in her body, and there it was — the screams and the sound of broken flesh.

"Sit down here," she said.

"We're near an abandoned house," Liu Chenguang said, pulling her down to sit. "There are some trees ahead of us–"

Aili shook her head. "None of that matters," she said, trying not to sound unkind, but her head was going to explode with the noise. She took off the blindfold and looked.

In the dim light of the stars, the battle was shadowy and unclear, for which she was profoundly grateful. She looked for the copse of trees where she remembered Chenguang had been trapped, but there were several and of course, it had been a thousand years. The real trees and the trees of the ancient battle were no longer the same. She had come in from the top of one of the hills last time, probably where the demon was waiting now. She didn't care about that demon, though undoubtedly it would care about her once it realized she was breaking the array, but Zhu Guiren had said that demons wouldn't be alerted to her as a danger. She was just a mortal, not worth their attention. Her priority was destroying this evil thing.

It was evil. She hadn't really thought about it in that way before. As awful as Zhu Guiren was, she rarely thought of him as evil, but the array itself was an evil thing. They would break it tonight, she thought fiercely. Not one more day.

She stood up and tried to gauge where the battle was and if it looked at all familiar to her. The generals on their hillsides helped her reorient, but truly everything was changed around, not only her own different angle of view. There was a copse of trees not far from them; was that Chenguang there?

"Hong Deming."

She turned around and saw an older man in blue cultivator's robes, handsome and proud, only the faintest hint of gray in his hair and beard. His sword was strapped across his back, and he stood next to a beautiful man in traveling robes. Zhu Guiren.

"Hong Deming," the cultivator said again, more fiercely.

She saluted formally. "Taiqian," she responded.

Liu Chenguang whispered, "Aili?"

"It's all right," she said softly. "I know who I am."

"How dare you call me Taiqian," he said, but it was said weakly. Taiqian looked at her with such weariness in his eyes.

"Taiqian," she said more gently, "get away from Zhu Guiren. Walk with me." She put her hand down to Liu Chenguang, and murmured, "They can't see you or hear you, Liu Chenguang, but I still can. Tie your hand to mine and come with me. Wake me up if I seem to be getting…away from myself."

She felt Liu Chenguang's hand tie the ribbon around both of theirs — loosely, so that she could free herself quickly if she needed to — and felt the tug as they began walking. Nothing else was solid around them: the shadows of the men dying and killing moved and shifted everywhere; the trees seemed to change their positions; the bloody stream was partly beneath her feet and partly above her head, as though she was swimming in the blood cauldron. To one side, Zhu Guiren stood, a fixed point, but everything else was slowly tugged toward a new pole.

Zhu Guiren, Hong Deming, Liu Chenguang if she found him — they alone were not real here. All the souls surrounding them were real, the souls of the dead who had fought the same battle and died the same deaths for a thousand years. Because Zhu Guiren's soul wasn't in the array, he didn't notice that Taiqian had walked away from him, nor could he see Aili. Taiqian was more solid than Liu Chenguang in Aili's sight, but she knew that Liu Chenguang was there; she could feel the weight of her, always tugging on the ribbon as they walked together. Every so often Aili said, "Liu Chenguang," and she would hear her voice respond, "I'm here."

Taiqian said, "Who are you talking to?"

"It's Liu Chenguang, Taiqian," she said. "Do you know what has happened?"

"I don't know. It seems that things happen, and then they happen again. But things can only happen once, can't they?" He looked at her, questioning. "I'm so tired."

She nodded.

"Liu Chenguang is dead," he said suddenly. "Zhu Guiren lied to me."

"I know. He lied to all of us."

"But I can never– I can never stop doing it," he said, confused as a child. "Even though I know it's always the same, even though the end is never different, I have to keep doing it. I kill Liu Chenguang. I cut him and make him bleed, I cut off his arms and legs, and then, I cut off his head and the fire comes. There's never any other ending."

"Do you want another ending?"

"Yes," he said. "I wish I could stop doing it. I wish I had never done it."

Aili felt Taiqian's hand grab her shoulder.

"I see you too. I see you dead, every time. And I step over your dead body as though you meant nothing to me. I wish that I could tell you that wasn't true. I wish that I could go back and never meet Zhu Guiren, never bring Liu Chenguang back with us, so things could have been what they should have been for you." His face twisted as though he was trying not to cry. "Are you a ghost?" he asked. "Are you Hong Deming's ghost come to haunt me? But everything is haunted, all the time, forever."

"Liu Chenguang," she said, needing to know what was real.

Liu Chenguang's voice came, "I'm here."

Aili couldn't see her anymore, but she could feel that Liu Chenguang had taken her hand. Knowing Liu Chenguang could hear her too, she said, "Taiqian, it's all done now. It's long gone for me. For Liu Chenguang, too. We forgive you. I'm not here to haunt you. I'm here to set you free."

He said, "Is Liu Chenguang here too?"

"She's here."

"Can I speak to him?"

"She can't hear you or speak to you," Aili said. Given how Taiqian felt about

Liu Chenguang, it was just as well, she thought.

But to her surprise, Taiqian said sadly, "If he could hear me, I would also tell him that I am sorry. I was tricked. But even if I hadn't believed Zhu Guiren's lies, I was not kind to him. He had a burden none of us understood, and I failed him as his Taiqian. For no reason except I was tired and didn't want another disciple, I didn't like him. I should never have taken him as a disciple, not because there was something wrong with him, but because my abilities were limited. I was too old to change for him."

"I'll tell her," Aili said. "But she was your last disciple. Taiqian, when Crane Moon vanished from the earth, it was only Liu Chenguang who remembered you."

"I never truly treated him as my disciple," Taiqian said. "I am sorry. Tell him."

This was what it meant to be a resentful ghost, Aili realized — forever tormented by failures and pain, always lost among the most terrible version of one's life and death, never able to make amends or receive redress, never to be free of it. She looked up at the thousands of men on the battlefield, trapped in this reality for a thousand years. At last, she said to Taiqian, "It's good to be sorry for mistakes, Taiqian, but it's more important to try to do something different. Something better."

"What could it be?" he asked sadly.

"Bring me with you when it's time," she said. "Just bring me with you."

"Time has no meaning here. It is always time."

The phoenix fire was now part of the horizonless, perspectiveless world, mixing with the blood and the ghosts. Zhu Guiren was firm and solid against it, his outline clearly marked, as Taiqian stepped over a body and stood next to him. Aili looked down and saw Hong Deming.

"Liu Chenguang," she said, panicked, but she could no longer feel or hear her. The only remnant of Liu Chenguang now was that she couldn't freely move her left arm.

Hong Deming was lying on his back, his eyes closed. There was blood on his mouth and all over his torn robes. Aili saw himself — a young man, handsome once, like the thousands of others who had died and would die on the battlefield, his long hair clotted with blood, his body full of wounds, all of his dreams and hopes and efforts come to nothing. There was a sword next to him. En.

Aili twisted her right hand and called En to it; the En that had lain on the ground disappeared. Carefully, she said, "Liu Chenguang, I can't see you or hear you or feel you. If you're here, I need you. Come closer to me."

She felt something touching her, as though arms were around her. She looked down and saw Liu Chenguang, an arrow in his lung, breathing shallowly through lips thick with blood. *"Chenguang,"* she said, panicked, then she felt Liu Chenguang's lips on hers and closed her eyes to focus on that. She reached up her left hand, shaking, and felt Liu Chenguang's hand against her shoulder. "Stay," she said. "Stay there till I tell you to move, I need you close to me."

The hand against her shoulder touched her face, gently.

Liu Chenguang said, "Let me hold his hand."

Zhu Guiren said, "That's a dead man, phoenix. Holding his hand isn't going to change anything."

Liu Chenguang looked at Zhu Guiren, and he looked back.

Liu Chenguang said, "Please."

Aili saw that Zhu Guiren's eyes flickered — as though something had hurt him or confused him — but it passed quickly. "Zhu Guiren," she tried, but he couldn't hear her.

Zhu Guiren laughed and put Hong Deming's dead hand in Liu Chenguang's.

"Chenguang," she said, shaking all over now, and she felt Chenguang's arms holding her tightly, Chenguang's body nestled against her. "Untie my hand," she whispered. When her arm was free, she touched Liu Chenguang's back with her left hand, feeling the warmth of her wings, and said, "Be careful."

Aili reached out with her left hand and called the phoenix whip.

Taiqian began to cut Liu Chenguang. His blood spilled softly on the ground. Aili made a whimpering sound, feeling the warmth of Chenguang's embrace. She had to think. It would be soon; what could she do to block it, to undo the final seal that held the array together?

"Taiqian, stop cutting. Stop now," she tried, but it was as though he didn't hear her at all.

She said, "Liu Chenguang, please. Can you hear me?" and felt Liu Chenguang reach up to kiss her, but Liu Chenguang remained on the ground, bleeding, almost unconscious now.

She said, "Chenguang, step back."

Liu Chenguang let go of her, and she knelt next to Liu Chenguang and kissed him.

He opened his eyes; Aili couldn't tell if he saw her.

"Liu Chenguang," she said, "I love you. I will be with you again. Don't be afraid."

She cried out, "Chenguang!" and felt Liu Chenguang's hand on her head, stroking her hair.

"He's unconscious," Taiqian said.

Zhu Guiren's voice came, "Dismemberment and decapitation. In that order."

Taiqian argued, and Zhu Guiren's persuasive voice smoothed over it, and Aili tried to think through all the madness of her heart. The agitation of the world surrounding them grew even greater. The few of them — Taiqian, Zhu Guiren, Liu Chenguang, and Hong Deming — were the only stable things; everything else was a wash of patternless color and senseless movement.

When Taiqian's sword came down for the first time, she tried to block it with En.

The second time, the phoenix whip.

She couldn't block the sword.

Liu Chenguang screamed only once. His body was now so mutilated that if she looked down, she knew she was very likely to lose her mind.

"Chenguang," she sobbed. Aili knew that Liu Chenguang was nearby, but she couldn't touch her anymore. "Chenguang, I can't feel you anymore. Stand away from me. I don't want to hurt you."

The third time, she screamed in rage and loss and frustration that she was here for nothing, for nothing.

On the fourth cut, she threw herself in front of the sword. It came down anyway. She felt nothing but a sharp tingle in her skin.

She turned herself on top of Liu Chenguang's body to face Taiqian's sword, her eyes streaming with tears. As the last strike came down, she held up her hands full of phoenix fire and called out, "Eftahede."

The sword went through her hands, through her body, through Liu Chenguang, and the world exploded.

CHAPTER 16
MEETING SECOND

Liu Chenguang watched Aili live through their deaths again in the empty, silent field, only the night wind in the grass around them, and became more and more desperate to touch her, to bring her back. When Aili held up the phoenix fire and cried out her true name, she leapt over to catch her as she dropped to the earth, wrapping them both in her wings as they rolled in the grass. The air, the earth, all beings shook as though a great earthquake wrenched the foundations of reality. From the hillside, she heard a shriek of pain and rage and the cawing of many crows, flying off into the distance.

Aili was unconscious beneath her, breathing weakly; whatever she had done had taken enormous amounts of power. Liu Chenguang checked her pulse, and then tried to feel whether her meridians were damaged. She wished Tainu was there since he was so much better with cultivational injuries, but as far as she could tell, Aili was uninjured beyond draining all her qi. It would heal naturally, in time, but for now, she was unconscious on the cold, wet ground, and Liu Chenguang wasn't strong enough to bring her back to the warm inn.

She was shaken by the power released by the breaking of the array herself. This was far beyond what she had imagined. The very energy of the mountains and rivers had shifted, and the net of qi over the earth had been remade. Something had echoed in her as well — some things that had been caught and frozen in regret were free now to move and flow toward their true destinations.

Liu Chenguang looked at the woman lying beneath her and kissed her, very gently, holding her in her arms. She looked around for a place to take Aili, the best she could find, and she felt lucky that it was close, was a little shack that had probably once belonged to a farm. She apologized mentally to Aili and dragged her unceremoniously over. It was long abandoned, but the straw still inside was good enough. Liu Chenguang tried to get her comfortable on the straw, wrapped her body and wings around Aili, and slept.

Aili didn't wake that night or the next day, but Liu Chenguang's constant checks of her pulse showed nothing of concern beyond exhaustion. After she tried to make their little hovel more comfortable, she found some water which she dribbled into Aili's mouth and was relieved when her tongue licked at it, responding to reality appropriately. She also checked Tainu's location; that was more concerning. While they were in the array, he had suddenly gone far to the west, past Zai'an. Had he started flying for some reason? Had the time in the array been much longer than it seemed? Why was he going in that direction?

Sometime after midnight, Aili opened her eyes. "Liu Chenguang," she said immediately.

Liu Chenguang was already lying down next to her and holding her, but she said, "I'm here."

Aili looked at her, silently, her eyes a deep blue that Liu Chenguang could see even in the dark. "It's done," she said. "Isn't it?"

Liu Chenguang nodded, propping herself up on one elbow to look down at her face. "I feel it. I feel that something's broken. Something that needed to be broken — like a chain that I never knew was on me."

Aili nodded and said, "Yes." She reached up to bring Liu Chenguang's face close to her lips and kissed her, softly and then ever more deeply, pulling Liu Chenguang down to lie half on top of her and stroking the back of her neck beneath her hair. "Do you love me yet?" she asked with her little half-smile.

Liu Chenguang kissed her hand and nodded. She smiled at Aili again, teasing, "And I want to take you back to that inn, because there are things I want to do with you that I don't want to do in this straw."

Immediately, she realized she hadn't really been teasing after all. Her heart started racing when she looked at Aili's mouth and the shape of her hands, and felt the strength of her body, and realized that Aili's eyes were very serious about this. Before it could go any further, both of them froze. There was a sound of beating wings outside.

Aili looked up at the ceiling of the little shack. "Liu Chenguang," she whispered, "get your weapons and your talismans ready."

Outside, in the darkest part of the night, they heard crows cawing. Many of them — so many that they could hear the beating of their wings descending all around the little shed. There was no other sound.

Liu Chenguang looked out through a crack in the door. There were dozens of them, all silently sitting in the grass around the little shanty, all of them staring at the building where they were. She met Aili's eyes.

Aili nodded slowly and leaned to whisper in her ear: "Are you ready?"

Liu Chenguang showed her the deerhorn knives.

Aili smiled and kissed her cheek. "Be ready when I jump, I'll draw them away first," she whispered again. "Run for the river. If we're separated, I'll find you, just get to a safe place. Don't worry about me."

With only a moment's gathering of her energy, Aili lashed out at the ceiling with the phoenix fire whip, setting it on fire, and leapt upwards at the same time, gaining height through qinggong and then coming down on the other side of the ranked crows. As she landed, she flipped so that she was facing the demons and lashed out again, catching several in the flame.

While the crows were distracted, Liu Chenguang leapt out as well and made it to Aili's side.

"Run first," said Aili sharply.

Liu Chenguang ran, no need for pointless heroics. She knew that Aili was faster and stronger and would cover her retreat; she herself was Aili's vulnerable point. *But where to retreat to?* There was nothing in front of them but the high levee of the river, nothing around them but empty fields and shallow hills, nowhere to hide. The sense of unreality returned to her — the landscape where she and Hong Deming had died, the landscape with no cover, no safe place.

She ran and ran, hearing the caws and shrieks of the crows behind her, but other things, too. She risked looking behind her and saw that there were many demons in their mortal bodies chasing them, some fighting Aili, who was surrounded by a circle of them with their various weapons. Others were chasing her, and were getting closer. There were so many of them. For the first time she felt fear. She couldn't transform; if there was no safe place to run to, she wouldn't be able to get away.

Aili broke away from the demons surrounding her, using only the phoenix whips in both hands, each whip lashing out more than twenty feet on each side and setting all the grass on fire. When Aili caught up to her, Liu Chenguang saw that her face was set in rage and felt a sense of dread. Together they turned and ran, Liu Chenguang striving to match Aili's speed, faster than she had ever imagined she could run, but her heart was clamoring in her chest and even with qinggong, she couldn't defeat the flight of a bird.

"The river," Aili said sharply. "Can you swim, Chenguang? Be honest."

"No," she said. "Not well."

Aili swore and turned. "Behind me," she said. "Chenguang. Get behind me."

They were at the top of the levee, the river at their backs, with nowhere to go. The crows fluttered down around them in a multi-ranked half-circle and transformed, dozens of them; she had never seen so many demons in one place.

A woman stepped out in front of them. Dawn was just starting to lighten the sky, and by its light Liu Chenguang could see that she was very beautiful — smiling, tall, with golden skin, black hair braided with gold, and deep blue eyes. "Hello, my dears," she said. "Zhu Guiren sends his greetings." She turned to the demons surrounding them. "The phoenix is damaged and doesn't require a shackle. Neither of them can transform. Both of them are capable of healing themselves. No need to hold back, only avoid amputation and decapitation."

Liu Chenguang pushed out to stand in front of Aili.

"Liu Chenguang!" she said sharply, and tried to pull her back.

"Aili, jump in the river," she said, quick and low. "Go now. You can escape. You can come find me. Otherwise, there's no hope for anyone to come help us. They must have Zhu Guiren, and they probably already have Tainu."

Aili looked at her, already angry with her, she could tell, opening her mouth to argue.

Liu Chenguang reached up and closed her mouth by kissing her, smiling. "Go now," she said. "I trust you." It seemed as though time slowed down so that she could say what she needed — could look up to Aili's eyes and say, "You'll come. I'm not afraid."

She looked at her face so she would remember it when the pain would come. Then she pushed her, hard, from the top of the levee to fall twenty feet into the river's murky currents, and turned to face the demons, deerhorn knives in hand.

Aili had never been so angry while needing to focus on her breathing at the same time. The water of the Sorrowful River was so filled with silt that it was a deep yellow brown, completely opaque and gritting finely in her mouth and eyes. She knew that as long as she remained underwater, there was no possible way the demons would find her. But she didn't want to stay underwater. She wanted to get back up that levee and pick up Liu Chenguang and take her somewhere safe, and then yell at her for several hours.

However, this was not an option. The river was deep and wide here between the steep dikes, and without anything to stand on, she couldn't jump up even with qinggong. She would have to swim until she found some way out — a bridge, or a boat, or a dock, or anything sticking out into the water. The current was strong, and there was no easy way out. At least, not here.

She swore mentally, using all the best curses she'd heard during several months at sea and on a Navy base, and then began to swim purposefully toward the southern side of the riverbed. There, the levees had been breached — some deliberately as a defense against Kunoru, others accidentally as the entire levee wall had been weakened afterward. Nonetheless, it was more than an hour before she could find a place to pull herself out, and yell "FUCK!" at the sky. The phoenix whip came to her hand in pure rage, and she lashed at the river for no other purpose than to get her fury out at something she couldn't hurt. Then, she sat down and tried to think.

She whispered Liu Chenguang's true name and saw the path immediately move west. They had already taken her. She put her face in her hands and took several shuddering breaths, trying to get her terror for Liu Chenguang under control, trying to erase the images in her mind of Liu Chenguang on the stone couch, his blood falling softly into the basin, trying to think.

They had Zhu Guiren. Almost certainly, that was true — they had known how to find the seal of the great array, they had been able to begin to subvert it toward a new demonic owner. She was quite sure that that wouldn't be possible unless Zhu Guiren was incapacitated. He had said that his death would destroy the array, but the array had still been functioning. Therefore, he wasn't dead. He had said that powerful demons would try to take the array before his death. It was possible that since that the array was now destroyed, they would kill him anyway.

If they had Zhu Guiren, they almost certainly had Tainu as well. Tainu wouldn't have left Zhu Guiren; he would have stayed, as she should have stayed with Liu Chenguang. If Liu Chenguang wanted to try something like this, she could have said so; they could have jumped together, she could have helped her swim too. Of course, it would have been more dangerous and difficult with a weak swimmer but now…now. She clenched her fist and struck the ground next to her over and over, fire wisping out and suffocating in the mud. Damn her. No time, no time for this, no time to be angry or afraid for her. She had to move.

Would they all be brought to one place? She would have to hope so.

The golden white light to Liu Chenguang led her back upstream, along the course of the river. She shook herself out and began to run. Liu Chenguang couldn't transform. They couldn't fly with her. They had a head start, but they were on foot too.

Liu Chenguang couldn't kill anyone with her knives, but she managed to disarm two of the demons and use talismans on three before they took her down. She thought that this was probably a record for a phoenix. There was something so glad in her heart that she had been able to do something at last, and not only and always have to hide behind Aili and depend on others to defend her. Although she knew Aili would be furious, she also knew that Aili would come for her. This was the best plan. She could distract them and let Aili get away safely. Nothing could be done to her that wouldn't be healed.

"My dear," said the black-haired woman, walking up to her, "really, a pleasure to meet a phoenix who can demonstrate some self-respect when approached."

Two demons held her, one on either side. She had been injured — stabbed and slashed — but these had already healed. The black-haired woman reached out and took her deerhorn knives, calmly broke them between her hands, and threw them in the river. She then stood looking at Liu Chenguang. Just looking.

Liu Chenguang stared back at her, trying not to waver. But it was hard.

"Where is the other one?" she asked the demons holding Liu Chenguang.

"Answering Second, in the river," spoke up one of them. "Fourteen of the low ranked have gone to fly over the north and south shores to see where she comes up."

"Hmph," said the woman. "I want her. Until she is found, none of you return. If she is not found, none of you live."

Every demon there, crow or mortal-bodied, except the two holding Liu Chenguang, bowed their heads and immediately started running or flying downstream.

The woman walked around Liu Chenguang thoughtfully. "Show me the talisman," she said.

Liu Chenguang didn't respond.

The woman flicked her hand to hold a dagger and casually stabbed her in the eye.

Liu Chenguang screamed, and would have fallen to the ground, except she was being held upright by the two immobile demons. Hot blood dripped down her cheek, her eye blinded. In all her life, she had never had such an injury. Of course, she could and would heal from it, but the shock stunned her into tears and the tears hurt more because the tears flowed out through her broken skin, into her torn and mangled eye socket, stinging with salt.

The woman licked her dagger and released it, watching her.

"Third calls you the little phoenix, did you know?" she said, watching as Liu Chenguang sobbed and screamed. "He is quite fond of you in his way, or used to be. He told us that you can't transform anymore because you somehow have transferred some power to your lover — quite a bizarre story — so I can see that you are a creative little person, a problem solver. But my dear, don't delude yourself that you can change what is happening to you right now. There's no need to think I don't already know what I'm asking you. Third has already explained the talismans to me. I just want to see what it looks like…Just curiosity."

Liu Chenguang's eye had healed itself and she looked up, shaking, to see the woman's face very close to her — tipped first one way, then the other, as though trying to understand something. The woman brought her dagger out again, cut her own lips till they bled, and then drew the dagger's razor edge down Liu Chenguang's face. She traced a complex pattern for her own amusement, and then licked Liu Chenguang's blood while Liu Chenguang tried not to scream in disgust, feeling her tongue on her face.

"Hmmm," the demon said, her blood mixing with Liu Chenguang's in her mouth. "I've always wanted to try that, to see if phoenix blood heals if it's taken without your gift. Apparently not." She smiled and traced another design, this time below Liu Chenguang's throat, carving into the thin skin over her breastbone. "This is quite fun, how I can cut you and you'll heal over and over…There are many things we can do with your blood when it's taken unwillingly. No need to be concerned. Nothing is wasted. We're quite grateful." She put her head down on Liu Chenguang's breast and licked more, lapping up the blood that spilled from the wounds.

Liu Chenguang struggled to get away, to get back from her, to no avail.

"Look," the woman said to the other demons, "what character did I draw?"

"Answering Second, En," replied one of the demons obediently.

Liu Chenguang closed her eyes, determined not to scream.

The woman's voice said, "Bring her. We return to clan home."

One of the demons said, "Please instruct this person as to our preferred mode of travel."

"Walking obviously," she said. "This one can't fly. Feel free to carry her to go faster as you need, bind her, do whatever is needful, but whatever blood she spills between here and there comes out of your skin later. Bring her to Shancheng by tonight. I wish to speak with her further."

Liu Chenguang felt the woman's fingers on her lips.

"Little phoenix, tonight, I want you to transform. I'm very curious about those wings of yours. Please be ready to do so the first time I ask. Consider that I know how to make it happen, if you do not." The woman kissed her, a friendly peck on the cheek. "Until tonight," she said, and Liu Chenguang felt the shift in energy that meant she had transformed and flown.

The larger of the two demons holding her, a man almost Tainu's height, threw her over his shoulder and began to run with her, long loping strides. But not as quick as Aili, she thought, not as fast. Shancheng…they were staying near the river, then. She tried to think what to do, but her mind was panicking. Zhu Guiren had kept her unconscious while they cut her for her blood and had talked about this as though it were a great favor, but now she realized that perhaps he was right; perhaps other demons would be far worse. She had never been captured before, but Tainu had once told her that one of the reasons phoenixes needed to be so careful, needed to always hide, was that there were beings in the world, demon and mortal, who would enjoy having control of a being they could constantly torture that would never die, that could never escape from them. She had never really believed it until now.

She knew one thing, though. That woman could do whatever she wanted with her daggers, but there was no way she would ever do what she asked. Clearly, it would make no difference to the final outcome. And Aili would come for her soon.

The demons ran until they dropped, then handed her off to others. It didn't escape her that the demons were as terrified of the woman, Second, as she was, if not more so. None of them spoke to her and she had no opportunity to escape, trussed up hand and foot and tossed from demon to demon. She had no talismans left, even if she had had hands free to use one. At one point, she silently transformed and beat her wings, striking the demons with pure qi, but they overcame her again and bound her more heavily, this time with a sort of lined net that hurt her skin wherever it brushed her, a constant pain as they ran.

Their path, as far as she could tell, lay mostly along the levees on the north side of the river. Across from Shancheng, the demons were met by others in a small boat waiting for them and they moved back to the south shore. The building they took her to was right next to the river since it was now in flood — an ancient stone warehouse of some kind. She had stopped being able to think at this point. Despite her bravado, the thought of seeing that woman again terrified her.

Second was waiting for her in a large room with a couch and a window overlooking the river. The sky was threatening rain, an increase in the flooding. "It's just us, little phoenix," she said, sipping something while she sat on the low couch. Liu Chenguang had been thrown on the floor in front of her, the demon guards waiting outside the room's closed door. Second's hair had been re-braided with silver. "When we return to clan home, perhaps you'll see your friend Third again. Or the other phoenix. But for now, just us."

The woman put her cup down and said, "Transform."

Liu Chenguang got herself together enough to kneel upright, but said nothing.

The woman smiled. "Delightful," she said. She walked around her in a slow circle. At one point she reached out and touched Liu Chenguang's hair. "You know," she said, conversationally, "my spouse, First, has a terrible habit of destroying all of our strongest children. I wish he would remember to let them reproduce first, but he says it's so enjoyable to dominate those who resist, as opposed to the obedient, that sometimes he loses his control. It's something I've always found annoying about him. But I do see the attraction."

She knelt down in front of Liu Chenguang, very suddenly, so her face filled Liu Chenguang's field of vision. After her languid circling, the swiftness of the movement was terrifying. She reached out and touched Liu Chenguang's lips. "I'm not my husband," she said, "luckily for you. But I also appreciate the importance of dominating those who don't obey. If you would like to have a slightly less terrible time when we reach clan home, it would be better for you to learn obedience now, so that you don't draw his attention to you. He has had his fun with Third already. He'll be looking for something else to play with." She smiled, and put her finger inside Liu Chenguang's lips, stroking her tongue.

To her horror and shame, Liu Chenguang found that she couldn't even bite down. Even that small piece of self-defense was impossible for her.

The woman noted her distress, smiled, and added another finger. "You see," she said gently. "I could rip your tongue out right now, and there's nothing you could do about it. Perhaps it would grow back? An interesting experiment." She leaned over and whispered intimately in her ear, "Transform, my dear."

Liu Chenguang closed her eyes. The woman dug her nails into her tongue until the blood came, and she heard herself making terrible noises, choking and retching, while the tears ran down her face.

"Still no?" The woman got up and walked back over to the couch. "The hard way it is, then."

When she came back, she was holding a silver instrument that looked like a small, flexible wand with sharp teeth. Before Liu Chenguang was aware, she had struck her on the back with it.

Liu Chenguang screamed. The thing was full of corrupted qi, ripping into her skin and muscles, burrowing down like razored insects, tearing her meridians and spilling into both her mortal and spiritual body. The woman struck her again, and again, and again.

She would not transform, she would not transform, she would not do it. She clenched her fists and closed her eyes. She could feel what was happening — that the qi was trying to force her mortal body to transform in self-defense; it would be the first and normal reaction for any phoenix — but she wouldn't do it. *She wouldn't, she wouldn't, she wouldn't.*

Every so often, the woman would stop and look at her, always in silence, listening to her sob for breath, as she felt herself beginning to heal and the pain beginning to subside. Then, Second would begin again, moving from her back to her shoulders, her face, her belly, her legs and hips, anywhere unpredictable.

Eventually, Liu Chenguang lay quivering on the floor, unable to move or speak or focus her eyes. Her throat was raw with screaming. She realized dully that she was not healing as quickly as before.

The woman kicked her onto her back and looked down at her, smiling, and then knelt by her. Taking her chin in her hands, she said, "Really, you are quite a pleasure, my dear. Much stronger than you look." She kissed her on her forehead. "First will enjoy meeting you." She kicked her again, in the ear, and then left.

Two demons came back in and bound her, but left her lying where she was. Apparently, this was her prison for the evening. Shaking from pain and the on-going torment of her meridians, she closed her eyes, and tried to sleep.

Aili followed the golden light without stopping, calling Liu Chenguang's true name every few minutes to be sure it hadn't diverged, but it followed the course of the river on the north side faithfully, and then, at Shancheng, crossed back over to the south bank, such as it was with the river deciding banks were completely unnecessary here. It was well after midnight when she had reached that point — slowed down by the flooding, almost two full days without sleep, food, or rest — and she knew she was drawing heavily on her cultivation to keep going, but there was no question of doing anything else. This was where Liu Chenguang was; the golden light ended here, in this city, in this street, in this building, a stone monstrosity with no lit windows.

She was sure that she could go in and get Liu Chenguang out, but unless she had a place to go with her, there was no point; it wasn't any different than it had been on the bank of the river days ago. A safe place, a safe place to run with a phoenix, with pursuit behind them. Or a place where someone would hide them.

Aili looked back at the Sorrowful River, its golden-brown water sliding by, showing nothing that was underneath, and threw in a pearl. Then, she closed her eyes to gather herself. The pearl would bring Yisue for them, or it wouldn't. Either way, when she came out with Liu Chenguang, they would jump into the river. She could think of no other plan. She would help Liu Chenguang swim… they would be so slow. She couldn't think of that. It was the only option they had; she would not leave Liu Chenguang here for one moment longer. She looked back at the building and whispered Liu Chenguang's true name. She was there. There were no windows at ground level, and only one door.

Aili realized she was very, very angry.

She took a deep breath, grasped a phoenix whip in one hand and En in the other, and ran for the entrance, slashing down with a sword pulse against the wood and stone of the gate. Demons boiled out — crows and mortal bodies, wings and weapons — and she started killing.

Liu Chenguang heard the shouts and clash of metal and saw the reflected light of the phoenix whip on her window, flaring red and gold, and closed her eyes in relief. Aili had come.

They had only bound her with rope, ordinary rope, not spells, but she struggled to loosen her hands and feet. Quite a bit of her own blood had spilled during Second's time with her — enough to make the ropes both slick and sticky — and she rubbed her wrists against them until they let her draw her hands out, then she worked on the knots around her ankles.

She could hear Aili now, hear her voice, yelling for her. She called back, "Aili!" Her voice sounded hoarse from all the screaming she'd done earlier, that still wasn't fully healed, but she heard the clash of weapons around Aili coming closer and closer. She stood shakily, and started walking toward the door, but it suddenly blew inward, raging with phoenix fire, and Aili was there, her whole body wreathed in flame.

And then, the fire went out and Aili fell forward onto her knees. Liu Chenguang screamed. A sword bearing a talisman was thrust into Aili's chest. Second stood there, smiling, holding the sword lightly in one hand. She had moved so fast that Liu Chenguang hadn't even seen her. She saw Aili's mouth moving, trying to say her name, but it was as though she were paralyzed.

Second smiled again. "Look, little phoenix," she said, turning to smile at Liu Chenguang, "your lover came. As expected. Perfect." She wrenched the sword out of Aili's chest, and as the talisman fluttered down,

Liu Chenguang saw a black, oily mark left on Aili's body.

"The experiment is successful," Second said, and kicked at Aili's shoulder so she fell down on her face. En and the phoenix whip had both disappeared. "Third helped me design that talisman just for you, whatever it is you are." She squatted down and looked at Aili with great interest, then reached over to stroke her face.

Aili's eyes followed the movement of her hand, but she couldn't turn her head.

"So, this one broke Third's array. Fascinating. He didn't think she would be able to do it."

"Get away from her," Liu Chenguang said, but she was held by two demons again. "Aili," she called, trying not to scream. She knew that if Aili could hear her, she would want to know she was all right, that they weren't hurting her. She would never ever tell Aili about what had happened before she came. "Let me go to her," she said. "She's hurt. Let me help her."

"No," Second said, "I want her to heal on her own. I want to see how this works." She went back to the couch. "Shackle the hybrid. Rope alone is fine. She can't transform."

Suddenly, there were screams from below them: the first floor of the building.

Second frowned and stood again. "What is it? You, you, and you, go see and report."

Several demons ran for the door, but the screams were coming closer, and along with the screams there was a strange noise: a deep, slow, regular pounding, with space between each strike. The noise was coming closer as well.

Since Aili had already mostly destroyed the doors, Liu Chenguang could see down the corridor leading to it, and turning the corner from the stairs came a man. He was both tall and powerfully fat, dressed in a fashionable Federation-style suit and vest, his hair long and graying, and a thin, gray, beard hanging to his large belly in three strands. He held a walking stick in one hand, and this made the pounding noise at each of his steps — a great, deep, booming sound from the little half-height cane — making the stone walls vibrate and shudder.

The man walked deliberately and without haste toward the door of their room. The demons who attacked him from all sides simply were thrown back violently into the walls, broken and dead, as though they were touching something that could in no way be affected by their feeble efforts, something that paid them no more mind than an elephant pays to an ant. He neither looked at them nor raised his hand, but merely kept walking. His right eye was covered with an eye patch and his face was set in an expression of deep disgust, as if for some unfathomable reason he had been forced to take a detour through a narrow alley filled with stinking waste.

Behind him came a little boy with tangled white hair, filthy and completely naked. "Aili!" he yelled happily, peeking around the man's arm. "Aili, my uncle came to see you!"

CHAPTER 17
BEILONG

LIU CHENGUANG DID her best to bow toward the man. He ignored her completely. "This is the one?" he asked, looking down at Aili.

Yisue ran to Aili and shook her, his happy face suddenly a caricature of shock. "Uncle, uncle, they hurt her–"

The man turned to sweep his gaze across the room. His expression of disgust intensified. "Any friend you have here, take them to the palace and wait for me while I clean up this trash." He added, without looking at him, "And put on some clothes, you shame our family."

"Yes uncle," said Yisue, and he transformed. The room was suddenly full of white dragon scales.

Second yelled, "Retreat! Grab them–"

But Yisue already had Aili caught in his mouth, and quicker than water had come to Liu Chenguang. Yisue's uncle looked at the demons holding her. His glance alone threw them, bones broken and vomiting blood, into the stone wall. Neither of them moved again.

Liu Chenguang clambered on Yisue's back. "Go, go, go," she said. "Yisue, go quickly!"

As Yisue swarmed back down the stairs, she saw the carnage all around them, the demon bodies, but she knew that worse would be coming. Above her head, she heard the voice of Yisue's uncle. "How dare you, demon, do this on my banks?" he roared. "What makes you think you can disrespect me in this way? Do you think I am unable to control my own territory?"

Second said, "There is no disrespect meant–"

A great booming noise came, as though Yisue's uncle had struck the floor with the cane grown to the size of a tree. The entire building shook, and stones started to come down around them, and although they were still on the second floor suddenly they were surrounded with swirling, unstoppable water the color and texture of milky tea, rising and rising at a rate beyond belief — dozens of feet per second.

"Here we go!" yelled Yisue. "Take her," and he turned his head so Liu Chenguang could pull Aili out of his mouth and hold on to her. "Hold your breath!"

They were surrounded by the deep brown water, impossible to see through or around. Liu Chenguang closed her eyes, kissed Aili with a seal over her nose to keep her from breathing in the water, and held her breath, and held her breath, and held her breath, and finally she had to breathe. When she opened her eyes they were in a room made of stones, lit by pearls set in the ceiling.

She half-fell from Yisue's back, trying to keep Aili — still paralyzed and seemingly unconscious — from falling heavily to the floor. Yisue immediately transformed and knelt next to her, hovering over Aili's body.

"What happened?" he asked miserably.

"There were demons. They attacked us." She didn't have enough attention to go into it further. The wound where Aili had been stabbed was not healing; black tendrils seeped out from it into her body, weeping a thick black fluid. When she tried to check her meridians, she found that the rot was moving through them, pushing all the qi that remained into her extremities to be trapped there, unable to circulate. The pain must be intense, but blessedly, she was unconscious. Liu Chenguang almost wept in horror at the thing. If only Tainu were here…she didn't know how to do this.

Yisue said, "Liu Chenguang, Liu Chenguang, you can fix her? You're a phoenix, you can fix anything!"

But she couldn't fix everything. There were some wounds a phoenix couldn't heal — not many, but some — and cultivational injuries were healed by skill, not only blood. Besides, "A phoenix can't heal another phoenix. It doesn't work," she said helplessly, trying to circulate qi in Aili's damaged cultivation.

"But she's not a phoenix, she's a starfish," Yisue said.

Liu Chenguang took a shaky breath. "Yes," she said. "Give me something sharp." Yisue ran over to a rack at the wall and came back with a dagger. She slashed her hand and lay it down over the wound, then bit her lip and leaned over to kiss Aili's wound, closing her eyes.

She could feel her blood circulating against the rot, bearing qi with it, forcing it back, but it was difficult, difficult — as though she herself had become part of her own blood, imbued into Aili's body, seeking out the uncorrupted qi, strengthening it into walls, pushing the walls back, back, back, meridian after meridian, toward the central wound.

Yisue yelled as she fell backward from Aili's body, too exhausted to continue. Something rose up from the sword wound, a misshapen ball, sending its tendrils out toward her, toward Yisue.

BOOM!

The man who had rescued them entered the room with his cane and scornfully poked the thing with it. It instantly dissipated, not purified with qi, but simply melting into nothingness. "It was sentient," he said. "Disgusting."

Liu Chenguang tried to stand, but couldn't yet.

"Don't bother. Yisue, what did I tell you?"

Yisue looked down at himself. "I'm sorry, uncle," he said. "We were trying to save Aili."

The man knelt down next to Aili, surprisingly agile despite his bulk, and lay his large hand on the sword wound. "It's healing now. She'll need to rest for a while before she comes back to consciousness, though. And you look as though you could use a bath and a rest as well."

Liu Chenguang bowed awkwardly from her sitting position.

He stood and said, "The jiaoren will tend to both of you. Rooms will be prepared. When you feel ready, tell the jiaoren to bring you to my audience hall." He sighed. "And you too, Yisue. Let the jiaoren bathe you and give you clean clothes. If you want to live among mortals you'll need to do this. I don't understand why it's such an issue for you."

"There's no mortals *here*," he said rebelliously under his breath.

The man looked at him.

"Sorry uncle," he said.

Yisue's uncle swept out of the room, this time thankfully not striking his cane on the ground with every step, and several people entered: beautiful young men and women dressed in the style of the Feng dynasty, flowing silks and ribbons and golden ornaments in their hair. Several of them had visible scale marks on their faces, but this only made them look more interesting. Their hair varied in color, white, red, orange, and black; some of them even had hair of more than one color. Liu Chenguang was intrigued. She had never met jiaoren in their mortal forms before. Two of the men brought a stretcher to carry Aili, and they walked together into a different part of the palace. All of it was made of stone and lit with the shimmering pearls hung in nets and strings from the ceiling. The men brought Aili into a room with a bed and a bath prepared and departed.

One of the female jiaoren bowed to Liu Chenguang and said in a very soft voice, hard to hear, "My lady, please come with me. You also have a room we have prepared for you."

"Who's going to bathe her?" she asked, frowning.

Two of the women bowed.

She wavered, feeling uncertain about this, but Aili certainly did need a bath, and she wasn't strong enough to lift and bathe an unconscious Aili by herself. She nodded and said, "Take good care of her, please," and followed the remaining two female jiaoren into another room across the corridor.

The bath attendants provided her with all she needed and offered to wash her hair for her, and then to rub it dry and comb it into a semblance of decency, which she accepted gratefully. Laid out for her when she was dry was a simple layered cultivator's robe. She was deeply glad that Yisue's uncle didn't expect her to wear women's Feng styles, so elaborate and so easy to trip over, though she would have done her best for politeness' sake.

Despite his invitation to rest for a while, Liu Chenguang knew very well that this person was not one to offend or keep waiting. As soon as she felt her appearance was acceptable, she asked the jiaoren to take her there, just peeking into Aili's room on the way to see her comfortably clean and sleeping.

The room was huge, with enormous golden pearls set along the sides so there was a delicate warm glow over all of the furniture, carved rosewood tables and chairs. The floor was shining polished black, inlaid with pale jade in complex patterns.

"This insignificant person expresses gratitude for the great lord's kindness and care for strangers," Liu Chenguang said, offering her most formal salute before Yisue's uncle.

The dragon of the Sorrowful River snorted disdainfully. He had changed his clothing for court dress of the Fu dynasty — brilliant yellow and deep gold embroidered with vermilion and jade — and looked all the more impressive despite the fact that he was lounging quite casually on a carved wooden couch with his feet up on the railing. "The other one has given care to this king's relative. A debt is owed," he said. "His parents certainly aren't doing the job. Come in, come in," he added, sitting up, "there's tea and more here. I doubt the demon fed you well since she was trying to whip you to death, or whatever she thought she would accomplish by torturing a phoenix."

Liu Chenguang came to sit opposite him at the tea table. Jiaoren brought over the teapot and some small delicacies, though she didn't have much appetite.

"That one," he said, "she has a dragon's heart."

"What?" Liu Chenguang asked, confused.

"Yisue told me about their journey here. She is a dragon."

"Great king, this person is confused by your statement."

"You may speak informally, and address me as Beilong," he said. "I'll let you know when I need you to be polite."

Liu Chenguang bowed her head, slightly nervous at the prospect.

Beilong slurped some tea with evident pleasure. "It's nice to have someone to talk to besides the jiaoren. They're all very quiet, hoping to become dragons someday, but they won't because they don't have dragon hearts. They're just fish when you get right down to it. Fish that have cultivated mortal forms. A dragon heart is different. A dragon heart knows the reality of sacrifice and risk."

"I don't understand," Liu Chenguang said. "That doesn't sound good at all."

"Of course you don't understand, you're a phoenix," he said. "Phoenixes are always about new beginnings, forgetting what was, transcending loss, done is done and pain is pain. You don't understand such things."

"That's not true," she said. "Not for me."

He looked at her, and behind his jovial attitude she saw a hint of his true nature, his single eye deep and unfathomable.

She bowed her head.

"I'm older than you, or any phoenix," he said, "and I have seen much. Sacrifice is also part of reality. It's not usually the nature of the phoenix to grasp this aspect of existence. But I see that you have done so." He bowed in return. "Does she know?"

"I haven't told her. There's no need for her to know. It's not certain. Who knows what will happen?"

The dragon's eye glinted at her. "True," he said. "Who knows? This may not be your last cycle after all. You may be reborn again. You just don't know. That's a sacrifice as well, to not know, and to take the risk anyway."

Liu Chenguang poured both of them more tea.

Beilong asked, "Would you prefer liquor?"

"Not at this time. I need my mind clear." She sipped her tea, and said, "No one knows, not even my sibling. I didn't know it myself when I did what I did, but I suspected it might happen. It would only make sense that taking another being into rebirth with me through my own power, giving her part of my own self, that this would weaken my own ability to continue in my existence."

"On the other hand, it may not," Beilong said. "Your existence may be strengthened. This is the nature of sacrifice. It is one of the levers that moves the world in ways that can't be predicted. Sacrifice brings the element of desire into all that is, and desire moves the world into new and unexpected paths."

"But what does it mean," Liu Chenguang pressed, "when you say that she has a dragon heart?"

"Courage, sacrifice, desire, strength, willfulness, unpredictability and violence — these mark the dragon heart," he explained.

"That's not all of who she is," she said. "Not at all."

"Of course not," he said. "It's not all of who I am either. I am also the source of life for uncounted millions who have lived in my valley for all of mortal history, back beyond any possibility of memory. But they always think they have to buy safety from me or control me for this to happen because to them, the dragon heart is only power and violence and unpredictability. And I do not like being controlled. Neither does she." Sipping his tea, he added, "You should not keep secrets from her."

Liu Chenguang said, "Someday I'll tell her. Now, she's too upset about anything that might hurt me."

"Hah, possessive and protective as well! She truly is a dragon." He tapped on the table. "As I said, a dragon is also a source of life — the life of the mortal realm, growing and dying, creating and destroying. It is because we are far more mortal than you phoenixes are, more connected to the mortal realm, that we are so. This is true for her as well. It is her mortal soul that permits her to give a different life to you. This is why I wanted to meet her. I have things I wish to say to her later, when she is able to listen. Meanwhile, tell me what was happening with that trash of a demon. I have never seen such blatant disregard for my power and dignity. Not ever. How dare she, on my banks, torture a phoenix!"

Liu Chenguang could very easily imagine him lashing his tail in fury.

"There have been great sacrifices of mortals lately," he said. "My banks were breached and my bed has shifted. Countless thousands gave up their lives to me. An unwilling sacrifice is still a sacrifice. In return, I must protect my people from being preyed upon by demons like that one."

"It's a complicated story," she said, and began.

On her way back from talking with Beilong, she knocked at the door and said, "It's me."

Aili's voice responded, "Don't come in."

She opened the door anyway.

Liu Chenguang stopped in the doorway to look at Aili. She was standing with her face to the wall, one fist clenched — the very picture of anger and rejection. Her hair had come out of its braid when they bathed her and hadn't been put up again; she had rarely seen it down. She realized that she very much wanted to touch it and smiled. All she could think was, I love this person so much. "Aili," she said.

Aili turned to look at her, silently. "Liu Chenguang," she finally said in a voice that shook with anger, "you should leave. I'm going to say things I'll regret later."

Liu Chenguang ignored this and walked inside. She felt very light, as though she had discovered a great secret. The world was encircled with a wall and there were no doors in it. As long as a person tried to get through the wall they would always fail, and yet, the wall was much smaller than the world's vastness; all one needed to do was look in another direction. In the end, she thought, it turns out that I am still a phoenix, after all.

She noticed there was a table set with delicacies, apparently untouched. "Have you eaten?" she asked.

"No," gritted Aili. "I don't want to eat. Liu Chenguang, I am–" she took a deep breath, "I am so angry at you."

"I know," Liu Chenguang said. She looked up at her. "But I'm hungry. Aren't you?"

Aili said, "No. I am not hungry."

Liu Chenguang picked up a dessert that she loved, made of soft tofu with sweet syrup. "Have you ever had this?" she asked, and tasted it. "It's delicious."

"I. Have. Not." Aili frowned at her from across the room. She was wearing a Feng inner robe tied only at the waist, the thin fabric showing the shape of her body — her broad shoulders and the curve of her breasts. Her dark gold, unbraided hair tumbled down just past her shoulders, thick and not very long. It made her face look more gentle, even though she was so angry, with her eyes narrowed and her fists clenched at her side, ready to fight.

Liu Chenguang stood silently by the table, rolling the sweet tofu on her tongue and reveling in looking at her.

"What is it?" Aili said at last. "Why aren't you talking to me?"

Liu Chenguang said, "I really think you should taste this."

"No. I don't want it."

Liu Chenguang walked over to her with a spoonful.

"I said I don't want it."

"Yes you do." She ate a little bit off the spoonful herself.

"No. I don't."

"Yes. You do." Liu Chenguang smiled at her and offered the spoon. When Aili wouldn't take it, she tasted some more, just a little, just touching it with her lips.

"I don't." Aili was looking down at her, her eyes still narrowed, but her voice was wavering.

"You do." Liu Chenguang held the spoon up to her mouth.

Aili took the spoon out of her hand, very carefully, and laid it down on the little table next to the wall, never looking away from her eyes.

Liu Chenguang looked up at her, her mouth partly open, not able to smile any more, feeling dizzy at being so close to her, at what would happen next, her own heartbeat pounding in her ears. "Aili," she said, and closed her eyes, feeling Aili meeting her lips, slowly licking at the sweetness there and in her mouth, tasting her and exploring her — her mouth and down the line of her throat. All her body went soft with yearning, so Aili had to put her arms around her and hold her upright. Still kissing her, Aili picked her up and quickly turned to press her body hard against the wall, her robe coming all loose in front so she could feel the heat of Aili's body through the thin fabric.

Aili whispered hoarsely, "Arms around neck, legs around waist," and so she did.

Since there were no windows, there was no day or night in Beilong's palace, but the jiaoren seemed to have some sense of times for waking and sleeping and knocked to bring breakfast to them sometime after they had slept, tangled and sweaty in Aili's bed. Neither of them had ever lived in a place that had this sort of service before and both of them felt very embarrassed to be lying there, naked and trying to hide under the blankets, but the jiaoren seemed to literally not see them, laying out the food on the table as well as washbasins, cloths, and clean clothing for both of them, then departing in silence.

Aili whispered, "They all seem to have bulgy eyes. I feel like they're looking at me even when they're not," and Liu Chenguang laughed.

After breakfast and getting dressed, Liu Chenguang brought Aili to Beilong's audience room again. He was already there, and this time, so was Yisue — clean and elaborately dressed in the style of a Mitang chieftain, his white hair braided with gold — practically dancing with excitement.

"Aili Aili Aili!" he yelled, and launched himself at her, grabbing her around the waist.

"Yisue!" she said, equally happy, and picked him up to spin him around. "Yisue, thank you for coming to us," she added more seriously, then bowed to Beilong. "Thank you for saving us."

Liu Chenguang was pleased to note that she seemed not at all intimidated.

Beilong said, "You have a dragon heart."

Aili said, "I promise you that I do not."

Beilong snorted with laughter, a vast sound that hinted at a creature much larger than could be contained in the room around them. "Hah, you are a good one." He stood up and stretched. "You have been good to my nephew, and so I wished to meet you. You have a dragon heart, but you are not a dragon. There are things you can do that a dragon cannot do, but you will do them in a dragon way."

Aili didn't respond. Liu Chenguang could tell she was confused.

"We will have time to talk more. I will learn you better. For now, I wish to ask you a *favor*," Beilong said. He put a great weight on the word. "My nephew needs to be cared for better than his current caregivers can, since they will not leave the deep sea, and he is drawn to the edges of the land. He is running wild and does not know how to be a dragon, nor does he know how to be with mortals. He wishes to be among them, and thus needs to learn the dragon's proper role among other beings. He cannot stay here with me forever, and he will not learn from me." He casually reached over and smacked Yisue on the back of his head.

Yisue grinned at him.

"You see?" he asked, making a terrible frown at Yisue. He flipped up his eye patch so Yisue could see his scarred and missing eye, and Yisue yelled with laughter. He turned and formally bowed to Aili.

Liu Chenguang watched in awe.

"I ask if you would take my nephew to foster and teach him," he said, remaining in a bow. "If you will care for him until he is ready to take his place among dragons and mortals."

"What about his parents?" Aili asked, frowning.

"Parenthood among dragons is not like mortals," Beilong replied impatiently. "Yisue's parents beneath the great sea have already let him depart. He will need a new home to grow to adulthood."

"Does he want to?" Aili asked uncertainly, looking at Yisue,

"Yes yes yes yes!" yelled Yisue. "I want to!"

She smiled at him and said to Beilong, who remained bowed, "I am willing, but I don't know how long my lifetime will be — how long it will take him to grow up."

"Hah," said Beilong, and stood upright. "It is done."

Liu Chenguang and Aili both stood still, looking at Yisue. Aili met Liu Chenguang's eyes, and Liu Chenguang nodded.

"Now," said Beilong, "we move. Your phoenix and I spoke last night about the other phoenix and the demon with whom you concern yourself. I have a second favor to ask you: go destroy these demons, their nest."

"That's something I would do for free," said Aili.

Liu Chenguang smiled.

Beilong said, "Indeed you would! But I am laying it on you as well. I will give you what help I can."

"Can you come with us?" Aili asked. Liu Chenguang had described to her Beilong's power — how the demons had fled before his face and were destroyed by his glance.

He shook his head. "A river cannot run uphill. No demon makes a nest where I can reach them. While I could come with you in my mortal body to the mountains, away from my bed and floodplain my power is limited. I would not be able to do much for you. But, I know that their nest is somewhere in the mountains above Ximersia, where I run narrow and deep. I will bring you to Ximersia, and I will give you what I can to help you. Return to the river at any time for safety. The jiaoren will be waiting to protect you if I am not there."

"Can I come?" Yisue asked.

"No," said Beilong and Aili at the same time.

Yisue pouted.

The palace seemed to exist in a strange netherworld beneath the Sorrowful River. When Beilong walked outside with them, Aili looked up and saw that the sky was a deep, swirling mass of brown and gold and white, like an ever-moving painting. Light did not come through it; it was far darker here than it was within the pearl-lit palace.

Beilong turned to Aili and said, "Take this." He gave her a flask full of swishing liquid. Consideringly, he continued, "Your power is that of the phoenix fire and a mortal soul. You are a mortal cultivator. There are other ways to find the qi of the world, in the powers of the mountains and the rivers. This is all qi. When your cultivated qi is exhausted, drink some of this. It will feel different for you, but will enable you to keep fighting. Fighting is what you will want to be doing!"

He slapped her on the back so that she almost fell over, and whispered, "Don't give any to the phoenix. It's not good for her. She's not of the mortal realm."

Aili nodded. "What about demons?"

"Hah, no idea. Demons fear the river, as they should. Water is life and movement and transformation. Demons cultivate the barrenness of resentment. I can't imagine it would feel good for them. But it is not a weapon." He stepped away. "Let's be off. Stand back."

Aili and Liu Chenguang stood against the outer wall of the palace. Yisue, glum, stood next to them.

Beilong transformed.

The yellow dragon filled all their vision, so enormous she couldn't take it in, the one glaring eye larger than a house, its body fading into the distance. It spoke in a voice that made their entire bodies vibrate, so large and deep that it was almost not a sound. "Get on," he said. "With me, you don't need to hold your breath. This will be quick. You," he said to Yisue, "go inside. When I return, I want you to recite two new verses from the Great Classic."

"Goodbye, Aili," Yisue said sadly. "Come back soon. Goodbye, Liu Chenguang." He turned reluctantly and walked back into the palace.

Aili and Liu Chenguang had to use qinggong to leap up to Beilong's back, and then they were off, moving upstream through the shifting, impenetrable waters.

CHAPTER 18
CLAN HOME

ZHU GUIREN STOOD over him, cutting him again. Tainu stared at the ceiling, trying not to look at his face. There was beginning to be pain now, pain that didn't go away. For a phoenix, injury was always temporary, and thus a phoenix didn't get used to pain; it was new every time. But now, there were things in his body that didn't heal, and thus he was getting used to them: the slashing cuts, the bedsores, the weariness of not being able to move his limbs from their fixed places. He knew that this meant whatever First had in mind for him would come soon. There was not much time left. Very soon, though not in the mortal realm, it would be possible to kill him.

He was not afraid to die. He had lived a very long time. He suspected that when the time came, he would even be grateful to have it over. This must be how his beloved family had felt — how so many mortals felt, tormented by a life that went too long and too far into pain and loss and memories — that a time would come to leave. That was all right. It was only for his demon that he was afraid to go. For his beloved one, who would suffer alone after he was gone, who would never forgive himself for what was happening right now.

Suddenly Zhu Guiren screamed and collapsed on the floor next to him, convulsing.

Tainu yelled, "Demon! What is it!"

But Zhu Guiren was beyond answering, bloody froth at his mouth.

First stood up, frowning. "Check him," he said shortly.

Another demon knelt next to Zhu Guiren and tried to check his acupoints, then shook his head. First walked rapidly over and passed his hand over Zhu Guiren's body. "Ah," he said. "His cultivational structure has been ripped again. There is a serious—" He jumped backward, and the other demon began backing up as well, as quickly as he could, as Zhu Guiren's body transformed.

There was a being lying there now, a glittering silver creature sprawled on the floor, something between a lizard and a cat, perhaps fifteen or twenty feet long, with a smoky mane tangled over its long neck, and bearing an impossible thicket of horns on its head, clear and shining as icicles just before melting, some several feet long. It was missing its left front claw, and its left wing hung at an awkward angle. The creature cried out and thrashed in pain.

Tainu begged, "I can help him! Let me help him, please!" He was terrified now. The demon had returned into his true body while in the mortal realm; he was extraordinarily vulnerable, anyone could kill him with hardly any effort, his true body unsheltered and unshielded by the mortal one. He tried desperately to pull himself out of the shackles, but of course, nothing happened.

First walked over to him and looked down, those red-veined black eyes boring into his own. After a moment he leaned down to him. "If you attempt to heal his heart, I will kill him immediately," he said softly. "Do not doubt how fast I am." He reached out and touched the shackles on his wrists and ankles, which disappeared. "The one on your neck remains. That is enough to keep you from transforming."

His ankles and wrists also had sores; he rubbed them quickly, then stumbled off the couch over to where the demon had subsided into quivering unconsciousness. "Demon," he said, standing near the great head, "I'm here, it's me." He slipped his hand, already covered with his own blood, into the crystal-fanged mouth and let his head lie, just for a moment, against the forehead of the creature. It was near his head's height as he knelt next to it. One of the ice horns grazed the top of his skull, sharp as a razor, and as cold. The glittering silver scales sent a shower of light all around him. He reached out to stroke the mane, softer than smoke; his fingers could barely feel its fineness. "You've grown so big," he said, his eyes filling with tears. Even with all that was happening, he was glad he was able to see his true body one time — how the lithe quickness of his childhood had become power and beauty.

The body shivered, shimmered, shrank back into Zhu Guiren lying unconscious on the ground. Tainu knelt next to him, awkwardly because his body wasn't flexible anymore, and held out his hand, forming his true name silently in his mouth, putting whatever qi he could still summon into it, feeling the damage to the demon's meridians. He could feel the block that First had placed around the demon's heart, but it was not something he could have broken even if he wanted to. In his current state, bled and weakened, it was far beyond his power. The demon's meridians had been torn — some of them completely severed, others violently jerked out of alignment. The damage was spreading through his cultivational body like wildfire, demonic qi flooding everywhere within him, ripping him apart.

Tainu drew deeper into himself, pouring it into his demon from the last reserves he had of his own power, closing the bleeding meridians, and pushing the demonic qi back where it could be contained, to keep him alive, to keep his mortal and spiritual bodies from disintegrating in pain and madness. At last, Tainu fell down over him, gasping, blood trickling from his mouth and nose. He had nothing left, and he didn't think Zhu Guiren would ever be able to cultivate again, but he would live.

Zhu Guiren opened his eyes and looked up at him, confused. "What happened?" he asked. "What is it?"

Two demons grabbed Tainu and made him lie down again. First re-established the shackles, then walked back to his chair. "Continue," he said.

Zhu Guiren frowned and shook his head. He stood up with difficulty, trembling as though his body pained him. Then, he took his knife out again, and continued.

At some point later, an unimaginable amount of time later, Tainu lay alone in absolute darkness, body and mind, heart and soul. This was the time he should sleep — when the lights were out and the demons had left, when no one was cutting him or hurting him — but he couldn't. There was too much pain. He had used all of his qi for his demon, and his mortal body was deteriorating far more quickly now with no chance to rejuvenate or heal himself. He wondered, if they didn't take him to the spirit realm, if he might just continue living forever like this, like a piece of meat being sliced every day. What had Zhu Guiren said so long ago? Meat that doesn't die? Dying would be better.

He heard someone approaching. Even though everything was dark, he knew. A thread of warmth came into his heart. "Demon," he said softly.

Zhu Guiren stood next to him, then sat down on the stone couch. "I remember being like this," he said. "I remember holding your hand while you slept."

"You did," he said gently, remembering. "Would you like to now?"

He felt Zhu Guiren's hand tentatively entangling with his, interlacing with his fingers.

"I don't feel anything," the demon said at last. "I thought I might."

Tainu felt his eyes tearing up again, but weeping wouldn't help anything. He said, "Demon, will you listen to what I have to say? I don't know if I'll have a chance to tell you anything in the future."

"All right," Zhu Guiren's voice came indifferently.

He took a deep breath. "Come closer," he said.

Zhu Guiren leaned down. He could feel the warmth of his face near his lips in the absolute darkness. "Arciniang," he whispered. "I want you to remember this. I love you and will always love you. You are beautiful to me. You have been the best thing in my life. I don't regret anything. Will you remember that?"

"All right," he said again. His face remained near. "Is there more?"

"Yes." He didn't want to miss this opportunity; who knew if they would have any more time, ever again? He knew that there was almost certainly another listener — First might have anticipated that Zhu Guiren would come to him privately — so he tried to keep his voice as quiet as possible, but he couldn't not speak. "First wants to kill you. Be careful of him, please. Don't trust him."

"Of course he does, and I am, and I don't," he said calmly.

Tainu said, "That's good, that's good. I want you to be safe." He breathed and tried to think how to say it, wishing he could move a hand to touch him. "Demon, I know you don't feel anything for me now–"

"That's true."

"But there may come a time when you feel things again, and I know that you'll feel badly about what's happening right now. I want you to know that I know in your heart you don't want this. I want you to be able to forgive yourself. You have to promise me that you won't harm yourself, and you won't let anyone else harm you. Promise me."

"Why would I need to promise you that?" He made a little sound of annoyance. "Don't worry if it's on your mind. My life is always my own highest priority."

"Good," Tainu said. "Your life is also my highest priority."

Zhu Guiren paused. "Even now?" he asked uncertainly. "What about your life? Don't you want to escape?"

"Of course," he said. "But if I can't escape, if I can't have what I want, then just preserving your life is my wish."

"What do you want?"

It was dark, and he couldn't see Zhu Guiren's face, but he remembered that tone of voice well enough, imagining him frowning, trying to understand something that confused him. He smiled a little.

"I want you to have your heart back, and for us to live together, and love each other, and be happy," Tainu said. "That's all. That is my only wish. If I can't have that, between your life and mine, I would choose yours."

Zhu Guiren shook his head; Tainu could feel the movement of the air. "You're a phoenix," he said. "You're not going to die."

Tainu had given this a lot of thought since First had talked to him. First's plans couldn't be fully predicted, but he had said he intended to cultivate the resentment of a phoenix. There was only one way in which that could happen. "I think that First intends to kill me in the spirit realm, and for you to do it." He could feel Zhu Guiren's body grow still, the vibration of his breath ceasing in the darkness. "If that happens," he said, "for your own sake, please, refuse to be the one. Refuse. Let someone else do it." He couldn't risk letting him go without saying this, without being very clear. He was very much afraid that if his demon killed him with his own hand, he truly would commit suicide later no matter what he said now.

"I won't do it," he said. "I promise."

Tainu thought that there was an overtone of anger in his voice.

"That would be…too much. That would just be him trying to control me, demonstrate his power, be entertained by my obedience. I won't do it."

"All right." Tainu sank back, relaxed. His mind felt at peace now; he wanted to rest. If his demon was angry, he would get stubborn. He could trust that, at least. No one could make him do it if he refused. "That's good."

"Is that all?" Zhu Guiren asked after a long silence, still close enough to him that he could feel the warmth of his body. Their hands were still interlaced. It was a comfort to him. "I remember that you were good to me. I would free you if I could because I remember that. But I don't have the power to do it. First set your shackles himself. He's far stronger than I am, and I can't break those wards even if I tried. I wanted you to know that I would do it if I could. Because I remember," he said, with that directness so characteristic of him.

It made Tainu smile. "It's all right," he said. "I'm glad to know that you would if you could."

Again, Zhu Guiren asked, "Is that all?"

"That's all," he whispered sleepily. "Just remember that I love you, my demon, my Arciniang, always remember it."

"All right." Zhu Guiren bent closer, uncertainly, and then, to his surprise, lips touched his forehead. "I don't feel it, but I know that I loved you too. I'll remember what you said. So…so sleep well."

"Will you stay with me until I fall asleep?" he asked. He knew in his heart that he would not have this again.

"All right," Zhu Guiren, said, one last time.

He felt him there, holding his hand in the dark, until he slipped into sleep. When he woke again, the demon was gone.

Beilong brought them to the reaches of the Sorrowful River above Ximersia at evening, depositing them on the southern bank and disappearing silently back into the water, which looked far too narrow to hold him. Aili thought that probably the actual size of his body was too large for the mind to encompass and that this was just an imprint, a suggestion to the mind of "dragon."

Liu Chenguang whispered and looked up. Here, far to the north of the wide floodplain, the Sorrowful River ran deep and fast and turbulent in a steep gorge, with only a narrow bank a few feet wide, where they stood among tumbled rocks between the water and the stone walls.

"That way," Liu Chenguang said, pointing slightly east of south into the steepest mountains.

Aili looked at her seriously. "I'm not sure you should come," she said bluntly.

Just as bluntly, Liu Chenguang said, "It's a little late to say that now, Aili Fallon." She smiled as if to take the edge off. "Let's go. My qinggong actually isn't as terrible as you think it is. I just like it when you carry me."

They spent days climbing the cliffs and wandering among the peaks, trying to find a way to where Tainu was. Undoubtedly, it was in a fairly inaccessible area since the demons could fly in and out; the opening to it might be very small, large enough only for a person to crawl through. Even when Liu Chenguang said, frustrated, that Tainu was right *here,* here seemed to be beneath their feet.

One night, they huddled together under some low trees to keep warm, without a fire. Aili knew Liu Chenguang was almost frantic with worry.

"If only Tainu were here," Liu Chenguang said. "He's the one who can manage wards and spells, I don't know how." She slammed her hand down on a rock next to her and said "Ouch. If I was the one captured, I know he could find me."

Both of them had been racking their brains to see if there was anything Zhu Guiren had ever mentioned about his demonic home other than that he never wanted to go there again, but they couldn't think of any clues at all.

"Did you ever come here with Zhu Guiren?" Aili asked, reaching for anything. "Before?"

"We went to the southern sacred mountain, once," she said. "He left me there for a week at one of the temples. It was the only time in all our travels that he left me alone for more than a few hours. But that's the closest we came."

"It surely couldn't have taken him three days from the southern peak? It must be closer than that…"

"But he could fly then, if no one was watching him."

They looked, dejected, at the ground.

"I could just try to blast down through the rock somehow and see?" Aili was running out of ideas.

Liu Chenguang gave her the look that idea deserved.

"All right," Aili tried to work it out the way Zhu Guiren might have. "What marks might demons leave? What clues? What do demons…like?"

"Resentment," said Liu Chenguang automatically.

"There can't be that much resentment here. There's no mortals nearby at all, no towns or villages or cemeteries…Can you sense a place with strong resentment?"

Liu Chenguang closed her eyes and breathed deeply, then held up one finger and pointed it slightly west of south. "That way," she said. "It's quite strong. Further down the slope, not at the peak."

They picked their way down the mountain slowly, without qinggong, to follow every subtle hint that Liu Chenguang's senses could give about their direction. "We're close," she said several hours later, deep into the night. "We should plan as though we'll find the entrance. What should we do? Just…walk in?"

Both of them looked at each other.

"I honestly have no other idea," said Aili eventually. "We've had this much trouble finding one entrance, I doubt there are more. Will they sense us? Will there be guards?"

Liu Chenguang shook her head. "I don't know. Let's assume so?" She shivered. "What if they have more of those special talismans that are just for you?"

Aili said, "Well, we can only go see and try. We'll just…attack frontally. Try to use your wings to block talismans for me?"

Even in her anxiety about Tainu, Liu Chenguang seemed pleased that Aili had actually asked her to do this. It showed in her face; Aili kissed her lightly. "I'll be advance guard," she said, "and if we need to retreat, I'll cover. Remember what Beilong said. The river is safety. All we need to do is get to the water." There was a substantial ridge of mountains between them and the Sorrowful River, but it was better than nothing as a goal. "Even if we're separated," she said anxiously. "No matter what. You go straight to the river, promise?"

Liu Chenguang nodded. "You have the water Beilong gave you?"

Aili patted the flask at her side as she stood. "Let's go," she said softly.

The entrance was not magically invisible, but nature had done a good job. It was a narrow crack in a rock face, overlapped in front by a jutting boulder, impossible to see unless you were coming at just the right angle or already knew it was there. It would also be easy to defend from attackers, but there were no guards at all. Aili found this incredibly suspicious; surely there was at least a ward that was alerting the demons of intruders as they crossed into the rocks, but there was nothing to do except go forward, creeping sideways in the dark along the unlit cave wall.

Gradually, light showed in front of them after the tunnel had widened and gone through several sharp bends. Like Beilong's palace, it was lit with jewels hung from the ceiling — not pearls, but rubies and sapphires, producing an uneasy, shifting purple light. Aili liked this even less than the darkness. She reached out to find Liu Chenguang's hand and pull her nearer. The shadows produced by the swinging, irregularly placed jewels seemed to constantly be on the edge of solidifying into a hand or weapon coming toward them, and the air of resentment was stifling. Aili started shivering with nervous energy, ready for anything; she stopped herself just before pulling out the phoenix whip time and again for something that was only an illusion of the light.

Liu Chenguang stopped and pulled her closer. "It's affecting you," she breathed in her ear. "I can tell."

Aili nodded, nauseous. Liu Chenguang reached into the air beneath her own right hand and plucked hard, then wrapped Aili's hand around something she could feel only as a warm caress on her palm. "Feathers. Hold them, put them in your clothes, against your skin," she whispered. Aili slipped them inside her shirt, where they felt comforting and real.

As they turned the corner, someone stepped out in front of them, a true person. Zhu Guiren.

They both stopped and stared at him. Neither of them knew what to say.

Zhu Guiren's face was dreadful in the purple light. His hair had been cut short, so that all the planes of his face were sharp and shadowed, and his eyes were bruised and dull. He looked at them and said, very quietly, "My ward told me you came. I set it out past the entrance, well back, because I thought you might come for him. I disabled the inner ward so I would be the first one to find you."

When they didn't respond, he said, "Are you here to take him? Can you break the shackles?"

Liu Chenguang moved in front of Aili to block her with her wings. She said, "Zhu Guiren, if you know where he is, take us to him."

He immediately turned and started walking. They followed him down the twisting tunnel, which began to branch off, and he unhesitatingly took turn after turn after turn, in silence. The lights shifted from purple to a sickly orange, and he started to walk faster. "It will be dawn soon," he said. "You need to take him now."

Aili thought, *what's happening? If he's free to move why hasn't he freed Tainu himself?* But what other choice did they have except to follow him? Her hand was half-twisted, ready to call a weapon; Liu Chenguang clearly didn't trust Zhu Guiren at all, and stayed firmly between them, not letting Aili get near.

They came into a dark cavern, so unutterably black that the darkness seemed solid, something they needed to push against to enter. "He's here," said Zhu Guiren. "Can you break the shackles?"

Liu Chenguang rushed over, able to sense where Tainu was as she whispered his name, and Aili followed her scent in the air. Zhu Guiren came behind her, which made Aili's skin crawl, but he only stood behind them as though he would watch, although there was nothing to see.

"Aili," said Liu Chenguang, "En."

She brought En out and held it up. The golden light fell on Tainu's exhausted, ravaged face. Liu Chenguang made a whimpering noise and brought her fist to her mouth. "He's not healing," she said unnecessarily. The oldest scars were pale on his dark skin, but in the warm light of En his skin was mostly red. "Zhu Guiren, take the shackles off him, now, please, please now."

Zhu Guiren shook his head. "I thought you would," he said in a disinterested voice. "If I could, I would have already. They're still making me cut him every day, even though he's unconscious almost all the time now."

Aili turned to him slowly. "What did you say?"

"I can't undo the shackles. I thought you could."

"The other thing," she said, her voice shaking in a whisper.

"They're cutting him every day, even though he's unconscious."

"Who? Who cuts him?"

"I do. First insists that it be me." He looked at her calmly while saying it.

She slashed at him with En. He dodged, but not as easily or quickly as he had in the past; he was injured somehow.

"Aili," hissed Liu Chenguang sharply, "get Tainu out. That's what we're here for. That's what we need to do now."

In a nightmare of time passing, Aili tried.

She tried with En; she tried with a dagger made of spiritual qi, then with hooks of qi to tear the shackles out of the stone; she tried with the phoenix whip, even knowing it might take Tainu's hand off. She tried with her blood. She tried with Beilong's water, which hissed, rageful, when it struck the stone couch. She tried with her bare hands; the shackles burned them, as though they were coated with acid.

Zhu Guiren watched it all, his face unmoving.

Aili looked at Liu Chenguang. "I can't," she said at last. "I can't get them off."

Liu Chenguang's face grew horrified, then empty. "Aili," she said. "Kill him."

Zhu Guiren finally showed interest. "What?" he asked, frowning.

Aili understood, but she shook her head. "No, Chenguang. No."

"There's no other way. No other way, Aili. If we can't rescue him, send him into rebirth, then he'll be free." She looked at Zhu Guiren, her expression tortured. "We can't leave him here to go through this forever."

Zhu Guiren shook his head. "You can't kill him. That's…he wouldn't want you to do that. He told me. He told me, don't kill him."

Aili held En up to see him better as he spoke. For the first time, he seemed discomposed, his eyes dazed and uncertain.

"He specifically told me–" he said again. "He made me promise, don't kill him."

Aili looked at Liu Chenguang. "Chenguang, he said not to kill him…"

Liu Chenguang shook her head. "We can apologize to him later if it's not his intention," she said, "but believe me, Aili, he wouldn't want this, no matter what Zhu Guiren thinks he said."

Aili lifted En, then let it fall. "I can't, Chenguang."

"It won't take dismemberment now," Liu Chenguang said in a voice of forced calm. "If he were anything but a phoenix, he'd be dead already, long ago." She held her hand near his heart, and tears fell off her chin, glinting in En's light. "He has nothing left, Aili. No power left at all. He needs to be reborn. Just…just do it. Decapitation is the…safest and quickest way."

Aili looked at her. "Chenguang," she pleaded. "No."

Liu Chenguang stepped back. "I'm sorry, Aili," she said, "but if Zhu Guiren is forbidden, and I can see why Tainu might have forbidden it, you're the only one." Her voice was shaking, but her tone was inarguable. "The only one who can. He'll– he'll be back, don't worry. It just feels bad to you because you don't understand how it is for us. Rebirth is just…normal."

Aili looked at her, remembering Liu Chenguang's mutilated body on the ground, and then cleared her mind. "All right," she said. She positioned herself for a clean blow at his neck, and raised En, praying that he wouldn't wake up as the sword came down.

But as the sword whispered through the air, Zhu Guiren's halberd blocked it, En staggering in sparks, the harsh music of spiritual weapons clashing through the darkness. "No," he said, his face contorted with the effort. "No. He said no, don't kill him. He said someone else could do it. He said…not me."

Aili said, "Did he say not me?" She twisted En and tried to come at Tainu from another angle, but her heart wasn't in it, so she didn't even come close before Zhu Guiren blocked her again. "Maybe I count as someone else that can do it?"

"No, but I'm sure…I'm sure…" Zhu Guiren struck the halberd at her, quick and vicious. "He said…"

Aili realized, as they spun and struck at one another, that there was more light now and she could see him. His face was troubled, confused, his eyes unfocused; something was very wrong with him. The jewels in the cavern were starting to glow a rather cheerful, calming blue color — like a morning sky. She swore as the light grew stronger.

Zhu Guiren had managed to back her away from Tainu and corner her with a swift series of attacks from his halberd, but it was only because she was distracted. She could tell that he was far below his normal performance; his injury, whatever it was, must be serious. She flipped over his head and ran back toward Tainu. Something like a spear of qi dashed past her shoulder and almost hit Liu Chenguang, which enraged her.

"That's enough, children," came a cheerful voice. "Third, come here."

Zhu Guiren immediately stopped fighting and walked toward the owner of the voice: a tall, pale man with black eyes and a mane of white hair. He looked delighted to see them all. "Third," he said, and briefly trailed his hand over Zhu Guiren's chest in passing.

Zhu Guiren shivered back from his touch, but showed no other concern. His face grew calm again and his eyes cleared.

The white-haired man nodded toward Aili and Liu Chenguang. "You'll have to tell me why you're here and my wife is not," he said. "She hasn't returned from hunting you."

Aili leapt back toward Tainu, her sword raised. The man laughed and threw a talisman, but Liu Chenguang blocked it and it fell harmlessly to the ground.

More demons entered, but none of them attacked yet. The man waved his hand negligently and a protective net of purple light enclosed Tainu, who remained unconscious. "None of that, now," he said. "I have plans for that one. Now that I have another phoenix, no need to put it off."

Suddenly, a cloud of something dark, shot with red like old blood, surrounded Liu Chenguang. She screamed and fell to her knees, then down to the stone floor, unconscious.

"Take her," he said to Zhu Guiren. "We'll clean up the couch before putting her there. Just bring her along for now."

Aili ran toward Zhu Guiren, phoenix whip raised, but at the last moment whirled and sent it at the white-haired man.

He raised a hand and caught it, laughing. "Quite nice, quite nice!" he said. He moved quickly — so quickly she didn't see him move at all — to stand directly in front of her face, still holding the phoenix whip. His hand was burning slightly, a stench coming from the skin, but he seemed uncaring. "Here you are, my dear," he said smiling, and slapped a talisman on her throat.

The sick pain rushed through her and she collapsed immediately, but she could still see, still hear. Zhu Guiren walked over to Liu Chenguang and picked her up. The white-haired demon removed the protective net and reached out to touch Tainu's shackles, one by one. They all disappeared. The demon leaned over to slap Tainu's face, over and over, until his eyes opened blearily; Aili saw the moment when he realized that Liu Chenguang was in Zhu Guiren's arms, and she saw how he closed them again in utter despair.

"Demon," he said, his voice hoarse and croaking. He didn't say anything else. Zhu Guiren's eyes were fixed on him, expressionless.

The white-haired man tugged roughly at Tainu until he sat up, then stood, leaning against him. The man put his arm around Tainu, almost lovingly. "Are you ready?" he asked. He stroked Tainu's shoulders, gently, and kissed him. Blood came away on his hands and mouth.

Tainu didn't respond; he didn't open his eyes again.

"Third, give the little phoenix to them," the man said, gesturing at the other demons. "Ninth, choose four others, you're coming. Tie her up. Rope is fine, she doesn't need a shackle. The hybrid doesn't even need to be tied. The talisman is enough."

Once the demons had tied up Liu Chenguang, who was still unconscious, and one of them had picked up Aili, who was still unable to move, the white-haired man said, "Now this one. Tie him to carry."

Two demons came over to Tainu and lay him down on the ground to tie him.

"No," he said, when they were done. "You're not the ones that will carry him. Third," he called again. "Bring him."

Zhu Guiren walked over to Tainu and picked him up, cradling him gently against his chest, but his face was still blank. "Not like that, Third," called the white-haired man, seemingly in high spirits. "Over your shoulder, like a sack."

"No," Zhu Guiren said. "This way."

The white-haired man stood still and looked at him, then came over to him and looked in his eyes. "Hmmm." He reached out with one finger and touched Zhu Guiren's chest. "Still good," he said, as though he had determined that some sort of machine was still in running order.

Aili stared at Zhu Guiren, unable to conceive of how he could be there, holding Tainu's bloody unconscious body, not fighting, not running, not…doing anything. Did he have a plan? What was happening? She was close to total panic. They had Liu Chenguang now, but they hadn't shackled her yet; it wasn't too late to get her away, except she herself couldn't move, paralyzed by the talisman, waves of pain crashing through her and blurring her vision.

"Asking First," said the demon called Ninth, a woman with black hair cut short and vividly purple eyes, "please instruct these as to where we are going? Should we prepare for a journey?"

"No need." With a sharp movement of his hand, First opened a red-black slash in the air. "Come," he said, and he stepped forward.

The demon carrying Aili, much like a sack over his shoulder, followed after Zhu Guiren and the demon carrying Liu Chenguang had gone first. When he put his foot down after stepping through the break in the air and threw Aili on the ground, she saw the golden-edged razor grass, and the deep green sky, and the crystal blue rocks of the spirit realm.

CHAPTER 19
TAINU

AILI HAD BEEN thrown on the ground near Liu Chenguang, who was still unconscious. Behind them, Ninth and the lesser demons made a half circle with First in the center, facing them.

"Third," he said, "bring the phoenix here. Put him in front of me."

Zhu Guiren hadn't thrown Tainu on the ground. He carried him gently to First, and carefully laid him down.

"Not like that," First said. "Make him kneel up."

Zhu Guiren pulled Tainu into an upright posture but he couldn't seem to stay there, though his eyes were open. Tainu looked only at Zhu Guiren, as though there was nothing else in the world to look at. Aili wasn't even sure that his eyes could focus to see as far as where she and Liu Chenguang were lying in the grass. Finally, Zhu Guiren managed to get him to kneel, and stood back with the other demons, his single hand and his clothing covered in Tainu's blood.

Aili, struggling fiercely, managed to finally move her hands.

Immediately, one of the demons noticed. "Asking First," he said, "this one can move now."

"How interesting!" First knelt down next to her and touched the talisman.

She screamed out loud at the shock of agony.

"And she can make noise now, too." He frowned at her and slapped her face. "Well, I want to examine her more closely later. We can't risk losing her. Tie her."

He stood up again and went over to Tainu, who was having difficulty kneeling upright on his own, swaying back and forth. He pushed gently on his shoulder and Tainu fell to the ground. First laughed.

Aili said, "Stop it." The words came out quietly; she seemed to be unable to put force behind them yet.

First looked back at her. "Very interesting," he said. "Make sure she can't get away."

She felt the demons tying her feet and hands tightly as she laid on her stomach, trying to wrestle away from them.

"Third," he asked, "why can she resist the talisman?"

Zhu Guiren said, "I have no idea. But we haven't had a chance to test it previously. It's all trial and error."

Aili realized that underneath her belly, pressed against her skin as she lay on the ground, the feathers Liu Chenguang had given her were almost burning hot, sending a sense of warmth all through her body. It was beginning to wear away the choking tightness of the talisman on her throat, and the paralysis was weakening as well. She stilled, trying not to give away that she was more and more capable of movement. She was tied, but that was temporary — rope was only rope. She risked a glance over at Liu Chenguang, who was still unconscious. This was worrying; what had they done to her?

First poked Tainu with his foot. "Phoenix," he said, "any last words?"

"Not to you," said Tainu. He struggled back up to his knees. His eyes were clearer now, and looked toward Zhu Guiren.

First watched him, then smiled and spoke at last: "Third, kill the phoenix."

Zhu Guiren straightened up. "No," he said. He stepped back, out of the circle of other demons.

"No?" First seemed amused. "I will give you one more chance."

"I will not," said Zhu Guiren. He looked calmly at Tainu, then at First. "Someone else can do it. It doesn't have to be me."

Aili yelled in shock. "Zhu Guiren! You can't– You have to protect him–"

One of the other demons slapped her face to silence her, but she still struggled and fought to get away, trying to bring phoenix fire against them, but the talisman still kept her from calling En, or any weapon.

First looked at her, smiling. "Later for you, my dear. As Third said, you are indeed an interesting experiment." He walked over to stand next to Zhu Guiren. "Please observe. This is also an experiment."

Tainu looked very fragile, his arms tied painfully behind his back, his ankles tied together, forced into a kneeling posture, the posture of someone awaiting execution. His expression was calm. He looked only at Zhu Guiren. "Demon," he called, "look at me."

Zhu Guiren turned to meet his eyes.

Tainu's bloodstained face was very gentle as he smiled at him. "Now look away," he said. "Don't watch. Remember what you promised me."

Zhu Guiren did not look away. He kept looking at Tainu's face.

First said, "Ninth, there are several vacancies in the ranks above you. Kill the phoenix, and I will consider you for promotion into one of them."

Ninth stepped forward from the surrounding half-circle of demons. "Please instruct this person as to the preferred mode of death," she said respectfully.

First seemed to consider. "Killing a phoenix is no easy matter, even here," he said at last. "Blood loss before the fatal strike is crucial." He smiled. "Let's start with slashing both wrists and the throat. Then, immediate disembowelment. After that, decapitation on my word."

Aili screamed again and struggled harder; two additional demons came over to hold her down. "Zhu Guiren!" she shouted. "Zhu Guiren, wake up!"

"I'm not asleep," he said, sounding slightly insulted.

"Zhu Guiren!"

Tainu said, his voice suddenly stronger, "Aili, don't blame him. It's not his fault. Don't you watch either." He kept looking at Zhu Guiren. "Demon, please, stop watching."

Zhu Guiren did not obey.

Tainu closed his eyes.

The female demon leapt forward, two small knives in her hands. She freed Tainu's hands and slashed his wrists to the bone in one quick movement, then slashed his throat. Bright red blood poured from all three wounds. Before he could fall over, she changed one knife to a short sword, and stabbed and tore at his stomach several times. Tainu screamed at last, long and hoarse. Darker blood and other things poured and slipped out. He fell forward on top of them, his limbs twitching against the golden grass.

Aili couldn't stop screaming. She could feel the demons holding her down, pushing against her legs and back to hold her on the ground as she thrashed in a desperate frenzy, but Zhu Guiren stood there, calmly, looking serious but in no way upset.

"Zhu Guiren! Let me go, I might still be able to save him—"

Zhu Guiren looked at her, frowning, then looked back to Tainu's body.

First turned to Zhu Guiren. "Third," he said gently, smiling. "Come here."

Zhu Guiren came a step closer.

First put his hand on Zhu Guiren's chest and murmured something.

Zhu Guiren suddenly threw his head back and screamed. Screamed without breath, as though he was tearing out his own throat with his pain as he ran toward Tainu. Aili stared in shock and horror.

First stepped in Zhu Guiren's path and casually threw him aside, seemingly without effort, certainly without weapons. "Do you see?" he said to Aili, strolling over to her. "Let's see what he does now." He turned to Ninth, standing next to Tainu's dying body. "Decapitation," he ordered.

Before the demon's sword could come down on Tainu's neck, Zhu Guiren had cut off the other demon's arm, then slashed her nearly in half with his halberd. He knelt next to Tainu, keening wordlessly, trying to pick him up and hold him with his hands and body covered in Tainu's blood.

"Zhu Guiren!" Aili shouted. "Let me go. I can help!"

"Too late," said First, satisfied. "He didn't need decapitation after all. The bleeding before we got here must have weakened him significantly. We'll have to add this method to the records for future reference. Although, I don't expect we'll need to kill phoenixes in the future. With his death, the refuges will dissolve. We'll be able to capture them on rebirth again, as we used to do. Interesting…I'm not sure the phoenix death produced any resentment at all." His tongue flicked out, as though tasting for something in the air. He added, kicking Aili in the face, "Now watch and see what Third does. He's been totally destroyed, I think. His death will produce outstanding resentment." His eyes glowed with anticipation, like coals showing the patterns of the flame.

Aili looked, horrified, at Zhu Guiren trying to cradle Tainu's broken body against him. "You did this to him?"

"Of course," he said.

Zhu Guiren's cries had words now; he rocked back and forth, calling Tainu's name over and over, crying for him to come back, saying he was sorry, sorry, sorry. Then, without any pause, he stabbed himself in the throat with a dagger of ice and smoke.

Aili screamed again. First laughed.

Because he was laughing, he didn't notice that Aili froze in place, but the demons sitting on top of her did, and relaxed. Tainu was suddenly kneeling down next to her. He reached over to her, and she felt that tingling sensation — a ghost trying to be heard. His voice was not distant or strange; it sounded just as it did when he was alive, but very agitated.

"Tell him!" he was shouting at her. "Tell him!"

First looked over at the demons holding Aili. He snapped his fingers, opening a slash in the air. "All of you, go," he said. "Go assist Second. Tell her we have the phoenix and the hybrid, and the refuges are destroyed as we planned. She should come home now."

The demons stood, bowed, and transformed to fly through the gate back to the mortal realm.

Zhu Guiren was too distraught to have hit a fatal point with his first stab. He pulled the dagger out of his own throat, gurgling with blood, and readied himself more carefully, closing his eyes and laying the dagger's edge along his jugular vein.

Aili understood at last what Tainu wanted. She screamed, "Zhu Guiren! Tainu is here! He says remember your promise!"

Zhu Guiren opened his bloodshot eyes and shook his head.

"He says–" she yelled. "He says that his name is Tielende! He wants to hear you say his name. He says he loves you. He says you promised!"

Zhu Guiren held the dagger at his own throat, his hand shaking, his mouth moving without making sounds. It was possible that he couldn't make sounds; blood was pouring from the wound in his throat.

"He's here," she said. "He's right next to you. He's trying to touch you." Tears streamed down her face. She could see Tainu — the deep distress in his features, trying desperately to embrace Zhu Guiren, to hold his hand back.

"I can't feel him," Zhu Guiren rasped, voice thick and bubbling. He laid Tainu's body down, very gently, and stood up. "I can't hear him. I can't feel him."

First frowned. "What is–"

Before he finished, Zhu Guiren had a sword embedded in First's chest. He drew it out, then slashed him across the stomach, then his throat, then his wrists. First winced. His body shifted, becoming far less human-seeming and more monstrous, cold and furious.

"Zhu Guiren!" Aili screamed, struggling.

First came at Zhu Guiren with a sword in one hand and spear in the other, but Zhu Guiren dodged out of the way and raced to her, slashing down to break Aili's bonds. She rolled over; he had also slashed her skin, but it would heal quickly. She screamed in rage and attacked along with him, a phoenix whip in each hand.

Zhu Guiren's energy was fading quickly. He was bleeding heavily; Aili grabbed him, swiped her own bleeding wrist across his throat, and spun back toward First, who came at her, his teeth bared in a grimace. She whipped him again, hard, but once more he caught the phoenix whip in his hand. This time, she let him pull her close and stabbed him with En, sending a sword pulse of qi into his body. He growled and slashed at her with his dagger hand, and she left En buried in his chest, flipped back, and held her hands in the demon-quelling form, sending more qi into his body through En. First raced at her, but veered off toward where Liu Chenguang still lay on the ground. Panicked, Aili leapt to meet him, but she wasn't fast enough.

Zhu Guiren got there first, standing over Liu Chenguang's body; he had something in his single hand that she didn't recognize, but he used it to throw spear after spear of qi at First. Several caught First in the torso and abdomen, but he ripped them out and crushed them in his hands. He leapt bodily at Zhu Guiren, bearing him down to the ground next to Liu Chenguang and lifting his clawed hand to tear out his throat. Zhu Guiren was still, looking upward at the sky as though this didn't matter much to him anymore.

Aili could hear Tainu shouting at her, could hear that he was terrified for Zhu Guiren. He ran over as well, his ghostly hands trying to pull First off of him. To her shock, she realized that First could feel Tainu, even if he couldn't see or hear him. First whipped around and growled at the air, yelling something in the demonic language, and then turned to spit in Zhu Guiren's face. Zhu Guiren screamed in rage and began fighting again, just as Aili reached them. She threw herself on First's back, reaching around his throat to slash it thoroughly with her dagger of qi, and then wrapping the phoenix whip around his neck like a garrote to drag him off Zhu Guiren. Gasping, Zhu Guiren raised his single hand and let it fall back to the ground again, weakly.

The stench of First's burning flesh was heavy in her nostrils, but he was both strong and unbelievably resistant to pain. He suddenly threw himself backward so that he landed on his back with her underneath him, and then twisted around, hissing and slashing at her over and over again with the two daggers in his hands — her arms, her throat, her face. *It will heal, it will heal,* she thought to herself, her mind rapidly going through her options before she reached behind him to stab through his spinal cord, En grating on his bones.

He screamed and scrabbled back behind him with his hands; they grew very long, claws extending out, and he grabbed En and threw it at her, shouting a curse in the demonic tongue. Just before it impaled her through the forehead, En disappeared, dissolving into a shower of qi.

Aili called En back, but it didn't come. She backed up quickly, trying to draw First away from Liu Chenguang and Zhu Guiren on the ground.

Liu Chenguang had sat up at last, her hand on her head.

"Zhu Guiren! Heal Zhu Guiren!" Aili shouted. Her own wounds were healing slowly, poisoned with corruption, she realized.

But Liu Chenguang instead ran toward her, trying to use her wings to block a talisman that First had thrown. Even with qinggong she was too late. Once again, the talisman caught Aili, brushing her shoulder, and she felt the instant power of it on her, freezing her meridians, stilling her muscles. First watched Liu Chenguang catch her, rolling over and over to protect her with her wings, which in the spirit world were visible — red and gold, each feather limned with light.

First turned from them and walked steadily toward Zhu Guiren, holding his hand out for a sword.

Liu Chenguang stared down at her, terrified. "What– Aili– Tainu?"

Aili couldn't respond; Liu Chenguang's wings were protecting her, slowly nullifying the talisman, but too slow, too slow.

Suddenly, she was choking on thick, silty water; Liu Chenguang had grabbed Beilong's flask and dumped it out on her. Aili gasped, trying to drink, assuming that was what the water was for, since that was what Beilong had said, but a lot of it was going into her nose and her eyes and her ears as well. Sand as fine as air mixed in the water, gritty and tasteless against her teeth and tongue. There was nothing sweet or refreshing about this water — mountains and rivers, eyes and ears and nose and mouth and breath and body — and she choked and choked and got it down at last.

Liu Chenguang rolled off her and ran for Zhu Guiren, and Aili stood up, shaking her head in confusion. The dragon was imprinted on her mind: the dragon that was too large for the mind to hold. When she moved she felt that immensity moving along with her, a huge shadow with her small, frail body, following her and obeying as though she were holding the sticks of a shadow puppet. Or perhaps, she was the shadow, and something was holding her. There was the small and colorful world, and there was the great and unseeable shadow behind all the delicate and solid lines that tried to divide one thing from another.

There was another shadow, shapeless, huge, bending down over Zhu Guiren, and next to it was a small, bright star. Zhu Guiren was a puppet — a small broken puppet — and the shadow was reaching into him and tearing out his heart.

Aili yelled, and in her own mind, it was a roaring noise of waterfalls and boulders crashing in the flood. She threw herself on the shadow, tearing it with her claws of qi and her teeth of fire and the weight of her being. The shadow tried to flee, but she was much faster, much larger. *Trash*, she thought scornfully, and ripped it to shreds, tiny screaming pieces of shadow fleeing in all directions, but her being was a flood that captured all the pieces, the sliding silt that sealed them beneath. Each little bit of it was captured under her own shadow and torn and torn and torn until it could never become one being again, until it would dissolve into the greater existence. The bits of shadow she had ripped apart faded softly into the earth, harmless now.

Aili stood still, quivering with violence and rage and power, her eyes closed until she felt that fade from her as well, and she was only herself again. She opened her eyes to feel Liu Chenguang's arms wrapped around her. Zhu Guiren was lying on the ground, Tainu's ghost trying to hold his hand. Everything felt very still. Aili collapsed to her knees and Liu Chenguang stayed with her, calling her name, keeping her from falling into unconsciousness.

Zhu Guiren knelt back down next to Tainu's body. He could feel that Liu Chenguang was placing blood on his wounds, trying to heal him now that Aili was settled and conscious again, but he merely stayed still, uncaring. It was better if he was bleeding and in pain, but he had no energy to stop her. Kneeling was not enough. He laid down, pulled Tainu's body close to him, and closed his eyes, unspeaking.

Liu Chenguang knelt on the other side. "Tainu," she said. "Tainu." She shook the body a little bit.

Zhu Guiren pushed her hand away.

Aili said, "He's still here."

Zhu Guiren didn't move. That Tainu's ghost was here was a comfort, but soon, even his ghost would be gone. There was nothing to hold him to existence. Tainu had died without resentment, satisfied that his demon was still alive. He buried his head in Tainu's neck and let the hot tears pour down.

Aili's voice came. "Tainu says he loves you so much. He doesn't want you to be sad. He's not afraid of death. Only of leaving you behind. Only that you'll mourn him too much."

Zhu Guiren made a high-pitched whining noise because there were no words to answer that. But Tainu was still here, Tainu could still hear him. How could he say his last words to him and have them be bitter? The words of his heart: *don't leave me, I will never stop mourning you, I will die even if I'm alive.*

"I love you," he said instead. "I love you. I'm so sorry– I'm so sorry I failed you. I wanted to keep you safe, I wanted to make you happy–" He found that he was sobbing, gasping for air. The world was black, because he would not open his eyes again; he would not open his eyes and see that Tainu was now not in it.

"He's touching you," said Aili. It sounded as though she were crying too. "He wants to know, can you feel it?"

He tried, he really did, but there was nothing. He shook his head.

Aili said, "He asks, can you say his name? He never heard you say his name."

Zhu Guiren whispered, "Tielende," and felt the connection — the golden light inside him that meant it was a true name buried forever in his heart.

Liu Chenguang's voice came, also choked with tears, "Look. The refuges. The refuges are dissolving."

Zhu Guiren didn't want to look, but the refuges were a part of Tainu, the last part that he would be able to see. So he looked, and everywhere throughout the landscape, bright golden beams were springing up to the heavens, from the hills and mountains and plains, far into the distance. There were so many — dozens that they could see from where they sat. So many refuges that he had built, with his blood and his pain and his love.

"The refuges are him," he said as they watched the sky be striped with light.

"Zhu Guiren," Aili said suddenly, her voice tight, "Tainu says, if you really want it, he will try to stay for you. Otherwise, he says he is ready to go."

Zhu Guiren's throat was healed now, but he choked. He managed to get out, "Yes. Tainu, yes."

"Aili, what are you talking about?" Liu Chenguang asked.

Aili said, "I don't know." She wiped her eyes. "I'm just saying exactly what he's saying. Zhu Guiren, he says you need to use his blood to set an array. Right now. It has to be before the refuges fully dissolve."

Already, some of the beams of light were thinning.

"Liu Chenguang, you have to come here." She moved Liu Chenguang's hands as though she were sitting with her palms pressed against someone else's. "He's here. Tainu says you are cultivating with him. He wants you to send him qi. His hands are against yours now. He says you can't feel him yet, but if it works, you should soon feel that the qi is circulating with another body. He asks, do you understand?"

Liu Chenguang nodded, her eyes determined.

Zhu Guiren knelt by Tainu's body, reaching out to touch it and then drawing back. There was already blood everywhere, the terrible wounds of his death and the wounds he himself had given him, all those days, carved into his skin one by one with his own hand. He couldn't even cry anymore. His hatred of himself was so great that he wanted to stab himself, over and over and over, until he had as many wounds as Tainu. It would hurt less than this. But Tainu wanted him, wanted him to do this — this one last terrible thing. "I can't," he said. "I can't do this to him."

He felt Aili next to him, speaking quietly. "Tainu says he doesn't want to say your true name, so instead he says this. He wants me to say exactly this. Only exactly this." She closed her eyes. "I want to stay with you. This is only my body, that would be reborn anyway in a few centuries. This is trying to bring about an early rebirth. That's all it is. When my body dissolves, the array will bind me here, to you, until there is a new spiritual body for me. Don't be afraid. Just do it, my demon. I need you to do it right now."

Zhu Guiren listened. The tears started rolling down his face again, but he reached into Tainu's ravaged body through the great wound in his belly, trying not to feel it. He brought his hand out full of thickening blood, and began to sprinkle it on the earth, chanting. He saw the smoke spider creature leap out and bind something invisible near Liu Chenguang. *Was it Tainu's soul? Had he captured Tainu as he had captured so many others for so many centuries for his own needs, caring nothing for their suffering?* The spider didn't go anywhere else before it leapt back to his hand and disappeared.

"I feel something," said Liu Chenguang suddenly.

Zhu Guiren's head whipped up.

"Zhu Guiren," said Aili, "he's telling me to burn his body with phoenix fire. It has to be right now. Get back." She raised her hand.

Zhu Guiren stumbled backward, and she slashed down with the phoenix whip. The body didn't burn, but like the refuges, it dissolved into a pillar of golden sparks, rushing upwards into the sky.

Suddenly the pillar bent; all of the pillars, all of the golden, dissolving refuges, bent and coalesced into the invisible person whose palms were held against Liu Chenguang's.

Liu Chenguang shouted in surprise, spreading her wings. The influx of qi was so enormous that she blazed with light, too bright to see. Aili covered her eyes, but Zhu Guiren strained his eyes toward the light, eager, hopeful. The light grew brighter and brighter, more focused, as if all the light in the world pressed down into a blazingly brilliant star sitting opposite Liu Chenguang. Her bright wings were a black silhouette against that sunfire, and it compressed and compressed, brighter and brighter, until it was a pinprick too brilliant to even imagine, simultaneously all colors beyond the world's holding and no color at all, burning existence around it.

And then, it disappeared.

Liu Chenguang collapsed, her wings crumpled beneath her.

Zhu Guiren felt a hot, burning sensation in the palm of his single hand. It grew and grew, hotter and stronger as though a fire was burning through his skin — a searing star of flame.

Just as suddenly, the heat went out.

Shaking, he unfolded his fingers. In the palm of his hand was a very small red bird — smaller than a hummingbird, not nearly as big as a sparrow. He raised it up to the level of his face, and it opened its golden eyes and stretched out to rub its bright-feathered head delicately against his nose. Then it settled down in his hand, and went to sleep.

CHAPTER 20
AFTER

Tainu woke up in a warm place, feeling very tired. He looked up and saw the face of his beloved one, his demon, and it all came back to him.

His demon had fallen asleep too, lying still in the golden grass outside the refuge, but was still holding him in his hand, loosely cupped so that he could move and flap his wings if he wanted to. Cautiously, he stretched out his wings and hopped out of his demon's hand. He didn't yet have all his flight feathers, so he continued to hop up to his face and nestled close to him, close enough to feel the warmth of his breath. Gently, softly, he called, "Arciniang."

He opened his eyes. He looked so tired, so hurt, and withdrew from him, afraid.

"Arciniang," he said, "please don't let it hurt you so much. I'm here…"

His demon nodded and held his hand out to him again, but didn't speak as he sat up.

From his new, higher vantage point, he saw Aili sitting a little bit away with her back to them, her sword ready in her hand. Liu Chenguang sat next to her. The two of them were talking quietly.

"Liu Chenguang," he called.

Liu Chenguang turned to him and walked over, kneeling so that she was next to Zhu Guiren. She asked, very gently, "May I take him? I need to bring him into the refuge now."

The demon jerked slightly and nodded, holding out his hand.

"I'll be back," Tainu said, "wait for me, don't worry."

But he didn't respond.

Once they were in the refuge, Liu Chenguang let him out and he sighed, stretching his wings. "This is better," he said. "I'll grow quickly so I can come back out sooner."

Liu Chenguang said, "Tainu, Zhu Guiren is…not in good shape."

"Why? I'm back…"

"Like you told me with Aili," she said, "this is not normal for him. He can't understand that it's really you and that rebirth is what we are accustomed to. And this isn't a normal rebirth. You were dead, Tainu. You were truly dead. He saw your dead body, he touched you when you were dead, his hand was filled with your blood. That's what he remembers now. That's all he can think of. You were a ghost that Aili spoke to." Her eyes filled with tears. "You were dissolving. Do you remember it?"

"I remember." He remembered it — the sense of dissolution, of the spaces within him growing and the pieces of his soul shrinking and scattering. "I came back for him."

Liu Chenguang nodded. "He hasn't spoken since," she said. "I didn't want to bring you into the refuge until you two were able to talk because he's in so much pain. I don't think he can bear to be here with you. His cultivation system is completely haywire with a mix of corrupted and natural qi. And…" She stopped.

"I know," he said. From First's sick pleasure in tormenting the demon, he could well imagine what had been done to him when he was powerless to resist it, what had been involved in breaking the connections between his mind and his heart. *I can't be with him in that way anyway, not until I'm grown,* he thought. *We'll have time.* But a little anxiety wrinkled into his heart.

He tried the transformation, and it worked; he already had enough spiritual power back for that. "How old do I look?" he asked, his voice piping high.

Liu Chenguang smiled. "Around four," she said. "You're so cute."

"If I go out to talk to him, do you think…you and Aili could give us privacy?"

"Let's make a plan first," she said. "How long do you think it will take you to cultivate to adulthood?"

His heart sank. This was hard to calculate; the time in the spirit realm didn't match with the mortal world well. "A year at least," he said. "Maybe more. Between one and three years." Once, a year would have been a blink of an eye to him; now, it seemed forever. He wanted to be back in the world, back with his demon.

"He can't stay here that long," she said. "He's more or less defenseless right now."

He nodded, dejected. His emotions were rather childish at the moment too.

"We'll set up a phoenix gate here. Aili can do it," she said. "We'll be able to come back and forth."

"Where will you all be?" he asked.

"Aili and I will go back to the Common Federation," she said. "She wants to be with her mother. If he'll come with us, Zhu Guiren as well. I don't think he should be alone, and I don't think he should be in the Daxian Republic. Try to convince him."

He nodded and squared his childish shoulders. "All right, then," he said.

When they left the refuge together, Tainu saw his demon sitting right next to the outside wall. Liu Chenguang took Aili's hand and they walked further away.

Zhu Guiren's eyes followed them and then turned, reluctantly, to him. "Demon?"

Zhu Guiren started crying silently, looking at him.

"Arciniang," he said, coming over and sitting next to him, "it's still me. I'm just small."

"I know," he said hoarsely. He wiped his eyes with his single hand. "I'm so sorry."

Tainu decided to use a different strategy. He simply couldn't have this conversation in the body of a four-year-old child. It was too strange. He transformed back. Already, he was slightly bigger — a sparrow rather than a hummingbird. *I should probably stay in my true body here as much as possible, the cultivation will be faster.*

"Arciniang, can you take your true form too?"

The demon's eyes were startled, but he nodded and immediately transformed. The creature of ice and smoke was there before him, the air around him glittering with silver sparks. Tainu hopped up onto his right claw, then onto his snout so he could look into his eyes. He laughed. "Demon, you really always do have the same expression." He felt so tiny next to him. "I love you so much."

His demon closed his eyes, which in his true body were not black, but a very deep blue that was almost indistinguishable from black until seen very close, like ice over a deep lake. "How can you still love me?" he asked. "I've failed you in every possible way."

Tainu shook his feathered head, not knowing what to say. At last, he said, "You didn't fail me at all. You didn't. None of that was what you wanted to do

to me. You brought me back at the end. And now, can't things be good again?"
He knew he still sounded like a four-year-old; he couldn't help it — that's how
his emotions were at the moment. "I have you back, and you have your heart. We
have each other."

His demon looked at him and gently laid his head down on the ground. "I'm
getting cross-eyed looking at you," he said. "You're so little."

Tainu smiled, though it didn't show in his bird form. "I'll get bigger as
quickly as I can," he promised.

"I'll stay here until you do."

Tainu thought about it, hopping off the demon's snout and a little way away
so he didn't have to get cross-eyed. Then, he laughed and fluttered his wings;
the primaries had come in. He flew up to the end of one of the icicle horns and
landed there.

"That's also an awkward way to look at you," his demon said, but his voice
sounded a little lighter.

Tainu fluttered back down. He said, seriously, "Demon, I want to complete
my cultivation as quickly as I can. And that means I should probably be in the
refuge as much as possible, and not paying attention to anybody. If you were
here, I would want to always be with you." This was true, and he thought it was
better to say it this way than to emphasize that Zhu Guiren shouldn't be alone
in the spirit world right now for his own safety, for his own healing. He needed
Aili's protection and he needed to be with other people who would talk to him
and distract him from his pain, not waiting for a bird that was hiding in a hole,
trying to cultivate.

The demon nodded his head. All his movements were very regal, with the
weight of the icicle horns.

"You're very beautiful," Tainu blurted out.

The demon put his head down on the ground again and didn't say anything.

Feeling a bit as though this wasn't going at all how he had hoped, Tainu said,
"Will you come visit me? Aili and Liu Chenguang can bring you. Will you stay
with them? Then when I come back, we can be together."

The demon was silent, and then he said, "I don't know if– if I can…If you
will want me."

"Why would I not?" His heart felt a little desperate. "I will always love you.
I will always want you."

"I'm not like I was," he said. "I don't have any power. To protect you, or do
anything else. I don't– I don't have…I'm not like I was before."

Tainu wished so strongly that he was able to take on an adult form right now, to take him in his arms, but as a four-year-old or a baby bird there was no such reassurance he could give. All he could say was, "I love you and I will always love you," as seriously as a sparrow could say it. "I love you in your mortal body and I love you in this one. I love you with power and without. I love you because I love your heart and I love you with whatever body I have."

Arciniang looked at him. "I love you too," he said, at last. "I love you, Tielende."

They brought Zhu Guiren back when Tainu had grown to the size of a falcon. When Zhu Guiren arrived, he flew up high in delight, and spiraled down around him, spilling golden qi all over silver scales. He could see that his demon was smiling inside even though it was hard to tell with his true body; smiles didn't really fit on that face. He raised his icicle horns and let Tainu dive in and out around them before they settled down together, Tainu nestling between his forelegs.

"How is it in the mortal world?" he asked.

The demon said, "Aili and Liu Chenguang are living in Sand Island with the little dragon. He's going to school there. Aili's mother is there too."

"And you?" he asked.

He hesitated. "I'm there a lot. Not all the time. I have a project I'm working on."

"That's good," he said, smiling. "That's very good. What is it?"

"A surprise. I'll show you when you come back."

"Are you cultivating?"

"Aili's teaching me how to cultivate natural qi, the way she learned at Crane Moon," he said.

Tainu smiled inwardly.

"You did that, didn't you?" the demon said, nudging him with his snout until he laughed and had to spread his wings to keep his balance. "That time in the flood, when you said it was preventative…you planted a new cultivation system in me."

"It worked!" he said, jubilant. "I didn't know if it would. That's why I didn't tell you. I put it in the place in your side where your old cultivation system was already destroyed. It wouldn't begin to grow into your meridians unless your old cultivation system became completely nonfunctional."

The demon's head swung back and forth, the icicles cutting a swathe through the silver glitter from his scales. "Tainu, how did you do it?"

"I don't know," he said. "Someone told me once that phoenixes are all intuition and no skill."

"That must have been a very rude person," the demon responded.

"The rudest person I've ever met," he said. "But I think the only person in the world it would have been possible for me to do that for, because…"

The demon tilted his head to one side, considering.

It brought back very ancient memories for Tainu.

"Because?"

"Because we were as close as it's possible for people to be," Tainu said simply. "Because I love him so very much."

The demon looked down again.

Tainu transformed into his mortal body. He was now somewhere around nine or ten years old, he thought. It was hard to tell without a mirror or any other human people around to compare with, but that seemed to be the size of clothing he wore; he had long ago asked Liu Chenguang to bring him a wide variety, to have it as he grew. He stood in front of his demon and said, "Look at me, Arciniang," very seriously.

He looked, and away.

Tainu said, "Demon, my mortal body is still here. Someday, I'll be grown again. I don't want you to reject me then. I don't want you to be afraid of me or think of me as a ghost."

Zhu Guiren said, at last, "It hurts me to see you in your mortal body."

"Because I died in it?"

"Because I hurt you in it," he replied. "I did it, with my own hand. No one forced me, I wasn't controlled, I wasn't a puppet. I could have refused. It just…" His lip curled, showing his crystal teeth. "It wasn't convenient for me to resist. I weighed the costs and consequences and chose to hurt you. Even knowing who you were, even remembering…everything…"

Tainu's heart ached for him, but he said, "Arciniang, I made this mortal body to be the one that you knew." He walked over to stand next to him and put his forehead against the ridge over his eye. "Do you hate it?"

He felt himself getting teary inside. It was true the mortal body had been his choice; it was true that a phoenix had great control over the mortal body, more than a demon or other spiritual creature. He could have remade a different body for himself, but this body — this was the body his demon had loved. He wanted so much to stay in this body. It wasn't only a piece of clothing that he could change or not change. He understood, now, why Liu Chenguang had reshaped her mortal body to be identical to the one she met Hong Deming in after his death.

Softly, his demon said, "I don't hate it. I could never." He pushed against Tainu, and he almost fell down.

The spirit realm time was not like mortal time. When the demon came again, he was close to sixteen, lanky and gangling, and his true body was much larger than any mortal bird. He didn't show Arciniang his mortal body that time. It felt too embarrassing; adolescence brought all those feelings and bodily responses that he wasn't sure he could control, plus pimples and general awkwardness. Who wants to show their life's love what they looked like at sixteen? In his true body, however, he was aware that he was quite gorgeous, and so he flew all around his demon, draping him with his long plumage of blood and sunlight, golden qi glittering to match the demon's silver scales.

"Will you show me your mortal body?" Tainu asked as he rested between Arciniang's forelegs after showing off. "Just…I want to see you."

Arciniang nodded and transformed, and there he was: Zhu Guiren's clear dark eyes looking at him, arms wrapped around his wings and covered with his feathers as they lay on the ground together. His hair had begun to grow long again, well past his ears toward his shoulders. Tainu found himself itching to touch it with his hands. Just as well that he was in his true body at the moment. His true body didn't have gender, and it also didn't have hands; embarrassing things could thus be avoided. He allowed himself to run his beak through his hair, just once. He then spread his wings and bowed, feeling like a very red-tinged peacock, but he wanted to do *something* to show him his appreciation. His demon laughed.

"I miss you," Zhu Guiren said, abruptly. "I miss you so much."

"I miss you too," he said. Truly, it had been a bit of a shock to see Zhu Guiren again in his mortal body. He felt such a yearning toward him, not only because he was sixteen years old, but because, because, because…His heart beat with it. "Soon," he said. "I'm cultivating as fast as I can."

"I know," his demon said, and transformed back to his true body. It was a relief to both of them. Tainu flew over to nestle under his chin, and they were able to sleep together like that in the sunlight while Aili and Liu Chenguang kept watch with their backs to them.

When his demon came again, he was almost done. His body was in his early twenties.

He thought a great deal about how to manage this. He was old enough now, and certainly he wanted certain things, but he didn't want to move too fast, and he didn't want his demon to be pressured, and he didn't want to be rejected or have everything be awful. He thought it would be best to appear in his true body, his tail feathers nearly ten feet long and sparkling with gold and sunlight every time he moved; it would be good for his demon to see him like that first, and then he would realize that now it was awkward for him to cuddle. The demon's true body was a good size too, but they wouldn't fit together very well, so then his demon might just go ahead and ask him to transform, and then it wouldn't feel as though he was pressuring him at all.

He was extraordinarily nervous.

It was all thrown off because Zhu Guiren appeared in his mortal body to begin with, so there he was feeling very awkward, standing with his head several feet above Zhu Guiren's, and desperately wanting him.

But instead of asking him to transform, Zhu Guiren just reached out and touched his feathers as though in wonder. "You're so beautiful," he said. Where his hand touched his feathers, it nearly disappeared into their softness, and golden qi spiraled out all around him, encompassing him in Tainu's aura.

"You never said that before," Tainu blurted out. "Wasn't I the same before?"

"You were beautiful then too, but now you're yourself again." He looked up at him. "Aren't you?" he asked softly.

He nodded his head. Now, he felt very embarrassed. Out of an intense desire to change this conversation, he asked, "Demon, would you like to fly with me?"

"That would be embarrassing," he replied seriously.

He reached down and very carefully ran his beak through Zhu Guiren's hair; he had to be careful about it because his beak was now larger than Zhu Guiren's head. "You can ride on my back," he said. "Not embarrassing at all. How can you be offended when I'm being so friendly and helpful?"

Zhu Guiren laughed, which was the best sound in the world, and Tainu knelt down to let him clamber on to his back. "What if the feathers fall out?" he asked conversationally. "You don't have a saddle or anything."

"I'll dive and catch you, of course," he said, and spread his wings and leapt up into the air. He could hear Zhu Guiren laughing with joy, and he remembered that his demon hadn't been able to fly since he lost his hand. He must have missed it.

He very carefully swooped down to a place he thought would be safe — a place with another refuge at their backs, but far away from Aili and Liu Chenguang. He wanted privacy for this.

Zhu Guiren slipped off his back and they looked at one another.

He took a deep breath and transformed.

Zhu Guiren's eyes filled with tears as he looked at him. "Tainu," he said softly.

He nodded, feeling his heart in his throat. "Demon," he said. "It's me. I missed you so much."

Zhu Guiren walked steadily toward him, never taking his eyes away, though he also didn't stop crying, and then his arms were around him, hugging him fiercely. "So long," he said, burying his face into his shoulder. "Tainu, it's been so long. I've missed you. I've missed you."

Zhu Guiren turned his head so his lips were against his throat and kissed him; Tainu felt his whole body shiver with it, and Zhu Guiren stiffened against him.

"Oh." Tainu had forgotten how it felt. He had forgotten what it was like to have his demon love him. He thought he remembered, but he really hadn't.

He sank down to the ground, pulling Zhu Guiren down with him, feeling his weight, the softness of his hair spilling around him. His demon kissed him harder, reaching down between his knees to push them apart so he could lie between them.

"Arciniang," he gasped, but he couldn't get out any other words. Zhu Guiren's hand was touching him everywhere that he was most sensitive — all the places that he had dreamed of since his mortal body cultivated into adolescence.

"Oh," he said, sharp and surprised, and reached up to tangle his hands in Zhu Guiren's hair and kiss him, everything about them entangled in one another, and he wasn't afraid. He wasn't afraid of this. He wanted this so badly, for so long.

His demon's voice trembled against his skin, calling his name, and Tainu was too breathless with joy to answer.

CHAPTER 21
The Mortal Realm

A few weeks after they had left Tainu in the spirit realm, Liu Chenguang showed Zhu Guiren around Little Daxian, including the apothecary where she had worked. She looked at it consideringly. "You know," she said, "if you still have access to your gold, I'd rather just open my own. And I can study Federative medical traditions too. There's a college nearby."

"You can study here?" he asked. "What kind of things?"

"Oh, all kinds," she said breezily.

Since Zhu Guiren knew the Liu Chenguang of old, he knew this meant that she had no idea. "Aili, what can you study here?"

"It's not in Easterly," Aili said, walking slightly behind them, holding Yisue's hand. "There's a college in San Toma. I don't know what they study. I didn't even graduate from high school."

"Why do I have to go to school then?" Yisue asked immediately. "It sounds so boring."

"Because you're five hundred years old and functionally illiterate in two languages. That's why," Aili said. "I'm going to go back to school too. We can go look at the college together some time, Zhu Guiren."

He nodded, slumping back into indifference.

Aili and Liu Chenguang looked at each other.

Yisue yelled "DUMPLINGS!" and ran down the street.

Liu Chenguang said, "I'll catch him," and ran after him.

Aili and Zhu Guiren walked together; he felt about as comfortable with Aili as he felt with anyone except Tainu, who was different, and who he couldn't think about now without hating himself, and who he couldn't stop thinking about. She was able to be quiet when he wanted to be, which was most of the time now. He hadn't ever cut her into pieces to collect her blood, either, which made things feel less awkward for him.

After they had walked aimlessly for a block or so, following Yisue's white hair down the street, he made an effort and asked, "Why are we living in Sand Island instead of here if you both like Little Daxian so much?"

Aili replied, "When Liu Chenguang and I met with his parents, they were very clear that Yisue needed to have frequent access to the ocean, even if he doesn't swim every day. If we were in Easterly, he'd just have the estuary and the port, and they're kind of dirty and filled with heavy machinery and lots of people. A child or a dragon in the water would be noticed for sure. Sand Island's got a beach, at least, although the water's really shallow."

She added, "I've been thinking that we might need to go up to Fallon again." She said this easily now, although Zhu Guiren remembered that when she had first mentioned Fallon at the dinner table a few weeks before, she had seemed to choke. "My mother's going to sell that land. I don't want it, but when we have the money from that, we should find some other place that has good ocean access for him so we can go stay there sometimes, near his coast and his dragon gate."

"Why don't you just keep the land in Fallon?" he asked, without much interest.

Aili looked at him, her expression complicated in a way he didn't understand. "I burned Fallon to the ground. Bad things happened to me in Fallon," she said. "Like what happened to you at the clan home."

He flinched. "Oh." he said. Then, rallying, "How do you know what happened to me at the clan home?"

"I don't know the details," she said, "and you don't need to tell me at all, unless you want to. But I know they hurt you. That's what happened to me, growing up."

"Oh," he said again. He was silent for a while more, then, "When you go there, I'll go with you." He added, "We don't have to wait for you to sell that land to find another place. I've got plenty of gold."

After Aili and Liu Chenguang were in bed, and the dragon child was asleep, and Aili's mother had finished puttering around in the kitchen, Zhu Guiren slipped out of his own room and went to the beach to look at the water. He couldn't sleep much, these days. He couldn't cultivate either. All he could do was wander and try to get away from the pain and the memories: the pain of what he had done, and the pain of what had been done to him. He knew that these two things were intertwined, but couldn't separate them. They were one thing. Even his memories of Tainu were poisoned by this pain; he couldn't think of them being together without the sharp claws tearing inside.

Occasionally, he tried to cultivate resentment, but trying to reach out to find the suffering and loss that permeated the mortal world just made him feel sick. And he couldn't do it anyway. Liu Chenguang had confirmed it; his cultivation had disappeared. Of course, he still had the meridians of his mortal body, the ones that every human being had, the liver and heart and all those things, but the well of qi — the center where he had gathered and stored corrupted spiritual power — was gone. He sometimes wondered if he was even a demon anymore. If he didn't cultivate resentment, then what was he? If he couldn't produce a spiritual weapon or use spells, at best, he was a long-lived mortal with good martial arts skills.

He looked across the still waters of the bay toward San Toma. The lights were out everywhere, since the country was still at war and there was anxiety that Kunoru might attack with planes or ships, so at least the stars were bright. He tried to remember what it had been like as a child, before he had learned to cultivate, and couldn't, really. They were started on cultivation very young at clan home, and his earliest memories had been broken by First as his punishment for freeing the phoenix. There wasn't much there, but he did remember that he used to love to look at the stars. That was how he had developed his system of symbols and calculations, trying to predict and understand the movements of the stars and planets. He looked at the stars now and imagined that he was back at the beginning and everything was still to come, rather than all over, all done, all ruined.

In the end, they all drove up to Fallon together. Liu Chenguang didn't want Aili to have to be there alone, and after all, the whole reason for going was to give Yisue a chance to swim in his own part of the ocean again. Aili refused to let Zhu Guiren drive, which he found irritating, but not worth arguing about. Yet.

Fallon was green again, after the burning. Aili walked quietly toward where the white house had been, Zhu Guiren remembered. Liu Chenguang went with her, holding her hand.

Yisue stood with Zhu Guiren. "Uncle Demon," he said.

"What?"

"Why is Aili sad?"

"This was a bad place for her," he said. "She doesn't have good memories." He added, "Should you call her Aili? Is that respectful?"

"That's how I first met her, so she said that's ok if that's what I want," he said comfortably.

"I have never in my life told you to call me Uncle Demon. You can call me Zhu Guiren like everyone else." *Except Tainu,* he thought with a sudden pang.

"I like Uncle Demon," said Yisue, "so that's what I'll call you."

He wondered what Aili saw when she looked at the burned places. The phoenix fire was not like normal fire; there was nothing left. The eucalyptus trees that he had stood under when he told Tainu about the array — those were gone.

Tainu had said, *We'll try together. Come back and finish your dinner, demon.*

Zhu Guiren said, "I need to walk, stay here," and ran away from Yisue and Aili and Liu Chenguang to the hilltop, then over to the other side of the hilltop where they wouldn't see him, and curled up in the grass.

The worst thing, the worst thing, the worst thing about everything was that even his dreams of Tainu were tangled up in all of what First had done to him, and what he had done to Tainu. Even the good things were ruined. How could Tainu come back to him? How could he let him be near? All his best memories, all that there had been between them, even those good feelings and good memories were corrupted now; there was no pure thing left in him that wasn't tainted, disgusting, horrible, not one memory or feeling or desire.

He must have lain there for a long time. Eventually, Aili came and sat next to him silently. She didn't say anything. He pulled himself up eventually and wiped his eyes.

She continued to be quiet, so he was able to say, "I don't know how it can ever be better. I don't know how he can love me." He thought maybe he needed to say more, but then he thought Aili understood.

After a while, she said, "It's different for everyone, I think. Everyone has to find their own way through it. But someone told me once — it was very important for me to hear at the time — that just because bad things happened to you doesn't mean good things can't also happen. That things were done to you is nothing you need to be ashamed of. And if you've done things you're ashamed of, it's better to do different things to make amends than to live in shame about it." She paused and seemed to struggle about whether to continue. Then, she finally said, "People hurting you is just that, Zhu Guiren. It's got…nothing to do with Tainu, with loving him. It's the opposite of that. Don't even put it in the same category. Let things that hurt you be things that hurt you. Let loving Tainu be loving Tainu. Let him love you too."

He shook his head. "I don't deserve it," he said. "I don't deserve him loving me."

Aili said, "No one blames you. We all know, Zhu Guiren, that you would never have hurt Tainu of your own accord. Even with First torturing you, you still tried to get Tainu away from him. You let us in. Can you give yourself some credit for how much you also love Tainu and how strong you were to resist First? And you also had to survive. Would Tainu be happier now if you had fought back so much that they killed you? Can you imagine how that would have been a better outcome? Without you, how would we have brought him back? Without you, Zhu Guiren, he wouldn't even have tried to come back."

He didn't say anything. None of this made him feel any better about any of it. Without him, would they have captured Tainu at all? Tainu would have been safe and hidden, as he had been for thousands of years, except for him.

"Zhu Guiren," Aili said sternly. "Stop finding ways to make everything your fault. You're not the source of all the evil in the world. You're really not."

Zhu Guiren looked up at her, surprised at her tone. She sounded very…the word that came to mind was *commanding.*

Where had that come from? Zhu Guiren frowned.

"What do you think Tainu will want, when he comes back?" Aili asked. "What will he want most of all?"

Zhu Guiren tried to think. "He said once that he wanted me to be a free-range demon."

Aili smiled. "What does that even mean?"

"Not…not like the other demons, not in a clan where I had to live like that."

"So, you should find a way to be a free-range demon," she said. "Because I think what Tainu would want most of all would be to come back and find you living a happy life. Because he loves you so much, and that's not ever stopping."

Zhu Guiren nodded and stood up. "So now you've been here," he said, rapidly changing the subject. "What do you have to do to sell it?"

From Fallon, they drove west to the great bluffs above the ocean. Zhu Guiren desperately wanted to drive the curvy road along the cliffs, but Aili still wouldn't let him. She was showing off for Liu Chenguang; Zhu Guiren very reasonably pointed this out and Aili ignored him while Liu Chenguang smiled at her. Yisue was hanging his head out of the window and letting his tongue flap like a dog. Zhu Guiren decided that he was very done with these people, and he should figure out how to be a free-range demon somewhere else.

"Here!" shouted Yisue suddenly. "Here, here!"

There was a little "For sale" sign off to one side of the road, on the ocean side. Down the cliff from the sign was the rocky beach with the crashing waves, and out to sea was an arched rock.

"Well," said Aili, driving up to the sign and parking the car, "this does seem pretty perfect. I wonder how far back the property line goes."

There was a good amount of grass-covered bluff between the road and the cliff, but Zhu Guiren was mesmerized by the glitter of the light on the ocean. He found himself settling into a cultivational posture and just watching it. Far below, he saw Yisue run naked into the violent surf and then come up again in his dragon form, blending perfectly with the foam and spray. Yisue leapt and cavorted in the waves and Zhu Guiren watched him, his eyes half closed, seeing the intertwined patterns of wave and dragon, the light and the water, the rocks and the tide, the complex unpredictability of the predictable movement.

Liu Chenguang watched Zhu Guiren, clearly curious; Aili put her finger to her lips and drew her away.

Zhu Guiren didn't know how long he sat there, but gradually, his body felt different — lighter, more relaxed, as though something dark and painful was leeching out of it.

He startled and realized that the light had changed; the sun was going down. From the brilliant white glitter the light on the water was now more golden-red, and the shadows were long. He looked away from the ocean, blinking his eyes to clear them, and saw that Aili was going through a simple sword form behind him, her eyes closed, holding En and moving gracefully through the pattern, over and over again. He thought he would like to try that; he hadn't seen a sword form quite like that before. He couldn't produce a sword, but he could just hold his hand out and pretend. He set himself behind and slightly to one side of her and began to mimic her movements. Soon, he had it well enough to also do it with his eyes closed. It felt very peaceful. Then, he heard more movement, opened his eyes again, and realized that Aili was going through the form again but many times faster, so that her sword became a flickering light in her hand.

He could do that, so he did it. Even though he didn't have a sword, still it felt oddly like he was flickering too with the swiftness of the movements, like the light on the water.

Aili laughed and put the sword down, not looking at him. "Yisue's back," she said to no one in particular. "Yisue, where are your clothes?"

He was stark naked. "Forgot them on the beach," he said.

"Well, go get them. We have a long ride back in the car and I don't want you naked."

"Too late, tide got them," he said, sounding very satisfied.

Aili said, "Well, then, the blanket it is."

"What blanket?" he complained, following her back toward the car. "What blanket are you talking about, do you mean the picnic blanket? But it's all *itchy* and it had *bugs* on it…"

Zhu Guiren heard their voices slowly drifting away. He turned back to look at the ocean and saw Liu Chenguang coming up from the beach as well, using qinggong to leap up the cliff instead of the narrow, curved path. She had found some abalone shells, which glowed in the sunset light.

She smiled at him. "Come here," she said, "let me check you."

He frowned. Liu Chenguang checked his pulse, and then carefully laid her hand over his abdomen, not quite touching it, the way that Tainu had done sometimes.

She smiled. "Very good," she said.

"What?" he asked, following her as he walked back to the car with her.

"Nothing," she said. "Nothing much."

Edna Lee brought her daughter over, a fat little baby sitting up and waving her hands at everyone and making babbling noises. Aili, her mother, and Yisue were absolutely enchanted. Liu Chenguang was standing with her back to a wall looking very freaked out; Zhu Guiren felt like Liu Chenguang looked.

He cleared his throat. "Ah, Liu Chenguang, don't we need to go check on the clinic?"

"Yes. Yes we do," she said, and fled with him outside.

They walked down the street to the storefront Zhu Guiren had rented to become Liu Chenguang's clinic. She had decided she didn't need to stock a full pharmacy since there was already a good one in Little Daxian, but there was a space for consultations, two table-beds for acupuncture, and today, there would be a delivery of furniture — the many-drawered cabinets that would hold her equipment and some of the more basic, frequently-prescribed materials for prescriptions.

Liu Chenguang said, "It's good to get you out of there, Zhu Guiren. Edna keeps asking if you're married."

"I heard," he said, annoyed.

"Aili's tried to explain, but she's never met Tainu so she doesn't really understand," she said. "Aili just says you're spoken for. But I guess Edna has some friends who are really in the market for someone as good-looking and sweet-tempered as you are."

"Shut up," he replied absently. They sat in the clinic drinking tea, waiting for the delivery truck. After a while Zhu Guiren decided he might as well ask. "So," he said in a voice as casual as he could make it, "Aili tells me you've been with fox spirits?"

Liu Chenguang spat her tea on the floor. "Why on earth would you– Why is that your business?" she asked, pouring herself more tea.

"Well," he said, "last time I was up at the ocean…by myself, you know… I was cultivating, and I think I met one? But I'm not sure."

Liu Chenguang's eyes grew wide. "What happened?" she asked.

"Well," he said awkwardly, "this very good-looking man…he just kind of… showed up. And then he…well, he tried to kiss me. And when I said no, he kept trying to kiss me anyway."

"Sounds like a fox spirit," she agreed. "And?"

"And nothing. I finally convinced him to leave." This had actually required a certain amount of physical intimidation, but he got there in the end. "But the thing is…"

"Mm?" Liu Chenguang sipped her tea again.

He was sure she was laughing at him, but this was important. He needed to ask someone — someone who might know.

"The thing is, I was interested," he said at last. "And I never…Never except Tainu. Had that feeling. So I am…is that part of what fox spirits do? Make that happen to you?"

"No," she said. She seemed to understand why exactly he was so upset, even though he was trying not to show it. "It's not just a fox spirit thing. It's normal, Zhu Guiren, to be attracted. It doesn't mean you don't love Tainu. It's a choice to love someone this way. It wouldn't be a meaningful choice if there was literally no one else in the world that you could possibly be with, as though Tainu were the last man on earth." She reached over and patted his shoulder gently. "There's nothing wrong with you at all, and nothing to be ashamed of, and it doesn't mean that you've betrayed Tainu somehow just by having feelings of attraction. It's just a way that you can remind yourself that you love him, because you are committing yourself to him and telling the fox spirit or whoever no thanks."

He nodded, thinking it over, and sat quietly, drinking his tea. "I miss him so much," he said at last. "So much. Last time I was in the spirit realm he wouldn't show me his mortal body at all."

Liu Chenguang smiled kindly. "He must miss you a lot too," she said. "He'll be ready soon."

Some months later, Zhu Guiren was alone in the house. Liu Chenguang was at the clinic, Yisue was at school, and Aili had gone out for a walk with her mother. He went into the little back yard to check the "Victory Garden," which he thought was the stupidest name ever for a bunch of vegetables, but Aili's mother had a good time with it.

He was kneeling down trying to look between the vines for ripe tomatoes when he heard Tainu's voice. "Demon?"

Zhu Guiren froze, then carefully got up, brushing off his knees, and turned around.

Tainu was standing there, looking shyly at him. He must have come through the phoenix gate that Aili had set permanently in the back corner of the yard. He looked just as he had when they first met in this body: in his late twenties or early thirties, tall and well-made, if a little on the slim side, skin a warm deep brown, high cheekbones and generous mouth, beautiful eyes looking only at him.

Zhu Guiren leapt over to him so quickly that Tainu almost fell over before he was caught in Zhu Guiren's arms. "Tainu," he said. "Tainu, you're really back? You're done now? You're back here?"

Tainu smiled down at him. When they had made love in the spirit realm, he had still not quite been to his full height and weight, but now he was just very slightly taller than Zhu Guiren. "I'm back," he said, and kissed him.

Zhu Guiren held his face and kissed him back, first on the lips, but then carefully on his eyelids and his ears and his nose, everywhere, all the precious places he had missed touching and seeing for so long. He found his eyes growing wet, and he could taste that Tainu was crying too.

At last, he said, "No one's home now. Come on, let me show you the house." He took his hand and brought him inside the little wooden house, showing him the kitchen, and the dining room, and the library-study-living room, and then his own bedroom, which was small and held only a bed and a shelf for his books.

He saw Tainu frowning at the size of the bed and laughed. "Don't worry," he said, "we're not staying here."

"We're not?"

Zhu Guiren dragged him down the hallway, laughing madly the whole time, but he felt so happy inside that he couldn't keep it in. "Definitely not," he said. He left a note for them on the dining room table and then brought Tainu outside, where he hot-wired the car. He had been doing this for a while, and Aili never said anything about it, but she also didn't give him his own set of keys, so this was how it was going to be. "Get in," he said, patting the passenger seat.

Tainu laughed too and sat down. "Where are we going?"

"It's a surprise."

When he pulled up at the ocean several hours later, it was just the right time. The sun was glittering on the water. Tainu came out and took a deep breath, energized by the qi, just as Zhu Guiren had hoped he would be. "What a wonderful place," he said. "I've never been here before…this part of the world."

"I didn't think you had," he said happily, "Aili said you just came to the Western Federation on the ship where she met you, for the war, so I thought you probably hadn't been up here before." He held his own hand against his handless arm to keep it from shaking as Tainu turned in the other direction, looking back at the bluff running up toward the high hills. There was a little house there — really just a one-room cabin.

Tainu looked at him. "Is that where we're going?" he asked.

He nodded, feeling anxious and trying not to let it show.

"Well, let's go up," Tainu said, taking out the groceries. "The milk will spoil if we leave it in the car."

Zhu Guiren carried the groceries since the hill was steep and he thought Tainu might be tired, but he came up easily and quickly enough, looking around at everything.

"The view's even better from here," Tainu said approvingly.

From the grass in front of the cabin, they could see out across the panorama of the bluffs and the little rocky castles and great cliffs of isolated rock scattered through the deep blue, glittering coastline.

"Is that the dragon gate, that arched rock there?"

Zhu Guiren nodded again. He still couldn't manage to say anything, his throat was dry.

Tainu turned and opened the door to go inside.

The cabin was not large, but it had a good kitchen and a large bed and a table and a wood-burning stove.

Tainu ran his hand over the door frame. "This was built pretty recently," he said. "Nice work."

Zhu Guiren smiled, still nervous. He'd forgotten that Tainu knew how to do so many things; he probably knew how to build houses too. "Do you like it?" he asked at last.

"I do. It's very nice," he said. "I especially like the bed." He went over and sat on it, smiling at him. "Why are you still standing in that doorway, demon?"

Zhu Guiren didn't say anything. Finally he said, "Aili's mother made the quilt."

"Very pretty." He held his hand out. "But I want you now," he said, simple and demanding.

Zhu Guiren just looked at him.

Tainu stood, went to the center of the room, and turned around slowly. When his eyes came back to Zhu Guiren again, they were shining. "You made it," he said. "You made it?"

He nodded. "There's a sawmill up the river. It's redwood, and the house was easy, really. It was figuring out how to get running water that was the challenge. That took me forever to engineer," he said, knowing he was babbling, and then Tainu was holding him and laughing and crying a little bit at the same time.

"It's so beautiful," Tainu said, holding him. "Arciniang, you made this. It's so beautiful." He bowed his head down onto his shoulder. "I've never had a home before. No one has ever made a place for me before, ever. A place to share with me."

Zhu Guiren put his arms around him and said, "This is for us to be in when we need time together, or to cultivate together, or whatever. Whatever we want to do. I was thinking that you wouldn't want to live up here always. It's so lonely, you want to be near your family, but there's no place there that I could build a house for you, and I wanted to build something for you. Just for you." He held him tighter. "When we go back, we'll look for a house there together. I didn't want to buy one without you seeing it too and helping to choose. But this will be our special place."

"Yes," Tainu said, and smiled at him again. "You've thought so much about it."

Zhu Guiren took a deep breath, feeling how their bodies fit together as they held one another; he was more than ready now. "I've thought so much about lots of things," he said, and kissed him, and pulled him over to the bed.

THE AUTHOR HAS SOMETHING SHE WOULD LIKE TO SAY

Thank you for sharing the adventures of Liu Chenguang, Aili Fallon, Zhu Guiren, and Tainu. I hope you're as happy as I am that they've found one another and begun their lives together. They've come to a point where they can rest, but for beings that are immortal or nearly so, there will always be more to come.

Once again, I want to highlight the wonderful stories to be explored in the Chinese genres of danmei, xianxia, and xuanhuan which inspired me in these books. Works of Mo Xiang Tong Xiu (MXTX), Priest, Rou Bou Bu Chi Rou, and others are now being published in official English translations, and I hope that you'll enjoy them as much as I have.

With much gratitude, always, to my wife Teresita, to our child and our shared extended family, and to all the readers and writing community that share all these imaginary worlds.

If you enjoyed the book, please leave a review or star rating. This helps other people find the book and know if they'll enjoy it or not, and it's greatly appreciated! And if you'd like to stay in touch, read book reviews or musings on the writing and publication process, and get first news about future books, free short stories or novellas, and more, please sign up for my newsletter on my website, jcsnow.carrd.co.